AND THE RIGHTEOUS SHALL PUNISH

ALEXANDER FORBES

KAIYA GAZED UP AT THE HANGED MAN. BENEATH UNYIELDING boughs the traitor surveyed his final place of struggle, throat bitten by the noose of justice – a collaborator and a symbol to all the people of Leth that retribution came swift and unforgiving. Six years that retribution had waited, patient and restrained, stirring inside those who suffered the consequences of loyalty. But now its time had arrived.

Kaiya gazed up at the hanged man, and the hanged man gazed down into her.

She knelt on the glossy black side street beside an old, six-storey terrace house. Leth was full of buildings like it, given its history of architectural repetition, but the southwest quadrant deserved its reputation for playing host to the most historical array of buildings in the town. Even the original fort still stood, the only connection to the top of an ancient wall that had guarded them for so long, failing only once in its duty.

Her father had taken her there twelve years ago, but the view remained imprinted on her mind: a plain stretching to the western horizon, broken in the north by the river, rising to hills and meadows in the south, and watched over by the mountains beyond. Behind her the rooftops and sprawling lanes of Leth hearkened back to a time when the wall had been more than ornamental sentimentality. And beyond, farther to the east, the Tarkinians brooded. Had they been preparing, even then, for the day that Leth would finally succumb?

Kaiya grimaced at the hanged man's ceaseless staring.

She turned her attention back to a detached, hexagonal road tile, its natural darkness replaced with a cloudy quality. The surface was charred, probably from *Allied Atlantica* and the final days of fighting. She examined the base – sure enough, the repellent layer had been damaged. Her mother had always complained about their fragility. One explosion, even faint, could disrupt the temperamental technology.

Kaiya removed both the protective and circuitry layers and held the repellent layer close to her eyes. She had seen this injury too many times in the last few years. It was always very small – a subtle dent in a layer that required absolute flatness. She placed the injured layer against a tile mould and prodded the edges with her electroscalpel. The layer rippled as it reconfigured itself. A simple procedure. She inspected her work and replaced the four components of the road tile. Given the relatively minor damage, the surface would only take two days to regenerate.

Kaiya returned the road tile to its slot and started work on the next. The process was not demanding, just boring. She distracted herself with glances towards the hanged man, and found herself drawn to a holoboard resting on a terrace house wall. It was full of joy and smiling faces. An advertisement she'd not seen before.

RAPTURE
free yourself

The holoboard morphed again, back to its traditional snack

food and drinks. Kaiya held the electroscalpel and road tile, mesmerised. There was something calming about the advertisement. Maybe it would return...

"Beautiful day," came a man's voice.

Kaiya turned her head towards a uniformed *Allied Atlantica* soldier.

"My apologies," he drawled. "I didn't mean to scare you."

She gripped the electroscalpel tighter. "I've seen you before. You've been watching me."

If the soldier felt any embarrassment, he didn't show it. "I can't deny that, miss. Though, it is my job to patrol the southwest quadrant and... ensure peace." He looked at the body of the hanged man. "It appears I've not been very successful."

His face was too young to have seen much active service.

"I wouldn't worry about him," Kaiya indicated to the corpse. "Collaborator."

"You knew him?"

"I've never seen him before in my life. What are you trying to say?"

"How do you know he was a collaborator?"

"People don't just walk around hanging other people for fun," she said. "Someone knew what he was and did something about it."

"Makes sense," the soldier said.

"Don't patronise me."

Kaiya separated the road tile's top layers, doing her best to ignore the intruder.

"Would you care for some assistance, miss?"

"No," she said, before reconsidering her tone. He was a soldier, after all. "I'm fine, thank you."

She shoved the repellent layer against the tile mould, and ran her electroscalpel around the edges.

"Are you part of a team?" the soldier continued. "I've seen other road teams around the city. It's a big job."

"I prefer to work alone."

The soldier continued to watch her as she worked. If she just stopped giving him attention, surely he would go.

Instead he approached again, and knelt nearby. He took out his own electroscalpel and began to remove a road tile.

"What are you doing?" Kaiya said.

"We are a reconstruction team. I've been trained—"

"No, I don't care. Stop it!"

The soldier removed the road tile and examined its charred protective layer. "If you stimulate the circuitry layer in the right way, it can program its own healing."

Kaiya shook her head. "No, that's not the right way. You never stimulate the circuitry layer."

"Why not?"

"Because it's not the right way. Stop it!" She stepped forward and made to snatch the road tile out of his hand. He pulled it out of reach.

"Watch."

He lay the electroscalpel against the circuitry layer, applying tiny surges here and there. Still attached, the repellent layer began to rearrange itself. "See, it works."

"I never said it wouldn't work," she said. "Of course it works! It's still the wrong way."

The soldier removed another road tile. "I don't see why. The application takes longer, but I don't have to detach the repellent layer. It evens out."

Kaiya sat back down where she had been working. "It doesn't matter. The circuitry layer might have developed a fault. You have to treat the layer with the problem."

"Not necessarily. The layers interact. The entire thing works together. It was designed to heal itself."

Kaiya shook her head and separated another tile's repellent and circuitry layers. Jaw clenched, she resisted the urge to use her electroscalpel on the stubborn soldier. Not that she would even reach him. But still, it was a nice fantasy.

He watched her, prodding circuitry, in no rush to leave.

"Have you been in this job for long?" he asked.

Kaiya stared resolutely at her current repellent layer and began to flatten it. She had, thank you very much, and she didn't need some Atlantican ruining her work and pretending that was fine.

"You're angry."

"Really," she said. "What gave you that impression?"

The soldier examined her. "I apologise. I'll do it your way if it means so much to you."

Kaiya stopped and looked back towards the hanged man and the holoboard behind. The advertisement had returned, and the odd need to watch until the very end.

RAPTURE
free yourself

It faded, leaving a tingle on her skin and a renewed consciousness of the soldier's presence. "No," she said, rubbing her forehead. "Forget it. Doesn't matter."

The soldier continued to watch. She wished he would stop.

"Three years," she said. "I've been doing this for three years. Mainly road tiles. Sometimes other basic bioelectrics. It's not that exciting, but it's money, and I'm good at it."

"I can tell. You have some passion for it."

She smiled. "I'm not sure I would call it passion. But things should be done right."

The soldier caught her tone and placed his electroscalpel against the circuitry layer, grinning. "I agree."

A woman walked by, body pulled in towards itself, trying to make herself invisible. She held hands with a small girl who struggled to keep up. Kaiya understood that desire to be on the street for as little time as possible.

"Shouldn't you be patrolling?" she asked.

The soldier shrugged. "Isn't much to patrol. Although..."

He glanced up at the hanged man. "I could be wrong."

Kaiya followed his gaze.

"Why do you suppose that he is still there?" she asked.

The soldier replaced a road tile and stayed silent, waiting.

"People like him are worse than Tarkinians," Kaiya began, then shook her head. "Forget it. You're Atlantican. You won't understand."

She shoved a road tile back into place.

"I suspect the authorities have not been notified?" the soldier said.

Kaiya shrugged. "You're the authorities."

"Not for matters like this. I'll let the police know."

"You do that."

The soldier gave no reaction, and continued on with his section of the side street. When would he leave? Atlanticans could never take a hint, and she didn't need help from a soldier, of all people. He didn't even heal tiles correctly.

"You're ok with him staying there?" he said.

"Absolutely. The collaborators should know what's coming. And the people should know that the collaborators will be punished. The police sure as hell won't do it. And you lot won't either... off in northeast quadrant. Might as well be in a different world."

The soldier simply looked at her and began to remove another road tile.

"Will you *please* leave me alone?"

She glared at him, electroscalpel gripped tight. The soldier shifted his gaze and placed the tile gently back onto the street. Kaiya watched the electroscalpel in his hand, heart rate increasing, and shifted her weight ready to flee.

"Of course, miss," he said, and stood. "Please feel free to seek our assistance at any time. We are here to help in any way."

Kaiya scoffed.

The soldier departed with a final glance at the hanged man.

Finally alone again, Kaiya replaced the tile the soldier had been about to heal, and looked up at the holoboard. The *Rapture* advertisement had returned. She turned off her electroscalpel and watched, content simply to ponder the calming emptiness each viewing gave.

Her thoughts drifted from that damned soldier to other questions she had spent so long trying to pack away.

Where was Kormac?

***

Kaiya ambled up the centre of the boulevard, head down, half-attempting to count the damaged road tiles. From time to time she looked up and stared into the empty distance, familiar terrace houses looming from both sides. The boulevard ran straight from the town square to the southern gate, and not a single vehicle could use it. Even with all the teams and extra people working, it would take ages for cars to be functional again. It was indicative of the state of transportation all throughout Leth.

Still, the silence astounded her. At least she didn't have to close her bedroom window every night to keep out the whine of poorly-tuned magnetic pads.

A woman emerged from a front door and gave a surreptitious glance at her surroundings before hugging herself tight and striding up the footpath. The glowstone anticipated her movement and illuminated the way ahead, fading back to its dull, perpetual glimmer.

What business did she have, being out at night?

Kaiya frowned to herself. She had to break that mindset.

Her own building beckoned, its high-balustraded entrance steps faded with time. The glowstone footpath registered her as she approached, obliterating that magical atmosphere of urban silence she'd never experienced until the Atlantican arrival a week prior.

Perhaps she should have spent the past three years damaging the road tiles instead of healing them. She could have had a good night's sleep.

Kaiya took the first step towards her front door.

"Tilda!"

Her best friend sat on the landing, head resting against the balustrade.

"Where have *you* been?" Tilda said.

"I've been working in southwest quadrant." Kaiya hugged her tight. "I've been meaning to see you. I promise."

"Don't worry about it. I understand."

Of all people, Tilda was the only one who could say that and mean it.

"What's wrong?"

Tilda looked strained. "Can we go inside?"

"Of course."

Tilda picked up her large duffel bag.

Kaiya tapped her identity card against the security module. "It's a pity they haven't fixed the Network yet. You wouldn't have had to wait."

They walked into the outdated entrance hall. The light panels on the walls sensed their presence and glowed faintly.

"Apparently the Network is completely destroyed," Tilda said as they climbed the stairs of faded-blue carpet. How many years since the oaken handrails had been polished? The light panels followed them, lower levels fading back to nothing as they progressed to the fifth storey.

Kaiya opened the door to her apartment. Tilda dropped her

duffel bag onto the hallway. "Thanks," she yawned. "Can I stay a while?"

"Of course." Kaiya locked the door behind her and checked it several times. "You know I love it when you stay."

Tilda hugged her. "Thank you," she whispered.

"What's wrong?" Kaiya asked again.

"It's nothing. I was just worried about you."

Kaiya restrained herself from saying any more.

Tilda made herself comfortable on the couch while Kaiya changed. She rubbed her face over the sink and sighed, expelling the exhaustion of daily existence. How long had Tilda been waiting?

"Have you eaten?" Kaiya asked, looking in at Tilda from the central corridor.

They went about raiding the cupboards, searching for the simplest meal possible.

"Don't you have any *marashta*?" Tilda asked.

"The tinned stuff? That's disgusting."

"It's better than no *marashta* at all!"

"If it's not the real stuff, it's not worth it."

Tilda rolled her eyes. "Perfectionist," she whispered slowly in a sing-song voice.

Kaiya gave her a light backhand below the shoulder.

"I'll do some shopping tomorrow. Promise."

Tilda groaned. "God, what I wouldn't do for the Network to be back up."

"We could just go out, if you—"

"No," Tilda said. "I don't want to go out."

Kaiya was taken aback. "Ok."

"Let's stay here. Take a movie."

Kaiya glanced at Tilda, who made a great show of searching through one of the cupboards. "Well, it's not like we're going to get any channels, so we don't have any other options. I'll have to refill the VC, though. Its scent is weak."

They decided on the last few frozen meals left. Tilda gave a pointed look and Kaiya reiterated her promise to go shopping again.

"You have to take care of yourself," Tilda chided.

Kaiya escaped to the living room. She had been putting off refilling the Vision Caster, but she'd have to pull things together if Tilda were staying. Get rid of some of the mess.

The inky black screen rippled as she pulled out the scent receptacle, double checking she had chosen the right one. There would be no repeat of the mistake she had made the first time her mother had entrusted her with maintaining the device. Scent fluid in the kinaesthetic receptacle didn't go down very well, apparently. The Vision Caster had been rather upset about that – not to mention her mother – and refused to function properly for three days, even after it had been cleaned. Her mother had to clear one of its memory chips to erase the traumatic experience.

A road tile was simple. Its biological component was primitive and had only one purpose – to heal itself. But the Vision Caster was almost alive, as far as Kaiya was concerned. Her mother had tried to explain it, but Kaiya couldn't grasp the complexity of the bioelectrics.

Something she would have learnt in university, if she'd been able to go.

Kaiya emptied the thick fluid until it fit the narrow acceptable range, and touched the receptacle so it slid back in. Excited, the inky black began to dance around, darting back and forth in the direction of the refilled receptacle and away into every inch of the device.

This was a very happy Vision Caster.

She commanded it to complete a scent reset. The receptacle had been empty. No wonder the other senses had been dulled – the primary functions had attempted to compensate for lack of a fluid. She sat on the couch and experienced the Vision Caster's reorganisation. It would have figured out within a day that the receptacle had been refilled, but Kaiya was in no mood for over-saturated scents while the device completed its own process. The Vision Caster experimented with variations on the seven primary odours in all intensities. The process was different every time, depending on how the internals had decided to rearrange themselves, but she had to make sure the Vision Caster didn't make a mistake. The experience was quite lovely when the scent of jasmine in full bloom filled the room, but not as enjoyable when replaced with flatulent canine.

Tilda entered with two plates and placed them on the coffee table. Kaiya prodded her food with a fork and began to eat. "So what's new in northwest quadrant?"

Tilda chewed for a while before answering. "Nothing. What have you been up to?"

Kaiya frowned at Tilda's lack of news, then told her about the hanged man and the soldier.

"You didn't even know him," Tilda said.

"It doesn't matter. He deserved it."

Tilda stared and dropped her fork. "But you don't even know what he did."

"That doesn't matter. He was a collaborator."

"It does matter. It does!"

Kaiya clenched her jaw. Tilda was getting too upset about it.

"What *kind* of a collaborator was he? Maybe if he were someone like Bennett, I could understand, but everyone had to work with the Tarkinians to some degree."

Kaiya shook her head. "I don't want to talk about it."

"Kaiya—"

"I don't want to talk about it."

Tilda forked her food around her plate. Typical soft traitor. So quick to forgive and willing to forget. People like her should have understood.

They ate in silence.

But still. She didn't want to scare her away. She had forgotten how nice it could be to have company.

Sometimes.

Kaiya was looking at Tilda's sunken face when a knock came at the door. Tilda grabbed her fork tighter. Kaiya put her plate back down on the coffee table and shared a brief look with her, their previous conflict brushed aside in the face of a sound that carried six years of ominous reputation.

"I'm sure it's fine," Kaiya said, trying to convince herself as much as Tilda, who looked apprehensive.

Kaiya made her way out into the corridor and touched the viewpanel. A middle-aged man stood patiently outside.

Benjamin.

2

KAIYA STEELED HERSELF AND OPENED THE DOOR.

"Commissioner," she said, injecting as much bitterness into the word as she could muster.

Benjamin smiled dreamily, arms held behind his back. "Kaiya," he said, as well-mannered and polite as ever. "How lovely to see you." He looked thoughtful, as though mildly surprised by her appearance. Always with that sense there was some other conversation happening in his mind. "May I enter?"

Kaiya stood still and gazed at the uniform that didn't belong on him. "What is this?" she sneered. "A courtesy call? A friendly visit?"

He examined her, smile still light across his face. "Both, I would hope."

Kaiya maintained her position. "What for?"

"Why don't you let me in and we can discuss that?"

They stared at each other before Kaiya relented and stepped out of the way.

"Thank you," Benjamin said. He walked into the corridor and looked around slowly. "Not much has changed."

"Really? Where have you been the past six years?"

He didn't respond, but stared into the living room at Tilda, who gave him a weak smile. They greeted each other awkwardly.

"What are you here for?" Kaiya pressed.

Benjamin peered at Tilda a little longer before moving the expression to Kaiya. She knew that look. He was hiding something. "You don't trust me anymore," he said.

Kaiya shifted her gaze. Benjamin's eyes were too strong. Too searching.

"Why not?"

She folded her arms. "Because I don't."

"That's not a reason."

"I don't need a reason!" she said, and stepped onto the depressed floor of the dining room. She stared out a window onto the empty boulevard.

Benjamin watched her from the corridor. "You just don't want to justify yourself." He didn't sound angry. He sounded almost amused. So typical. What private, humorous commentary went through his head while everyone else existed in the real world? How could a man like that be Commissioner? He'd fall over the moment someone applied pressure.

Kaiya ignored him.

He stepped down into the living room and stood in front of the credenza, looking at the holos. "You haven't moved a single one," he said, and turned his attention back to her. He watched her, those uncomfortable eyes full of secrets boring into her with an intensity too great to bear. "You're not wrong, Kaiya. To mistrust us." He returned to the holos and picked one up. Kaiya struggled against the impulse to stop him from ruining everything's natural place.

"A lot of bad things happened under Bennett," he continued, "and we have a lot of... bad people, for want of a better expression. But we also have many good people."

"Stop it," she hissed.

"No, Kaiya, I will not." He replaced the holo with great care. "You need to listen to me."

She shook her head, gaze resolutely on the boulevard. "You are corrupt. You're a collaborator."

He gave a short, humourless laugh. "I don't think you really believe that."

Kaiya shifted her weight, jaw clenched.

"And it's an insult to the entire force. You know nothing of the people I now command. You know nothing of the sacrifices they have made. So be reasonable, Kaiya, and see each officer for what they are beyond their rank." He stepped closer. "I am still Benjamin, and you are still Kaiya."

She closed her eyes and rested her head against the cool glass.

"No. You're not. And I'm not."

"You have decided that?"

"I haven't decided anything," she snapped. "It's a fact. It has nothing to do with me deciding anything. But you don't get that, do you? Because you haven't had anything taken away from you. You are the one that has decided. You didn't have to be Commissioner—"

"I have been Commissioner for five days, Kaiya."

"That's not the point."

"No, I understand your point," he said, voice still mild.

Kaiya fell silent under his gaze.

He spread his hands and shrugged. "Perhaps you're right. Maybe I haven't had enough taken away from me. Maybe I didn't have anyone to lose in the first place. Except for friends. And colleagues."

Kaiya dodged his pointed look.

"I understand your feelings regarding Bennett. I wouldn't be here if I didn't. But Bennett is gone."

"He's still—"

"He's gone, Kaiya. I am the Commissioner. But you don't like that. Now you dislike me for taking your father's position. Or is it because I stayed in the force while Bennett was in charge?"

Kaiya looked back out onto the boulevard.

"I guessed as much. So tell me, Kaiya – what should I have done? Should I have quit? Or rebelled, like your father? Would those have been more acceptable to you? More... pure?"

"Yes! You should have stood up for something."

"Your mother never seemed to mind that I stayed."

"Yeah, well she's gone now, isn't she? Because people like you didn't fight back."

Benjamin bowed his head and smiled. Again with that damned internal narrative she couldn't hear. That inability to accept the gravity of what had happened and what was still happening. She had thought it endearing, once. Now it just irritated her.

"I would like to know something, Kaiya. Who should be the Commissioner?"

"My father," she said proudly.

"But he is not here."

"He should be. He will be."

"And until then? Can you tell me the name of the person you believe should be Commissioner?"

She refused to play his silly games.

"You can't, can you? Because you haven't thought about it. You want things to be the way they were before the Tarkinians came. Before people had to make choices."

"Before people became collaborators," she corrected.

He shrugged again, as if the distinction meant nothing. "Perhaps you're right. Maybe it would have been more noble for all of us who rejected Tarkinian rule to leave the force, but then what? Who would have been left? Those most loyal to Bennett? Look me in the eye and tell me that would have been better."

She refused to dignify the challenge. Her father had been

principled. She didn't need a lecture from a man who had worked under Bennett for six years and betrayed her family.

Benjamin watched her quietly.

"I have something for you," he said at last, voice gentle.

Kaiya's eyes flicked over and watched him. He didn't move. Just waited for her to come to him, which she did after a few moments of consideration.

Benjamin reached into his deep trouser pockets. "It was your father's," he said, pulling out a holodisc. "I found it in one of the storage rooms. Bennett must have put it there."

Kaiya flashed with anger to think of Bennett touching her father's possessions, invading the spaces that had belonged to him. She had tried her best not to think of Bennett's assaulting presence in the Commissioner's office.

Benjamin stepped away and sat down at the table. "Come see," he said. He turned on the holodisc as Kaiya took a seat beside him.

Her mother appeared above the disc, a candid smile across her face, and heavily pregnant. Benjamin offered Kaiya the holodisc, and she took it carefully, as if it might break. She stared at the holo of her mother, absorbing every detail, before moving on to the next one, which showed her wedged between her mother and father, staring blankly at a first birthday cake. She stayed with each holo for a great length of time, studying them in detail. She was sure she'd never seen some of them before – holos of her parents before she had been born. A flutter of shock ran through when she saw her mother and uncle Kytos standing by the Emancipator fountain in Leth's town square. They both looked so young. It had definitely been taken before her parents had met. Kaiya stared at Kytos. What would he look like now? It had been so long since she last spoke to him – a distant memory of her childhood. She couldn't clearly remember a time where there had not been some level of conflict between him and her mother.

Benjamin looked on as she continued to flick through the holos. At least half of them contained her. Birthdays and Christmases and school award ceremonies. Inauguration as Leth's Commissioner of Police. Even her and Tilda in the lavender fields nestled in the southern mountains all the way back in third grade. Kaiya steeled herself against the threat of hopelessness. One day soon life would return to the way it should have been.

"I like this one," Benjamin said as she flicked through. Kaiya smiled in spite of herself, and stared down at the holo of her and Benjamin. He must have memorised its location on the holodisc. She remembered that evening, her fourteenth birthday. Benjamin had made some joke – she wished she could remember it – and their faces had been captured in that moment, hers stuck forever between surprised shock and unguarded laughter, turned up and staring at a grinning Benjamin.

He hadn't even made Chief Inspector, yet.

"Thanks," she whispered, taking the holodisc. She turned it off and spun it idly in her hands. "Is this all you came for?"

The thread of acid she tried to keep in her voice didn't seem to have any effect on Benjamin. He was too clever for that, she should have known it.

He looked down at the table and back at her, weighing something in his mind. "It isn't," he admitted, and stood up.

Kaiya watched him pace in preparation for whatever it was he had really come to say.

"I thought you should know," he began, "given your interest in the matter. The provisional government in Akheron has instituted a court of priority. To try collaborators. It has special powers for both investigation and sentencing." Benjamin shook his head. "I can only suppose it is an attempt to curtail events such as last night. The limited news I get from Akheron indicates there have been significant protests there. Far larger than the disorganised, random attacks we have had. In any case, Bennett is to be sent to Akheron."

The news didn't sink in straight away.

"No..." Kaiya said. "What?"

She put the holodisc down on the table and walked over to the centre window. She tapped a short combination into the glass and felt a light breeze drift through. Benjamin's revelation sank through her consciousness, and started to burn.

"You're going to let them, aren't you..." she said.

"As distasteful as I find the idea of 'expedited' justice, Bennett will be sent in accordance—"

"No! You can't." She rounded on him, eyes wide, watching all her answers fly away to Akheron. "It's not right, he has to stay here. He has nothing to do with Akheron. They won't get it right."

"Kaiya—"

"It's not up to them!" she yelled, thumping the table with her fist. "Why are you so weak? He should be on the streets. He should be judged by the people who were affected. Where is he? Where is he now? Where are you hiding him?"

Benjamin took a deep breath and sighed. "You're seeing conspiracies, Kaiya. We're not hiding him. He is in prison."

"Which one?" she demanded.

"Which one do you think?"

He gave her another pointed look.

She nodded and licked her lips.

"Right. Right. I want to see him."

"Kaiya—"

"I want to see him," she spat through gritted teeth, staring at Benjamin. He returned her gaze, his own inscrutable. He was measuring her. "Stop it," she said. "How do you do that?"

"I just wanted to let you know, Kaiya." Benjamin turned and walked back out into the corridor. On the other side, in the living room, Tilda didn't hide her interest in their exchange.

"Wait," Kaiya said, following. "I need to know. Benjamin, I need to know. I need to see him."

Benjamin stopped by the front door. "Why do you think he will tell you?"

"I don't know. He just will. Please. I have to know. I just want to talk to him."

Benjamin shook his head. "No, Kaiya."

"You talk to him, then. Tell me what he says."

Benjamin avoided her gaze. He looked sad.

"You know something, don't you. What aren't you telling me?"

"Stop," Benjamin commanded, raising a hand. He looked straight into her, piercing the trickles of terror she knew had bubbled up through her eyes. "There are camps. Inside Tarkinia. The *Allied Atlantica* forces have been liberating them. I don't know much more than that, just that the operation is ongoing. I have nothing to do with it. No one in the force does. It was considered inappropriate, given Bennett's role in the Occupation."

Kaiya processed the information slowly. For the first time since Benjamin's arrival, Tilda stood, and walked over to the corridor.

"Camps..." Kaiya said.

"Yes." Benjamin stepped forward and placed his hands gently on her shoulders. "They're alive, Kaiya. The Atlanticans are bringing them home. That's all I know. I don't know how many. I don't know where from. I don't know if your parents are in there, or yours, Tilda, I just know that there is at least a little bit of something to be hopeful for."

Kaiya looked up into Benjamin's fine-wrinkled eyes. "I need to know," she whispered.

"I'm sorry. I can't tell you any more. I'm not *Allied Atlantica*."

She accepted the answer reluctantly and resisted the urge to embrace him. He was not still Benjamin, and she was not still

Kaiya. A small part of each remained, she could grant that, but they were no longer the people they had been. No space could be allowed for old attachments to flourish. She needed to steel herself for the coming return, and in time he would be hardened by the role he had assumed. Such things were inevitable.

Benjamin's hands lingered on her shoulders, as if waiting.

Then he left.

3

KAIYA WOKE, GENTLE RAYS OF SUNLIGHT DANCING THROUGH HER blinds. She had been dreaming of something pleasant – she recalled an image of Kormac and the lavender fields south of Leth – but already it was fading, replaced with a growing awareness of reality. She stared at the cream-painted ceiling, the sound of emptiness pressing into her ears. Seconds passed into minutes, and she surrendered herself to the lethargy sleep could not seem to heal.

She reached out, feeling for the control unit on her bedside table. She found the glassy panel and tapped twice. The murmurs of Leth seeped into the room as the blinds opened and the windows altered to full day mode, flooding the room with direct morning sunlight. Kaiya kicked herself free of the white sheets and rolled out of bed, pausing on the edge as she found her balance. She rubbed her eyes and thought about going back to sleep.

Something crashed in the kitchen, sending a rush of apprehension through her. It took a few moments to remember that Tilda was there. Still thinking of sleep, Kaiya opened her door and walked into the corridor. The pungent odour of mushrooms assaulted her.

"That's disgusting," she yelled. Something sizzled, as if it had just been placed in oil.

Tilda popped her head around the corner and smiled. "I made your favourite."

Kaiya rolled her eyes and ventured forth, wrinkling her nose. Tilda ducked back into the kitchen and, as Kaiya passed, ambushed her with a serving spoon full of mushrooms, thrusting them at her face. Kaiya jumped back, almost knocking the spoon out of Tilda's hands, and let out a scream of utter disgust. Tilda laughed and advanced, forcing Kaiya to retreat into the dining room. "Piss off!" she yelled. Tilda continued to laugh and returned to the kitchen, where she ate some of the mushrooms and placed the rest back into the frying pan.

Kaiya walked over to the windows and set them to open. They shifted to transparency, allowing a mild breeze to carry in the sounds of peaceful urban living, a far cry from the previous night's pockets of chaos. She surveyed the boulevard. Fire had gutted the second floor apartment of a building about twenty doors down on the opposite side. She couldn't see it very well from her position, but it was unmistakeable.

A little crowd was gathered outside the burnt building, chatting amongst themselves as police cleaned up the glass. Kaiya pushed down a spark of resentment for Tilda, who had pleaded for Kaiya to stay inside. Next time, Kaiya promised herself, she would do her part in bringing justice against the collaborators.

A pair of uniformed *Allied Atlantica* soldiers ambled down the footpath, all smiles and enjoyment as they began to talk with the crowd of onlookers. They really knew how to talk to anyone, Atlanticans.

Kaiya turned around and watched Tilda cook the mushrooms. "I want to go to the *Allied Atlantica* headquarters."

Tilda faced her. "Oh, yeah? Today?"

"Yeah. I'll get ready and we can go after you have your breakfast."

Kaiya walked into the living room and turned on the Vision Caster, switching between various non-existent channels. The Network was still down.

"I..." came Tilda's voice from the corridor, "I think I'll stay in."

Kaiya turned off the Vision Caster. "Really?"

Tilda nodded. "Yeah. I don't feel like going out."

Kaiya reined in her surprise. Tilda was always the one eager to be out and about, dragging her along to this, that, and the other. "Ok. I don't know how long I'll be. I'll bring home something nice."

"*Marashta*?"

Kaiya smiled. "Maybe."

The answer pleased Tilda, who hugged Kaiya and sang a ditty about her love for *marashta*. Kaiya laughed and began to think through what she would say to the Atlanticans.

A whole building full of soldiers.

Kaiya approached the eastern bridge, a majestic stone structure with ancient lampposts that had been rendered redundant with modern technology and were retained purely for aesthetic and sentimental reasons. Police patrolled the bridge, striding across glossy road tiles Kaiya had healed far too many times over the past few years. She had heard stories of people jumping into the river, so no doubt the police were keeping a watchful eye out for such behaviour.

As far as she was concerned, they were better off in the river than splattered across the road tiles. Less work for her. It was a good thing she'd never learnt water bioelectrics. The energy conductors had been injured by jumping, in the past, even if most bodies disintegrated before they reached the core infrastructure, and she couldn't imagine having to heal those monstrosities.

One of the officers faced her, eyes lingering, before finding a new target.

Kaiya hugged the thick stone balustrade and gazed down into the river. Silvery webs criss-crossed the eddying water, anchoring themselves to the top of dark, silent turbines with spiralling, curved teeth. Kaiya remembered the fear of her childhood, watching her mother dive into the water to perform maintenance feeding. Even turned off, the turbines would still brood with entitled expectation. Now they stared back at her, watching her, like they were calculating the amount of energy they could strip from her body. The compulsion to look always lingered. Kaiya forced herself to endure the avoidable fear.

Someone touched her on the arm, jolting her into consciousness and breaking the spell of the unrelenting turbines. She looked up at the face of an old man in police uniform. He should have been well past the age of retirement. "Can I help you, miss?" His gentle manner of speech and guileless eyes eased her wariness.

"No. Thank you."

The officer smiled and peered down at the energy conductors. For some reason Kaiya felt as though the old officer deserved an explanation, though she wasn't certain what the explanation would be for. "I should be going."

"Enjoy your day," he said, nodding at her.

She looked back as she walked away. The officer meandered along the sidewalk and car-empty road, smiling at passersby.

Kaiya left the bridge behind, the hungry turbines fading from her mind. She thought of Tilda's mushrooms and smiled. Tilda should have come. The northeast quadrant deserved her mocking presence. Manor quadrant, as she would say, her voice uncanny in its resemblance of those who lived there.

Kaiya stopped abruptly, averting a collision with a hurried

woman. Head covered by a shawl, she seemed to shrink into herself, as if pleading for the world to forget her existence. It took a few moments for Kaiya to realise the woman's head had been shaved, and when that fact penetrated her mind she glared. How anyone could submit herself willingly to the needs of the enemy was beyond her. They were the worst type of traitor and deserved to feel every sting of retribution. She had watched a whore collaborator punished just last night, and still carried a quagmire of exhilaration and disgust at the ritual stripping and shaving.

People like them needed to be marked.

Kaiya moved over to the sidewalk to avoid the traffic – roads in the northeast quadrant were still driveable. The hum of repellent layers announced a car behind her, which passed by with tinted windows. She watched it disappear around the corner.

The sound of humming faded as she pressed deeper into the northeast quadrant, a forest of red stone terrace houses. She had only been in the area a few times, to visit Kormac's mother. He had always felt more comfortable at Kaiya's place, so he said, and she retained that knowledge as a matter of pride. To think that he could be home, soon!

The sidewalks widened as the streets became narrow and one-way, containing quaint gardens and trees in an equidistant, alternating formation. Kaiya glanced around to see if anyone was looking at her, then knelt by the street, examining the road tiles. She didn't have the qualifications to work in the northeast quadrant, and she thought she understood why. There was something very different about these road tiles. She would have liked to examine them more closely. Their darkness was not quite midnight, and they were more translucent than the ones she worked with. She could almost see the repellent layer underneath.

A car passed by, and she stood up in shock. There had been no hum, or perhaps she just hadn't heard it. There was certainly no characteristic push and pull between the car and the road. She had only ever seen that kind of behaviour in Obsidian Tanks, and the last time she read about it, that technology wasn't yet available in consumer vehicles. She looked at the road tiles. Perhaps they were responsible?

Her mother would have known.

Kaiya filed away the new information and continued on towards the northeast quadrant CBD. Glass towers loomed low in the sky, monstrous and modern, ugly blights on the urban landscape of a town as old as Leth. They had no ground floors, and instead shaded a street-level courtyard, filled by people in business suits sitting at tables drinking coffee and eating sweets available from the mobile food stands. Holoscreens glowed at most tables, men and women speaking with business partners from across Nymosen and around the globe, if the languages were anything to go by.

Anyone who hadn't lived in Leth would think the war had never happened.

Bitterness burned Kaiya's throat. They were all collaborators, probably, their loyalty bought with the promise of assets retained. What was the difference if you worked for the occupiers instead? It was still the same job. She understood that. But at least she had done her best to sabotage her own work as much as she reasonably could.

She looked up, distracted by movement. A giant holoboard perched on the exterior of one of the buildings, angled down for pedestrian consumption. Above it, shimmering painted letters announced that the building – or, at least, its first few floors – belonged to Life Plus. The holoboard turned black, its advertisement having ended, but soon began to glow once more.

A flower bud appeared, and a thrill of excitement passed through Kaiya, soon replaced with utter calm. The flower bloomed and approached, spreading warm detachment as it entered her body. Infused with the scent of flowery meadows, light engulfed her, eliminating the tyranny of physical limitation.

She was a goddess. She could do anything.

The ocean lapped against a nearby cliffside, weaving through faint rustic music, and her skin prickled with electric warmth, the temperature of perfect comfort.

Her eyes watered as her soul thrashed against the confines of her body. Release beckoned ahead, just there, just out of reach. Ever so slowly fading. Something inside her grasped at it, and came up empty. It grasped again, panicked, searching for a final skerrick of the teasing purity that beckoned.

Senses fading, Kaiya's own voice whispered in her mind:

RAPTURE
free yourself

Tears rolled down her cheeks as the holoboard went black, and a fissure emerged in the core of her being, into which all sensation fell and burned. The advertisement began again, but she had been emptied of the capacity to connect, and she experienced nothing from the holoboard but a flat image.

Now she understood.

To live was to be imprisoned.

She looked around as her hearing returned to normal. No one seemed to have noticed the gargantuan display that had just occurred between her and the holoboard. This wasn't any technology with which she was familiar, this was something else. Something more than the Vision Caster.

She had thought an Extensive Vision Creator was only theoretical, but here it was, reaching in like any old Vision Caster, but solely to her. A unique and intimate relationship between her and the technology.

Perhaps that was *Rapture*?

She walked away from the courtyard, glancing back at the

Life Plus section. She would see the Atlanticans then come back. Just for a look. Just to see what it really was. No harm in knowing.

Allied Atlantica had set up their headquarters in a centuries-old, colonnaded edifice with eighteen steps leading down to the roundabout that surrounded the courtyard. She'd never met an Atlantican until the soldier who had shown so much interest in her, but they had a reputation for pageantry and tradition, so it was no surprise they had chosen such a building. A few soldiers lazed about on the steps, supposedly guards, and glanced at her as she strode up towards the front door.

Her skin prickled.

The bowels of the building arched into the heavens. She had never seen a ceiling so high, with the old kind of windows lining portions of the wall below it, allowing light to illuminate the soft, polished surfaces. Whatever building this had once been, it had been transformed into an eclectic mixture of ancient and new technology. She walked through the automated scanner, which confirmed she posed no security threat, and approached a gleaming mahogany counter.

The young woman sitting behind it could have been a doll, for all the trouble she had gone to with her grooming. Kaiya couldn't see a strand of hair out of place. The doll woman smiled at her, revealing teeth that were far too white and far too straight to ever exist on a real person.

"Hi," she said, her voice lilting and high-pitched. "How can I help you?"

Kaiya almost did a double take. She had assumed a Nymian would be doing basic duties for the Atlanticans, but no, they had brought their own. Was this woman in the military?

Kaiya hesitated. "I wanted to speak to someone about the camps in Tarkinia."

The woman's glazed eyes revealed an absence of under-standing. "Certainly. Just one moment." She stood up and walked over to a phone on the other side of the square reception counter, out of earshot. They must have set up a private local-web. Unless the Network had been somewhat repaired and they didn't want everyone else to know. It wouldn't have surprised her.

A congregation of Atlantican officers and Leth police descended from dulled marble stairs at the rear of the atrium, sharing laughter. Kaiya couldn't help the flash of fury that tore from her chest, through her neck and back down until it tingled in her fingertips and filled her legs with expectant power. The image of Bennett leading a procession of police and Tarkinian soldiers up the southern boulevard slammed into her mind. She had forced herself to stay at the window and watch until every boot and Obsidian Tank had disappeared from her sight.

What schemes did they now discuss?

"Miss?" The doll woman peered up at her with an annoying simper. "I've spoken with someone from the bureau responsible for this matter, and they have informed me that access is restricted to those with a B-level clearance."

Kaiya stared.

The woman hesitated and looked at her doubtfully. "You... don't happen to have a B-level clearance, do you?"

Kaiya flicked her eyes back and forth between the woman and the posse of police and military officers. "Can I speak with them myself, please?"

"I'm sorry, miss, but that would be against protocol."

Kaiya groaned. She'd never seen a protocol that didn't stand in the way of people getting things done. "There's got to be some way I can talk to the people who know what's going on."

"I'm sorry, miss, but unless you have a B-level—"

"Ok. Ok."

The woman's doll face didn't move a touch away from her fixed expression.

"Thank you," Kaiya said dismissively. She retreated to a

bench near the massive entranceway and sat, defeated. Would Benjamin have a B-level clearance? The officers in the atrium were discussing who knows what with the police, so there was some degree of information exchange. Though Benjamin had made it clear that their cooperation was limited. There had been something more in Benjamin's voice. An annoyance that betrayed a flicker of resentment towards the Atlanticans. Perhaps this was the reason.

Benjamin should have let her speak to Bennett.

Kaiya looked out through the entranceway towards one of the side streets that connected with the CBD roundabout. A team of tile healers worked, chatting both amongst themselves and with a nearby soldier.

She stood suddenly, riding a wave of inspiration, and strode back to the reception. "Excuse me," she said. The doll face woman turned and donned the same simpering mask as before. "Would you be able to help me with something else? I met someone. A soldier. I'm wondering if you're able to help me find him."

"Of course."

Kaiya described the soldier as best she could, and the woman pulled out a holoscreen to narrow down the search. She showed Kaiya the two options and Kaiya selected the one she recognised, a worm of doubt burrowing its way into her stomach.

"If you take those stairs there," the woman said, pointing to a set on the front right corner, "he will be in section fourteen on level two."

Kaiya hesitated. "And I don't need any kind of security clearance?"

"Not at all, miss. We hope to strengthen the bonds of friendship between our two countries. It is important to be open and accessible to the public."

Kaiya scoffed inside but thanked the woman. If they wanted

to be accessible, then maybe anywhere but the northeast quadrant would have been better. And what was all this nonsense about the bonds of friendship? The sooner she didn't have to see a soldier, the better. Until then, she would do what she had to do.

She climbed the stairs and couldn't help a rise in apprehension as she passed a pair of soldiers deep in their own discussion. She glanced back at them as she rounded the half landing, but they didn't seem to show any interest in her.

The level two corridor had been outfitted with modern windows, all of them set to open. Kaiya stopped at the first one and looked out onto the roundabout and courtyard. From this angle, the Life Plus building was invisible. The murmur of the collaborator masses floated through the window, along with the occasional puff of breeze that struggled against the stillness of the day.

Kaiya held herself rigid as she walked up the corridor, alert to potential danger. The late-morning sun shone through onto the numbered doors, and she kept going until she found the one with a fourteen. This must be what the doll faced woman meant.

She knocked and waited, then her solder answered. They stared at each other.

"Good morning, miss."

"Hi," she said, trying not to appear too uncomfortable.

"Would you care to come in?"

Kaiya looked into the room behind the soldier, filled with messy desks and no one else. "I'd rather stay out here. If that's ok," she added. Best to be polite.

"Of course." He closed the door behind him and stepped over to the window. "This is a surprise."

"I need some... help," she declared.

"I take it you've spoken to reception? Or is it completely coincidental that you knocked on the door to my office?"

Kaiya forced a short laugh. "Yes. It's completely coincidental."

She shouldn't have come.

"I need information. The camps in Tarkinia..."

The soldier studied her face. "How do you know about that?"

"I... just do. The receptionist told me I needed a B-level clearance."

"That doesn't surprise me." he said, and shook his head. "I don't even have a C-level!"

"Oh," was all she said. She should have known this wouldn't get her anywhere.

"But... maybe I can help." The soldier looked uneasy. "I can't promise anything."

"No, I know, I know," she said.

"You have people you think might be there?"

"Yes. My parents and... a good friend of mine."

It was best she leave Kormac at that.

The soldier nodded to himself and looked out the window.

"Who else have you told about this?"

"No one."

"Good. Even here, not everyone knows. I think it's best that we wait until there's some certainty." He looked back at her and smiled softly. "I apologise. I understand you must be impatient for some news, after all this time. I am only somewhat familiar with... that night."

Kaiya looked away and through a haze of memory. "Yes."

Silence fell, the soldier standing patient and still. Kaiya perceived that he was waiting for some greater explanation of Leth's recent experiences, and weighed up her indignation at the assumption that he deserved it and her desire to keep someone who might be helpful on side.

"There was a Chief Inspector in the police," she said. "Before the Tarkinians came. Bennett."

The soldier indicated he was familiar with the name.

"Bennett and... the Commissioner at the time, they didn't get on so well. Bennett had been rejected twice for promotion to Assistant Commissioner. When the Tarkinians came, they overran the Nymian forces stationed here, but the police went into hiding. They fought back. It only lasted five days, but they were the best days of the whole war. The Tarkinians didn't know Leth. They've never been able to take it in any of their wars with Nymosen. At least, they hadn't been able to. We were the only border town ever not to have fallen. The Tarkinians had no idea of Leth's internal layout, so the police were able to pick them off one by one."

Kaiya sighed.

"And then on the sixth day, things changed. The Tarkinians suddenly knew all the police positions. Bennett had made a deal, and taken a bunch of police who had been supportive of him before the Tarkinians came. They made him Commissioner and he gave every other police officer who was hiding an ultimatum – return and serve, or be hanged. A lot of them returned, but there were some who stuck around, who didn't want to be involved with the Tarkinians or someone as corrupt as Bennett. It took the Tarkinians six months to get rid of them all."

"What happened to the Commissioner?"

Kaiya shrugged as nonchalantly as she could feign. "I don't know. No one does. I've heard rumours that they never caught him, but I don't think that's true. Other people say he's in the concealed prison, but if that were true the new Commissioner would have released him."

"You don't think—"

"No," Kaiya said, shaking her head. "No, I don't think so. You don't understand how much Bennett hated him. If I hated someone that much, I would want to see them suffer."

The soldier stared at her and nodded.

"Bennett didn't just place the force under Tarkinian command," Kaiya said. "He merged it with them. They made him a military officer as a reward for his loyalty. He could do anything he liked. For the first three years things didn't change much. The Tarkinians could be rough from time to time, but they left us alone, and Leth was more a base they used. It was Bennett that kept people in line, and his police would never be punished. Everyone put up with it to some degree, and everyone knew it was corrupt, but there were limits. Bennett's people never did anything too obvious or outrageous, but then one day Bennett was in the town square. A woman insulted him. He stuck an injectable straight in her face, in the middle of a crowd.

She waved her hand dismissively.

"Dead, obviously. But that was it. There were riots for three days. I was there. Everyone was there. It felt like we would win, but... of course we didn't."

She stared down from her dining room window as a Tarkinian frequency rifle tore a hole through a protestor's chest. There were a hundred such memories she could select at any given moment, all burnt vivid into her mind.

"The Tarkinians came on the final night, with the police, and they took people. The Night of Retribution. At least one person from every family, at random. The convoys were still leaving at dawn."

Kaiya bit the police officer's arm, and received a backhand for her trouble. She fell to the floor and struggled to stand, then collapsed back down with a boot in her face as they dragged her mother out the front door.

"There were two Occupations. The second one started that night. After that, everyone learnt their lesson, and no one said anything again."

4

Kaiya gave the soldier her address on a promise that he would tell her anything he could discover. She would have preferred the Network were still working so he could just call her, but sacrifices had to be made. Perhaps he would discover nothing and she would be spared another interaction... but then what was she really hoping for?

The Life Plus clinic beckoned. Projected people – walking advertisements – milled about the courtyard, speaking to anyone who would listen. Another trick of the Extensive Vision Creator technology – she'd never seen anything like it before. Kaiya walked through the motley assortment of tables and chairs, listening to conversations about blood prices, the risk involved in biotech derivatives, and the dissolution of a marriage. That conversation could surely have been held some-where other than a public courtyard. The man sitting at the table was obviously fine with everyone nearby knowing about his wife's infidelity. At least he was safe in front of the holo-screen. Who knows what havoc would have been wreaked were she there in person? For some reason she sounded far angrier than her husband. Perhaps this was fate punishing him for collaboration.

Kaiya looked around. There were no stairs and, it seemed, no lifts, until she noticed the near-translucent single-person tubes positioned throughout the courtyard. A well-dressed business-woman talking to a floating projection of a head stepped into one of the lifts and motioned for it to close. Had she not been watching closely, Kaiya would never have even known the woman had been there. Moments later the same lift appeared, a grey blur streaking down to the ground, and a slick-haired man stepped out holding a briefcase.

Of course the northeast quadrant had new lifts. Another benefit of their collaboration. Her mother would have brimmed with excitement at the prospect of trialling them. The first had been built in Akheron in the early years of the war. Just the news of it had set her mother off, jabbering on about principles of propulsion and implications for space exploration.

Kaiya stared around, trying to figure out which lift was for which business. There didn't seem to be any easily discernible marker, yet everyone knew exactly which one to use. She approached one. It was a wonder that more people didn't walk right into them. She stood by and waited for something to happen, then glanced around to watch what everyone else was doing. She made an opening gesture with her hand, and an archway into the lift appeared. Or, rather, melted away, revealing its glowing, opaque insides. Etched black lettering announced *LevDev Enterprises*. An inconvenient method of discerning ownership, she thought.

She strolled around underneath the Life Plus building, peering into lifts until she found the right one. She stepped inside and turned, searching for the command module. It didn't exist. Perhaps it was on the door. Kaiya made the same motion she had watched others make, and the arch disappeared, replaced with the exact same texture as the rest of the tube. Kaiya had only half-processed the feeling of entrapment when the world blurred momentarily and the archway reappeared. She stepped out into the atrium of the Life Plus clinic and looked back to see that the lift had already vanished. A translucent cylinder remained.

"Welcome to Life Plus." A woman about her age appeared, somewhat misty with a bluish tinge. "How can I help you today?"

Kaiya stared around at the grandiose atrium, considering her response. "I was wondering what this place is."

The projection nodded and altered her unceasing smile to a slightly different formation. "We are Life Plus, your partner in lifestyle design. We offer services both to heal the mind and unleash the heart."

"You mean *Rapture*?"

"*Rapture* is our flagship product, for those who are dedicated to living a life of unlimited bliss. We have a second service, though, for those who prefer to experience the secrets of their deepest desires." The projection's smile changed again, though the eyes never seemed to. "May I interest you in a complimentary sample?"

Kaiya looked out through the floor-to-ceiling windows at the pedestrians below. "Sure."

The projection led her past smiling clerks at the atrium's desk, each one looking up in the same manner just before she reached them. Kaiya arrived at a small, concrete room with a plain wooden door. The project motioned an invitation to enter. Kaiya hesitated.

The only light in the room came from that which the doorway permitted. No windows adorned the walls, no lights nor glowstone. From the little Kaiya could see, the floor and walls had been painted or rendered black. She stalled at the door, wary of the room, until the opposite wall began to glow. It was a colossal Vision Caster, except... not.

"Please, take a seat." The projection motioned to a single reclining chair in the centre of the room, much like the pictures she had seen of first class pod carriages. Kaiya entered the room, taking her time to examine the Vision Caster that was not a Vision Caster. It seemed to act in a very similar way, the contents swirling about inside, preparing to create some new experience for the viewer, but Kaiya had not seen a number of the patterns before, nor had she ever seen the white, silvery glow. Vision Casters were universally dark.

Kaiya suspected this was the Extensive Vision Creator that controlled the projections milling about in the courtyard. She sank into the chair and let out a whisper of comfort. Behind her the door closed with a click. She didn't know who had closed it, nor did she care. The chair seemed to mould itself around her body, filling her with a deep warmth and overwhelming desire to fall asleep.

She closed her eyes and heard the gentle lapping of wavelets against sand, the progeny of those waves that crashed further out in the beach. Seagulls flew about, talking amongst themselves, the same salty breeze that buoyed them tickling her face. She opened her eyes and stretched out in the sand, licking the salt off her lips and staring at the cloudless blue sky. She couldn't remember how long she'd been there – perhaps forever? – but she was there for a purpose, if only she could remember what that had been.

As far as she could tell the beach was private. Her tent was pitched near a little freshwater stream where the sand met the bush, though had she pitched it two hours or two years ago? Her only certainty was that the tent belonged to her, and that's all that mattered. She lay in the sand for an indeterminate length of time – she really couldn't tell – soaking in the warmth without ever feeling hot. The breeze cooled her, yet never so much that her skin rallied against it. If life were to end in that moment, the transition to oblivion would be as the softest satin carried through air, drifting in nonchalant abandon.

Kormac would return soon. Kaiya couldn't remember the time – did the sun ever move? – but it felt right that he would be by her side again, as had been the narrative of their eternal existence. She blinked and laughed as Kormac traced a finger down her side, achieving what the breeze could not. Kormac's touch sent her skin to a state of alertness, almost rebelling, yet just coping with the arousal and allowing its continuation. She curled her fingers through his short, sea-matted hair and pulled his mouth down to hers. They had always been connected in this embrace since time immemorial, if time had ever existed. Such a thought struck her as absurd, that constancy could be measured, as though one could divide permanence into anything other than more permanence. She closed her eyes and succumbed to the power of her and Kormac's desire, cheered by the restless waves and unchanging solar countenance.

When she opened her eyes again, she smiled at the swaying stalks of lavender, everlasting place of rest. Nothing existed but this hillock, nor had nor would ever. The sunlight danced through Kormac's hair, grown long from the eternity they had spent together here in the hills and meadows of purple stretching to the distant mountains that formed a ring around their sacred abode. The lavender tickled some ancient memory, or perhaps something that resided in her imagination, as if there had once been, perhaps, a field like this in some other universe.

Kaiya breathed in the scent of rich earth underneath her bed of grass. Kormac picked out stalks of lavender for a bouquet, the plants swaying as if calling for his touch, desirous of the great and only honour of pleasing their god's whimsy. New stalks grew as the lucky ones were picked, and soon he had fashioned a bouquet such that fields would rejoice at this harvest of the chosen.

Kormac released a stalk of the lavender into the air, where it floated along, never higher nor lower, worshipped by the waving of its siblings beneath. The floating lavender rearranged itself, growing wings of delicate purple swirl, transforming itself into the epitome of its purpose. The butterfly fluttered its fragile wings for the first time, and the breeze swelled to welcome a new member to the pantheon of the chosen. Soon Kormac had thrown his entire selection into the air, and butterflies lilted about, farewelling their as yet unchosen siblings. The hillock whispered a song unknowable, sketching its flimsy melody somewhere just beyond the comprehension of Kaiya's ear. The butterflies surrounded her, colouring the sunlight to hues of violet and the occasional smattering of gold. She stretched out in the grass, exalting her perfection, and the butterflies cocooned her, preparing to pick a chosen one for transformation.

She laughed, a cacophony of echoes responding in joy. The juts of jagged beauty gave birth to slivers of silvery harmonics bouncing around the glittering cavern. A smidgeon of snow blew in from the moonlit mountainside, settling on her hair and wings. She walked out onto the narrow ledge and surveyed the limitless expanse of mountaintops, the moon occupying its sempiternal quarter of the sky. Beneath her an expanse of darkness consumed the moon's glow. Since existence had begun she had never flown down farther than she could see, yet she knew there would never be an end if she did so.

The firmament flickered, and Kaiya felt a twinge of unremembered familiarity, a feeling that she had forgotten something. She gazed into the abyss, where a crack had opened and silvery stars trickled out, filling her eyes and mind with memory. Horror sank into her stomach, and she grasped at the fading world around her, as if its tatters could provide better nourishment than whatever she had forgotten.

Kaiya writhed in her seat, mouth open in a voiceless scream. Sensation returned with no thought to haste, and she rubbed at her wet cheeks, the remnants of her immortality lingering on the edges of consciousness and centre of her desire. The projection stood in front of her, smile as constant as a machine. An older lady, real, had joined them, holding a glass of water, which she offered to Kaiya. She refused it.

"Please," the projection said. "This will assist your brain as it readjusts." The real woman offered the glass again. Kaiya drank the water – at least, it looked like water – and began to feel the reality of life return, grounding her in an experience far inferior to the now-dwindling memories. She put the glass down, unfinished, her mind rallying against the return, scrambling to hold onto the memory of perfection. Better to remember it and live in a shadow than lose the shadow of the experience. Even as the thought of holding on materialised, she forgot what it was she wanted to hold on to. She was left with the knowledge, somewhere deep inside, that a better time had existed. The answer was there. Only Life Plus could offer a way back.

The real woman took the glass of water and left the room. The projection sat in her own chair now – where it had come from, Kaiya didn't know – and gazed at her, smile unbroken. Kaiya wiped away a few final tears and stared past the projection at the EVC, which she loved and hated at the same time. Whatever had just happened, she couldn't remember, but she knew that it had been wonderful, and she had to have it again. Even the thought of leaving the chair filled her with desolation, let alone the room, then the clinic, then the quarter, and back to the drudgery of existence. "Was that *Rapture*?"

"Not quite," said the projection. "You could call it a kind of *Rapture*, but this is our basic treatment at Life Plus, for those who are not yet ready to undertake a full surgical solution."

"Am I supposed to forget?"

"Yes. Unfortunately only the full surgical solution – true *Rapture* – provides the capacity to enjoy our treatment throughout the entirety of your life."

"Exactly like that? I don't even remember what happened…"

"No. Our basic treatment uses a similar process to *Rapture*, but in a much more concentrated manner. The intensity of the experience is unsustainable. We developed it on the way to developing *Rapture*, so it has been available for much longer. We believe that everyone should benefit from our research into purifying the human experience."

Kaiya pushed herself up in the seat and stared at the EVC. "What do you mean purifying the human experience? What does it do?"

"Our basic treatment unlocks the innate creative potential within every person, and brings it to the surface. It analyses your most secret desires and allows you to experience them in a state of pure bliss. Given the intensity of that experience, we have strict limits on its usage. A patient may only access our basic treatment once a week. The full *Rapture*, however…"

The projection leaned in close, making the hairs on Kaiya's arms stand tall.

"The full *Rapture* is a complete surgical treatment. We analyse your brain in a more detailed and thorough manner than the basic treatment, and devise a plan to expunge every moment that has caused you harm. It is a complete purification. Life with nothing but beauty, unadulterated by memories that stand in the way of you and your ongoing joy."

"How much is it? *Rapture*?"

She had already known the price would be prohibitive, but the projection's answer still deflated her. She pushed down her disappointment and maintained composure, a pretence of careful consideration. The projection gave a spiel about benefits and pre-payment options, as well as reduced costs for subscribers to regular basic treatment. The price of the basic treatment lifted her spirits, and Kaiya promised to consider her options, making calculations for how often she could afford it.

Already a longing grew inside her.

Kaiya ambled through the streets in the easternmost section of northwest quadrant. The cosy, vibrantly-coloured terrace houses oozed charm, ornate balconies poking out at irregular heights and intervals, plants hanging down from all sorts of nooks and crannies. The old concrete sidewalks had faded with age. Years ago – so her mother said – the residents had protested replacing the concrete with glowstone. Even the change to road tiles had been controversial, apparently, though the desire to drive comfortably won out in the end. Old, black-bodied lampposts with curved, hanging lights straddled the street. Even they weren't equally spaced. Nothing matched.

It made sense that Amelia came from a place like this.

Kaiya entered a quiet, one-way street, glancing at two teenagers making out on an old bench. They looked far too happy for her liking. She knocked on Amelia's front door and waited, listening to the hum of a balcony conversation further down the street, and the chattering of birds in a nearby tree. Its branches intruded upon balconies on both sides. The residents obviously weren't bothered by it. She wouldn't have minded a few leaves poking through her own window.

"Kaiya!"

Amelia flung the door open and pulled Kaiya into a deep embrace. "You're alive!"

Kaiya returned the gesture with a lesser degree of enthusiasm. "Of course I'm alive."

"What do you mean, 'of course?'" Amelia drew back with a look of concern. "I had no idea. You disappeared."

"I didn't disappear," she countered, and looked away. "I just stopped hosting."

"And never saw me again or told me why." Amelia's tone indicated there was no real anger behind her words.

"Well, I'm here now."

"Yes. You are. Come on." Amelia beckoned and walked inside.

The thrill of rebellious apprehension still ran across Kaiya's skin as she followed Amelia. Anyone could be watching, not that it mattered anymore. They sat by the square wooden table in the narrow, unassuming kitchen that had played host to so many secrets over the last three years.

"I was worried they'd found you," Amelia said.

Kaiya shook her head. "I'm too careful for that."

"I know." Amelia smiled. "You were my most reliable host. Why did you stop?"

Kaiya stared at the old red teacups that had touched so many secretive lips. "I just... didn't want to anymore. Sorry." She bristled at having to feign contrition, though she was sorry to some extent, in a more complex manner of thinking.

Amelia watched with her intelligent, prying eyes. Weighing something in her mind. "Have you seen what people are doing with the collaborators?"

"I wondered if you were involved," Kaiya said.

Amelia shook her head. "I haven't been. But I have been paying attention. Following events as best I can with no Network. There's obviously sentiment around, but it's poorly directed. Sporadic." She leaned back. If she had a cup of tea it would have been the moment that she sipped and studied the face of whoever sat opposite, holding back a question or statement that would lead towards a conclusion she had already drawn. "What do you think?"

Kaiya grinned. She knew Amelia's strategy. "You already know you're right."

Amelia gave a show of faux modesty. Where did all that confidence come from? She was only a few years older than her. "I think there's a space for leadership," Amelia said. "For people like us."

"For people like you," Kaiya said.

"Don't be silly. I was merely a conduit. You were my brightest node."

"You're flattering me. It won't work."

They shared a secretive smirk. Amelia knew full well that it worked. Kaiya couldn't deny that it lifted her spirits.

Amelia chewed her lip. Scheming again. "Why do you think no one ever found me?"

Kaiya shrugged and played along. "Because you're clever?"

"Now who's flattering who? Ha. I don't think that's it. It's... expectation. They didn't expect it could be me. That's why they never found me. Expectation is everything."

Kaiya waited for Amelia to pull her thoughts together. The lip chewing indicated there were large gears turning inside that brain.

"I've been compiling a list," she said at last, looking directly at Kaiya. "Of collaborators. People we know worked with the Tarkinians, and people we have reasonable suspicion of. It's still in the early stage, and difficult without the Network, but I've had people out and about. Asking questions."

"And you want me to help?"

Amelia shook her head. "That's basic stuff. What I really want to know is... what would a Commissioner expect? Right now. In this context. What would he expect?"

Kaiya allowed the question to sink in. Amelia appeared genuine in her desire to know.

"I don't know Benjamin as well as my father."

"I'm sure that's true," Amelia said, "but you still know him better than anyone I know or have access to."

Kaiya considered the question. "Benjamin doesn't let on much, but I think... I think he expects people to be angry. I think he's not surprised. But I think that... he knows something. That something's happening. Something that would distract everyone so maybe they're not so angry anymore."

Amelia stared at her.

Kaiya shifted in her seat. "Like... if people started returning."

"You think that might be what's happening?"

"I don't know," she said quickly. "It's just... an example. I think he expects that we'll find something else to think about."

Amelia leaned back in her chair and chewed her lip again. "But would he expect organisation? Would he expect something planned? Methodical?"

"I don't know..."

"It's all about expectation," Amelia said. "The Tarkinians won Leth because we never expected they could. Bennett and the Tarkinians never found me because they never expected someone like me to be orchestrating the resistance. And now the police... if I'm right, then they expect flareups. Isolated events. Easily contained. But what would they do if we were organised?" Amelia's eyes lit up the way they had when Kaiya first met her. A blaze of passion that had sucked her straight into the post-Night of Retribution resistance movement. "They know they've let the people down. If there's enough of us together, demanding justice, they're going to have to ask themselves the question – whose side will they be on now that the Tarkinians are gone? Us, or the collaborators?"

Kaiya's blood flashed with elation. Amelia was right. More importantly, Amelia understood. With Amelia at the helm, everything would turn out right. Benjamin would be forced to turn Bennett over. He would be forced to allow true justice to take its course, and Leth would at last be rid of the whores and collaborators.

Purified.

She had sought Amelia almost on a whim, as a distraction, but now her purpose was clear.

Kaiya leaned across the table and looked into Amelia's blazing eyes.

"There's something you need to know."

5

KAIYA TWIRLED STRANDS OF *MARASHTA* WITH HER FORK AS SHE SAT on a dining room alcove gazing out the window. More people had begun to venture outside, and the glowstone sidewalks were preparing themselves for another night of labour as late afternoon morphed into twilight. How many of the people down there would heed Amelia's call? How far had her message gone in one day?

Tilda eyed her from the dining table. She had already finished her *marashta*, the thinnest hint of leftover sauce coating the biodegradable container, and devoured a newscast on her tablet. Apparently people still sold daily newscasts door to door – at least, the trend had returned thanks to the Network's destruction.

"I want you to come with me tonight," Kaiya said.

Tilda's face fell. "I really don't want to..."

"But why? I don't understand. It's just people like you and me telling them we want justice. If hundreds of people like you don't show up, then they won't understand. They won't realise it's what the people want."

"Kaiya, it's Amelia. Do you really want to work with Amelia again?"

"Yes."

Tilda looked doubtful.

"Look," Kaiya said, placing her *marashta* to the side, "it wasn't Amelia's fault."

"I've never thought it was her fault. I just thought you might not want to be involved in that kind of thing anymore."

"Of course I do. This is what I need, Tilda. To do something, to make things right. The whole reason any of us went through what we did is because of those collaborators. Because of Bennett."

"I'm not sure it's that simple, Kaiya..."

"No, but it is, Tilda. It is."

Kaiya finished her *marashta* and began to pace. "Come with me. You'll see."

"What if it's not what you really need, though? I just..." Tilda looked back down at her tablet. "That court that Benjamin was talking about. I've been reading about it."

Kaiya shook her head. "It's unacceptable. No one in the capital cares about border towns. They won't give us what we need."

"I know, I know. But that's not what I was going to say. There are advocates from Akheron coming to Leth. Tomorrow. To take evidence." Tilda looked up at her, eyes probing gently. "They want to hear people's stories."

Kaiya stopped and took a moment to consider the implications.

"No. I don't want to see an advocate."

"But Kaiya—"

"Tilda," she said, "I don't want to tell them." She sat opposite and lowered her voice. "I don't want anyone else to know."

"They can help, though."

"No, they can't. They can't. And I don't trust them. We have to stop relying on other people. Akheron gave up on Leth. Bennett betrayed us. Now Benjamin's letting Akheron take the people who deserve to be punished here. We cannot rely on anyone but ourselves."

Tilda looked down at her tablet again, disappointed.

The sidewalks glowed at maximum, aware of the hundreds swarming southeast quadrant's CBD. Far more traditional in layout, Kaiya much preferred it to the northeast quadrant's attempt at modernity. Respectable seven-storey classical façades lined the outside of the roundabout, within which a cenotaph rose high from the grassy commons. Kaiya stood tip-toe, trying to catch a glimpse of Amelia, who was on a makeshift wooden platform that had been brought for the occasion.

Kaiya perused the faces of those present. She needn't have been concerned about the turnout, but the crowds should have been overflowing. The entire town should have been there in solidarity. People were obviously still afraid. Perhaps they would feel more confident after tonight.

Either that or they were collaborators.

She looked across at the police headquarters, and up to the Commissioner's lounge. The windows were dark. Benjamin either didn't think their voices important enough, or was too cowardly to let the people see him.

Accountability. That was the entire reason the lounge had been put in that position – so the people could see what happened. The office required some privacy, of course, but the people had a right to see who came and went from the Commissioner's section; to see who the Commissioner entertained, to whom he listened. Even Bennett had maintained its use, if only to flaunt his position in the Tarkinian army.

There was no way Kaiya could move any closer to the front.

She had hoped to be near Amelia, but a sea of bodies blocked further passage. Already people were closing in behind her, forcing her to hyper-vigilance of her surroundings. She watched those close to her, and noticed every stray touch against her body.

Disapproval roared from a section of the crowd. A line of helmeted police had approached from a side street in full riot uniform. The people jeered and hurled deserved insults at the faceless collaborators.

All throughout the crowd pockets of disgust and distrust sounded out at the appearance of more police. "Death to traitors!" yelled a lone voice.

"Traitors hanged!" another offered.

Within two minutes Kaiya chanted with the crowd. "Death to traitors! Traitors hanged!" rose from hundreds of mouths. Those closest to the police wore expressions of animal fury, their obvious desire to inflict this punishment barely restrained.

The police stood still.

Kaiya looked behind her. She was about halfway between the cenotaph and the rear of the group, which spilled from the roundabout into the street. Dozens of police lined the sidewalks behind them, silent and threatening.

Benjamin's window remained dark.

"People of Leth!" Amelia's voice reverberated through the CBD.

A roar of approval greeted her, and Kaiya pumped her fist in the air, the heat of passion coursing through her.

Amelia stood on the makeshift platform holding a microphone. Wireless receivers amplified her voice, held by individuals interspersed throughout the crowd. Combined with the reflection of the stone buildings, her voice sounded as though it came from everywhere.

"People of Leth, I thank you for your bravery." She stared out over the crowd, waiting for it to quiet. "When I discovered yesterday that we had been betrayed, I despaired. I despaired for our future, for our honour, for the legacy that we will leave. I despaired that even after the Tarkinians had gone, we would still be ruled by puppets. But people of Leth," she softened, raising a hand in placation, "I did not despair for long."

Kaiya cheered along with the crowd, replete with the knowledge of her own importance in bringing about this glorious event.

"I did not despair for long because I knew, deep inside, to the very core of my being, that we are a strong people." The crowd cheered as she clenched her fist. "We are a righteous people. We are a people who stand up when the call is made, who join together to fight injustice and demand that our voices be heard. We are a people who will not accept the duplicity of puppet masters who think they know better than us! Who pretend that they are the same as us, that they are one of us, when they are nothing more than the putrid sewers of collaboration!"

Kaiya punched the air again, eyes watering with the beauty of knowing that the people were with her. "Death to traitors!" she chanted with the crowd.

"You have heard it whispered, and I say to you that it is true. Bennett has not departed!"

A sea of rage smashed against the warm air.

Amelia pointed at the headquarters. "His shadow still lingers over this building. It lingers still on our streets and in the bones of our fellow citizens, those who still tremble at the sight of our treacherous police. It haunts them into submission. It forces surrender on their souls, all because this man has the gall to tell us that we do not deserve the chance to heal our own wounds."

Amelia pointed at the Commissioner's lounge, and Kaiya looked up.

Benjamin stared down at the crowd, face impassive. Beside him, an officer matched his gaze. The crowd turned their fury to the now-visible subject of Amelia's polemic.

"People of Leth," she said, "we are still led by collaborators! We are still subject to the whim of forces external to us. But we do not have to be. No, my friends, we do not have to be cowed into acceptance of the unacceptable. You have come here tonight so your voices may be heard by those who would deny you that voice. You have come here tonight to *give* a voice to all those who have been reduced to fear inside their own homes."

Cries of agreement punctuated the air.

"You have come here tonight, my friends, to say that we are ready to reclaim our lives. To reclaim our town. Our future."

The crowd swayed as it became restless. Kaiya chanted death to the traitors as pockets around her screamed in Benjamin's direction. If he had turned off the noise filter to listen, it didn't register on his face. He scanned the crowd slowly.

"Where is my son?" a man yelled from nearby, face boiling. Around him similar questions were directed to the Commissioner's lounge, giving voice to an undercurrent of trepidation Kaiya knew well. The crowd swayed with greater agitation, and a glass bottle arced through the air. It disintegrated against the force-shielded glass, sending a few small ripples along the surface.

Benjamin ignored it and continued to search the crowd.

"Commissioner Benjamin," Amelia's voice echoed. She faced the lounge and stared at him. "We come here tonight with a simple request. One that will prove to the people you purport to serve whether you are truly with them, or whether you are yet another collaborator puppet. Commissioner Benjamin," she said, holding a hand up to momentarily ease the crowd's restlessness, "will you release Bennett to the judgment of the people?"

Amelia swept her hand to indicate the gathered crowd, a signal that released a new wave of chanting. More projectiles arced up and disintegrated against the Commissioner's lounge, and Kaiya felt herself buffeted within the increasingly agitated mass of bodies.

The police lining the sidewalks of her street stood firm against an encroaching line of outrage. Benjamin had not indicated any recognition of Amelia's question, and continued to scan the crowd, speaking a few occasional words with the officer beside him.

A man at the rear of her section hurled a rock at the police, missing them. The police responded by unharnessing their energy shields and turning them on. Concave rectangles of shimmering, opaque light burst out from the metal handles, covering the majority of each officer's body.

The people raged against this escalation.

Kaiya's heart pumped. She had stopped her chanting, and her eyes hunted a gap through which she could run and find clearer air. A scream punctuated the evening from somewhere behind her, followed by a general roar of outrage.

Kaiya looked back up towards Benjamin. Right into his eyes.

He stared back at her, leaning his head towards the man next to him and whispering. Benjamin pointed, and the officer began to study her. The gaze lasted only a few seconds, interrupted by an explosion against the glass. Kaiya looked wildly into the crowd. A man held a force projector on his shoulder, already recharging it. The glass of the Commissioner's lounge rippled with electrical sparks, absorbing the energy.

Neither Benjamin nor the officer looked at her any longer.

The fragile thread of restraint snapped.

At the rear of Kaiya's section, police drew stun batons. A general howl of hatred reverberated through the street, and projectiles flew. The police marched forward, energy shields held high. Another explosion crashed against the Commissioner's lounge. Kaiya looked up and watched as Benjamin and the officer turned away from the crowd and disappeared deeper into the building.

How long could force-shielding sustain that level of attack?

Chaos engulfed the area, screams of remembered terror

rising from all around her. The police moved forward, intent on reaching the man with the force projector, their approach hampered by projectiles and an unwillingness of many to move.

Others panicked. Kaiya pushed forward, flailing against the backwards pull of eager hands. The police had formed a line, and while some pushed against it, others searched for any method to get past them to the apparent safety of beyond. A woman tried to climb over them, and was thrown back into the crowd.

Another explosion crackled through the air.

"Someone let me through!" a woman screamed from behind.

Kaiya pushed harder at the people in front of her, mind spiralling. Her head was clouded by the hot, thick air emanating from the crowd. Another explosion. Screams and heat. Bodies squashed against hers. Her nostrils flared with the scent of fear and sweat.

Ahead of her, some people had managed to break through the line of encroaching police, and ran forward without a glance behind. A group of protestors heaved against the police in a synchronised push, knocking a few over in the process. If the police had been trying to reach the force projector, that goal became secondary.

A protestor pushed forward against an officer, trying to punch, and collapsed as a stun baton crashed into his face. Energy shields became battering rams. People still chanted, but terror had taken hold in the hearts of most. "Let me through!" a woman yelled as she struggled against the line of police.

A stun baton lanced through the air and stabbed into her face. She collapsed, wailing and clutching the spot where her eye had existed only seconds before. The crowd pushed forward, and her voice disappeared beneath the crushing weight of fearful feet.

The push broke the line, sending a good third of the officers reeling.

Dozens of protestors ran through into the street beyond, while others stayed, trying to appropriate energy shields and stun batons from the fallen police, who redoubled their efforts. Sparks flew as stun batons were set to maximum. Bodies stormed together. The world spun.

She came ever closer to freedom.

A man fell to the ground, head slamming against the sidewalk. He lay motionless. A fallen police officer drew himself into the foetal position, letting out a strangled cry as five men let fly with fists and feet. He was soon rescued, his comrades meting out a relentless barrage of punishment. A flash of light burst from one of the stun batons as it smacked an attacker's throat, sending a wave of energy into his body. A flurry of blows drew blood from his mouth and matted hair, and the attacker fell to the ground with finality. Kaiya stopped. Their eyes met, but she sensed hers were the only ones that saw.

Freedom beckoned. She was close!

Kaiya stepped over the protestor's body, her own being shoved this way and that by those around her. People pushed against police as others pulled back from the swinging stun batons. Some old woman blocked her path, too afraid to charge forth into freedom. Kaiya grabbed the woman's dress and yanked hard, pulling her out of the way, then rammed her shoulder into the crowd, forcing her way to the front.

An officer stood a metre away, raising his arm.

The sight of space filled Kaiya's mind, and she lunged forward, tackling the officer to the ground. The stun baton rolled out of his hand, and protestors behind her seized the opportunity to rush forward. Cool air soothed the beads of sweat on her face. Pressure surged from all sides, and she crawled forward on hands and knees, desperate to free herself from the crowd's weight.

The officer she had tackled grabbed her foot and pulled backwards. Snarling, she shook her foot free and kicked his helmet. The hand withdrew and she stumbled forward onto her feet as others burst through behind her. Kaiya ran, and ran, and stumbled, and ran, the world blurring around her until she fell to her knees, gasping for air.

She looked behind her and realised how little distance she had come. She forced herself forward, the buildings on both sides shifting in and out of focus, her stomach churning. A cacophony of screams punctured the evening.

Sirens wailed in the distance.

Kaiya pulled herself over to the sidewalk and sat against the buildings, sorting through the jumbled sensations in her body. She watched as protestors surged past the police, only a few remaining to raise the cry of "Death to traitors! Traitors hanged!" The police ran forward, free of most resistance, and pursued the man with the force projector. Kaiya watched through half-closed eyes as the man realised he would be unable to outrun them and turned around, raising the force projector one last time.

Five police shattered, exploding in a rain of blood and disintegrated armour.

The man succumbed to an onslaught of stun batons.

Kaiya tried to stand, conscious that the police would eventually return, and fell straight back down. Head spinning, she stared at the roundabout, which swarmed with armoured police. They restrained those protestors who dared to remain, forcing them down and electrobinding both wrists and ankles.

"You alright there?"

A woman knelt down and placed a gloved hand on her shoulder.

"I'm fine." Kaiya knelt up and attempted to stand again. She collapsed into the woman's arms.

"I'm not so sure about that."

Kaiya grabbed reluctantly onto the woman's shoulder and managed to stand, albeit bent over as the world swam around her.

"Any better?"

"I'll be fine," Kaiya snapped, looking past the paramedic's face.

"Here." The paramedic rummaged through her belt pack and took out a patch no larger than half a fingertip.

"No!" Kaiya withdrew her arm and pushed back, a wave of nausea flooding her body.

"It'll help," the paramedic said. "Trust me."

Kaiya struggled as the paramedic grabbed her arm and applied the patch. A tingly warmth spread through her body as the world came into focus.

"Better?"

Kaiya ignored the paramedic and watched a line of police approaching from the roundabout, electrobinding anyone they came across. Anyone still alive. Dozens of bodies lay still on the ground, pools of blood coating road tiles or glimmering on the glowstone sidewalks.

The paramedic waited.

Limbs burning, Kaiya fled through the streets of Leth.

6

KAIYA PEERED THROUGH THE DOOR TO HER PARENTS' ROOM. FOR three years she had avoided entering, conscious that her presence would disturb its patient, melancholy peace. Already the musty air shifted, trembling towards the doorway that had contained it for so long. She stepped inside, surveying the reminder of her parents' existence. A nightie waited, unmoved, thrown carelessly onto rumpled sheets. A tablet lay on her mother's bedside table. And on the bucket chair in the corner of the room, draped over its back, was her father's uniform.

Kaiya stepped inside and drew a slow breath. Time had not disintegrated the lingering scent of a two-thirds empty bottle of perfume, or was that simply her imagination responding to the stimulus of her context and the chasmic desires of her imagination? Her father's uniform felt soft. Its crispness had disappeared long ago. Kaiya felt around inside the pockets but found nothing.

No, the object of her searching wouldn't be in there.

The tablet still possessed a charge, though nearing its final quarter. How much longer would it yearn for its owner, for hands that would recharge? Kaiya touched the tablet, and it gave the softest of vibrations, sucking at the heat energy in her finger. It knew the touch was not its owner's, but it did not complain.

Kaiya looked around the room and pondered where her father would have put his access card. Her plan would fail without it. Her plan might still fail with it – in fact, the likelihood of success was narrow – but she had to try.

She searched his bedside table, rummaging through an assortment of odds and ends. She pulled out a holodisc, still over half-full with charge – it had obviously been important enough to her mother that she had continued to use it until she herself had been taken. Kaiya turned it on and flicked through holos she hadn't seen before. Many of them weren't even true holos, but simply reconstructions of old digital photographs. She assumed the recurring child was her father, and that those were the grandparents who had died before she was born.

Kaiya sat on the edge of the bed, engrossed in the holos. Her father stood in the town square, long-haired and even younger than her, smiling with a group of loose-robed friends under an anti-war banner. Behind them a crowd of hundreds mingled, placards and other banners rising into the air. No one had ever told her about this. It had to have been around the time of the last war with Tarkinia. Perhaps even before.

Kaiya flicked through until she came to a section of five holos that didn't belong with the rest. They were first-generation, not as smooth as modern holos, and all taken at a beach. She stood on the sand, staring out into the ocean as a small wave crashed about her toddler feet. Kaiya searched her memory but came up empty. She couldn't recall ever being at the beach, or touching sand and seawater. Something tickled in her mind, a feeling that yes, she had been there before, but that was surely just her brain processing the new knowledge, trying to convince itself that the holo spoke truth. Creating a shadow memory in response; why it felt so familiar all of a sudden.

She continued beyond the holos of a past she could not remember, and appeared in no more. Nearly all of them had been taken well before she was born, and none later than those of her as a toddler, until she came across a single holo from ten years prior. Her father's inauguration. He stood proud on the ceremonial podium erected in the commons where Amelia had condemned Benjamin's treachery, shaking hands with the Governor of the Southeast Borders. A line of Chief Inspectors sat behind, watching and applauding.

Even Bennett.

Kaiya turned off the holodisc and shoved it back into the drawer. She couldn't allow herself to be distracted. The access card had to be somewhere in there, and she turned her attention to the wardrobe, rustling through a thick collection of dusty shirts and pants. They should have bought an apartment with more space. Her parents had talked about it for years, but always decided against it. No need, they said, despite the fact they couldn't even fit their clothes into the wardrobe.

Kaiya searched her father's pockets one by one, distantly fearful that some insect would be hiding within, ready to poison and kill her. There she was, letting her imagination run away again. She shoved her hand into the final pocket and stopped, feeling the cool touch of thin metal, and pulled out her father's access card. Smaller than her index finger, it had faded with overuse. A Commissioner would be expected to have regular access to the concealed prison, amongst other facilities of which she likely knew nothing.

She returned to the hallway and closed the door behind her, gentle, drinking in the sight of her parents' bedroom one last time. She would not open it again. Only when its owners had returned would it once more see the world outside of its four walls.

Tilda sat at the dining table, consuming another newscast.

She glanced up at Kaiya, unable to hide the scepticism on her face.

"Don't," Kaiya warned. They had already argued about this.

"Kaiya—"

"I need to know. Why don't you understand that? I need to know."

"I do understand," Tilda placated. "I just think it's a really bad idea."

"You're not involved," Kaiya said, sitting on the ledge between corridor and dining room as she grabbed her shoes. "I'm not making you do anything. You can think it's the worst idea in the world, it has nothing to do with whether or not I'm going to go do it."

Kaiya laced her shoes and tucked the access card safely into her pocket.

"How do you even know he'll be there?" Tilda said.

"Because Benjamin as good as said it." Kaiya stood up. "Look. If I don't do this now, I might not get another chance. Benjamin's sending him to Akheron and won't let me see him."

"Kaiya, please. I just... are you sure it's really about Bennett?"

"I don't want to hear any more of your theories, Tilda. I'm perfectly capable of figuring out what I need and what I want. I don't need any of your advice, that's for sure."

Tilda looked away, stung.

She deserved it.

———

Kaiya loitered outside a nondescript food factory deep within southwest quadrant. The narrow, curving street played host to a dozen or so pedestrians each minding their own business. She clenched the access card in her pocketed hand, knowing that she was beginning to look suspicious, and forced herself to walk into the factory, a flash of heat rising with the hairs on the back of her neck.

The five-storey factory was quiet. Kaiya looked up at the glass-encased upper levels that didn't extend all the way to the front wall. Each one contained a concentrated mass of crops at different stages of growth, the second level being almost ready for consumption. Fighting colours pressed against their glass containment, waiting for harvest. She couldn't see anything on the fifth storey, but meat production did require a different setup.

Offices and labs hid behind the doors directly in front of her, though she turned her focus to one of the lifts on either side of the travertine lobby. She stepped inside and motioned for the doors to close, then stared at the control panel. A voice asked her which level she would like to go to, and she advised it that she desired to visit the cellar. After a brief consideration, the voice asked for authority, and Kaiya tapped the access card against the control panel.

When the lift began to move, Kaiya's heart thumped harder. She relaxed her fist, not realising she had clenched it in the first place. She had worried the lift would not accept the access card, but deeper she travelled into the bowels of the factory, wondering if this meant the access card would work for every authority challenge. There would be questions to answer if it didn't.

The lift stopped and opened. Kaiya stepped out into a dimly-lit, rectangular corridor with rough stone walls, a single steel door looming at the other end. A wide glass panel set into the wall provided surveillance, and Kaiya donned her best air of authority as she strode past it, glancing at the two guards within. They stared at her as she passed, frowning, but stayed in their positions. No one could possibly be down there without knowledge and access, after all.

Kaiya stopped at the heavy door nearly twice her height and

a good two or more metres wide. What else they stored down there that required such a large door she didn't know, and she doubted she ever would. Her father had never mentioned the place. It had been her mother, in the early years of the Occupation, who told her of its existence, but neither of them had ever been there.

She tapped her access card against the panel beside the door and waited. It didn't register. She pulled the massive vertical handle, but the door didn't budge. She could just walk away and go back home, though the guards might be suspicious. She could run instead. But then, they likely had the power to stop the lift and bring her back down. No, she was there now, and she couldn't escape. She tapped the panel again, and the corridor lights switched to red.

Hot prickles overwhelmed as terror flooded her body, making every movement jelly. A panel of steel slammed down in front of the lift, and one of the guards stepped out of the office, striding towards her. Kaiya froze.

"May I see your access card, ma'am?"

Kaiya unclenched her clammy hand and gave him the access card. He put it up to his eyes and squinted.

"It's old," he said, assessing her. Why hadn't she thought of that? She would have been fourteen when that access card had been made. How could she have been so stupid? It was never going to work. She should have listened to Tilda.

"May I ask who it is you're here to see?"

"Bennett," she said.

The guard looked closer at her. "One moment."

He turned and walked back into the office.

Kaiya waited.

Time dragged, the red lights boring into her skull and reminding her every drawn-out second that she had failed. Any second now the prison door would open and police would pour out, dragging her inside so no one would see her face again. She would rot in the stench of her own decay as Bennett watched, laughing, and soldiers came to satisfy themselves inside her. Kormac would return and start a new life with Tilda, both forgetting that she had ever existed.

Nausea threatened to overwhelm her and she forced herself to step forward until she could see the police through the glass panel. They chatted, mouths moving soundlessly, as the one with the access card talked on a phone at the same time. He saw her through the window.

And smiled.

He ended his conversation on the phone and gave his companion an order. The lights returned to normal and the steel panel blocking entry to the lift retracted. The guard returned from his sojourn in the office, demeanour transformed, and handed her the access card.

"My apologies, ma'am. We are still having issues with the localweb. Leakage from the Network. Access privileges have been restored."

Kaiya looked at the card, dizzy with relief she hadn't finished processing.

"Thank you," she said, conscious of her voice's lack of authority. The guard gave her a final appraisal and returned to the office.

Kaiya walked back over to the oversized steel door, still recovering her stomach as she tried to appear unfazed by the torture of assumed failure. She focused her thoughts on what – and who – waited behind the door, fanning the tiny flame that had rekindled itself inside her.

Finally, she would confront him. She would have answers.

The panel beeped as she touched it with the access card, and the steel door emitted a series of metallic booms as it unlocked. Kaiya pulled on the handle, stepping backwards to give herself leverage, and grunted as she opened the door.

Beyond, the corridor continued in the same style as the one she stood in, only much darker.

As soon as she stepped through, the door began to close, trapping her in silence. The new corridor brightened. The floors were glowstone! She continued forward and stared up at the dark ceiling, polished in such a way as to reflect the glowstone below.

Equidistant steel doors with intercoms and glass viewing panels beckoned, six on each wall and one at the end of the corridor. Kaiya walked up to a viewing panel and looked inside. A man sat on the prison bed within, staring at her. The gaze shocked her until she realised that the glowstone's activation would have alerted whoever occupied each cell. The thought of it made her skin crawl, and she stepped away from the door to place her back against the bare wall, imagining some freak breakout.

Bennett may not even be there.

Kaiya cursed herself for jumping at shadows and began to inspect the cells. Eight of them were empty, which didn't surprise her. Whoever occupied the remaining five had done something so repugnant that even a maximum security facility was considered inappropriate. They would be at risk from not only other inmates but prison staff. There had been a case before she was born, her mother said, of a serial killer who butchered his child victims and publicly displayed their broken bodies. A decorated police officer was convicted of the crimes and imprisoned, awaiting trial. On the very first night the people rose up and stormed the facility, meeting little resistance from the guards.

His body was left on display in the town square for five days, treated in the same manner he had treated his victims.

Whether the concealed prison existed before then, her mother hadn't known. Those who knew of its existence even now were few and far between. Of course, people *knew*, if only by rumour and legend. If Benjamin were to put Bennett somewhere for protection, it would be here.

Kaiya stared through one of the windows at a sad-looking woman. Deep and thoughtful, she looked ever so familiar. The woman gazed back at her and smiled gently. Kaiya drew back, appalled at the woman's sincerity. Beauty could not exist in such a place of concentrated evil. What crime had she committed that allowed her to retain such a smile?

Having exhausted the twelve cells on either side of the corridor, Kaiya turned to face the final door opposite the entrance. It would be a fitting space for Bennett to occupy. She edged closer, slivers of nausea returning in fear both of finding him and not. What would she say to him, having achieved what she had assumed would be unachievable? The access card surely contained details of its owner.

Kaiya gazed into the cell as she approached, seeing nothing but the same basic furnishings as the other empty cells, and pressed her face against the glass.

Bennett stepped into view from the corner in which he hid, grinning at Kaiya.

She pulled back, acid pouring through her veins.

Bennett raised his hand so it was visible behind the glass, and pointed down through the door at the intercom. Kaiya hesitated as she searched for some kind of activation button, then realised she needed to insert the access card in a slot.

A tiny buzz of static floated through the corridor.

"It only works if you make it work," Bennett explained.

They considered each other. Bennett had seen better days, his face thinner than before, over a week unshaven, his hair already greyer. But still his eyes glinted as he let out a strained, caustic laugh. "Is this Benjamin's idea of a joke?"

"He doesn't know I'm here," Kaiya said.

Bennett's eyes widened and he nodded approvingly. "Your father's access card..."

"Yes."

He laughed again, bitter. "Then we don't have much time."

"What do you mean?"

Bennett stared at her and gave a disinterested shrug. "So the progeny of my predecessor—"

"Answer my question."

Bennett's face moved ever so closer to the viewing panel. "No," he whispered. "You interrupted my poetry."

"What?"

"The progeny of my predecessor peruses my prison. I thought it up just before." Bennett's face touched the glass and he grinned. "Do you like it, Kaiya? Do you like my poetry?"

"That's not poetry."

Bennett drew back with feigned shock. "It's not? Oh my, Kaiya, I do apologise that my brief foray into the arts does not meet your expectations. Truly, I am sorry."

Kaiya peered at the former Commissioner. "Why is Benjamin protecting you?"

"Wrong question," Bennett shouted, sending Kaiya back a few steps in shock. He gazed at her through the glass, eyes never wavering. "When did I become a poet?"

"You're not a poet."

"But I am! You may not wish to see me as a poet, but does that mean I am not a poet?"

"What on earth are you talking about?"

"Answer my question. When did I become a poet?"

"This is ridiculous."

"When did I become a poet, Kaiya?"

Kaiya bent down and screamed into the intercom. "When did you become a poet?"

Bennett fell silent, recovering from the sudden burst of sound inside his cell.

Kaiya stared at him, body raging with unspent fury. How did the cell door open? She pictured herself charging in and strangling that miserable excuse for life, smashing his head against the floor until a bloody pulp stared up at her on the edge of death, begging for mercy that would not be extended.

"I was born a poet," Bennett said. He no longer smiled nor met her gaze, but simply searched his own mind for some memory she could not see.

"You don't make a very good one."

It hadn't crossed her mind that perhaps Bennett would have lost a few threads of sanity.

"Maybe I'll improve."

"I doubt it. You don't even know what poetry is."

"And you do?" Bennett turned his attention back to her, lips curving.

"Answer my question," Kaiya said. "Why is Benjamin protecting you."

"Now, this is an interesting question. A curious one. Why do you think your father's lapdog would be protecting me? The last I heard, I'm being sent to Akheron to face an expedited trial. That doesn't sound much like protection, does it?"

"It's more than you deserve."

Bennett let out a sigh of satisfaction. "More than I deserve. Yes. What do I deserve, Kaiya?"

He stared at her through the viewing panel, face still brimming with arrogance, and Kaiya leaned forward until her nose touched glass.

"Pain."

"Yes! That's what I like to hear, Kaiya. Good girl. You want me to suffer."

"I want you to die."

"And if they sentence me to death?" he asked, savouring the final word in mockery. "In Akheron? That won't be enough?"

"No! Your death isn't theirs. It's ours. It belongs to the people of Leth. The people you betrayed."

"Of course," he said, lifting his hands as if to indicate he agreed. "Though, by the people of Leth you mean yourself, don't you?" His eyes flickered as he studied her. "Such a pity your access card doesn't... allow access. Ironic."

"Don't measure me by your standards. You're a monster."

"No, I'm not," he said. "I'm a poet. We established this already. Besides," he continued before she could say more, "you're a liar. I'm not."

It would have given so much satisfaction to slice his skin.

"You're disgusting."

"Everyone claims they're doing it for the people," Bennett said. "Do you want me to say the same? That all along I was working in the interests of the people of Leth? Because I will, if you like. I'll shout it out and say 'you don't understand, I was really protecting you!' To some degree that's true, but it would still make me a liar. We only ever see how bad things were, not how much worse things could have been, not that any of that is really why I did it. You see, Kaiya, I'm honest about my motivations. I can take ownership of my desires, but you're still looking for some outside authority to legitimate doing what you want to do."

Bennett's eyes pierced her own, flicking back and forth between them. Kaiya stayed silent, matching his gaze, cautious of the former Commissioner's sudden bout of lucidity. Perhaps those strands of insanity had been a ruse.

"And what do I want to do?"

"Kill me," Bennett said. He smiled.

"You say it as though it's a surprise to me. Of course I want to kill you."

"Then don't hide it behind your puerile worship of 'the people,'" Bennett said, impassioned. "You don't care about them! So why are you pretending? You don't want to just watch me die, you want to *make* me die. Isn't that the truth? Isn't that what you dream about? The only reason you don't want them to take me to Akheron is because you might miss out on being the one to do the deed."

"I care about justice! I care about the people!"

Bennett's face contorted in disgust. "You are a liar, girl. A petulant liar, as naïve as ever. Justice does not exist. The people do not exist. Stop hiding behind your lies and own your desires. I am a poet," he said, pointing violently to himself. "You are not."

Kaiya frowned, sensing that she was ill-equipped to respond to Bennett's confounding diatribe. How they had come to such a point was beyond her, but it dawned that the entire exchange had been a calculated distraction. Bennett knew full well why she was there. He had derailed her from the very beginning with his idiotic assertions about poetry, and strung her along on a wild goose chase that revealed nothing and left her none the wiser.

"What happened to my father?" she asked, forcing self-control.

Bennett shrugged. "What makes you think I would know that?"

"Don't treat me like an idiot. You wanted him gone."

"I wanted his job," he corrected. "There's a difference."

"You expect me to believe you have no idea—"

"Oh, I have an idea, Kaiya. I have an idea." His eyes gleamed with malevolence.

Needles of burning trepidation punctured her skin. "Tell me."

"Are you sure you want to know?"

"Tell me!" she commanded, slapping the steel door and hiding the sudden burst of pain that shot through her arm.

Bennett considered her through the glass. "Why should I? What do I get in return?"

"I'm not playing your games anymore."

"What game is that? You have nothing to offer me. That's all that matters."

Kaiya screamed and kicked the door. There had to be a way in. The access card had to do what its name said it did. Somewhere there was a button, or a switch, just something that would allow her to go in there and extract the information she needed.

Steel groaned behind her.

A police officer entered the corridor, flanked by the two guards.

Kaiya shoved her face up to the glass and banged on the door again. "Tell me, you fucking creature! Tell me!"

Bennett ignored her, still smiling as the guards approached. Kaiya turned and swung at one of them. The guard promptly grabbed her forearm and twisted it behind her. She yelped in pain as she struggled, but was quickly overcome and placed kneeling on the ground.

The familiar-looking woman stood behind her door, watching.

"So you're Kaiya," the officer said.

Kaiya looked up at the frowning man in his mid-thirties. A Chief Inspector. The same one that Benjamin had stood with at the previous evening's protest.

"You..." Kaiya said.

"Hello, Joseph," came Bennett's voice in sing-song. "Hey, Kaiya. I told you we didn't have much time. Why don't you ask him about your father? Rumour has it he knows a thing or two."

The Chief Inspector stepped towards the cell and ripped out the access card. The gentle hiss of static disappeared, as did Bennett's mocking voice. Behind the viewing panel, he shouted in silence.

"Who are you?" Kaiya demanded. "What do you know about my father?"

The Chief Inspector toyed with the access card and looked down at her. "You shouldn't be here," he said.

Kaiya despised him already, and kicked him in the shin. He gave no response at first, then returned the favour, kicking her in the same spot. Kaiya winced as slivers of fire sliced through her leg.

"I'm not Benjamin. I'm willing to stoop to your level. So if that's how you want to act, then go ahead. You'd better hope you're ready to deal with the consequences. Get up."

Kaiya avoided the Chief Inspector's gaze. There was something behind it she couldn't place. A fury that didn't come from a place of true anger. "What did he mean? What do you know about my father."

"This is neither the time nor the place," the Chief Inspector said. "Get up and come with me."

"Where?" she asked, conscious that she couldn't stall forever.

"Benjamin. That's all you need to know. Now get up."

Kaiya obeyed.

The southeast quadrant CBD had been placed under guard and closed to the general public. Kaiya stared down from the Commissioner's lounge at remnants of clothing and makeshift weapons. The bodies had been moved, but the memory remained, painted in coagulate red.

"Kaiya," Benjamin said, his voice gentle as he sidled up beside her. "Chief Inspector Joseph is leaving now."

She ignored him, eyes fixed resolutely ahead. Her shin still hurt, and Joseph had refused to answer any of her questions. The sooner he left the better.

Benjamin glanced across at her. "Kaiya?"

Joseph's voice floated in from behind them. "Forget it, Benjamin."

Benjamin turned to face the Chief Inspector. "I apologise, Joseph."

"It's not your fault," Joseph said, with an emphasis that Kaiya could not interpret any way other than an attack on her. "As you said before…"

When before was, Kaiya didn't know. The sound of a lift's opening and closing announced Joseph's departure, and her body lost a little of its stiffness. She refused to dignify that man's presence.

"Come sit down," Benjamin said, taking a spot on one of the leather couches.

Kaiya watched a patrolling police officer for a little longer before making her way to the couch opposite Benjamin.

"You've been busy," he said.

Kaiya folded her arms. "And?"

"And we should talk about it. You did break in to a restricted facility, after all. That's a serious matter."

"I didn't break in," Kaiya said, breaking the promise she had only just made to herself that she wouldn't rise to Benjamin's goading. "Your guards let me in."

"Indeed. They did allow you in, knowing full well that you were not the owner of the access card, as I directed them to. But you still went there in the first place and used it."

"So what are you going to do? Put me in prison?"

"Don't be silly," Benjamin said. "Although I always have that option if you choose not to cooperate with me."

"That's not much of a choice."

"But it *is* still a choice."

Benjamin watched her from his couch, relaxed.

"Fine," Kaiya said, wary he may not be bluffing, and conscious of how exposed they were in the Commissioner's lounge. "Are the windows open?"

"Of course. Do you not feel comfortable being seen by anyone? Or is accountability only for other people?"

"You're in a position of authority," Kaiya said, and shifted uncomfortably as Benjamin stared at her with no indication he intended to respond. "Whatever. I'm just not used to it."

"People rarely are. And few people actively enjoy being subject to such scrutiny. I admit even I was taken aback by just how vulnerable you are in this place."

Benjamin gazed around at the Commissioner's lounge, holding back a hundred thoughts for every one he expressed, the way he always did.

"I am disappointed in you, Kaiya. You knew I did not want you to see Bennett."

Kaiya steeled herself in the face of her unwanted shame. "It's not your place to tell me I can't."

"It is precisely my place. A rather important fact you've chosen to forget."

"Just because you're Commissioner now it doesn't mean you should be."

"I'm aware of your feelings," Benjamin said with gentle finality. "You've already made them clear to me. Until you can provide me with the name of the person who should replace me, and is available to do so, your opinion is invalid."

Kaiya bit back what she wanted to say and frowned, changing tack. "If you didn't want me to see him, why did you tell the guards to let me in?"

Benjamin shook his head. "You misunderstand me. It is a general direction, not a specific one. If they had called me and not Joseph, then I would have left you in lockdown and sent someone to pick you up. Joseph decided to let you in. I can only guess at why."

Whatever those guesses were, Kaiya could tell Benjamin felt they were correct.

"I saw Joseph last night. With you."

Benjamin nodded. "I know."

"You pointed at me, like you were showing him who I was. Why?"

"I was merely pointing out the daughter of someone we both respected. I have placed a great deal of trust in Joseph. That is why he is informed of anyone who visits Bennett. It is an authority I have delegated to him." Benjamin glanced outside, weighing something in his mind. "You accused me of being a collaborator, an accusation I do not think you mean seriously. But you are correct in implicating many of the people in this organisation. To some degree, every person within the walls of Leth is a collaborator. The trick is to sort out the passive from the active."

"No," Kaiya said, shaking her head. "There's no difference. And not everyone was a collaborator. Some of us fought back."

Benjamin considered her before continuing in disregard of her statement, "Do you know what happens when strong leaders take command of organisations?" he said. "They change culture. The identities of individuals within the organisation morph into something that resemble the ideals of the leadership. Now, if the change from one leader to the next is quite sudden, and each set of ideals is markedly different, there will always be conflict, and even though the new ideals will seep through, not everyone will be soaked, especially those who remain loyal to the old ideals. Do you understand what I am saying?"

Kaiya nodded, though it all sounded like a pile of typical collaborator justification.

"Your father led the force with a set of ideals, and then Bennett came with a very different set, and in a very different context. There were people who felt more affinity with his ideals than your father's, and they became the most loyal. Those who were left remained on the outer, unable to leave, but always at conflict within themselves between the prevailing culture and the one they used to enjoy. But you know what I've learnt about people in the time that I've been an officer, Kaiya? None of us are as strong as we think we are, and the context of our existence determines much more than we give it credit for. So what do you think six years of Bennett did to the people in this organisation?

How do you think Bennett's set of ideals influenced those who are still here? You saw it last night, didn't you?"

The scent of singed skin rose from her memory, along with the crackle of stun batons striking their targets.

"And now there is yet another Commissioner." Benjamin grinned at her. "I do not presume to put myself in the same category as your father. We are fundamentally different people. But my ideals are different to Bennett's, and that creates an environment of instability, in the beginning. In time, culture will change, identities will morph, but it does leave a significant problem, given the context: how to weed out those who still actively support Bennett, and change the behaviour of those who enjoyed their time under his leadership a little too much."

Kaiya struggled to speak at first, sighing in exasperation. "You're actually saying that if everyone else is doing something, it's ok to do it? That you can excuse what a bunch of collaborators did because Bennett's existence 'made' them do it?"

"I never said anything about excusing behaviour. I'm talking about recognising where behaviour comes from and differentiating between two types of people. There are people who want to free Bennett. People who were his allies and actively supported his engagement with the Tarkinians. These people exist right now, Kaiya, in this organisation, and they are working to undermine everything I do. There are other people who got a taste of freedom under Bennett, who liked the power. They didn't care who was Commissioner, they cared about what they could do with their position. You don't deal with these two types of people in the same way."

"Yes, you do! They are collaborators, Benjamin, and so are you!"

"I'm as much a collaborator as you are. In any case, your opinion is invalid. If you knew anything about what is happening in this building, you would support me."

"Then tell me. If you're so desperate for my support, tell me."

Benjamin studied her, sifting through all those thoughts he kept to himself. How anyone had decided he had what it took to be Commissioner baffled her. Benjamin belonged in analysis, not decision-making.

"I have told you enough. You simply don't grasp the magnitude of it. That is why I gave Joseph watch over who visits Bennett. There are too many lies and too few officers I can trust."

"How do you know you can trust Joseph? What if he's a collaborator?"

Again Benjamin weighed information in his mind. "There is no one in this building I trust more than Chief Inspector Joseph. If anything ever happens to me, remember that."

Her shin still throbbed distantly. "What do you mean if anything ever happens to you?"

"I've already told you that this place is fracturing. But you don't seem capable of reading between the lines. You used to be sharp, Kaiya. You used to think things through. I've had Bennett supporters trying to kill me, and you're sitting there accusing me of being on the same side."

"You're the Commissioner," Kaiya said, bristling at his disparagement. "You've got constant protection."

Benjamin shook his head and sniggered. "I have less authority than you think I do. You think that little protest your friend mounted last night – yes, I know exactly who Amelia is – you think that's all it was? Kaiya, that was an open rebellion. Why would I put fully-armoured officers in plain sight and in such a formation as to box in hundreds of people who hate them? That's not public protection – that's goading. Think! You used to be good at that."

Kaiya did as Benjamin asked.

"You watched. You could have done something to stop it."

"Even if I could have, I would not. It's better that people think we are corrupt and united, than divided. Not that I think most people see it so simply, but for the people who do see it that way, it's important. Besides, you may not be able to tell one officer from another in riot gear, but I can."

Benjamin smiled. "So you see, now, that it's not as simple as me protecting Bennett."

Kaiya studied him. Everything he said sounded too convenient. "If you're so concerned about someone letting Bennett escape, why not give the people what they want? Then they'd know you're different, that things have changed."

"Oh, Kaiya..." he said, amused. "I think that would prove the exact opposite."

She went to speak, but Benjamin held up his hand. "In any case, I won't allow Leth to sink any further into self-destruction. The Atlanticans have no interest in taking on a law enforcement capacity, so I've sent to Akheron for reinforcements. They have agreed to send a Civil Order Protection Taskforce."

Kaiya stood up and swore, kicking the lounge for good measure. "You sell-out! The Tarkinians leave and now you want to bring in a bunch of Nymians?"

"Kaiya, we *are* Nymian. Don't deny it! None of us were alive eight hundred years ago. I cannot for the life of me understand this absurd need for a separate identity."

"We're border towns, Benjamin. We *are* different. We've never been a part Nymosen or Tarkinia. Only dominoes that fall either way whenever they go to war. We might have been in Nymosen for eight hundred years, but only because the duke surrendered in the face of Nymian pressure."

Benjamin looked at her, face filled with incredulity. "Kaiya, listen to yourself. Eight hundred years ago! When have you *ever* cared about distinguishing yourself from the rest of Nymosen? If you want to discuss purity, start with yourself. Your mother came from Akheron."

"She *escaped* Akheron. That place is more corrupt than—"

"Kaiya," Benjamin said, staring at her with a rare flash of anger. "You've never been to Akheron. I don't know where you're getting these ideas from. Perhaps you do need to go away for a little while. To keep you safe from whatever it is that's distorting your mind."

Kaiya held back her retort and sat. Benjamin considered her and sighed.

"I'm sorry I didn't see you more often," he said. "And your mother. Bennett had his eye on me, I hope you understand that. I thought the less I interacted with you, the less likely he would be to do something harmful. To all of us. Perhaps I was wrong…"

Benjamin shrugged and gazed out the window. Kaiya followed his lead, watching the unmoving sky, exhausted. "There's something you're not telling me, Kaiya. I know it."

"There's hundreds of things you don't tell me."

"That's true," he said, chuckling, and looked back to her. "Is it something you would like to talk about?"

Kaiya shook her head, and Benjamin accepted the answer.

"There was a woman in there," Kaiya said. "In the concealed prison. She looked familiar."

Benjamin nodded slowly. "Yes, I know who you're talking about. She should be familiar. You met her, a long time ago. She was the Technology Director."

The memory came clear into Kaiya's head, the imprisoned woman younger, rounder, her smile broad and genuine. "What did she do that's so bad?"

Benjamin considered her, once more weighing something in his mind. "She wrote the virus that brought down the Network. Did you ever wonder how the Tarkinians came in so easily? Why all our communications and systems just disappeared overnight? That was her."

Kaiya frowned. "But why? I've never heard anything about this before."

"Why indeed," Benjamin said. "That is something I do not know. Something she will not reveal. Money, perhaps? I doubt that. In any case, that is one of the reasons she is there."

"She started the whole war," Kaiya said, trying to match the woman's smile with the atrocity of her actions.

"She enabled the war," Benjamin corrected, eyes flickering back and forth between her own.

Kaiya hesitated, her curiosity piqued. "What do you mean 'one' of the reasons?"

Benjamin nodded to himself. "Bennett may have masterminded the Night of Retribution, Kaiya, but she executed it. She devised the program that selected all those who were taken."

They sat in silence for several minutes, Kaiya's mind struggling to comprehend the depth of betrayal. Bennett had stood to gain from his actions, but what of her? What had she received?

"No one knows about her," she said, still numbed by the revelation.

"Do you think they would care?" Benjamin asked.

The question shocked her. "Of course they would!"

"Then why hasn't anyone asked about the people under Bennett? Or do the 'people of Leth' think he did everything single-handedly with a uniform mass of collaborators beneath him? Has no one thought to ask who his biggest supporters were? Who executed his strategies? The individuals, Kaiya, not the teeming mass you call collaborators."

Kaiya frowned and shook her head. "Bennett was the Commissioner. He made it happen. He was the figurehead – the symbol."

"Yes, he was," Benjamin said. "But he didn't make it happen all by himself. You know this already, but you haven't truly penetrated the implications. People rarely do when they are angry. That woman is the reason the Night of Retribution happened. Without her, it could not have been done. But yet it's still Bennett's fault? To some degree, yes, but people have a tendency towards placing the actions of many onto the shoulders of one. It's much simpler that way, isn't it? Conversely, people also do the same thing the other way around. And in the end, it's those in the middle who escape notice, because everyone is so focused on one person as reason, and all people as executor, when neither has full claim to those titles."

Kaiya stared at Benjamin. She had no more patience for this collaborator-justifying nonsense.

7

KAIYA KNELT, HOLDING A ROAD TILE IN HER HAND. HER SHIFT WAS almost over and she had filled barely a fifth of her quota. She stared at the road tile, moving it this way and that to see her glum reflection at different angles. Nearby, a holoboard scrolled through advertisements. Her shift had played out to the cycle of the holoboard, and she knew her few moments of relief would arrive soon.

When they did, she stared up, drinking in the unsatisfying faux-fulfilment of another *Rapture* advertisement. She had gone to the clinic, begged them for more, but a week had not passed. They had left her stranded in an ocean of pointlessness, her existence slowly fading into the road tiles for which she no longer cared.

Nothing had happened since she spoke with Benjamin two days prior. No news, no protests, no punishment, no happiness. No space to be silent with only herself, Tilda's continual presence becoming more frustrating. The only solace was the knowledge that in a mere few days she could return and feel alive once more; to recharge and grasp enough fortitude to struggle through another week.

She healed and replaced the road tile. That was enough. She no longer had the energy to pretend she was doing her work, so she packed her gear and walked away. Her meetings with Bennett and Benjamin played through her mind again and again, and that woman's smile. She couldn't stop the relentless churning of these most recent memories, nor did she possess any desire to stop them.

She relished the insights they had given her: Bennett was a madman, and Benjamin an apologist. It was as simple as that.

Kaiya ignored the few people who dared venture out since the arrival of the Civil Order Protection Taskforce. Benjamin had betrayed the people of Leth, just like Bennett, and left them all having to answer to these self-important police officers from Akheron who thought they could randomly stop and interrogate anyone they liked. Thankfully none bothered her, though a trio near the front of her building made no effort to hide their suspicious gazes.

Kaiya slammed the door as she entered her apartment, ignoring Tilda's hesitant welcome, and made for her bedroom, slamming that door as well. She unlaced her shoes and threw them onto the floor, the second one bouncing a metre away from the first, and collapsed onto her bed.

Thus would begin another evening of nothingness.

Her vision was split between bedsheets and the dark shadow of her arm. She traced the bedsheet patterns over and over again, mind flitting back and forth between memories she didn't want to entertain, but still enjoyed for their capacity to inflict pain that she deserved to feel. She was a coward. She should have been with Amelia right now, making things happen, standing in Benjamin's way, and there she was wallowing in the torment of her own mind.

A knock came at the door, which she ignored. Tilda stepped quietly into the room and Kaiya watched from the corner of her eye.

"Kaiya," Tilda said, sitting on the edge of the bed. "What happened?"

"Nothing."

Tilda played with the bedsheets. "Did you go to the clinic?" she asked casually, as if their argument about it had never happened.

Kaiya grunted her assent. That was all she wished to say on the matter.

Tilda must have understood, and repositioned herself closer. "I know you don't care what I think, but... I'm glad they didn't let you."

"I *don't* care what you think," Kaiya said. Whether or not that was strictly true, she couldn't be certain.

"Why don't we do something?"

"What do you mean do something?" Kaiya asked. "You never want to do anything. You just stay here. What do you even do all day?"

Tilda's lips thinned as she paused before answering. "If you don't want me here anymore, just tell me."

Kaiya refused to acknowledge the ludicrous statement, her eyes beginning to swim. Tilda should already have known that's not really what she wanted. The weight of cowardice and failure oppressed her. Amelia's protest had achieved nothing but more death. Bennett had given her nothing about her father. Benjamin still refused to give the people what they wanted, insisting on some distinction between different types of collaborator that didn't even exist.

Tilda edged closer and lay down, taking a few strands of Kaiya's hair into her hands. Kaiya began to sob, body heaving up and down on the bed. Why could she not just disappear? Fade into insignificance, retreat to some uninhabited portion of the world, or even just her mind?

Tilda continued to play with her hair, staying silent – something Tilda had never been good at in the past. She had always been the more boisterous of them, but time and circumstance had changed that. Maybe she would return to that state of being, but her disdain for leaving the apartment stood in her way.

"It's like no one cares," Kaiya said, "about everything that's happened. It's like everyone's just trying to forget about it."

Kaiya looked across at Tilda, whose face remained impassive.

"Aren't you trying to forget? With *Rapture*?"

Kaiya shrugged. "Maybe. I don't know. I want to and I don't."

Tilda moaned agreement. "Just specific things?"

Kaiya nodded, wiping tears away. "But it still happened, even if I could forget it. How does that work?"

"I don't know," Tilda said. "I think it's better not to find out."

"I wouldn't get full *Rapture*," Kaiya explained. "It wouldn't be fair to Kormac, or my parents."

Tilda studied her. "And what if..."

Kaiya shrugged with another sharp intake of breath, Tilda's voice trailing away. "They're coming back. You'll see. Yours, too."

She threw a weak smile at Tilda, who returned it, eyes doubtful. "I hope so."

They stayed together for a long while as Kaiya emptied herself of desolation. For all that Tilda refused to see the need to act against all collaborators, she at least stayed loyal. When Kaiya had recovered most of her voice, she told Tilda of her experience with Bennett and Benjamin, a story that she had withheld in some obscure retribution for Tilda's failure to agree on the question of collaborators.

"I think that I wouldn't want to be Benjamin," Tilda said when Kaiya asked for her thoughts.

"But do you believe him?"

"About what? That people are trying to free Bennett? That he doesn't have control over the police? I don't have any reason to think he's lying."

"But that stuff about different types of collaborator."

Tilda sighed. "I don't know, Kaiya. I don't try to say I know the answer. I just want things to go back to normal. I don't know who's right and wrong. Obviously Bennett's a bad person, but other than that, I think it's complicated. I know it's different for you..."

"Maybe," Kaiya whispered. It seemed bizarre that someone could truly not care about bringing the collaborators to justice. She was too tired to argue the point with Tilda, that 'normal' relied upon consequences for treachery. No 'normal' could exist without the complete destruction of those who had aided the Tarkinians, just as no wound could truly heal while the foreign material still festered.

"You know, I can understand why some people would become collaborators," Kaiya admitted. "It's easier. But what I don't understand is how these women, Tilda... these sluts, how they can go around sleeping with Tarkinians."

Tilda grimaced. "I don't like that word," she said.

"But it's what they are. Giving themselves away for whatever favours the soldiers offered them. It's disgusting."

"Kaiya, you don't know anything about them." Tilda sounded genuinely hurt, her face locked in a disconsolate frown. "I knew someone," she said. "In a relationship with a Tarkinian officer. They were very much in love."

"Who?"

"I'm not telling you, Kaiya. She's suffered enough, already, and she doesn't need Amelia's cronies looking for her. She already had her house burnt down."

"Good," Kaiya said. At least there had been some punishment for the transgression.

Neither of them said anything more. Kaiya rubbed her eyes, removing the final traces of catharsis, as Tilda's face maintained its frown. A trace of hope lingered once more in Kaiya's mind. The Taskforce didn't have to be the end of the matter. No, she needed to see Amelia. If Benjamin's position was weak, then that presented both an opportunity and a necessity for action. The rogue officers still loyal to Bennett would both prove to the people that they needed to rise up, and at the same time hinder Benjamin's capacity to stop them applying pressure. And if they did not act, then Benjamin's strategy – misguided as it was – may lead to the installation of a Bennett loyalist, and Bennett's release.

Three confident knocks at the door interrupted her thoughts.

She looked at Tilda, who had also tensed at the sound. They both lay still, somewhat stunned, until Kaiya crawled out of the bed and walked out into the corridor. Tilda followed, at least to the bedroom door, and half hid herself behind the wall, peeking through the doorframe.

The knocks came again.

Kaiya tapped the viewpanel and swallowed, her heart thudding harder upon seeing the *Allied Atlantica* soldier standing outside. The sight of him came as a shock, until she reminded herself that she *had* invited him there.

On condition.

She opened the door and greeted the soldier, looking back to Tilda for some level of support. Tilda decoded the visual message and walked over. The soldier wasn't so large that he would easily best them both, though he was better-trained than her, no doubt.

"I hope I find you well," the soldier said with a formal bob of his head.

Kaiya tried not to smile at him. "Yes. Thank you."

Tilda leaned against the wall where the corridor met the living room.

"This is the soldier I told you about," Kaiya said to Tilda, hoping to silently establish that they were to treat him as coldly as possible.

The memo didn't reach her.

"Tilda," she said with a smile.

"Jonathan." They shook hands with warm formality, and thus disappeared Kaiya's effort at depersonalising the Atlantican. She supposed the refusal to know his name would have been thwarted eventually, somehow. He looked back to Kaiya. "I don't think I actually know your name?"

Kaiya folded her arms. "You have news?"

The edges of Jonathan's mouth twitched an involuntary smile. "Yes," he said, smoothing his face.

Kaiya waited for him to say more, but he simply stood there, waiting.

"Why don't you come in?" Tilda said with a smile, her eyes a reprimand towards Kaiya.

"Thank you," Jonathan said. "My pleasure."

Kaiya stepped back into the dining room. "Might as well come in here," she said, taking a seat on the window–side of the table. Any barrier between her and the soldier was better than none.

Jonathan took a seat opposite her, and Tilda positioned herself not far away on the same side. Kaiya glanced at her, trying to express her disapproval, but Tilda simply grinned and directed her gaze back towards the soldier.

"So what's happening?" Kaiya asked, knees shaking beneath the table.

Jonathan laced his fingers and leaned forward in his seat. "I've done some asking around," he said. "Friends, people I trust, people with higher access. The good news is that there are convoys nearly here. We expect the first to arrive tomorrow."

Kaiya trembled. The information demanded silent appreciation. Across the table, Tilda had become more serious, still focused on the soldier.

"When you say convoys," Kaiya said, struggling to level her voice, "you mean... alive?"

"Yes," he said.

Kaiya leaned back and looked up to the ceiling, relief flooding her face. The rush of emotion came to her unexpected, though what she had expected, she did not know. "So they are from the camps? They've just been released?"

Jonathan gave the question a great deal of consideration. "Not quite," he said. "The Tarkinian camp system is complex. Each camp has a specific purpose, and they're spread out. These are only people from the outermost camps, ones that we liberated several weeks ago. At least, this is the information I have been given."

Kaiya hesitated, her joy slipping back to consternation. "You mean they've been free for weeks?"

"Some have," Jonathan corrected. "They... the people liberated have been... not well enough to make the journey until now. They were in the outer camps, so they were mostly young and strong, but still weakened by the experience."

"What do you mean outer camps?" Kaiya demanded. "What do you mean weakened? You're telling me you Atlanticans have known about this for weeks and not said anything?"

Jonathan avoided her gaze. "I assure you, miss, that I do not approve of this public relations strategy, as much as my superiors may believe they are minimising harm to the public psyche."

Kaiya scoffed. This was so typical. Withholding information, treating the people like incapable, irrational idiots.

"I understand," Tilda said, her voice measured as she glanced at Kaiya. "You have to forgive my friend. She is not particularly trusting of... people in your position."

Jonathan nodded, meeting Kaiya's glare. "I've noticed that. But I think I understand why. I've been learning about this Bennett character and the way people feel about him. I can see why people would remain sceptical even after he's gone."

Kaiya raised her eyebrows. "See, he gets it!" she said to Tilda. Her estimation of Jonathan immediately multiplied by several factors. At last, someone who could see things for what they were, even if his understanding of her distrust was incomplete. But only Tilda would ever know that.

Jonathan relaxed and smiled, while Tilda looked at him with concern. "What did you mean about the young and strong people being in the outer camps?" she asked. "Do you mean the... more useful people?"

He prevaricated before saying, "Yes. As I said, each camp has a particular purpose. The outer ones seemed to be manufactories. Road tiles, weapons, the usual stuff of war. As far as we can tell, anyone useful was put there, everyone else went to... inner camps. Ones that have only been liberated in the past few days."

"What did they make?" Tilda asked, her eyes intense. "Those inner camps, what did they make?"

Jonathan licked his lips and shrugged. "I don't know. I'm sorry. I was only given limited information."

He was lying. Kaiya knew it. Whatever the prisoners had been making in those inner camps, it wasn't something an Atlantican soldier wanted people knowing about. She leaned back in her seat and stared at Jonathan, rejudging him. He had kept his word. He sympathised with the plight of the people. And most importantly, he hadn't yet given any indication he presented any kind of physical threat, though that was always a fact that could change in seconds. Still, perhaps there was at least one face she could trust – to a limited extent – in the ranks of those who could turn at any time and subjugate the people once more.

"Why weren't the prisoners brought back straight away?" she asked.

"Where would they stay?" Jonathan asked, then shook his head. "Leth would not have had the capacity to care for so many people. It..."

Kaiya waited for Jonathan to continue. He was frowning. "I

see," he said. "You don't know. Miss, the convoys are not only for Leth. They have people from all over Nymosen."

"You mean other border towns?"

"No, not just border towns. Everywhere. Even Akheron."

Kaiya shared a look of incredulity with Tilda. "I didn't know Akheron had even been attacked," Kaiya said.

"It wasn't," Jonathan said.

"Then how are there people from Akheron in Tarkinian camps?"

"That, I can't answer. I've told you everything I know."

Kaiya tapped her foot as she mulled over the information. The soldier hadn't told them everything he knew, she could tell that much, but the parts he omitted were of no consequence. Sooner or later, the dining table at which she sat would be full. Her father would return to his rightful place, and Benjamin his. Her mother would continue her work on new bioelectrics. Kormac... well, she would never let him out of her sight. And perhaps Tilda, whose face betrayed a deep angst, would become boisterous once more when reunited with her own parents.

Jonathan had delivered on his word.

"Thank you," Kaiya said.

He smiled at her and relaxed. "You understand that this information is all very general? I can't speak for specific individuals. I don't know anything about where your families are."

"I understand," Kaiya said. His disclaimer was like any other – largely irrelevant. Something people said only to shield themselves from blame if catastrophe laid plans to waste. She looked across to Tilda. "Everything's going to be fine, see? We should celebrate!"

Tilda gave her a weak smile. "I'm not in a very celebratory mood. You feel free to, though," she added, indicating Jonathan with her eyes. "Maybe you could teach our new friend a thing or two about Nymian cuisine, hey? Have you eaten *marashta*, soldier boy?"

"I haven't," he said. "To be honest, I've been too afraid. It doesn't look particularly appetising."

Kaiya forced a smile as Tilda laughed. What was she playing at? Jonathan may have proved himself unlike the rest of his comrades, but that didn't mean he was someone whose company was desirable. "Maybe I can bring some back here," Kaiya said.

Tilda looked her in the eye. "That's no way to eat *marashta*, takeaway. You need the real thing," she directed to Jonathan. "From a chef who knows what they're doing."

"It's a bit early for dinner, don't you think?" Kaiya looked between Tilda and Jonathan, clasping her hands. She could have throttled her.

"I'll come back later," Jonathan offered. "How about that?"

He gazed at her cautiously. Beside him and out of his field of vision, Tilda's wide eyes gave clear support for the notion. Whatever game she had in mind, Tilda seemed adamant that Kaiya play along with it.

"Ok," Kaiya said, trying to make her smile seem genuine.

Tilda almost exploded with glee.

The restaurant had seen better days, as far as patronage went. Kaiya glanced around at the empty tables and scattered diners, listening to the buzz of inane chatter that accompanied these venues so perfectly. Tilda had refused to show her hand, simply laughing and insisting that everything would be fine. If nothing else, agreeing to the stunt had put a smile on her friend's face. That was something.

Jonathan eyed her from across the table, examining the menu, face looking even younger under the soft illumination of modest chandeliers and a glowstone ceiling. His maroon shirt shone beneath the lights, silky and reflective. Kaiya had never even considered that a soldier would bring suitable clothes for circumstances such as this, which begged the question – how often did soldiers go out dining with the local population?

She sipped from her glass of wine. The question was absurd.

"So the big question," Jonathan said. "Which one to have." He scanned the section dedicated to *marashta*, confusion obvious on his face.

Kaiya gave him a weak smile in response and called up her own menu from the circle in the middle of the table. She could immediately rule half of it out as completely unsuitable for someone who'd never eaten *marashta* before – too experimental. "You should probably stick with something traditional," she said. "All the ones on the top half of the first page. They're pretty standard. Or if you want to go *really* traditional, get the signature."

"Ok. That was easy." He swiped the menu projection away and looked at her. "What about you?"

"I always get the eastern cheeses."

"Always?"

"Yes," she said. Always meant always, the way she saw it. "It was created in Leth."

"I see. And that's important?"

"It is to me. Most of the regions have at least one variation of *marashta* that's considered theirs. It's just about the only thing left that differentiates us."

"But they're all based on the signature dish?"

Kaiya grunted agreement and sipped some more wine. It was like talking to a child, not that it was his fault. He was Atlantican, and hadn't grown up just *knowing marashta*. Like her children would know, one day...

"Everything's based on the signature dish. That's considered the very first recipe. You have the signature dish, then traditional dishes, then experimental ones. That's basically all you need to know. The signature dish is pretty much plain *marashta* lightly oiled and spiced. Obviously the taste depends on what kind of oil and spices you use, but anything that's just that is signature *marashta*."

Jonathan frowned. "Ok, I understand, but what is *marashta* itself?"

"Oh!" Kaiya said. She hadn't realised he didn't even know that much. "It's a synthesis of wheat and some other grains infused with an artificial complete protein. It's really old, one of the first proper modified foods that became popular in Nymosen. Whatever type of *marashta* you have, that *has* to be the base. You can do anything you like with sauces and other bits added on top of it, but if you change the ingredients in the *marashta* itself, it's not *marashta* anymore – it's a derivative."

Jonathan nodded slowly. "I understand. Do people eat the derivatives?"

"Some do," she said, relaxing, "but most people stick with the real thing. Even if they try experimental recipes, people like the idea that the base is always the same. Something that doesn't change."

"Pure tradition."

"Exactly. When you eat *marashta*, you're eating history."

She'd forgotten just how passionate one could be about *marashta*. How often did people have the opportunity to introduce someone into a completely foreign world?

"What is it?" Jonathan asked.

Kaiya realised she was beaming at an empty table, and brought her attention back to the maroon-shirted soldier in front of her. "Sorry," she said. "Just wondering how you'll react. Usually children grow up with it. I've never met someone who hasn't eaten it at all. At least, not anyone I've spoken to."

"So you haven't travelled much."

She lifted her hands as if caught. "No, I haven't. Leth has everything I could want, so why go anywhere else?"

Jonathan shrugged as he picked up his glass of wine. Kaiya

returned his smile and met his eyes, then averted her gaze with a pang of guilt. She shouldn't be there.

The waiter came and took their orders, then left them to sit in awkward silence.

Kaiya took a large enough gulp of her wine that she nearly emptied the glass before extending the conversational thread that had seemingly reached its end. "I might go to Akheron, at some point."

"Just to see the capital?"

"No, not that." She found herself strangely attracted to the notion of telling Jonathan precisely why, but held back. "Just some things I need to deal with there. Someone I want to find – someone I met during the war. And my uncle lives there, too, so there's always that, though I haven't seen him in years."

She was rambling. Giving away too much information. She barely knew this man.

"Why not?" he asked.

Kaiya shrugged. "I don't actually know. Some argument he and my mother had, oh... eighteen years ago? When I was six. I have no idea what it was about. They just stopped talking, and he stopped coming to visit us." There was too much she didn't know about Kytos. He had always existed in the back of her mind, somewhere, but seeing him in her father's holo collection – both collections – had reminded her how little she knew about her own family history.

"He's an uncle on your mother's side?"

"Yeah. I don't have a big family. Dad was an only child, and his parents are dead, and mum... I don't know. Left home or something. Came to Leth, became an engineer."

Something clicked in Jonathan's mind and he pointed at her as if he'd figured her out. "And that's why you have to do the road tiles a certain way."

Kaiya hadn't laughed like this for months. "I'd forgotten about that," she said. "But yes, she taught me how to heal road tiles. She was in the middle of a research project with the university when the Tarkinians came. Something to do with self-healing energy conductors. See, conductors get damaged over time, especially if there's an abundance of energy or a bunch of secondary material, like the conductors we have in the river, see the river used to be full of wood from..."

She stopped and smiled at herself, looking away. Hopefully her cheeks weren't as red as they felt. "Sorry," she said. "I get carried away."

"I was settling in for a good story," Jonathan said, receiving a self-conscious chuckle in response. "So you got your technician job through your mother?"

Kaiya shook her head. "It was after she left. I needed money, so I didn't have much choice. There was plenty of work in Leth for tile technicians."

"So you were working for the Tarkinians?"

She clenched her jaw and glared at Jonathan's innocent face. "No," she said. "Never. I was doing it for Leth. Protecting it from the Tarkinians. And I always did as much as I could to sabotage sections I knew the Tarkinians would be using."

Jonathan remained silent.

"Anyway," Kaiya said. She couldn't hold his ignorance against him. "It's not something I want to do forever."

"You want to work on self-healing energy conductors with your mother?"

"I don't know," she said. "Mum wanted me to study engineering, and I guess that would've been ok, but I always wanted to do history. Besides, I don't like water-based energy conductors. They creep me out, and most of Leth's energy comes from them. So I wouldn't have been very helpful with her research."

"Do you still want to do history? I thought the Tarkinians kept the university open."

Kaiya sighed and played with the tablecloth. The question

was too disconcerting. "I haven't even thought about it," she said. "It all seems... pointless, to be honest."

"History? Or university?"

"Both? I don't know. History, at least. I mean, what will I learn about? Every war between Nymosen and Tarkinia? It's not like anything changes, so what's the point? Am I supposed to become one of those people who goes around saying I have the solution, and if everyone would just listen to me, everything would be fine, and then as soon as the Tarkinians come, they shoot me in the face? I don't need to go to university to be able to tell you we'll end up at war with them again. And again, and again. Until one of us wipes the other out, which will never happen. So we're the ones who'll keep suffering – the border towns."

Kaiya leaned back in her chair and folded her arms. "Maybe I should just become a soldier, like you. Person with the biggest gun wins, in the end. Every time."

Jonathan sipped his wine as he watched her. Was this what he had bargained for? Perhaps after tonight he would leave her alone, and she could crawl back into her bed and just stay there until someone came and forced her to give a damn about all the people who didn't give any damn.

"I'd rather be the guy that got shot in the face," Jonathan said softly, the shadow of a grin on his face. "Cause at least I'd be right."

Kaiya peered at him. "So why are you a soldier?"

"Oh, that's a long story," he said, dismissing the question with his hand. "But I like to think I'm here as a builder, not a soldier."

"You *are* a soldier, though. That's like saying you're a rhinoceros, but you like to think you're a bird. You're still a rhinoceros at the end of the day."

Jonathan burst out laughing. Kaiya cracked an unwanted smile and covered her mouth with her hand, trying to resist infection. The attempt failed, and she joined her rhinoceros companion in a suspended moment of joy.

She wiped away tears as her laughter subsided.

"Maybe I'm a rhinoceros with wings," he said, still trembling with the remnants of mirth. "You can't say it *couldn't* happen."

"I suppose not. There's always some mad scientist prepared to create a new creature."

"That's what you could do," Jonathan said. "Become a mad scientist. Make rhino-birds, or fish-tigers. Rat-spiders!"

"That's disgusting," Kaiya said as she leaned forward, resting her elbows on the table. "Or you could combine them all into one super-creature. Anyway. It's getting silly, now."

"We can't have that, things getting silly!"

They laughed again as the waiter approached and placed two plates of *marashta* onto the table. Kaiya spread her napkin onto her lap and smiled across at Jonathan, who peered at the food doubtfully.

"I promise you'll be fine," Kaiya said, though she had no idea what she would do if he hated it.

Jonathan prodded the long, oil-shined strands of *marashta*, then began to twirl a small amount around his fork. They swung in mid-air as he surveyed them and closed his eyes, putting them in his mouth and beginning to chew.

Kaiya watched with beaming expectation.

"Ok," Jonathan said as he swallowed, "not so bad. It's... interesting. It's tasty, I'll give you that, but it's... weird."

"It's the texture."

"Yes!" he said. "That's exactly what it is."

"Trust me, once you get used to it, all you'll think about are the flavours."

"I hope so."

Kaiya began to eat her own *marashta*, mouth exploding with an exquisite array of delight. Truly, Leth's contribution to *marashta* cuisine was unsurpassed. She watched as Jonathan continued to eat his signature dish. He was obviously gaining confidence that this wasn't some grand conspiracy to trick visitors into eating something horrible.

Perhaps next time he would try a traditional dish.

"So," Jonathan began, twirling strands of *marashta* onto his fork and grinning up at her, "are you ready to tell me your name?"

Kaiya nearly choked on her mouthful. She had completely forgotten. "Oh, I'm sorry," she said, swallowing as fast as she could. "You must think I'm so rude. I'm Kaiya."

Jonathan nodded and repeated her name. "Only took half a week and dinner. Not so bad."

Kaiya smiled to hide her utter embarrassment. Her earlier reluctance seemed childish, now, though Jonathan was still only an exception to the rule. No doubt the rest of his soldier buddies were walking proof never to trust them.

And she still needed to be on her guard. Exceptions didn't always stay exceptions.

"I've really monopolised the conversation," she said, realising that she knew barely a thing about Jonathan. "I haven't had a conversation like this in... years."

"A conversation like what?"

"I don't know," she said, playing with the *marashta*. "Normal? With a stranger, maybe?"

"Am I a stranger?"

"Everyone's a stranger," Kaiya said half-jokingly. "These days, at least."

The *marashta* didn't taste so divine, all of a sudden, and the glowstone lighting lost its glimmer of mysterious beauty. Jonathan gazed at her between mouthfuls of *marashta*, holding back whatever thoughts went through an Atlantican soldier's head.

Tilda had been wrong to force this on her.

Every moment with Jonathan was a moment of further impurity.

Somewhere to the east Kormac sat in a convoy, or a camp, waiting to return. How could she justify the betrayal of his waiting – of her waiting – by fraternising with this man who sat in front of her? This... soldier. Every night of her solitude had been a punishment to be endured, a symbol of her loyalty. A constant reminder that one day, if she was patient and steadfast and true, the silent walls would sing with the whisper of those who belonged within. That she, undeserving she, had been left the freedom to wither in the absence of those who would give sustenance, while those for whom she was absent held to the thinnest horizon of hope.

Somewhere to the east Kormac thought of her.

And she had the gall to sit with a soldier and laugh.

8

KAIYA LEFT HOME BEFORE TILDA WOKE. THE SUN SAT LOW IN THE east, making the streets and sides of buildings shimmer in its early morning glow. The quiet of dawn lingered, and Kaiya kept her ears pricked for any sound other than the pad and echo of her own footsteps. There was no one else around her on the shadowed boulevard. Only when the central bridge came into view and she turned onto the riverside road did she see anyone. Early morning joggers, relaxed-looking police officers, an old man with a walking stick sitting on a bench, staring out over the river, arm extended as if he were used to someone else sitting beside him.

The river flowed along, free of the debris that had once littered it years before her birth. Kaiya walked over to the railings and stared down into the water, the energy conductors staring back into her. Measuring. Brooding. Their razor-teeth turbines spun and spun, sucking energy from the webs that floated above, always searching greedily for more. The mountains could collapse into the river, and still that would be insufficient. A thousand souls could succumb – a million – and still the turbines would hunger, insatiable.

What would it be like to fall? To feel one's body disintegrate against the threadlike feelers that fed the turbines? Many had found the answer to that question, but how those people could give themselves to such a creature mystified her. There were other ways, so why choose the only one that guaranteed the world would forget you had ever existed? Surely one would wish to leave a legacy, to say that they had been there, that they had lived. For what was such a death if not an act of performance? It was the audience that mattered, not the actor's final bow.

Kaiya started walking again, peeking back down at the energy conductors every so often until she reached the eastern bridge. Officers patrolled its length, and it had been repaired to a state that allowed vehicular traffic once more, not that the morning presented much of it.

The convoys would have to enter through the eastern gate, which stood just south of where the river flowed out of Leth. Where they would go after that, who knew. The only thing for it was to wait at the gate. Perhaps the *Allied Atlantica* soldiers guarding it would allow her to sit outside the walls for a while and watch morning embrace the landscape. She had only thrice been to the east, but no one ventured too far in that direction. Even in the peacetimes.

The riverside road curved around and became a T-intersection, either pushing ahead into the heart of southeast quadrant, or turning left and going straight to the east gate. Other streets – tiny, one-way features barely deserving of the name – snaked off from different points around the T-intersection, leading to an eclectic jumble of buildings and alleyways. No city planner would ever have designed such an atrocity. But Leth had never been planned, nor did Kaiya think it would still be Leth had it been so.

An unusually large group of soldiers milled about on the edges of the intersection. There was no doubting this is where the convoy would stop. Kaiya couldn't think of any other explanation as to why so many Atlanticans would stand around chatting casually in the same place. She slowed her pace as she approached, trying to catch any stray snippet of relevant information, but all they did was joke and laugh about sitcoms she'd never heard about, or complain about how boring they found Leth.

A few of the soldiers eyed her as she entered the intersection and turned towards the eastern gate in the distance. She wasn't going to spend her day fielding soldiers' stares, and if she waited outside she would see the convoy sooner. More civilians were beginning to venture into the morning, going about their daily business, keeping mainly to themselves. More cars hovered out onto the newly-healed road. After so many weeks without the regular sight of a car, Kaiya wasn't sure she liked this aspect of the return to normal.

The ancient gate loomed ahead, left hand tower missing half its top. There was no real gate, anymore, given how ineffective it would be against any modern weapon, and the road to Tarkinia was visible through the empty frame, but it was still a symbol of pride for the people of Leth.

Even if it had been used to keep them *in* for the past six years.

The shimmering, Tarkinian energy barrier had gone, replaced with two loafing *Allied Atlantica* soldiers who looked uninterested in being there. Kaiya approached with a smile and asked about the possibility of leaving, but they were having none of it. They dismissed her without much thought, like discarding a petty annoyance, and returned to their torpid vigil.

The sun crept ever higher, glistening on the river that flowed down through the fields that met the horizon.

Kaiya returned reluctantly to the T-intersection, searching for a place she could sit. A park, perhaps, where no one would complain about her presence. She turned down one of the snaky streets that was more like an alley, caught by a quaint shopfront that had a pair of small, wrought iron tables waiting for patronage. Overflowing flowerpots hung from a latticed feature attached to the faded sandstone wall, and windows provided a view into the snug cafe inside, each with more flowers sitting behind them. Kaiya walked into the entrance recess and opened the door, stepping into the warm, polished room.

A middle-aged woman greeted her with enthusiastic charm, and Kaiya sat on the cushioned wooden bench by the wall, gazing around at the medley of colourful decorations and mismatched tables. The woman had a familiar accent Kaiya couldn't quite place. Perhaps from the north of Nymosen. In any case, Kaiya supposed it was a good time to have breakfast anyway, and relaxed amongst the gentle pinprick warmth that some people's voices always seemed to engender.

"Any time let know when ready, ok?" the woman said, her tone embracing. She walked away, greying hair in a bun that placed her fashion sense two decades in the past. Nymian wasn't her mother tongue, that was for sure. She was *really* from the north. Some of those border towns did have their own dialects, after all.

Kaiya traced the menu circle built into the centre of the tabletop, and the menu beamed up from within. She touched the air and pushed lightly, adjusting the menu so it faced her and hovered a little lower. The cafe was called *Cecilie's Coffeepot*, and boasted an offering of 'fine food and delicious delicacies from Tarkinia and the exotic beyond.' Kaiya stopped there and looked up, scanning the cafe. The bun-haired woman grinned at her from behind the counter, cutting into what looked like a fresh caramel slice, though that was a Nymian dessert. Kaiya considered the door, but she had already made herself comfortable, and it was just food. She'd simply make sure she ate something from the 'exotic beyond' section. It wasn't like the woman was Tarkinian herself.

The menu was full of dishes she'd never seen. Kaiya read the descriptions slowly, marvelling that someone had ever thought it would be acceptable to put certain ingredients together on the same plate. Even had she wanted a Tarkinian dish, they all sounded horrible.

A suited, elderly man with a trimmed moustache entered the shop and held his arms wide for the woman Kaiya figured must be Cecilie. Cecilie matched the gesture and met the man in the middle of the cafe, where they embraced with great affection and began jabbering away in some other language. Kaiya tensed at first – it sounded a lot like Tarkinian – but it was a bit lighter, not quite as guttural as the Tarkinian she had heard for the past six years.

Kaiya smiled at the gesture and returned to her menu, watching the pair surreptitiously as she half-pretended to read. Cecilie made coffee for the man, and they shared a multitude of small, crescent-shaped biscuits, discussing something with great animation and drama. Cecilie laughed and laughed, her voice filling the cosy room, and glanced over to Kaiya, who quickly averted her gaze and swiped the air to reach the next section of the menu.

Coffees. By the dozen.

She didn't even like coffee.

Kaiya explored the next section of the menu, an equally gigantic list of desserts, before returning to the 'exotic beyond' breakfasts. For such a small cafe, it certainly had a substantial selection. She rescanned the list and read her selection once more, trying to make sure she really wanted it, then waited for Cecilie to notice her.

"What like?" Cecilie asked as she approached, holding an interactive holodisc to record the order.

"Um, can I get the... borcevepaki?" Kaiya said.

"Ah! Borcevepaki!" Cecilie said, pronouncing the word rather differently. "Course, course. Want oskhel with? Side?"

Kaiya hesitated, looking back at the menu. Cecilie pointed at the oskhel. "Make small one. Very good with. Complement."

"Ok. Yes, please. Thank you."

Cecilie beamed. "Very good. Want coffee start?"

"No thanks. I don't drink it."

"Eh?" Cecilie said, shocked. "No drink?" She turned and started speaking in her own dialect to the elderly man and they laughed. Kaiya's ears warmed.

"I sorry," Cecilie said with good humour, turning her gentle eyes back to Kaiya. "Eat this foods before?"

"No, I haven't."

"Ah. Make very good, then. Wait, it sees in will!"

Cecilie walked away and through the arch that led to the hidden back of the cafe, leaving Kaiya to ponder what her last statement had meant. The elderly gentleman sat at the counter, sipping his coffee and nodding to himself as he stared amusedly at Kaiya with no compunction.

Kaiya turned her attention back to the menu and read through the desserts, pinching the words to bring up holos of each dish. Two scarved women entered the shop, and Kaiya froze. They were definitely speaking Tarkinian. She watched them sit at a table near the window, comfortable in the space surrounding them. They obviously came there often. *Cecilie's Coffeepot* was proving to be quite the hub of un-Nymian activity.

It must have done a roaring trade over the past six years. No wonder it looked so fresh.

Collaborators.

She returned to the menu, trying not to stare at the scarved women, and had to reread a section she had distractedly passed over. *Marashta*. The Tarkinians had *marashta* as a dessert. Kaiya pinched up the holo of the Tarkinian *marashta* and stared at it, astounded that anyone could make such an awful attempt at changing their national dish. It wasn't *marashta* at all! The long strands were coated with a sugary sparkle, then covered with a ridiculous array of dessert toppings.

What a travesty.

By the time Kaiya's breakfast came, the cafe was half full. "Hope enjoy," Cecilie said with infectious warmth, presenting Kaiya with a large plate and smaller bowl. Crisp-looking balls of dough infused with diced onion waited next to miniature sausages and two pieces of pocketed, golden bread. Kaiya cut into one of the dough balls as she looked at the bowl of oskhel, an appetising stew of vegetables heavy on tomato. At least, it looked like tomato. Who knew what went into food from the 'exotic beyond?'

Kaiya began to eat, and the entire cafe lightened along with her mood. There could be no other way to describe the food than delightful. She quickly sampled the other aspects of the two dishes, the little sausages exploding with juicy flavour.

The elderly man at the counter – already on his second coffee, and still picking at the crescent-shaped biscuits – began to watch her again, nodding. This time Kaiya smiled at him, and he raised his colourful mug in recognition. More Nymian-speaking patrons had arrived, but half of those in the shop spoke other languages, which wasn't so bad except for the ones speaking Tarkinian, which still gave her the creeps. She had known there were immigrant enclaves peppered throughout Leth – not that she'd ever been to one before – but she never imagined there would be a Tarkinian living in Leth, let alone two or more.

She would have to let Amelia know about that.

"How like?" Cecilie asked as she did the rounds of the ever-more boisterous cafe.

"I... You're Cecilie, right?" Kaiya asked, making sure.

"Yes, that me."

"I can't believe I've never had this before," Kaiya said. "What is this meat?"

"Ah, that secret recipe. Generations pass down. Only place whole Leth! No persons find in farm, this right here made."

Kaiya listened carefully, nodding to indicate she understood Cecilie's broken Nymian. She must have had her own farm somewhere in the back, or in a basement, a private lab to grow her own meat. Not many would make such a substantial investment.

"You must have had very good business the last few years," Kaiya said, attempting to make her probing sound as casual as possible.

Cecilie grimaced dramatically as she sat down. "No, not so good. Tarkin come, want free, free, free. Hard do sale, custom no want come." Cecilie shook her head and leaned across the table. "Some best custom here Tarkin, get scare, no want other Tarkin know here. Tarkin keep pressure, see, '*vat* join, *vat* join,' want Tarkin here say things, give know-stuffs."

Kaiya nodded as she decoded the information, taking a few moments to figure out what 'know-stuff' meant and wondering what '*vat*' was in Cecilie's language.

"Tarkin complain, always food not how like home." Cecilie harrumphed and indicated the cafe around her. "No make food Tarkin, make food Nym," she said vehemently, gesturing at Kaiya. "Tarkin food different Nym, no different Tarkin. Uh... uh... *zabra voj!* Sorry so, Nym no good."

Cecilie called out to the elderly gentleman, who ambled up to the table and sat down. He nodded as she rattled away, making grunts of acknowledgement.

"Cecilie say Tarkins used to food here, but Nyms, to it you not used. Cecilie made shop for Nyms, not Tarkins. Only shop in whole of Leth for Tarkin food, lots of Tarkin customer, get scared when soldiers come want information, try tell them make Nym enemy."

"But why would there be Tarkinians here in the first place?" Kaiya asked.

The elderly man sipped his coffee as Cecilie stood up. "Excuse," she said, rushing off to greet some newly-arriving familiar faces.

"Leth only safe border town with Nym, for hundreds years," the elderly man said. "Leth not so like Tarkin, but that ok. Better than make life in place that fall to Tarkin, then fall to Nym, then to Tarkin, then to Nym. Every time happen Tarkin told 'go, Nym now.' This why I come here many year ago with my son and my son wife, Cecilie."

"You're from Tarkinia?"

"Yes, from east, far away." He grinned as he waved to some indeterminate point in the distance. "Cecilie no Tarkin, she like you – border town, Tarkin and Ropruss. Always the soldier come, fighting, fighting. We say 'no more,' come here. We no like big city central Tarkin, we want small place. Leth never fall – Leth have reputation."

Kaiya ate the oskhel as she listened. She had heard stories about the way Tarkinians were always waging war against the country on its other border. The old man's tale made sense. He was obviously enlightened and had tired of Tarkinia's warring ways.

"You wouldn't prefer Leth were part of Tarkinia?" she asked.

The elderly man shrugged. "I no care about the politic. I just want live, and drink good coffee. In peacetime we visit old family, they visit us. We have good friends here, Tarkin friends, Ropruss friends, Nym friends, border friends. We keep that, we happy."

He returned to his coffee, face placid as he watched the other patrons, and Kaiya tore off a piece of the pocketed bread in front of her. When her father returned she would ask him about this place – ask if he'd known they were there. The fact anyone could travel between Nymosen and Tarkinia even in peacetime was news to her, though she couldn't see any reason that a Nymian would want to go there. Of course a Tarkinian would want to come once they realised the nature of their own society.

As long as they had made that realisation, she supposed they were fine.

To an extent.

The two scarved Tarkinian women stood up and called out to the elderly man as they approached. He held their forearms tight as he greeted them loudly, speaking in rushed Tarkinian. Kaiya focused on her food, savouring the unique sausages that made it so difficult to linger on the suspicion that Tarkinians deserved.

"Hello," one of the women said with a heavy accent and a polite bob of her head. Kaiya reflected the woman's timid smile and continued to chew.

"You first time here, no?" the man said after the Tarkinian women left.

"Yes," Kaiya said. "I don't usually come to this area."

"Well, it lucky morning, then. You find best cafe in all Leth! No one do coffee like Cecilie."

"Or breakfast from the exotic beyond."

"*Lak nershta*," the elderly man said, raising his mug as if toasting. "You tell friends we here, ok? Thursday nights you come, always party in street, we start again now Tarkin gone."

Kaiya smiled politely, filing away that she needed to avoid this area on Thursday evenings. Bad enough there were Tarkinians walking into the shop so openly – who knew how many would crawl out of their holes for a street party? She studied the mixture of faces in the cafe, some laughing, some pensive, and realised there was one person she hadn't seen.

"Tell me," Kaiya said, "if it's not too personal... where is your son? Cecilie's husband?"

The elderly man shook his head dramatically and said something in his own language. "He no here now. He die eight year before. Why ask you?"

"Sorry," she said, embarrassed. "I wondered if maybe... when they came to take the people, they didn't take the Tarkinians here."

"No, no," the man said, "they take all. Some family no affect – we no know why, but we know they no on system, see, so no one know they here. That save, maybe? Or some people lucky, maybe that all."

Kaiya nodded, still scanning the room. His explanation made complete sense, after her encounter with the former Technology Director.

"When Tarkin come, Tarkin here go out say 'what you do? Why you do?' but no listen. Other Tarkin say 'you no Tarkin, you as same Nym.' *Zabra voj...*" the elderly man gave another dramatic shake of his head and sipped his coffee. "I want know," he continued, "why you let this Bennett *grenkal* be Commissar?"

Kaiya almost choked on her final mouthful of sausage. "What?" she said, swallowing fast while heat rose in her cheeks. "What do you mean let him? I didn't want him there."

"No, no," the man said, "no understand, maybe I no say right. No mean you, mean all peoples. I think, early, he no live. How can live, when so bad? Someone assassin, for certains, but... no, no one assassin. All people they say 'Oh, him I hate,' but... eh, no one assassin. You no think that strange? Make me think not all hate him like say."

"It's not so easy to kill a Commissioner."

"Eh," he said, dismissing her explanation with a shrug. "Happen all time Tarkin. It not so hard, you have right weapon. Need only will. I no understand, Leth peoples proud, see, but this Bennett *grenkal*, he no Leth. He Tarkin. He Nym. He Ropruss. You is understand this?"

Kaiya nodded and looked the elderly man in the eye. Something had always nagged about Bennett, always irritated her. Something more than his ambition, that she had never been able to articulate, but this old foreigner had put his finger on it, and she understood: Bennett had never been one of them.

———

Kaiya walked up the boulevard dividing northeast and northwest quadrants, arms folded. A group of boys played soccer, yelling out to each other for passes and groaning every time a play didn't go their way. Kaiya moved over to the sidewalk to avoid the spectacle, but a stray kick sent the ball in her direction, and it bounced off her shins and into the wall of the building.

Kaiya stopped, momentarily stunned by the necessity for action. The boys waited expectantly, ignorant of everything that was happening outside their game. All of them would be missing someone, that was guaranteed, and yet anyone unfamiliar with the Night of Retribution would never have guessed, seeing the careless ease with which they claimed ownership of the boulevard, like nothing had ever existed but their present pocket of the universe.

Kaiya kicked the ball as hard as she could, sending it over their heads. Two of them ran after the ball, and another lifted his arms in annoyance.

The convoy had come, but neither Kormac nor her parents were amongst it. People had swarmed to the T-intersection, pushing against *Allied Atlantica* soldiers, who were forced to call for reinforcements.

Slowly, the people of Leth were finding out that their loved ones were returning.

The seven buses with tinted windows didn't stop at the intersection. They turned left, heading further into the southeast quadrant to stop in front of the hospital, where dozens of nurses appeared, ready to bring the prisoners into the glass-walled hospital atrium. One by one, Kaiya had counted them, dishevelled and weary, being led into the atrium as people stood on their toes and cried out names.

Two hours of watching, of hope rising, then reality sliced it away, leaving her empty.

One of the boys yelled an insult, but Kaiya ignored it, continuing on towards Amelia's side street. She left the boys to play their silly, selfish game, and scowled as she rounded the corner. The same teenagers who had been there a few days before were on their bench again, kissing happily as if nothing else mattered.

As if it didn't matter that every moment of their pleasure was void until every person whose moments had been stolen was returned.

"You don't look happy," Amelia said as she opened the door to Kaiya's knocking.

"Oh, just... never mind."

Kaiya stepped inside, arms still folded, and sat at the infamous dining table while Amelia double-checked to see if anyone was watching.

"You're alright after the other night?" Amelia asked.

"Fine. You?"

"Couldn't be better." Amelia fussed about with a pot of tea she had just brewed. "You want some?"

"I think I've had enough of tea."

Amelia smirked. "You can never have enough tea." She finished pouring and sat opposite Kaiya, stirring in several large teaspoons of sugar.

Kaiya couldn't repress a grin. "You spoke well," she said. "The other night."

"Oh, you liked that?"

"Everyone did."

Amelia sipped her tea with a mischievous grin. "Not everyone. Just everyone that matters, wouldn't you agree?"

"Of course." There could be no argument there.

"And to what do I owe the pleasure of your company today?" Amelia asked.

Kaiya looked around at the unassuming kitchen that had seen so many hushed conversations and hatched plans. "I want to do something. I want to do something important, something meaningful. I'm sick of being scared and I'm sick of collaborators getting away with their crimes."

"You've already done something important. You hosted Nymian soldiers, Kaiya. You provided sanctuary to those fighting back. I've already told you there was no one else I trusted more in that capacity."

"But it's not enough," Kaiya said. "I just... let people stay. I want to do something real. Myself. I don't want to just watch people like you do it, I want be in there, I want to stand up and do the right thing."

Amelia nodded. "Like the other night."

"Exactly. Except... maybe we can actually make a difference. The police are never going to listen to us, and no one from Akheron will care. We have to go out and make these collaborators pay. I..."

She struggled to think of the words, the old Tarkinian man from *Cecilie's Coffeepot* swimming in her mind. "We have to make Leth safe again, get rid of everyone who isn't loyal first and foremost to this town. Cause if we don't, it'll happen again. I don't want to become another one of those border towns that keeps switching between Nymosen and Tarkinia."

"Quite right," Amelia said, sipping her tea. She leaned back in her seat. "The list of collaborators is nearly complete. I have names – hundreds, maybe even close to a thousand. A few sections in northwest quadrant haven't been done yet, but I'll have those reports soon."

"What are you going to do?" Kaiya asked.

"Give the people what they want," Amelia said with a shrug. "It depends on the severity of the crime. We'll mark the whores, but as for the others... a few arsons, a few hangings, some beatings. After that, they'll be begging forgiveness."

Kaiya nodded, heart thumping with renewed vigour. No matter how disheartened she felt by collaborators and apologists, Amelia would always be there to remind her that all throughout Leth there were loyal people ready to stand up for the silent majority. There could be no pursuit more noble and just.

"Some of the collaborators have gone into hiding," Amelia continued, "but I have people searching for them."

Kaiya leaned forward in her chair. "When do we start?"

Amelia hesitated. "It's all about expectations," she said. "Like I said the other day. The only thing I want you to worry about is three days' time. We're going to rally again, but better prepared. More people. I didn't plan the other day properly. This time we will force them to listen to us."

"Why three days?"

Amelia traced her finger over a line on the table and a holoslide popped up, projecting the image of a stern man with black hair. "He's from Akheron," Amelia said, indicating the projection. "Some government representative. Apparently he's in charge of the Civil Order Protection Taskforce. He wants more people to go see the advocates sent by Akheron."

"As if an advocate can do anything or even cares!" Kaiya said.

"Exactly my thinking."

Kaiya stared at the holo of the man. "How did you get that?" she asked. "The Network is completely down."

"The Network is a Nymian invention," Amelia said. "I will not use it any longer. There are other ways to get information – old ways, even if they're a bit slower. Leth used to have its own network, but there are people trying to repair it, even if the hardware is old. They've managed to hijack some of the Atlantican communication nodes, and the advocates from Akheron have terrible security systems, that's how we found out this traitor is coming. No one knows that we know, Kaiya. That's our advantage."

Amelia traced her finger back over the line on the table, and the holoslide disappeared.

"And how do we deal with the Taskforce?" Kaiya asked.

Amelia chuckled and smiled. "They'll be too busy figuring out who was responsible for the previous night – that's something I don't want you involved in. I have a specific plan for that. And if the Taskforce does show up, we will be more than capable of fighting back." Amelia leaned forward. "See, I'm stupid, Kaiya. I didn't see what was right in front of my eyes. I knew the police were still corrupt, but I didn't realise how ingrained it was. We can't ask for anything anymore – we have to take it. And that's exactly what we're going to do."

Kaiya burned with indignant exhilaration. She could already taste victory. "The police are weak," she said, trying to prove how helpful she could be. "Benjamin doesn't have control, he said so himself. There are factions that want him dead, and want Bennett released."

Amelia smiled. "Good. I knew I could rely on you."

Kaiya glowed inside.

"Tell me," Amelia continued, "what do you know about the concealed prison?"

Kaiya hesitated. "What do you mean?"

"Everyone knows it exists. I thought you might know something about it. There are some pieces of information that I just can't seem to find anywhere..."

Bennett's knowing laughter echoed in Kaiya's mind. He knew something that he wouldn't tell her, as did Joseph, if Bennett was to be believed. "No," she said. "Dad never told me anything about it."

That wasn't strictly a lie.

Amelia studied her, tracing patterns on the teacup. "I see," she said.

Kaiya looked away, afraid of Amelia's intelligent eyes. There had been a time, at that very table, when a man lied to Amelia. The energy conductors – so Kaiya had heard – were given a good feed that evening.

"Your sister will be back soon," Kaiya said.

Amelia continued to study her, considering hidden thoughts. "You knew, didn't you. The other day, when you told me what Bennett would expect – how the people would react if everyone returned. Your little hypothetical that turned out not so hypothetical."

Kaiya's mouth started to dry.

"But yes," Amelia said, tone lighter, "I imagine so." She smiled at Kaiya. "And I can meet your Kormac."

Kaiya had fantasised about such events, and gave a tiny laugh, relieved that Amelia no longer pursued a thread of suspicion. "Maybe. Or maybe I'll keep him all to myself for a while."

Amelia smirked and looked suggestive. "You could do that, yes. I think that would be... understandable."

Kaiya mimicked Amelia's expression, hiding the sliver of discomfort that snaked its way across her skin every time she considered the inevitability of such activities.

"Tell me what you want to do," she said, changing the subject.

And Amelia began to talk.

Kaiya lay in bed, eyes heavy, the convoy's arrival playing over and over in her mind. Somewhere beyond her walls there were families that were together for the first time in three years, and she felt nothing for them. How could she? No one who mattered had been in those buses.

"Did you ask the old man his name?" Tilda asked, lying beside her on top of the sheets.

Kaiya sighed. "I didn't even think of it."

"You should go to the thing on Thursday night," Tilda said. "I think it would be good."

"I'm not going to a street party with Tarkinians, Tilda."

"You said they were fine."

"They are, but that doesn't mean I want to see them on the street. If you think it's such a good idea, you should go."

The words bore no malice, but Tilda frowned. "Maybe..."

They lay in stillness for a while longer, like they had so many times over the years.

"I know you're trying to help," Kaiya whispered, "but I'm really not up to doing all this stuff."

Tilda looked right into her. "I know. I'm just trying to... encourage."

Kaiya grinned softly. "What about you? You won't go anywhere, you're worse than me."

"Well, take it from someone who should know better," Tilda said. "I don't like it when you close yourself off to everyone. You get... moody."

Kaiya laughed and looked archly at Tilda. "I guess that's why you sent me off to dinner with a soldier?"

"You didn't have to go," Tilda said. "I didn't make you."

Kaiya stared at the ceiling. "I suppose you're right."

"I'm always right."

They both laughed as Tilda deflected Kaiya's backhand to the thigh.

"Admit it," Tilda said. "You enjoyed it."

"I'm not admitting anything," Kaiya said. "We had dinner, he learnt about *marashta*, that was it."

"I never suggested there was anything more! What, you think I was trying to set you up? I'm not that stupid."

Kaiya grinned. "Are you sure?"

She yelped as Tilda kicked her in the shin and smothered her in friendly punches.

"Admit it!" Tilda said. "Admit it, admit it, admit it."

"Ok!" Kaiya said, laughing as she curled into a ball. "It was fine. I enjoyed it. It was just a bit... sad."

"Sad?" Tilda repeated, relenting.

"Yeah. I just wanted it to be Kormac, that's all."

Tilda smiled softly and began playing with Kaiya's hair. "I know. I just..." Tilda sighed, her smile fading into a frown. "What if he doesn't come back, Kaiya? Or your parents. What happens then?"

"No," Kaiya said, shaking her head. She turned over onto her side and gazed at Tilda. "Of course he's coming back. They all are. And dad will be Commissioner again, and mum will go back to work, and your parents will start making music again. Everything is going to go back to normal. You have to trust me, Tilda."

Tilda looked doubtful.

"Please," Kaiya said, squeezing Tilda's hand. "Trust me. Come with me to the convoys. We'll go together whenever each one comes. I know they're coming back, I just know it."

Tilda's mouth quivered, her eyes watering. "But what if you're wrong?" she said. "I've managed for this long, I don't want to get my hopes up for nothing. I don't want to... lose them all over again."

"You won't," Kaiya said, eyes glowing. "Just imagine it, Tilda, everyone together. We'll have a... a big party, a celebration."

Tilda began to cry in earnest, doing her best to hold back the tears. "Don't, Kaiya. Please."

"What?" Kaiya said. Tilda's emotional state made no sense. "Everything's going to be fine."

"They're musicians, Kaiya!" Tilda choked on the words. "And they're old. What use would the Tarkinians have had for old musicians? No one ever thinks they're important."

"No, no, you can't think like that," Kaiya soothed. "I know they're coming back."

"So what?" Tilda said. "What then? Do you really think everything's just going to be back to the way it was? You don't know anything about what happened in there. What were the Tarkinians doing with them?" Tilda rolled onto her back and palmed away her tears. "I don't want some... shadow, Kaiya. I don't want them to come back and then they're not the same anymore."

Kaiya shook her head. "Don't say that."

"What if Kormac wasn't the same person, anymore?" Tilda continued. "What would you do then? What if he came back and he didn't want you anymore? Or... something was wrong with him, or—"

"Stop it, Tilda. Just... stop."

Kaiya's voice fell to a whisper and Tilda gasped with grief.

There was nothing more to be said. Kaiya had forced herself to abandon the fears that Tilda now resurrected, burying them under layers of expectation and gambled joy. It did not do to dwell on the nightmares that now roamed free of their shallow grave, and Kaiya stared across at Tilda, steeling herself against the contagion of hopelessness.

"It'll be better in the morning," Kaiya said, and Tilda nodded, her face shining with the tracks of tears.

Kaiya rolled onto her back and stared at the ceiling, wishing that were true.

Nothing was ever better.

Soon Kaiya found herself on the top of Leth's wall, gazing into the west. Somewhere out there Akheron stood by the coast, on the other side of Nymosen. It may as well have been the other side of the world. Giant stalks of lavender swayed in the early-morning breeze, covering the plains all the way to the river, which wended its way from the mountains in the north.

On the other side of the river was dirt.

Kaiya walked along the top of the wall, peering down into the laneways below and across into the windows of buildings that had long ago grown higher than the wall. Everywhere there were people, standing motionless but for a gentle swaying. In the streets, in bedrooms, in parks and cafes, the people stood and swayed, waiting.

Her father took her hand.

She was a little girl again, skipping towards the giant work of engineering that allowed the wall to continue over the top of the river, great pillars thrusting down into the water to support the bridge that connected the wall on either side.

They stopped on the middle of the bridge and Kaiya surveyed the divide between dirt and lavender. Branches floated down the river, gifts from the great forest that grew within the mountains, and were disintegrated as they passed under the wall and through the filters that protected the energy conductors from harm.

Kaiya looked up to her father and smiled.

He looked back down at her, eyeless. Faceless.

A soccer ball bounced off her shins and rested on the walkway above the wall. A faceless boy stared at her and pointed towards the northern mountains. Kaiya's gaze followed. In the distance, the water bubbled, speeding closer and closer to the wall, thickening and transforming into a rich, boiling expanse of blood.

On one side of the river, the giant stalks of lavender wilted, and on the other, the ground began to shake. A hollow clattering rang out over the field of dirt, and jagged shards of bone erupted from the ground, fed by the now-overflowing river of blood.

The boy who had kicked the soccer ball climbed onto the top of the ancient parapet and looked down into the river, before allowing himself to fall. Kaiya raced to the parapet and stood on her child toes to watch the boy disappear into the river of blood below.

She turned around.

Her father had gone.

Kaiya went to pick up the soccer ball, but when she did so it deflated in her hands. She stared at it, unsure what to do, and decided to throw it over the edge into the streets of Leth. The misshapen plastic arced through the air and landed on a four-way intersection filled with swaying people, and exploded.

Bodies disintegrated.

And everyone stopped swaying.

Now they turned to face the river. Those on the street walked towards it, while those trapped by windows and walls smashed their way to freedom, falling soundlessly onto the streets below. A middle-aged woman climbed over the balustrades by the river and fell into it. The blood-soaked silvery webs shot up and grabbed her, pulling her into the mouth of an energy conductor.

Kaiya watched as all across the riverside, people jumped and fell. The sun was disappearing, replaced with a great storm from the east, rolling clouds approaching Leth raining fire and ash. It passed over the eastern gate, and a great bolt of lightning annihilated the structure that had stood for over a thousand years. Buildings began to fracture, turning to dust and swirling up into the clouds.

She understood what she had to do.

Kaiya climbed up onto the parapet and stared down into the crimson river. Body after body fell, disappearing in great flashes of red, while ash rained down from the clouds that now covered the eastern half of Leth. Kaiya stepped forward and found herself unable to move, held back by arms much older than her own.

She struggled against them, screaming soundlessly, and turned her head to look at her assailant.

Her father had returned, still faceless but horribly aged, with sagging skin and an aura of death. Great wounds gaped in his body, blackened with decay. Kaiya kicked at him, but she was too small, and he held too tight.

The storm approached, roaring victory. Below, everyone had

disappeared into the river. She was the only one left. She struggled harder, wriggling about and using every tactic she could
possibly think of to free herself. Why did he not understand that
this was the only way? The wall was beginning to shake.

Her father lost his footing, and they both fell to the floor of
the bridge.

Kaiya took her chance and climbed the parapet once more,
stumbling in her rush. Her father reached out, but he came too
late, and Kaiya fell back-first into the river, staring up into the
sky as her father's faceless body shattered in the onslaught of
the storm, tearing apart to become yet another component of its
ever-growing hunger.

Kaiya laughed as the energy conductors erased her corporeal
form.

She woke up to Tilda shaking her.

"Kaiya!" Tilda said.

Tilda sat on the edge of the bed, eyes wide, illuminated
softly by the bedside lamp.

Kaiya groaned and rubbed her temples. "What?" she
mumbled, looking outside. "What time is it?"

Tilda glanced over to the holographic time display that had
appeared above the beside table upon hearing the question.
"Nearly two a.m. You have to get up."

"Why?" she asked, pushing herself off the bed and wiping
hair out of her face. She had dreamed about something
strange... what was it?

Tilda walked over to the window and tapped a combination.
The window changed its status, morphing from a rectangle of
solid black into transparency. The boulevard was dark, with no
lights on the opposite building, but behind it, in the distance,
floodlights spilled into the eastern sky.

"You can't see it properly from here," Tilda said.

Kaiya put her feet on the floor and stood up too quickly,
reeling with dizziness. "I know," she said, understanding the

implication of what Tilda had shown her. "How long has it been there?"

"I don't know," Tilda said. "I couldn't sleep, so I reset the window and saw all the light."

Kaiya changed hurriedly, feeling around for the clothes she had already worn that day. "Are you ready to go?" she asked.

Tilda looked away and didn't respond.

There was no time to argue.

Kaiya went out into the corridor and put on her shoes, Tilda following behind. "Is it safe at night?" Tilda asked.

"I don't know. I don't care. I'll be fine."

Tilda looked at her with a small frown and Kaiya hugged her. "Trust me," she said, and left.

The boulevard felt different at night. The buildings looked older, with harsher shadows and menacing facades. Kaiya strode along the centre of the road, not wanting to draw attention to herself. The glowstone sidewalks always lit up at night without anyone's presence, just enough to make visible the path before and behind, but stepping onto it would be like a target.

Kaiya rounded the corner onto the riverside road. The benches were empty, but the river shimmered, as it always did in darkness. She ignored the strange desire to watch the energy conductors ceaselessly feed, their silvery webs lit up like glowing spiderwebs covering the water. There was no time to waste on such frightening frivolities.

As she approached the easternmost bridge, it became apparent that she wasn't the only one who had noticed the arrival of another convoy. Several people were walking across the bridge, ignoring each other, and lights shone through unblackened windows, some of them showing residents watching from inside.

Kaiya turned with the curve of the road towards the T-inter-section. In the distance, a crowd had already appeared, along with it the noise of shouting. Soldiers milled about, ready to interrupt any threat to the peaceful conclusion of prisoner transfer from bus to hospital. Kaiya walked faster, glancing down the alley that hid *Cecilie's Coffeepot*, until she reached the edge of the crowd.

She wished she were taller.

A hand grabbed her arm and she spun, shocked, insides twisting as she realised it was an Atlantican soldier.

"No pushing," he said with a heavy accent.

Kaiya scowled at him and shook off his hand. He eyed her for a few more moments before turning his attention to others he thought displayed unruly behaviour.

At the front of the crowd a commotion erupted as a woman rushed forward, shouting. A line of soldiers stepped away from the rescued prisoners to halt her approach. One of the prisoners stopped – it looked like a young man, from where Kaiya stood – and stared at the woman.

He stepped forward, ignoring a nurse who called out to him, and walked towards the woman. The soldiers eyed him and exchanged a few words, then withdrew from the situation, letting go of the woman. She rushed forward and enveloped the man with her arms, falling to the ground with him. His arms hung limp by his side as she rocked him back and forth.

The distance was too great to hear, but Kaiya imagined the woman was crying.

Everyone else continued their clamouring, and more people had now appeared behind. Kaiya steadied herself as people pushed and pulled, trying to keep her gaze on the buses and hospital atrium. The young man who had been reunited with his mother was taken inside by a nurse, the emotional woman trailing. Once, twice, three times more, a lucky spectator found the target of their searching.

Kaiya tried her best to see the faces of everyone who left the buses, eyes drawn to every man who could be Kormac, or her father, or Tilda's father, every woman who could be her or

Tilda's mother. So many wore hooded cloaks, faces hidden from the crowds as if they had something to hide, ushered along with great haste by the nurses.

Time dragged on, and the two buses at the front of the convoy drove away, emptied. Three remained. Kaiya screamed in frustration. More would come, she had to remember that. Tilda had stopped hoping, but she had to continue. She had to carry the burden for both of them.

From the rearmost bus, prisoners stopped emerging. A nurse stepped forward and waited, offering her hand to someone inside. After several long moments of hesitation, the offer was accepted, and a man came into view, the hood of his cloak hanging down over his back. Kaiya struggled to see, heart leaping at the initial view she received, then quickly settling back down as she realised the figure was far too thin to be Kormac.

The man let go of the nurse and stood up straighter, shaking his head at another offer of assistance. He walked towards the atrium, gazing at the *Allied Atlantica* soldiers and then into the crowd.

Kaiya's heart almost stopped, along with all sensation of life and existence.

She had been wrong.

9

KAIYA PUSHED DEEPER INTO THE CROWD, IGNORING THE CRIES OF indignant annoyance that followed her. She offered brief, half-hearted apologies as she charged through, but her focus remained on Kormac, who was walking into the hospital atrium.

She kept losing sight of him from her position in the crowd, and he disappeared behind a clump of nurses and soldiers. Kaiya's approach towards the front of the crowd was hindered by an irate man who grabbed her arm and swore as he pulled her back, declaring she deserved to go to the back of the line. Kaiya stumbled and regained her balance, shaking her arm free of the man and turning to face him.

Her first inclination was to give him a good whack in the face, but the need to find Kormac before he disappeared into the hospital's bowels pressed harder in her mind. She turned around and started to push back through the crowd, then felt herself being pulled back once more with a force far more violent. She fell to the ground, gasping in shock, and curled into a ball as someone kicked her in the back.

An uproar surrounded her, and denouncements flew, some directed at her and others at the man who had kicked her. Kaiya clambered to her feet and turned to face the wild-eyed man who had found her journey to the front so offensive. He glared at her, struggling to advance while two other men held him back.

Somebody pushed her from behind, and Kaiya fell towards the man, who kicked at her wildly. Kaiya returned the favour, connecting with his knee, and turned just in time to raise her arms against a deranged woman's punch. The area exploded with shouts and violence as all at once people began fighting. Kaiya held herself close together, trying to defend against stray punches while she edged ever so closer to the front. The soldiers were coming, and spared no measure to stop the uproar, slamming people to the ground and prodding with stun batons.

The space around Kaiya began to thin, and she ran forward, hoping for some small gap between the soldiers. She stopped suddenly, the wind knocked out of her by a fist in her gut, and fell to the ground, staring up at a soldier with a charged stun baton.

"Stop!" Kaiya pleaded, raising her arms above her face. "Please, listen to me!"

The soldier placed his booted foot on her abdomen and pointed the stun baton down at her, waiting.

"My fiancé is in there," Kaiya said.

The soldier considered her, then removed his foot and gave a curt nod towards the hospital atrium. Kaiya scrambled off the ground before he could change his mind. When she entered the front doors another three soldiers rushed forward in alarm, raising their frequency rifles and ordering her to stop.

Kaiya complied, and repeated her plea.

An orderly stepped forward from within the crowd of chattering nurses, and the soldiers lowered their weapons, still eyeing Kaiya with suspicion.

"Name?" the orderly asked.

"Kaiya."

The orderly stared at her. "Kaiya who?"

"Kaiya Brown," she said reluctantly, and the orderly frowned at her, motioning for one of the soldiers.

"Take her in. If the patient recognises her, she can stay."

The soldier nodded and indicated in the direction of the lifts. Kaiya went there with him, looking back at the orderly, who had already forgotten her and moved on to a clump of nurses sharing data on a holocloud shining up from each of their tablets.

"Reception," the soldier said to the lift once they were inside, and the doors closed.

They reopened a few seconds later, and Kaiya walked out into an explosion of noise. Soldiers stood interspersed against the walls, surveying a packed waiting room. Cloaked figures slumped against the walls or sat in the middle of the floor, all the seats having long ago been taken. Orderlies and reception staff packed behind the wide desk, holding multiple conversations with nurses, doctors, and other allied health professionals, each position denoted by shirt colour.

Kaiya followed close behind the soldier as they weaved a slow path through the rectangular room. Even as one rescued prisoner left through the corridors leading out of the reception, another emerged from the lifts, sometimes accompanied by a nurse or orderly. The nurses already there knelt in front of the new arrivals, making rushed decisions about where each one would be sent. Kaiya watched a nurse scan one of the former prisoner's faces and speak a ward assignation before quickly moving on. Taking the patient to the ward was someone else's responsibility.

Someone shouted nearby, and the escorting soldier stopped, Kaiya almost walking into his back. A nurse screamed and fell backwards, holding her arms up in defence as one of the new patients lunged forward at her. He was quickly restrained by two soldiers, but flailed about, cursing and accusing everyone of being part of an elaborate conspiracy. Another soldier had to come and hold his writhing legs before a nurse could rush forward with a tranquilliser ray. The patient roared as he noticed the tiny cylinder in the nurse's hands, thrashing as it came into view above his thigh. Its workings were invisible to Kaiya, but the man became still within seconds.

"Can you see your friend?" the escorting soldier asked.

Kaiya scanned the room and shook her head. Between the constant movement of nurses striding here and there, and the relocation of patients into the corridors to other wards, catching any glimpse of Kormac was impossible. Even freezing time and searching in stillness would have taken a considerable effort. The soldier began to move again, wending steadily towards the reception desk.

Kaiya looked down as they approached, surreptitiously examining the faces of those on the floor. Far and away weariness was the most common expression. Very few eyes travelled up to meet her own, the majority fixed at the floor or on something in the distance that wasn't really there. Jonathan had said they were liberated weeks ago, and hadn't been well enough to make the journey until now, but there was something disturbingly immediate in the faces of the strangers.

It couldn't have been weeks. Jonathan must have been mistaken.

The soldier stopped at the back of the reception desk clump, standing patiently as others yelled over the top of each other to attract the attention of the orderlies and reception staff, who were doing their best to maintain composure under an endless barrage of demands.

Kaiya moved gradually closer to the front, still surveying the reception for any sign of Kormac. Her eyes moved across the fixed chairs and rested on a girl with cheeks that placed her as not yet a teenager. The girl's unkempt hair fell across her face and past her shoulders, frayed and tangled, but she brushed it aside as she noticed Kaiya's gaze. They stared at each other, the young girl hunched over and covered by a too-large cloak, eyes curious yet guarded. Kormac fled Kaiya's mind for a small window of precious time, and she gave what she hoped was a welcoming smile.

The girl sat up straighter, evidently surprised by the attention, and her lips edged up in the merest flicker of recognition. She twirled a few strands of hair idly around her finger, still studying Kaiya with curious eyes that were now not so guarded, and the cloak slipped from its position, revealing a stomach swollen with child.

Kaiya's shock eliminated her smile, and the girl pulled the cloak back around herself, turning away and shaking her tangled hair so it once more covered her face. She stared back down at the floor, making herself as unnoticeable as possible.

"Miss?" the soldier said.

Kaiya continued to stare at the girl until the soldier queried her again.

"Sorry," she said, turning around with another quick glance behind her.

"Name?" asked a receptionist.

Kaiya gazed, mind still on the girl behind her. "My name?"

"Name of patient," the receptionist said. Someone nearby told Kaiya to hurry up.

"Kormac Balenne," she said.

The holoscreen automatically searched for the name as soon as she said it, and the receptionist reversed the image towards Kaiya. "This him?"

"Yes," she said. Kormac stared back at her from the holoscreen.

"Ward five six." The receptionist leaned back and called out to someone, "Catherine! Visitors, five six."

The nurse named Catherine motioned for Kaiya and the soldier to follow. The receptionist was already speaking to somebody new. Kaiya weaved her way to an impatient-looking

Catherine, who glared around at anyone who stood in her path as they moved towards one of the corridors.

"That girl," Kaiya said, looking back, her line of sight obstructed by constant movement. "Someone should see her, she's... pregnant."

Catherine scoffed. "She can join the queue," she said, and punched the button for the lift.

Kaiya travelled up to the fifth storey, stomach turning nervously.

The lift door opened, revealing a heavily-windowed corridor much quieter than the chaotic reception. Catherine led them forward while Kaiya stared out onto the dimly-lit south-east quadrant. They were on the southern wing of the hospital, then.

Catherine indicated towards ward six and left before Kaiya could even think to thank her. Not that she would have, with that attitude.

Kaiya entered the ward and scanned it from the doorway, flushing with apprehension. Extra beds and chairs had been jammed into the already-cramped space, each one containing a patient. Most lay still, but a few sat upright, either completely ignoring her entrance or staring directly at her. There was no in-between. Kaiya stepped forward slowly, approaching the first bed on one side so she could see who was in it.

Not Kormac.

She continued around the room, conscious of the staring and trying to minimise the noise of her footsteps. Two of the men were sleeping, and she had to remember that it was still the early hours of morning. The ward was quiet, and no doubt more of the patients would be looking forward to sleeping after what-ever journey they had just been on.

Kaiya came to the next bed and stopped, heart jumping in a jumble of ecstasy and fear.

Kormac lay still, eyes closed, face pointing away from her. His mouth rested slightly open, and as Kaiya stepped closer she could hear the slow, ragged thread of his breathing. Traces of grey peppered his unevenly-cut hair. She went around to the other side of the bed and picked up an empty chair, taking care to place it softly back on the floor.

She returned her attention to Kormac.

Their eyes met.

He looked at her without expression, face gaunt, and Kaiya couldn't help the tears that sprang up in her eyes. She palmed them away as she laughed at herself, trying to smile at Kormac, who continued to stare. Kaiya leaned forward, resting her interlaced fingers on the hospital bed, and studied the jagged traces of his haggard face.

None of her dreams had been like this. She had dreamt of processions and fanfare and cheering crowds, a celebration of all those who had fought and conquered in their own little way. Those who had suffered for the wrongs of traitors.

The soldier cleared his throat. "Excuse me," he said to Kormac, quite politely. "May I confirm that this is, indeed, your fiancée?"

The possibility of Kormac betraying her had never crossed her mind, but the lack of an immediate response twisted her insides. Kormac continued to stare at her, unmoving, and she met the gaze, trying to impart some psychic message that he could speak now. Her lips quivered, mind racing against the possibility that she would be taken away. Removed from his presence.

Kormac stirred, face unchanged, reaching out to touch her hand.

A tentative gesture.

Kaiya wrapped her own hands around his one, holding it up against her lips. His bony fingers tightened within her grip, and he gave the most hesitant shadow of a smile. Kaiya leaned forward, resting her head as near as possible to his, not bothering to hold back the tears of relief that spilled onto the white bedsheets.

The soldier nodded, and left the ward.

Everything would be better, now.

———

Kaiya woke to the sounds of murmuring. Something rolled on wheels along the corridor outside, and a short peal of laughter echoed from the same area. She lifted her head from its position on the bed and leaned back into the chair, moving hair out of her face and rubbing her eyes. Kormac still slept.

Few of the other patients did.

The light from the windows in the corridor indicated morning had well and truly begun. Kaiya looked around at the ward, watching as a few of the patients ate their breakfast. Most had finished, placing their trays on the inbuilt bedside cabinets that only stood by the beds that were normally present. One of the men passed his tray to his neighbour, who took it willingly and placed it on top of his own.

A few of the men glanced at her with a nod, but most ignored her presence. Four of the men were having an open conversation about the quality of the breakfast menu, the rest of those present chuckling from time to time.

"The bread could have been heavier," one of them said with a grin. "It had none of that crunch I enjoy so much."

The men murmured their amused assent.

"My egg was fresh!" another said to a great exclaim of disgust. "If I'd known we were coming back to such conditions, I think I'd have stayed!"

A few laughs rang out amongst the same murmuring of assent.

Not to be outdone, another man spoke up, "I've no idea why you're complaining. I look at my plate this morning, and what do I see? Cheese and eggs! Sausages! Real bread and butter! Mushrooms!" The final word engendered another exclamation of overly-profound disgust. "I look at this, and I'm appalled. Where is my suckling pig?"

Laughter rang through the ward. Kaiya smiled to herself, unsure what was so funny about the bizarre observations.

"Waiting for you, I heard," the fourth man offered, "in Ledophas."

The light-hearted chuckling died down, a few grunting cautious appreciation of the joke, before they all fell into a dark silence. Those still eating stared at their food, chewing slowly. From time to time someone would spend several minutes examining a piece of bread, or the slice of cheese, before savouring another bite.

A doctor entered the ward, calm and unhurried, heading in Kaiya's direction. He smiled at her.

"So you're awake," the doctor said.

Kaiya nodded and looked back to Kormac. The doctor walked over and surveyed him, tapping and making notes on a tablet. "Now... I need to talk to your fiancé about a few things, and I think it's best if we do that... well, as alone as we can be, given the circumstances. Why don't you go down and have some breakfast?"

Kaiya quickly weighed the wisdom of challenging the doctor's request-veiled order, and accepted there would be little point in doing so. She nodded and stood, lingering a few seconds to take in Kormac's thinned face.

When she looked back from the entrance to the ward, the doctor was waking him.

Kaiya stepped into the lift, and felt a deep pang of loss.

The hospital cafe overlooked the southeast boulevard on which the buses had stopped not so many hours ago. Light gleamed off the polished white floors, and Kaiya sat on an uncomfortable metal chair by the window, looking down at the slow trickle of cars and hospital visitors.

She sat staring for some time, lost in her own thoughts. The previous day seemed so long ago. Amelia would be making her plans at this very moment, Cecilie her wide range of coffee. All over Leth people were going about their morning business, not understanding how deeply the world had changed.

Kaiya shifted in her seat, restless, and traced the menu circle on the plain wooden coffee table. There was an unease she couldn't quite shake, but that was probably just her disrupted sleep, or the fact of her location. Hospitals always gave her the creeps.

She made her selection and tapped the menu holo back down. The circle glowed, waiting to be deactivated upon arrival of the order. Kaiya leaned back as comfortably as she could, which wasn't much, and watched the scattered patrons, wondering how many were there for the same purpose as her.

Across the room, by the north-facing windows, a woman sat alone, sipping from a cup. Kaiya swallowed, bitterness stinging her throat, and stared at the woman's shaved and uncovered head. Another whore collaborator, sitting there at ease in complete comfort, not an ounce of shame. What right did she have to be in the same building as people like Kormac?

Kaiya tried to look away, but found her gaze returning every few minutes, unable to accept that one of those sluts could so freely walk about with so little resistance. She surveyed the room, searching for signs of shared disapproval. Most present focused on their food and inane conversation, but there were others who showed a certain level of interest in the whore, their faces tight with displeasure.

As they should be.

Kaiya's resolve solidified. Leth needed Amelia more than ever.

A glum waitress arrived bearing a tray with Kaiya's food,

setting it down on the table. The menu circle faded, and neither Kaiya nor the waitress spoke a word to each other. Kaiya began to eat, still glancing from time to time at the shaved woman so proud of her collaboration.

Halfway through the meal, Kormac's doctor entered the cafe, scanning. Kaiya watched him approach, wary, and felt her appetite disappear quite suddenly.

"Enjoying your meal?" he asked as he sat.

Kaiya studied him. "I was."

The doctor traced the menu circle and made an order with great efficiency, not even looking at the options. He obviously knew the menu well.

"I hope you don't mind," he said. "I've been here since two, haven't eaten anything."

Kaiya stayed silent. She did mind, thank you very much, not that it mattered. She watched him look out the window, his eyes shadowed but still keen.

"Your Kormac is doing well," he said.

A jumble of nerves untangled inside her, one she hadn't realised was there. She took a deep breath, filling her lungs, and sighed.

"He's strong," she explained.

The doctor grunted. "I don't doubt that. Not one bit. I do want to discuss a few things, though. Ordinarily we would have this conversation with someone more... someone with a closer *legal* standing, strictly speaking, but we've not been able to reach Kormac's mother, and we need to keep the patients moving, unfortunately. There's only so much space here, and the Atlanticans aren't being very cooperative with telling us when the next load will arrive."

Kaiya bristled at the idea that she was not the one most suitable with which to discuss matters relating to Kormac. How they could contact his mother with the Network still down was yet another matter.

"Kormac has given consent, though, and he does appear lucid enough. First, I need to confirm that you are happy to have Kormac discharged into your care—"

"Of course," she said.

"...understanding what that entails," the doctor continued, pausing to frown. His eyes flicked between her own, and he softened his voice. "The Atlanticans have done a fine job of getting people back up to an acceptable starting point, but that's all it is – a starting point. It's going to take a while before Kormac can engage with a regular diet. Do you understand what that means?"

Kaiya nodded, lying.

"We only have the capacity to provide a week's worth of supplements, for now, but if you come back next week, we'll hopefully have engineered some more. When Kormac is discharged, the nurse will give you seven packets. The important thing to remember is one packet a day, halved, twelve hours apart. This is very important," the doctor said, eyes penetrating. "One packet a day, halved, twelve hours apart."

"What happens if he doesn't have them?" she asked.

The doctor leaned back and shrugged derisively. "I wouldn't recommend trying to find out. If I can't be certain that you will care for Kormac in the manner that is required, I *will* bar you from—"

"Ok, I get it!" Kaiya said. "I didn't say I wouldn't. I just wanted to know what would happen."

The doctor didn't look too convinced. "Your fiancé has a great deal of pride," he said. "He's going to try to convince you and convince himself that he doesn't need the supplements, like he tried to convince me just before. You *cannot* allow that to happen. Whatever he says, make sure he has them."

"Yes. Ok. I understand."

The doctor gave a satisfied nod. "As much as that pride of his will hinder a recovery, it's also an ally. I have a lot of hope for

Kormac. His movement is satisfactory for his condition, as are his bloods. He's lucid. He's demonstrating positive mental traits that should assist his readjustment. All I need from you is to be consistent with the supplements. He won't eat a lot in the beginning – he can't – so they are vital to rebuilding his diet and supporting healthy brain chemistry."

Kaiya frowned. The doctor had never told her why any of this was necessary. "What about the guys in his ward?" she asked. "They were all eating breakfast."

The doctor pursed his lips in consideration. "Different circumstances. I think that's best left for you and Kormac to discuss. At the right time."

The answer didn't give her much satisfaction. It wasn't an answer at all. The same glum waitress appeared with the doctor's breakfast, and Kaiya glanced back at the whore with the shaved head, who was playing a tablet-projected holo game.

Every sight of her filled Kaiya's body with pinprick fury.

She looked back to the doctor. "Did you ever treat a Tarkinian?" she asked.

The doctor finished his mouthful while frowning at her. "That's an odd question."

"Is it? They used this hospital, didn't they?"

"Occasionally," the doctor said. "But it was still a civilian hospital. And yes, I did treat a few Tarkinians over the years."

Kaiya stiffened. "How does it feel knowing that you might have helped them kill someone you knew?"

The doctor eyed her cautiously. "I'm not sure I'd put it like that..."

"Then how would you put it?"

Kaiya stared at him with a shaking warmth of righteousness.

"I wouldn't put it any way," he said, a hint of warning in his voice. "I don't think about it."

"What do you mean you don't think about it? You collaborated with them, you must have—"

"Excuse me?" the doctor said. "I'm a collaborator? For doing my job?"

"You helped the Tarkinians," Kaiya said. "You can't deny it."

"And you're so pure? You're telling me the only thing you ever did was fight the Tarkinians?"

"Yes!" Kaiya said.

"What gives you the right to go around accusing people of that?"

"The fact that I didn't give up! It's people like you that—"

"That's enough!"

The doctor smacked his hand down on the table, glaring at her. The cafe's already low chatter fell almost to a whisper, and the hairs on the back of Kaiya's neck prickled with the recognition that people were watching. Her ears burned.

"You know I can deny Kormac's discharge, don't you?" The doctor's eyes smouldered. "So have a good think about what you're accusing me of. You want to talk about people like me? Maybe we should talk about people like you."

Kaiya began to stand in protest.

"Sit down," the doctor said. "I'm not done with you."

The façade of his former friendliness had evaporated, and Kaiya stood still, eyes fixed outside. She had nowhere to go – his threat still lingered fresh in her mind.

Kaiya sat, refusing to look at the doctor.

"I don't know who you think you are," he said, "but I will not be spoken to like that. Ever. Especially in my own hospital, and not from someone like you."

Kaiya clenched her jaw. Someone like her?

She could have granted that he had been forced to treat Tarkinians, that he'd been too weak to stand up against them, but someone like her? Now she understood exactly the kind of person he was. And he was the one treating Kormac!

Amelia needed to know about the doctor. Maybe he was already on her list of known collaborators. But the ones in authority were all excellent liars. The corruption of Leth would never be undone while they still held all the power.

"If I were you, I'd be having a good hard look at my priorities. At the end of the day, I don't care about you, but I do care about my patient, and if you're the one who he's going to be with... then I sure as hell hope you're ready to deal with it. The last thing your fiancé needs is your self-absorption."

Every muscle in Kaiya's body was tight.

This collaborator would pay, eventually.

"So can I go back to Kormac, now?" she asked.

"He's seeing the psychologist," the doctor said with flippant aggression. "Rather uncooperatively, I might add. Do what you want. Just get away from me."

Kaiya glared at the doctor as she stood up and walked away. He ignored her, focused on his breakfast.

So Kormac was giving them trouble. Good. They deserved it. The fact he was strong enough to resist their attempts at brainwashing warmed her. It was a scam, most likely, put in place by the doctor himself to quell any questioning of his behaviour and his ongoing allegiance.

Still, she would wait a while before going to see Kormac. She didn't want to push someone that corrupt any further.

Unwilling to wait in the cafe, Kaiya returned to the second-floor reception. The previous night's chaos had dissipated, leaving a handful of people sitting on chairs and waiting, with only one receptionist to process them. Kaiya sat for a while, wondering how long it would be before it would be safe to return to Kormac.

A girl's face came into her mind, clear as the moment she had seen her.

Kaiya looked around the reception as if she were doing something forbidden, then approached the counter, catching the receptionist's attention.

"I saw a girl last night," Kaiya said. "I don't know her name, I don't know anything about her, but I wondered... I thought maybe... if she were still here, if no one has come for her, maybe I could see her..."

The receptionist eyed her cautiously. "You're not family?"

"No. I know it's strange, but..."

The receptionist nodded. "I understand."

Kaiya described the girl and the receptionist searched through the database. The hospital must have had its own localweb.

"Is this her?"

Kaiya gazed at the melancholy face. "Yes."

The receptionist chewed her lip. "Look... we don't have anything here about any visitors. No communications with family. No information regarding guardianship... I think that the circumstances can warrant a little bending of the rules."

Kaiya was taken aback. "Really?"

"Do you know how many people I have in here with no visitor records, since that first load yesterday morning?" the receptionist said. "I'd rather make that one less."

Kaiya listened to the receptionist's directions and went off towards the lift. A few butterflies somersaulted in her stomach. What was she doing? She didn't know anything about the girl, and why would the girl want to see her in the first place?

She stepped out of the lift onto one of the higher levels. Colour assaulted her eyes. The corridor's window-side wall was bright orange, opposite an equally bright purple wall that contained doors. Everywhere there were painted turtles and butterflies and giraffes and a humorous-looking lizard with a frilled neck. Kaiya walked forward, looking in through the open doors – each of which was painted in a different colour and had its own animal – to the mostly empty beds beyond.

The beds that didn't have patients were untidy, as if slept in, but anyone still in a bed was obviously in no state to leave it. Kaiya tried not to stare, but it was difficult not to. Nurses tended to the young patients, scanning them with medical instruments and reading data from their tablets. A boy not yet in his double digits lay still within a glass cylinder, flat on his back and staring up at nothingness. Wires and tubes penetrated his body. Three doctors stood around the cylinder, bodies blocking the lower half and talking in low voices. They moved around to examine the boy's head, revealing the absence of his legs.

Kaiya's intake of breath must have been loud, as all three of the doctors turned to face her.

"Can I help you?" came a voice from the corridor.

Kaiya turned to face a nurse as the door to the three-doctor'd room closed. "I came to see someone," she said.

What an inane thing to say. Of course she was there to see someone.

"You're family?" the nurse asked.

"Not quite."

The nurse peered at Kaiya and checked her tablet. "Well, the children are in the activities area, if you'll come this way?"

Kaiya followed the nurse down a connecting corridor and into a huge room full of chaos and colour. A clump of younger children played in one corner, where toys had been strewn across the floor. Some played games of make-believe in pairs or small groups, while others talked to themselves, inhabiting each of the characters in their imaginary world, while still others made no sound, simply staring at the toy in their hands as if they weren't sure quite what to do with it.

Two open doors led to secondary activity rooms. Behind one Kaiya could see a Vision Caster, with the largest group of children sitting in front of it, mesmerised by the all-encompassing sensory experience of taking a movie. Kaiya remembered the movie from her own childhood.

The other door led to a quiet room with comfortable chairs and plenty of reading tablets. There were even shelves of old paper books which looked like they belonged in a museum, from the little that Kaiya could see in her position.

She entered the main activities room, quickly determining that the girl wasn't there. The most likely candidate would be the Vision Caster, but a long glance around that room didn't provide any glimpse of the girl either. The nurse followed her attentively to the quiet room.

The girl sat on a couch, feet on the cushion, legs drawn up into a ball.

She had covered herself with the cloak.

"Thank you," Kaiya said to the nurse, who eyed her doubtfully and left.

There were other children in the room, some engrossed in reading, others in colouring, but a handful sat quietly like the girl, examining their own thoughts with vacant eyes. Kaiya walked towards the girl, smiling at the few other children who noticed her. She stopped in front of the couch, conscious of seeking consent.

"Can I sit with you?" she asked.

The girl looked up and eyed her cautiously. Her hair had been washed, though it was still mostly tangled. It was difficult to see how it could be rescued, in such a state. She gave a slight nod, and Kaiya sat on the other side of the couch, trying to make herself seem friendly.

"I'm Kaiya," she said. "I saw you last night."

The girl stared at her. "I know."

Kaiya cursed herself. Of course the girl knew.

"How are you?"

The question sounded lame as soon as it left her mouth. The girl said, "Fine," and Kaiya fumbled about in her mind for the right thing to say.

"What are you doing?"

"Nothing."

The bluntness of the response made Kaiya uncomfortable,

and she looked away. How did she keep walking into situations without a proper plan?

"It must be good to be back. Better than there, I mean."

The girl shrugged. "Yeah."

"Did you get a good sleep?"

"Guess so."

Kaiya went silent, watching the girl's head loll over onto the couch.

She had managed this very poorly.

It would have been so easy to leave – she didn't owe this girl anything – but something inside her refused to dignify the notion. Instead she glanced at a nearby bookshelf. She had never read a physical book before, though Tilda's family owned a large collection of them. They were museum pieces, not something to uselessly take up space.

"Do you like stories?" Kaiya asked the girl.

The girl's eyes flicked back to her. "What kind of stories?"

"I don't know," Kaiya said. "Why don't I have a look."

She went over to the bookshelf and flicked through the spines of the books, the girl watching. There was no particular order to them, no organisation based on target age or type. Kaiya took out and replaced thick books and thin books, short ones and tall ones, until she came across the largest one on the shelf. It was a deep red, with dated artwork and intricate patterning. She took it out and flicked to the table of contents.

She glanced doubtfully at the girl, who was most certainly too old for such a book. "Do you like fairytales?" she asked.

Something sparked in the girl's eyes. "My mummy used to read me fairytales," she said.

Kaiya studied the girl. By the time she had been the girl's age, 'mummy' had been long gone from her vocabulary. But if the girl had been taken in the Night of Retribution...

She stared at the round hump poking through the girl's cloak and pushed down her hatred for the Tarkinians.

"Did she ever read you *The Tale of Little Ava*?"

The girl shook her head.

Kaiya smiled and returned to the couch. "That was one of my favourites when I was little. Would you like me to read it to you?"

The girl hesitated before nodding in agreement and sitting up more attentively. She moved closer as Kaiya turned to the correct page and propped the book up between them. A quaint, two-dimensional picture showed the fairytale's titular character tied to a tree trunk while cruel-looking goblins laughed.

Kaiya glanced down at the girl, whose attention was focused on the picture, and began to read:

Once upon a time there was a little village by an enchanted forest, and in that village lived a boy and girl. They were best of friends, being brother and sister, and played together every day. They ran and danced and wrestled, and come nightfall they would stand on the path outside their house, waiting for their parents to return.

Like all parents of the village, they warned their children that the enchanted forest was not to be entered.

'You must never go in there, Ava,' the girl's father said. 'The forest is a cursed place, ruled by goblins cruel.'

The forest frightened Ava, for strange things were said to happen in the shadows beyond where eyes can see. Every year on midwinter eve, the villagers gathered to tell stories of disobedient children who wandered away and never returned. Ava's brother always said the stories didn't scare him, but Ava knew that underneath his valorous heart lurked the same fear that invaded her own.

One day Ava stood waiting as night fell fast around her. The cold made her shake, but her brother stood tall, saying no weather could penetrate his bones. 'Shall I face fire,' he said, 'my skin will not melt. Shall snowstorms descend, a furnace I'll be. Shall the lightning crash down, or the floodwater rise, yield I shall not, for the strong oak of the forest am I.'

His words comforted Ava, who was younger and needed protection. Her parents had hunted that day, going forward into the forest as villagers so rarely did. When heard she did a masculine scream from yonder where trees began, Ava knew trouble had befallen them.

'The goblins!' cried the man. 'The goblins have taken our kin!'

A great wail erupted from all around, and the villagers came out to mourn.

'Who will save them?' came a cry. 'Who will go into the forest?'

No one spoke up, for all were afraid, and all knew that to venture the forest was foolish.

'Not I,' said the lumberjack, the strongest of the village, 'for my strength is needed to keep us warm.'

'Not I,' said the priest, the wisest of the village, 'for my wisdom is needed to keep us pure.'

'Not I,' said the doctor, the cleverest of the village, 'for my wits are needed to keep us healthy and safe.'

No one stepped forward, and Ava despaired, for her parents had served the village for years and now no one wished to assist them. Then thinking how sad life would be with no one to read stories or play with her hair, Ava stepped forward so the village could see her.

'I will go,' Ava said, 'for I am neither strong nor wise nor clever, and the goblins will not think to look for a child.'

No one protested, for all were too scared, and their thoughts were with their own children only.

'Are you not scared?' came the voice of a woman.

And Ava said, 'Yes, fear crawls through my skin, for my feet have no knowledge of forested darkness.'

Then her brother stepped forward with chest puffed out nobly, and cried, 'Do not fear, for I shall protect you. I'm strong and I'm brave and I learn sword every day.'

Ava rejoiced, and so did the people, though they all thought secretly that the children would fail. Many wishes were made, and the villagers stood round to farewell the brave younglings.

'Take now this hatchet,' the lumberjack said, 'for you shall need fire and protection.'

'Take now this holy symbol,' the priest said, 'for you shall need guidance and hope.'

'Take now this salve,' the doctor said, 'for you shall need tenderness and healing.'

And with these gifts of the village, the children departed, walking into the darkness of the enchanted forest. Soon the village dwindled behind them, and their eyes adjusted to the gloomy surroundings.

'What way shall we go?' asked Ava of her brother.

'Yonder,' he said, with a confident point, and so they departed.

The shadows of night made curious shapes, and the moon peeked through leaves only ever so slightly. Ava imagined she saw wolves and yowies and the shining eyes of goblin-kind. They moved behind trees and cackled at them softly. She told herself it was nought but the rustling of branches.

For many hours they walked, until Ava's legs were sore.

'I must rest,' Ava said, 'for I am weary and have need.'

So they found a little clearing where the ground was dry and a small tree had fallen. Ava's brother took the lumberjack's hatchet and began to chop at the tree, until he had made a tidy pile of wood that would see them through the night.

With leaves and broken twigs he built a cheerful fire, and Ava sat close as she shivered.

'Sleep safe, little sister, I shall keep watch and my fire shall guard you from cold.'

And so Ava's eyes closed, and when next they did open, morning sunlight was shining, and the cheerful fire smouldered.

They set out again, and now that morning had arrived, the enchanted forest looked not so frightening to Ava. Ants marched boldly, while birdsong lilted through the air, and creatures small and furry scurried about, startled by the footsteps of these strangers.

For half a day they walked, and Ava grew confused, as the trees looked all the same.

'I fear we are lost,' said Ava to her brother, and clutched at the priest's holy symbol.

There came a great crashing behind them, all of a sudden, and Ava turned wide-eyed to see a tall man of the forest.

'Who goes here?' said he, and Ava's brother stepped forward to reply.

'We seek the goblin camp, good sir, to rescue those dear we have lost.'

'How know I your words to be true, that you be no shape-shifting wood sprite or harpy?'

'Good sir,' said Ava, 'lay your eyes upon this symbol, given to us as sign of devotion. We tell no lie and offer proof that we are true servants of the divine.'

The man of the forest accepted her gesture and drew out his own symbol matching.

'These paths are treacherous, and your journey is folly, but your heart is young and strong and must learn these lessons hard. Go yonder and stay straight, you shall come to the camp of the goblins.'

His words filled Ava with foreboding as she trudged on through the forest, and when she turned back to glimpse him, he had disappeared. Ava's brother strode forward with renewed vigour, and Ava worked hard to stay close.

As the afternoon wore on, and shadows began to descend, Ava declared they should prepare to rest. Her brother, however, insisted they keep moving, and this they did do, Ava reluctant but accepting.

'Look here!' cried her brother, stopping all of a sudden.

They had come upon a centaur wounded, writhing in pain on a bed of dry leaves.

Ava ran forward with no second thought, taking the doctor's salve to the side of the centaur.

'But wait!' cried her brother, stopping her hand. 'We shall have no drop left! Ava, what if we need it?'

'This poor creature needs it, more than us now. And should we not use it for certainty than keep it for chance?'

She knelt down by the centaur, who thrashed with mighty dread.

'Fear not, dear centaur, I've salve to close your wounds.'

And upon hearing Ava's words, the centaur ceased his movements. Ava leaned forward and opened the salve, covering the wound 'til not one skerrick remained. When at last it was done, the centaur did stand, giving a bellow of triumph.

'Not soon shall I forget this great act of kindness. If ever you need my hoof or my bow, think of me softly, and the stars will carry your voice.'

The centaur galloped away, and Ava's brother took out the lumberjack's hatchet, ready to make camp once more.

'But now we have no salve!' he moaned, and was glum for the rest of the evening.

Side by side they fell asleep, and the stars faded in Ava's eyes.

When suddenly they awoke, Ava cried in desperate terror. The goblins had come, eyes shining with evil. They laughed and they joked, voices black with horror, until the biggest one shushed them and stepped forward to speak.

'Who dares to venture so deep in our dominion?'

'I do!' cried Ava's brother. 'The son of those you took some two nightfalls ago.'

The goblins cackled and the biggest one roared, 'The village is yours, and the forest is ours, whoever comes within forfeits life – this agreement is known! You shall come with us to the goblin camp, where you will feed my kin at breakfast!'

The goblins all cheered, and it came to pass that Ava and her brother were taken to the goblin camp, bound as hunted animals. Upon their arrival, Ava was tied to a tree, as was her brother, and the lumberjack's hatchet was taken as loot.

'We have us more trespassers!' came the big goblin's voice. 'Tonight now we rest, and tomorrow we feast!'

A great fire roared in the centre of the clearing, and the goblins all lay down to sleep.

Ava looked round at the sleeping figures, and saw that her brother had been rendered silent with a magical herb. He had struggled mightily against the goblins, and could not be trusted to stay still. Now his head drooped, and Ava was alone.

'Oh, what am I to do?' said Ava to herself.

'Nothing but to wait,' came a voice from the tree beside.

A girl younger than Ava looked across with moonlit eyes.

'I did not see you there,' said Ava, 'but for what, pray, shall we wait?'

'Either rescue or the cooking pot, and by this time I long for either.'

The girl looked sad and weary, and Ava took pity on her. 'You speak as one who has been here long.'

'I have,' she said, 'for three nights now, and horrible have they been. The goblins are a torturous bunch, for they season their food with fear. And while I pity that you now share my fate, I am joyed to hear your voice.'

Ava now felt not so victim herself, for the little girl had shown a suffering far greater than her own. Said Ava, 'be not resigned, young sister, there's hope still to be found,' and raised her eyes into the heavens and whispered for the centaur to hear her plea.

A gentle breeze stirred, but no response came to assuage her fear.

So Ava told stories, and the little girl laughed, until dawn broke the murky black sky.

When all the goblins had arisen, they began to poke and prod their three young victims, cackling that soon they would eat them. The magical herb no longer affected Ava's brother, but neither did he struggle, for he had learnt that from his effort nought would arise.

A great cookpot was brought and placed on the fire reawakened, and goblins chanted round in a circle.

'We love the youngster's flesh,' the biggest goblin said to Ava, 'so juicy and fresh and tasty, you'll make a perfect morsel!'

The goblins began to untie the little girl and Ava's brother, and Ava panicked as she watched.

'Wait!' she cried, attempting to stall, and the goblins turned all to face her. 'Before we go to the depths of your bellies, one thing I would know. To my mother and father what did you do?'

The biggest goblin laughed and pointed to the ground, where bones aplenty were strewn. 'Look here, young child, and observe on the ground, the bones of your ancestors a-lying. Your quest was all in vain, and its price is your blood and your life!'

The goblins lifted Ava's brother and the little girl above their heads, ready to throw them in the cookpot, but then through the trees came a crashing of hooves, and the centaur galloped into their midst.

'Depart, goblin fiends! These children I shall guard. On pain of righteous death, begone and never return!'

The centaur made a fearsome sight, and the goblins ran away in terror.

Soon the children were free from their bonds, and safely secured upon the centaur's strong back.

'The only worthwhile promise is the promise that is kept,

and when I heard your prayer upon the stars, I rode as fast as wind allowed across benighted forest.'

'Your debt is paid,' said Ava, 'great centaur, may I ask? A small favour, if you'd be so kind, to take us to our village?'

'No debt exists, young human, for in terms of debt I do not think. I will take you to your village, and give you to their care.'

The centaur galloped long and hard, an astounding feat of strength, and finally they arrived at the edge of the forest mere moments before nightfall came.

'Here shall I leave you, and if ever you come again to forest, speak to the stars – I will find you and protect you, and we shall go galloping together again.'

Upon the return of the children, the village cheered and rejoiced. Although Ava and her brother had not rescued their parents, they brought with them a new treasure, one whom the villagers began to question.

'From whence did you come?' asked a woman.

And the little girl said, 'On far side of forest, where another village once lay. It is now but a memory, and no home do I have, for the goblins set all there on fire. Will one of you protect me from harm?'

There was pity all 'round, but nobody spoke, for all thought solely of the duties already owned. But little Ava's journey had taught her many things, and though she felt great trepidation, she stepped forward bravely to speak.

'I'll protect you, little sister, though I'm not strong, nor wise, and not always am I smart. But what I have is loyalty, and kindness for your heart. I'll make your favourite foods and read your favourite stories, and every Sunday after next we'll go a-flower-picking in the meadows.'

Ava's brother had not spoken since waking from the magical herb, and still no words he offered. His face was very sad, and Ava turned to him and said, 'Brother, you are brave and strong, but now is the time to lay aside these worthy traits. Let us head to home and rest, for we have many days of toil ahead.'

And so it was that the children did just that, and Ava kept her promise to the little girl. The house they filled with meadow flowers – lavender, I hear tell – and the scent of pies made all who passed by envious of those inside. Though Ava's brother spoke never again, he worked hard every day, and sometimes in the evening he would listen to his sister's stories.

They nourished the little girl's heart, giving her peace and health and joy, and now every time the little girl smiles, Ava remembers that life is a gift.

A moment of magical silence followed Kaiya's reading, and she glanced down at the girl, who looked back up at her, eyes enraptured. It had been so long since the days of fairytales. Kaiya could barely remember those nights, but a deep nostalgia pervaded the air around her, as if she were passing on her own mother to the girl.

"Did you like it?" Kaiya asked.

The girl stayed quiet but nodded with vigour, and Kaiya smiled at her, heart swelling with warmth.

"What's your name?" she asked gently.

The girl hesitated before finally saying, "Masuma."

"Masuma," Kaiya said, holding the girl's eyes with her own. "I haven't met a Masuma before."

"I haven't met a Kaiya," she said.

"Would you like me to read another?"

Masuma nodded again and Kaiya turned back to the contents.

Beside her, Masuma edged closer.

10

KAIYA PICKED UP THE PREVIOUS NIGHT'S PLATES FROM THE DINING table and took them to the kitchen, grimacing at the morning sun. The mess of her and Tilda's *marashta*-making still littered the kitchen benches, but the effort had been worth it. Kormac had enjoyed the home-cooked meal, even if his response was somewhat muted.

And the *marashta* had tasted good, to her delight, though that was Tilda's touch, most likely.

Kaiya yawned and began to fill the dishwasher, eyeing the collection of empty packets that sat in droplets of oil all over the benches.

"You're up early," came Tilda's voice from behind.

Kaiya groaned agreement. "Speak for yourself."

"I'm always up early. Anyway, I figured you'd want to spend as much time as you could in bed."

Kaiya turned and gave her an arch look. Tilda smirked.

"Not funny," Kaiya said, and went back to stacking the dishes.

"Oh, come on. Don't be such a misery guts. I'm just joking with you."

Kaiya ignored her.

"What's wrong?" Tilda asked.

Kaiya didn't know how to answer. She wouldn't have woken so early, if she'd had her way, but sharing a bed again proved itself an odd experience. She hadn't expected that.

"Just didn't get much sleep," Kaiya said. "Kormac kept waking, having nightmares or something. It's fine..."

Tilda was silent for a few moments, and Kaiya braced herself for what she already knew was coming.

"I told you he should have stayed in the hospital longer."

"They don't have space, Tilda, even if there were no more convoys coming. But there are more coming, and who knows when the next one will be?"

"Kaiya—"

"You don't understand, Tilda." Kaiya turned to face her, trying to show the gravity of the situation in her face. "I don't trust the doctors there. I think... I think some of them were full-on collaborators."

Tilda's face fell. "Kaiya—"

"I know what you're going to say."

"You don't know what I'm going to say."

"It's fine, Tilda. Everything is fine."

Kaiya walked over and gave Tilda a tight hug. She was trying to understand Tilda's refusal to accept the ongoing risk of collaborators, but perhaps that was something she could forgive to some extent.

"I know you're just trying to help," Kaiya said.

"I was thinking about it last night," Tilda said, "about if I should go. I know how much you've wanted Kormac back. I don't want to get in the way or be a burden."

Kaiya pulled away. "What are you talking about?" she said. "Don't be ridiculous. You can stay as long as you like, you know that."

"Well I can't stay forever."

"Who says that? Why can't you stay forever? Why would I want someone who makes such good *marashta* to leave? That's what you can be. My chef."

Tilda smiled and shook her head. "I'll keep that in mind," she said drily, "if I decide I need a career change."

"What career?"

Tilda rolled her eyes. "Very funny. Cause yours is going so well?"

"At least I have work. Sometimes. When I show up."

They both laughed softly, and Kaiya began cleaning the benches, Tilda assisting.

"I know you don't trust the doctors," Tilda said, "but maybe there's someone else Kormac can... I just think that maybe he could talk to someone. Someone he doesn't know."

"Why would he want to talk to someone he doesn't know? He has me."

Tilda glanced at her cautiously. "Yeah, but... what if he doesn't want to? What if he doesn't want you to know certain things?"

"Like what?" Kaiya shook her head. "He just needs time, Tilda. He'll tell me when he's ready. Like you will, eventually."

"What do you mean?"

"Don't play silly," Kaiya said. "It's not like I can't hear you when you're crying. You never say anything. Maybe you should go talk to someone, if you think it's such a good idea?"

Tilda looked away. "It's not important. Everyone in Leth has something to cry about. I'm no more special than anyone else. Maybe you're right..."

Kaiya glanced at Tilda and left it at that. Why couldn't she just admit she was afraid of not seeing her parents again? All that talk about accepting they were already gone... it wasn't like Tilda at all. For some reason the thought of Tilda's parents shifted Kaiya's mind to Masuma, and she wondered whether her parents had come looking for her yet.

Their failure rankled Kaiya.

"Do you have plans today?" she asked, trying to draw a line under their previous conversation. "Going out, like usual?"

"Ha. You're on fire, this morning. I think I'll do something different today and stay here. Shocking, I know."

Kaiya grinned, hiding her perplexity at Tilda's continued failure at engaging with the outside world. "Kormac wants to see his mother, I think, so that will be interesting," Kaiya said.

Tilda's mouth edged up in a smile. "Manor quadrant," she mimicked.

Kaiya choked back her own laugh as Kormac walked into view in the corridor. "Hey," she said, dropping an empty can back on the bench and walking over to embrace him. "You're up early."

He stood still, as if unsure what to do in response. "I've been waking up early every day for three years," he said. "I'm used to it."

Silence fell. Kaiya didn't know what to say, and her mind was focused more on the fact that Kormac hadn't returned the embrace.

"You know what," Tilda said, "we should have a special breakfast. Another celebration."

Kaiya looked up at Kormac's face and forced a smile. "That's a good idea. What do you feel like eating? You didn't have much last night. You must be hungry."

Kormac frowned and closed his eyes. "I think I'll go out. Just... have a walk around. I'm not hungry."

"Ok," Kaiya said. "Yeah, let's do that. Just let me get out of my pyjamas, and we can go."

"I just... I just want to go by myself for a while."

Kaiya swallowed. "Of course. That's a good idea. You should, you totally should."

Tilda had turned her back on the scene, making herself busy by cleaning loudly.

The smattering of premature grey in Kormac's hair glistened in the morning sun. What was he thinking? What happened now? They had only been one night reunited. She was mad to think things would go back to normal so quickly.

He just needed time.

Kormac went back into Kaiya's bedroom and changed, reemerging in a grey tracksuit that hid the majority of his body from view. It was far too baggy for him, his head protruding from the neck hole like a kitten from a lion's den.

Kaiya held out a glass of coloured water. The doctor's prescription.

Kormac eyed it with distaste.

"You have to drink it, Kormac," she said, though she wished she could convince herself of it. She had argued with Tilda about whether or not it was a plot to poison those returning, but Tilda had overruled her in an unusual display of vehemence.

She hoped Tilda was right. That she could trust her.

Kormac took the glass and drank, stopping halfway as he semi-choked. His face indicated just how disgusting the liquid was. He finished it with a groan and handed back the glass, before giving a weak smile and hesitating where he was.

"I won't be long," he said softly. "Just... feel like walking."

Kaiya leaned forward and kissed him on the cheek, squeezing his hand affectionately.

"I love you," she whispered.

Kormac smiled softly, eyes locked onto the wall, and walked to the door.

After he left, Kaiya sat on the alcove by the window and watched him amble down the boulevard. He was heading towards the river, hands in pockets, and Kaiya began flicking through everything she had said and done since he came home, looking for some trace of a mistake.

"Everything will be fine," Tilda said, coming over to stand by

Kaiya. They hugged each other while Kaiya kept her gaze on the boulevard, watching until she could no longer see Kormac.

He had said he wouldn't be long, so she waited, head resting on the opened glass. There was a minuscule swell in the air that cooled her sun-soaking face, making her drowsy. She really had slept poorly, and her eyelids drooped, try as she did to watch for his return.

After a brief and hazy nap that barely seemed to last four minutes, she started awake and stared down at a familiar figure walking up the boulevard. Her body tensed a little at the sight of Jonathan, who was making his way towards the front door of her building.

Kaiya raced to her bedroom, drawing a bewildered Tilda out of her quietude.

"It's Jonathan," Kaiya explained. "Your bloody soldier boy."

Kaiya took off her pyjamas, searching the muddled bedroom floor for something decent to wear.

Tilda stood by the door, looking amused. "My soldier boy?"

"It's not funny," Kaiya said. "I didn't tell him about Kormac. He doesn't know I'm engaged."

Tilda rolled her eyes, sighing Kaiya's name in exasperation.

"I didn't encourage him!" Kaiya said. "He's the one who keeps pestering me."

"Except that you went and got his help finding out about the convoys, so... you kinda did. And what do you mean he keeps pestering you? He came by once to give you the information you wanted. This is the first time he's 'pestered' you and you're making him out like some stalker."

"I didn't ask to see him."

Tilda shrugged dramatically. "So he's interested in you! So what? Isn't that a good thing? Not every soldier is the same."

Kaiya fumbled with the button of her blouse and glared at Tilda. That had been a low blow.

"You don't know anything about soldiers," Kaiya said. "Of course they're not all the same. But they think the same."

Tilda pursed her lips, and a knock came from the front door.

"How do I look?" Kaiya asked.

Tilda stared at her, stunned. "Are you kidding me? Now you care about how you look? Make up your mind!"

"Shut up."

Kaiya scowled at Tilda, who quickly positioned herself at the dining table and picked up her tablet, pretending to read.

Kaiya opened the front door

"Good morning," Jonathan said cheerily.

"Hi," Kaiya said, with no great warmth.

They stood awkwardly on opposite sides of the doorframe.

"I thought I'd see how you were," Jonathan said. "You looked unhappy when you left the other night."

"Oh, that," Kaiya said. "It was nothing. Just... thinking about things."

Jonathan studied her. "Is everything fine? I hope you don't mind me coming here."

"No, she doesn't mind," Tilda called from the dining room. "We were just talking about you, actually."

Kaiya could have murdered her.

Jonathan smiled, looking past Kaiya into the dining room. "Yes. The one who doesn't like going out."

"That's me," Tilda said. "But happy to entertain at home. Why don't you come in?"

Kaiya tried to hide her displeasure at Tilda's childish games, but she couldn't take it back now. She didn't want to be rude. Jonathan looked at her for permission and she stepped back into the corridor, indicating towards the dining room.

"Make yourself comfortable," she said. "I'll get us something to eat and you can get to know Tilda better. She's been dying for some male company. Haven't you?"

Tilda scoffed. "I'm a woman with needs, Kaiya. Is that such a crime?"

"Depends!"

Amused, Jonathan stepped down into the dining room.

Kaiya went into the kitchen and opened the pantry. She had made sure it was stocked with anything Kormac might desire. Tilda and Jonathan chatted about inanities – the usual stuff of introductions – while she searched for some kind of snack that Tilda wasn't so fond of. That could be her punishment. Now that Jonathan was inside, it wouldn't be easy to rid him without being rude.

Kaiya smirked as she pulled out a fruitcake with a copious amount of sultanas.

Tilda hated sultanas.

Kaiya gave her a massive piece with a grin, and received raised eyebrows in return.

"You eat sweets early," Jonathan said.

"Everyone does," Kaiya said. "There's no correct time of day for sweets, especially cake. It's all the time."

She pushed a filled plate towards Jonathan, and immediately worried that he may not like it. Not that his opinion mattered. She was just being polite, that was all.

Jonathan thanked her and began to eat, murmuring in approval. Kaiya's fast-grown bundle of nerves eased at that, and she glanced at Tilda, who was focused on picking out the sultanas with a dessert fork.

"Thank you for helping me," Kaiya said to Jonathan. "With the convoys. My... my fiancé returned yesterday."

If the revelation that she was spoken for dismayed him, he didn't show it on his face. He didn't give any indication of emotion at all, in fact, upon hearing the news.

"I'm glad to hear it," was all he said, and he nibbled at the cake. "So you live here?" he asked Tilda.

She shook her head. "Just staying. Making sure this one doesn't get in too much trouble."

Jonathan grinned. "And how's that working out for you?"

"Don't get me started," Tilda said with a dramatic sigh. "She's out of control. You should really look into her, you know. Maybe you need to take her away for questioning."

Tilda smirked and stabbed a sultana with her fork, holding it up for Kaiya's viewing pleasure.

Kaiya ate some cake, cringing with embarrassment.

"I'd love to assist you," Jonathan said, "but unfortunately we have no jurisdiction here. You'll have to sort this case out for yourself, miss."

"Pity," Tilda said. "She doesn't much like listening to me."

Kaiya rolled her eyes. "So how long are you staying?" she said to Jonathan. "*Allied Atlantica*, I mean."

"Depends. Could be a month. Could be half a year. Personally, I hope it's the latter. I'd like a chance to see the rest of Nymosen."

"Leth not good enough for you?" Kaiya asked.

"Oh, don't get her started," Tilda warned.

Jonathan flicked his eyes between them, grinning. "Leth is fine. Just small. I want to go to the other border towns, and I want to see Akheron. I've always wanted to see Akheron."

"There's nothing there," Kaiya said. "Just a bunch of old towers."

"You've been?"

"Well, no... but everyone knows that."

Jonathan skewered his slice of cake. "I see."

"Don't listen to her," Tilda said. "Akheron is magnificent. I wouldn't want to live there, but it's nice for a visit. I think everyone should go there at least once in their life. Kaiya's just stubborn."

"I am not," Kaiya said, and Tilda snorted, choking on her cake. Kaiya smiled. "Serves you right."

"Why don't you like Akheron?" Jonathan asked.

"Because I don't like Nymosen," Kaiya said. "Leth doesn't belong in Nymosen. We should be independent. It goes back hundreds of years – I wouldn't expect you to understand."

Jonathan frowned. "Back to the duke's capitulation, right?"

Kaiya's eyes widened. "Yeah. Exactly."

"But... I thought Leth was allied with Tarkinia, back then. That the duke surrendered to Nymosen because Nymosen threatened to invade it for supporting Tarkinia."

"What history book have *you* been reading?" Kaiya asked.

"I could ask the same question!"

"You're wrong," Kaiya said. "We've never had anything to do with Tarkinia. We were always our own little town until the Nymians took over."

"Eight hundred years ago," Tilda reminded her pointedly.

"It doesn't matter."

Tilda held her hands up in resignation.

"Well," Jonathan said, "if you say so. But that's not what I learnt..."

Kaiya chewed on her cake, leaving that thread of conversation alone. Whatever the Atlanticans were teaching their children, it was way off the mark. Amelia would be interested in that piece of information.

"Will you get to see Akheron?" Tilda asked. "Does the army give you the opportunity?"

"Of course. We can ask for leave—"

Jonathan stopped speaking at the sound of the front door opening.

Kormac walked into the corridor, eyes to the floor, and closed the door quietly behind him.

"There you are," Kaiya said, standing.

Kormac turned around and gazed into the dining room, eyes flicking between the three of them. "Yes," was all he said.

"Do you want some cake?" Kaiya asked.

Kormac thought about the question as he sat down to remove his shoes. "No. I don't think so."

"Did you have a good walk?"

He stared at the dining room floor and grunted affirmation. "It was nice. Quiet."

"I'm glad," Kaiya lied. She had to keep reminding herself that it would just take a bit of time. Next time he'd want her to go with him.

"Why are there Taskforce police here?" Kormac asked. "Everywhere I went... police."

"It's... complicated," Kaiya said. "Come sit down with us."

Kormac stared at Jonathan. "You're Atlantican."

"Yes," Jonathan said. "I am. I... hear you've recently returned."

Kormac gave a brief nod. "I guess we have you to thank for that."

"I only wish we could have got there sooner," Jonathan said.

Kormac sneered. "I was under the impression you could."

Jonathan clenched his jaw and looked at the table, Kormac still staring at him.

"I think I should go," Jonathan said with a smile to Kaiya and Tilda. "Thank you for your hospitality."

"Why are you here?" Kormac demanded, his voice gaining in strength. "What's going on?"

"Kormac—" Kaiya began.

"You've been sleeping with him," Kormac said. "You've been sleeping with him."

Kaiya froze as the bottom of her stomach fell away. "What?"

"I'm not stupid," Kormac said, beginning to pace. "I knew something was going on. I knew it. I could feel it. You wanted me to find out, didn't you? That's why you made sure he was here when I got back."

"He's here with me," Tilda said, placing her hand on the back of Jonathan's neck. "I invited him."

Kormac stopped and looked at Tilda, shaking his head. "No, no, you're lying. You're lying!" he yelled, picking up the empty chair at the head of the table and throwing it against the wall.

Kaiya's body screamed with concrete adrenaline. She watched, stuck in her position, as Jonathan stood up and confronted Kormac, hands raised in placation.

"Get away from me!" Kormac said, stepping back against the wall.

"I'm not trying to hurt you," Jonathan said, edging closer. "Listen to me. I haven't—"

Kormac bellowed and used his arm to scoop up and fling the holoholders and vase that were on top of the credenza. The vase smashed against the floor, and Kaiya stood, legs weak.

"Kormac, please," she said, eyes filling with frightened tears.

Jonathan stayed where he was.

"You admit it!" Kormac said to Kaiya.

"What are you talking about, Kormac? He's a soldier! I would never sleep with a soldier!"

Tilda looked at her sharply as she stepped forward to the head of the table. "Kormac—" she begun.

"This is why it took you so long to come!" Kormac said to Jonathan. "Now it makes sense. Now it makes sense. You're working with them, aren't you? You're working with the Tarkinians. You've been on their side the whole time."

"We're on your side," Jonathan said.

"You could have come. You could have come. I know it. That's what you've been doing here, you've been setting a trap. It's a trap, you're bringing everyone back into a trap."

"No one's bringing anyone into a trap," Jonathan said. "There's no trap. No one's trying to hurt you."

Kaiya edged forward, repeating Kormac's name until she finally had his attention. His eyes bore into her soul, pools of lost and panicked fury.

"Kormac, listen to me. Please."

She stepped forward, and her foot crunched a broken piece of chair. Kormac glanced down as if he'd never seen it before.

"You know I would never, ever betray you. I've been waiting for you. You know that, right?"

Kormac stared at her.

"And you've been waiting for me, too, haven't you?" Kaiya said. "You've been thinking about me. Like I've been thinking about you."

He frowned as if he had a headache, rubbing his hand through his hair. "Yes," he whispered, then repeated it with more confidence.

She smiled at him encouragingly, trying to mask her own apprehension. "Everything is ok, now. You're with me. I haven't gone anywhere. I haven't found anyone else."

Jonathan took a step forward, and Kormac yelled for him to stay back, going on about some alliance between the Tarkinians and Atlanticans.

"Go," Kaiya said to Jonathan. "Please, just go. He's only like this cause you're here."

Jonathan looked askance at her. "You're blaming this on me?"

"It's not about blame," she said, frustrated.

"He needs help, Kaiya," Jonathan said. "He needs someone to restrain him and—"

"You don't have jurisdiction. You said so yourself. Please, just go."

Jonathan stayed for a long few moments then sighed and straightened himself proudly.

"I'll come with you," Tilda said as he walked towards the front door, and Kaiya watched them leave.

The room was silent.

"Kormac?" she said softly.

He pressed his temples between fingers and thumb, face pained. Kaiya took another step forward and repeated his name.

"Who is he?" Kormac asked.

Kaiya watched his face squeeze as he tried to understand what was happening around him. "Just a person," she said. "He told me that the convoys were coming. He was just here to see if you had come back, that's all."

Kormac sat down on the floor, leaning against the wall and pulling his knees up to his chest. He hid his face behind his hand, still rubbing the front of his head. "I thought that..."

His words disappeared, and Kaiya moved closer, kneeling down beside him. How he could have thought something so ridiculous was beyond her, but she didn't want to say anything that might push him away so soon. "I'm sorry," was all that she could utter. Perhaps it was her fault, deep down...

The front door opened and closed quietly, and Tilda looked in from the corridor, face inscrutable. She shook her head with resignation and disappeared deeper into the apartment.

This was none of her business.

"I want to see my mother," Kormac whispered.

Kaiya touched his knee with hesitant sympathy, saying nothing. It was time to put on the armour again and face the infinite depth of his mother's disapproval.

The energy conductors stared up out of their watery grave, goading Kaiya.

She stood with Kormac by the balustrades of the eastern bridge, watching the sun glisten off each silvery web that floated gently side to side in the water. Kormac looked relaxed, and held her hand. Whatever had happened in the dining room, he felt more open now. More receptive to her affection.

She cuddled against his too-thin arm, and the sun's warmth mixed with that rediscovered sensation of momentary contentment, when all that existed was her and him and the breeze and the water.

"They need feeding," Kaiya mused.

Kormac murmured a wordless enquiry as to how she could know such a thing.

"They just... get a certain look," she said. "When they haven't eaten enough. They become... lethargic. Like you can tell that they're struggling more than usual to do the conversion. I don't understand the bioelectrics. Mum tried to explain it to me, once, but it was too complicated, and I didn't want to know."

The first chance she had, Kaiya would ask her.

"It's not actual food, like we need food to survive," Kaiya said. "It's just a bio-enriched fuel that helps them heal. They get damaged over time from the process of converting material into energy. That's what mum was working on. Self-healing for water-based conductors."

Kormac gave a soft grin. "I know. I remember. You must have told me fifty times."

They departed from their position and finished crossing the bridge, dodging cars. There was something disgusting about the gradual return of the cars. Where did anyone have to go? What were people doing? Leth should have been at a standstill, demanding the justice that was owed them.

She squeezed Kormac's hand tighter. He was back, now. She had to stop thinking about everyone else. Kormac was all that mattered. And soon her parents would be home, maybe even in the next convoy, and she needn't concern herself with whores and collaborators. She could cocoon herself in her own little world. Amelia would deal with the problem.

The first red stone terrace house came into view, signifying the beginning of the more exclusive area of the already-exclusive northeast quadrant. The streets narrowed, and birds tweeted from tree branches. No wonder the people here had been so comfortable working with the Tarkinians. It was easy to comply when you had so much privilege at stake. She'd even heard rumours that half the quadrant had never been affected by the Night of Retribution, simply buying their way out of it.

Kormac's mother should have done the same. Kaiya would never forget that failure.

"I feel... strange," Kormac said, pausing as they ambled down his street.

Kaiya's heart had been thumping along harder with every step towards his front door. "Why?" she asked, grateful for a few snatched moments before the confrontation, and the possibility of avoiding it altogether.

"I don't know," Kormac said, frowning. "Nothing makes any sense."

He started walking again and Kaiya pondered what he had meant.

They stopped in front of the crimson, newly-painted front door, and Kormac's hand tightened against her own. She gazed at him, smiling, and pressed the doorbell. The sound of chimes tinkled in response.

They waited.

"She might not be home," Kaiya said, trying to mask her hopefulness.

The door opened, and she looked up at Kormac's mother.

"Good morning," she said cheerily, smiling down at them both. The expression looked completely foreign on her face. "How can I help you?"

Kaiya frowned. What kind of game was she playing?

"Mum?" Kormac said, hesitating.

His mother looked at him sympathetically. "I'm sorry, young man, you must have the wrong house. I'd love to help, but the Network is down for some reason."

The realisation of what Kormac's mother had done fell like an avalanche in Kaiya's body.

"No..." she said. "You have to be kidding me..."

Kormac's mother peered at him with a look of dawning realisation. "You're not someone famous, are you? I feel like I've seen a holo of you before."

"This is not happening..." Kaiya said. "I cannot believe this."

Kormac's face betrayed his difficulty at processing his mother's strange behaviour. "Mum?" he said again, confused.

"She doesn't know it's you," Kaiya said, glaring accusatively at Kormac's mother. "You had *Rapture*, didn't you?"

Kormac's mother looked almost apologetic, smile still stretched across her face. "I'm going to have to ask you to leave, please."

Kaiya struggled to express herself amidst the horror of the woman's selfishness. "Are you kidding me?" she said again. "This is your son! Your son!" Maybe if she said the word enough it would sink into her skull and force her to remember.

Kormac stood still.

"If I cannot remember you, then I had good reason to remove you from my life," his mother said. "Please leave me in peace."

She went to close the door, but Kaiya stepped forward and pushed it further open, sending her several steps back into the entryway. Kaiya advanced and watched the woman's eyes widen with fear.

"You're not getting away with this," Kaiya said.

Kormac grabbed at Kaiya's arm, but she shook him away. Of all the things imaginable, this had never crossed her mind. The damned woman had been a coward, before, but now she was downright subhuman.

"Kaiya!" Kormac said, grabbing her arm again, his grip weak.

Kaiya stopped in the middle of the small vestibule, staring at Kormac's mother, who cowered on the floor against an expensive, polished cabinet, arms held protectively above her head. Kaiya stepped backwards and turned to Kormac.

What was she doing?

Kormac looked frightened, and she pulled him into an embrace, though whether it acted more to quell his fear or her own she couldn't tell. "She doesn't remember you," she said, and began to move them both back outside. "Just trust me. I'll explain everything."

She took a final look at Kormac's mother, who still sat on the floor, and closed the door behind them. Kormac looked back at the closed door as Kaiya led him to one of the ornate benches a short way down the street. Far enough away so as to not be visible from his mother's house.

They sat, and she explained *Rapture* to him. His face barely moved.

Kaiya studied it as he processed the information.

"I don't understand," he said. "How long has this been going on?"

"Not long," Kaiya said, "as far as I know. Not long here, at least, in Leth."

Kormac frowned. "I thought it sounded familiar," he said. "There was a person in the ward, who came to visit us. I didn't know if she was a doctor or a nurse or... what. But she was talking about... this treatment. I wasn't really listening. She kept saying that it was free, that the Nymian government would cover the cost for everyone who came back from Tarkinia."

"You can have the *Rapture* treatment for free?"

"That's what I remember," Kormac said. "I wasn't paying attention. I guess I am now."

The revelation piqued her curiosity. She couldn't deny the trace of envy of those who had the money for *Rapture*, but the idea of forgetting Kormac was beyond comprehension. If she were having it, she'd make sure they left him there, whole and complete. The rest of the world could disappear, just as long as he stayed clear.

Perhaps they could do the same for him...

"I went there," she said, "to the clinic where they do it. I talked to them."

She told him of the experience, or what she could remember of it. Everything was unclear, now. She knew something had happened in that room, that she'd seen something wondrous and beautiful, but... if only she could remember it. Surely if she went back there, she could see it again.

Maybe she could see it forever, if only she had the money.

"I want to go there," he said.

Kaiya brightened. "You want the *Rapture*?"

Kormac looked at her. "What? No, I want to talk to them. Why would I want that? Why would I want to forget... people? Forget you?"

The addition at the end of his sentence reassured her, and already her mind raced with the possibility of what their lives could be with *Rapture*. "But maybe there's a way they can do it differently," she said. "Maybe it doesn't have to be like your mother's."

"No," he said. "Never. I'd rather kill myself than get *Rapture*."

Kaiya drew back in shock. "What's that supposed to mean?"

"Exactly what I just said. It's... not right. I don't like it. Didn't you see her, Kaiya? She was a completely different person. It's like they took out everything that used to be her, and replaced it with someone else. Why would I want to do that?"

"It's not like that," Kaiya said. He couldn't be right. She was sure of it. "They just... take away the bad stuff. It's not *Rapture*'s fault that she doesn't remember you, Kormac, it's her fault. That's why I'm so angry with her. Because she obviously wanted them to..."

She stopped there, realising the magnitude of what she was saying in her effort to protect *Rapture* from criticism, but Kormac had understood. He bent over and placed his head in his hands, back heaving as he cried. Kaiya drew him into her arms and he acquiesced.

She searched for something to say, but what could there possibly be? There was no appropriate response to the absolute betrayal of such forgetting. If it had been her own mother...

But it wasn't, and her mother wouldn't have. Kormac's had always been selfish.

Kormac cried himself out in Kaiya's arms, the sound mingling with whispering birds and leaves. She stayed silent, mulling over the revelation that Nymosen was offering free *Rapture* to all those returned. Kormac was still in shock, that was all. He always did this – react too quickly, push back in response. He would see the benefits in time. She would help him.

Maybe it would take time for her to save the money required, but Kormac could start a new life any day. They would be together again without the barriers and limitations of pain and loss. Kaiya touched her nose to the top of Kormac's hair and felt herself overcome with the wider implications.

Her own parents would be offered the treatment as well.

Suddenly the dream of that reunited dining table, the party she had talked about to convince Tilda, all of it seemed closer than ever. They would sit all around, Kaiya and Kormac and Tilda and all of their families, knowing that nothing had ever been any different to what it was in that moment. The people at the clinic, they would make it work. They would find a way to reconstruct the past six years into a seamless narrative. They might even modify the treatment they had given Kormac's mother. Anyone who could do what they did had the power to reinstate a memory previously rejected.

Kormac would understand in time.

"Let's go there," Kaiya said, tracing patterns on his arm. "I'll show you where they do it. We'll talk to them. I know you'll understand once we get there. Please trust me."

One basic treatment was all it would take.

Kormac rubbed his eyes and they stood up, lingering to hold one another. Already he was changing, coming back to her.

Returning to the world they inhabited together and rejecting the world of frightened loneliness that had pervaded him since his return to where he belonged, with her.

She held his hand and they walked together to the northeast CBD, Kormac giving a final, saggy-browed glance back at his mother's home.

His home no longer.

The sight of all those rich collaborators in the CBD court-yard didn't bother her so much, anymore. Their punishment was coming, steady and quiet. If Amelia's plans came to fruition, then this very night the purging would begin, with the grand uprising to come next evening. Just thinking about it gave her a warm glow. The water shall be purified, so the Emancipators had said, and the righteous shall punish.

Kaiya stopped in the middle of the courtyard. Kormac was drinking in his surroundings, staring at the suited office work-ers, the cylindrical transport tubes, the *Allied Atlantica* headquar-ters. Kaiya watched his face scrunch up in consternation, as if he couldn't quite place what it was he wanted to say.

"Everything's..." he began, but shook his head.

Kaiya took his hand. "I know," she murmured. She knew exactly what he was thinking. He saw it, too. He saw the corrup-tion, he saw the depth of collaboration, he saw the truth of the matter – that even though the Tarkinians had gone, the people were still at the mercy of oppressors and despots.

"Come on," she said, and led Kormac to the tube directly under the Life Plus clinic. Kormac looked around at the tube with interest, and Kaiya smiled at the expression on his face when their journey came to an abrupt end. A few things had changed, at least. On the margins.

Upon arrival, projections from the EVC welcomed them.

"Welcome back," said the same young woman from her first visit, as a middle-aged woman greeted Kormac.

"Hi," Kaiya said automatically, then wondered if politeness

really mattered with EVC projections. How did the machine decide what each person saw?

"I am pleased to see you again," her own projection said. "Have you come for your weekly?"

She glanced across at Kormac. How much could change in a week! She wanted to scream 'yes,' to run inside that concrete room right at that moment and allow herself another shot at perfection, but Kormac needed her. He needed her to bring him along, to comfort him onto the journey towards *Rapture*. Just one basic treatment, and he would understand.

"Actually, we wondered if we could speak to someone about the *Rapture* treatment," she said.

"Certainly," her projection said. "Please follow me."

Kaiya looked back at Kormac and beckoned. "Where did your projection go?" she asked.

"I dismissed it," he said with a sour expression. "How dare they play on people's feelings like that."

"Like what?"

Kormac looked at her sceptically. "Don't pretend like you can't see what they're doing."

She let his statement go and followed her projection past the reception and up an aisle towards a well-apportioned office that looked out over the roundabout and the passersby below. A woman – a real one – welcomed them, and Kaiya gave the best, most polite smile she could. One could never abandon the notion of a possible discount for simple likability.

"Good morning," the woman said, and indicated an opulent couch perpendicular to the window. "Please sit."

They did so, and Kaiya grew uncomfortable at Kormac's reticence.

"I'm Alethea," the woman said. "Make yourselves at home. Here at Life Plus, we are all one family united in the pursuit of perfection. The EVC tells me you are interested in joining our family."

Kaiya's eyes widened. "But it never said anything."

Alethea chuckled and held up her left forearm. It glowed like a tablet. "I had this implanted when I became director of Leth branch. The EVC communicates via localweb. Now I can carry her around with me. We're never apart."

Kormac shifted beside her. "You... put it inside you?" he asked.

"Just a basic audiovisual communications device, yes. No touch receptors, but I've no need of that. EVC translates my wishes perfectly through voice command."

Alethea grinned.

"I think it's great," Kaiya lied, and Alethea gave a grateful nod.

"I guess people like you don't really care what you do to your body," Kormac said.

The hairs on the back of Kaiya's neck stood tall.

Alethea considered Kormac. "We have a progressive view of humanity, yes. Our bodies have always been imperfect. While we at Life Plus only deal with the human brain, we are supportive of our sister companies who continue to push the other limits of what it means to be alive. I believe we have a bright future ahead of us. A future of superior lifestyle design never before available to the human race, and I hope that you will consider joining us in this quest."

Kaiya needed no more convincing, and shared a smile with Alethea. "I had my first basic treatment last week," she said, making sure Alethea knew at least one of them supported the efforts of Life Plus.

"I'm aware," Alethea said, holding up her forearm again. "And now I take it you are interested in the next step?"

"No," Kormac said before Kaiya could respond. "We're not here to listen to this. I want to know what can be done about this *Rapture*. You made my mother forget me. You... completely erased us," he said, indicating Kaiya as well. "I was... *there*... for three years, and I come back, and you've gone in and changed everyone that I dreamed about every night. You took away my family. That's what you did."

Alethea looked at him with great concentration, her expression having changed upon the revelation of Kormac's previous whereabouts. "So you were in Tarkinia..." she said. "I have heard... rumours. I know how difficult it—"

"You don't know anything about Tarkinia," Kormac said, every word a rapier.

Kaiya stared between the two silent combatants, her body rigid with apprehension.

"EVC," Alethea said to her forearm, "please close my door."

Kaiya watched the glass door close, and silence pressed against Kaiya's ears as she stared through the glass walls at the everyday office life beyond. This EVC technology did far more than she had ever thought to give it credit for.

"I apologise for misapprehending your presence here today," Alethea said. "It is so rare, after all, that we have complaints against our service. May I ask specifically what it is you wish to discuss?"

"I want you to reverse it," Kormac said. "I want you to put my mother back the way she was before."

Alethea gave nothing away on her face as she stared at him. "That's not possible."

"What do you mean that's not possible?" Kormac said. "If you can do it in the first place, then you can do it backwards!"

"It's... not that simple," Alethea said. "But I tell you in all truth, the *Rapture* treatment is completely irreversible."

A silence descended in the room as Kormac's face went still. The shock of the realisation sent Kaiya's thoughts reeling, but she pulled them back after several moments. "I don't think you mean completely, though," she said. "Right? I mean... surely you can adjust it. If things aren't quite perfect."

Alethea gave a curt shake of her head. "The process is solely extractive. And one time only."

"That can't be right," Kaiya said. "Just a modification. Putting someone back that shouldn't have been erased. She wouldn't have chosen to get rid of him if she'd known he'd be back."

Alethea frowned. "You don't actually know how it works, do you? Let's just say that we tried that, in the early years. Making adjustments. Doing manual overrides. We tried and... we failed. Let's put it that way." Alethea shifted in her seat and licked her lips. "The process, now, is completely automated. No one chooses what stays and what goes. The technology does not discriminate, and it reads a human mind far better than any other human could. It *knows* what needs to go, and it has never been wrong."

Kaiya leaned back into the couch and mulled over the significance of this correction to her understanding. How did the machine decide? Could the machine be fooled, even? Were there levels of intensity? What if there were specific events that one could live with, even if the machine disagreed? Or people whose influence could be handled? But then, that was the nature of *Rapture*. It wouldn't matter once the events or the people were gone.

"I don't believe you," Kormac said. "There's no way a treatment like this could come to market with such glaring holes. The regulator would never allow it."

"You call them holes," Alethea said, "but I call it foolproof. As long as our patients understand the risk of our procedures, they are free to enjoy its benefits. Our service is... much-needed at this point in time."

Kormac shook his head. "You shouldn't be allowed to do this."

"But it's what the people want," Kaiya said "Kormac, you can't deny them the right to make a better life for themselves. I know that it hurts, what your mother has done, but maybe the answer isn't trying to change her back... maybe the answer is having the *Rapture* yourself."

He looked at her as though she were a complete stranger. "And you're so confident that you'll still be there, after I have it?" he asked.

Though it didn't sound like a question for which he needed an answer.

Kaiya looked away. Time, she reminded herself.

"No, I don't accept this," Kormac continued. "This madness is *not* the answer. Maybe I need to go and force the memories back. It's not like we're jars, and you can take out this one and that one. You can't suck the memories out into nothingness – they have to go somewhere! They're still in her. She just needs some encouragement."

"I would not recommend this course of action," Alethea said. "There is some... conjecture... as to exactly what would happen were someone to force a memory back into a patient's mind."

"You mean you don't *know*?" Kormac said. "You have all these patients and you don't even *know*?" He raised his hands in frustrated resignation and stood up. "Look, forget it. Let me go. I'm done with you."

Kaiya followed his lead and looked back to Alethea in apology. Alethea commanded the EVC to open the door, and Kaiya made to follow Kormac.

"You know what," he said, turning around. "I *do* have one more question. Have you even had *Rapture*? Has anyone that works here had *Rapture*?"

Alethea watched him carefully, eyes flicking over his face. "Life Plus regulations are such that unfortunately—"

"Right," he said. "So you haven't. That's all I needed to know."

He stormed out into the corridor.

"Sorry," Kaiya said to Alethea before striding to catch up. "Kormac, wait!"

He stopped and rounded on her. "What? What do you want?"

She pulled back ever so slightly. "I... I just want to help. I want you and me to be good and—"

"Are you blind, Kaiya? Are you stupid? Why would you even want me to think about getting *Rapture*? You want me to just forget? As if everything I've ever done or been through meant nothing? That's my *life*, Kaiya. I'm not going to throw it away just because you want easy answers."

"It's not about easy answers," she said. "It's about the *right* answers."

Kormac continued into the atrium and towards the tubular elevators.

"Kormac, stop it!" she hissed, and he followed her direction, stopping in the middle of the atrium with his back to her.

Kaiya was conscious of the real people watching, and the projections remaining blissfully unaware.

"Just... hear me out," she said, approaching. "I know that you're angry right now. But please trust me. Even if you decide you don't want the full *Rapture*, please just come with me for the—"

"You're joking, right?" He turned around, face painted with scorn. "I'm not going to let myself be poisoned by these criminals. I don't want to be someone else. I want to be me, and if you don't like who I am anymore, then that's your problem, not mine."

The murmuring of people pretending not to listen crept into the space they inhabited together, and Kaiya palmed away a few stray tears. She had to be patient. Time, that was all. He was still there, she knew it. She had felt the connection on the bridge.

"Are you coming or not?" Kormac asked. "Cause I'm not waiting around while you get zapped by some machine, or whatever happens in your *weekly*."

Kaiya swallowed and gasped. "I need this," she whispered. "Please. I need this."

Kormac shook his head and walked over to one of the tubes, waving it open and disappearing inside. Kaiya took a deep breath and rubbed her eyes again, before turning around and coming face to face with her personal projection.

The projection smiled, and Kaiya followed her to the concrete room.

Someone had put up wind chimes. There were no balconies facing the southern boulevard, so they had to be inside a nearby sound-opened window. That was the only explanation that made sense to Kaiya. She stood by her own window, set to full open mode, and listened to the chattering chimes as a crisp breeze chilled the tip of her nose.

In the distance, from the riverside in lower northeast quadrant, and from the heart of southeast quadrant, came the glow of burning houses.

Stray screams scattered the shifting breeze, each one a cold lance on Kaiya's skin. She couldn't deny the piercing quality in the voices, the trademarks of wretched torment, but neither could she deny the exhilaration of desire to be out there amongst Amelia's force. Each one of those in present agony had been responsible, in their own ways, for the agony of their fellow citizens, the true people of Leth.

"They deserve this," she said to Kormac.

He eyed her from the bed, where he sat. For several hours after her return, he had refused to speak to her, but soft words and cautious glances conquered his taciturnity. He had touched her, fingertips hesitant on her back, and kissed her lightly on the neck. Thus was she forgiven for her transgression.

"Why?" he asked.

Kaiya stared at the crowd approaching southern boulevard ever so slowly. "Things got worse after you went. After they took you," she corrected. "It wasn't like when you were here. People started... watching each other. We weren't allowed to be anywhere in a group of more than three people, and the police were *everywhere*. All the time, always asking questions. But you couldn't go anywhere by yourself, it was too dangerous."

A woman cried out in the distance, and Kaiya looked down across the boulevard at a second-storey apartment. "Do you remember the Parker family?" she asked, looking back to Kormac.

"Across the road? Wasn't he..."

"Yeah," she said. "One of the ones who didn't go back when Bennett became Commissioner."

Kormac nodded with slow realisation. He had stayed with her that night. "I remember that. I never met him..."

The image came into her own mind. Waking up one morning several months after Bennett's rise to see the man's head staked to the door of the Parker building. "Anyway," Kaiya said. "It was the eldest daughter's fifteenth birthday, only a few months after they took you, and... well she had four kids, the mother. Meant you couldn't ever have anyone over, cause you'd be in a group of more than three excluding immediate family in the home. But they had a party anyway. She invited me, you know..."

Kaiya looked back down at the second-storey window that had been dark for over two years.

"I was too scared to go. I watched the people come, one by one, spaced apart, like we all learnt to do, but someone reported them, and... that was it. They came at night, seven of them. Police. I don't know all the details, but I know they... took it in turns with the girl."

Something exploded in the distance, and the sky brightened with flame.

"When they'd finished with her, they strung her up naked from a tree by the river so everyone could see, and flogged the rest of the family and the guests the next day in the town square. The only true punishment is public, Bennett said. So he made sure everyone knew what had happened."

Kaiya looked to Kormac, connecting with his distant, haggard eyes. "Someone reported them," she said. "Someone let that happen. Someone I probably know, even in passing. I don't care what anyone says, whoever they are is just as bad as the people who did it. That's why they deserve it, Kormac. Because it wasn't just the Parker family. It happened everywhere. And people *let* it happen, trying to get into the police good books, or get back at people they didn't like. That's why this is good," she said, pointing towards the burning buildings. "Every single collaborator deserves to die, and Leth will never be at peace until that happens."

Kormac stood up and walked over beside her, watching the distant violence with a weary calm. "Do you think you could do it?" he asked. "If it was up to you. Could you be the one to kill a collaborator?"

"Of course," she said with no hesitation. "Gladly."

He looked askance at her, just for a moment, before turning his attention back outside.

"You have such conviction," he said. "I wish I could be so certain."

"Certain about what?" she asked.

The sound of justice marched ever closer.

"Anything," he said. "I... I used to imagine what it would be like to be back. I tried to be realistic, to say that things would have changed, but all I could ever think about was how things used to be before the Tarkinians came. I couldn't even imagine Leth like it had been when they took me. All I could see was before. Except for you. You were there, even though we didn't even know each other then. I... told myself every day that one day it would be like that, like how I pictured it. Convinced myself that's what it would be like when I came back. Except that it's not."

Frequency rifles rang from somewhere near the river, and a trio of Taskforce police came into view on the boulevard, running towards the sound.

"You were..." he whispered, and Kaiya placed her arm around him, giving all the closeness and comfort she could muster. "You were like an idea more than anything. You were perfect. And all I had in me, all I had that kept me going, was this image of you and Leth and... peace. Except that it's not real. I don't know where I am, or what to do, or who to be, and it's like there's nothing to latch on to."

"You have me," she said.

"But who are you?" Kormac said, brows drooping heavily. "I don't... I don't know that I could ever do that. Kill someone. Even if they deserved it. I've seen too many people die, and I don't want to believe that you could do that. I know the image isn't real, the image I had in Tarkinia, I know you can't be perfect, and I can't be perfect, and Leth can't be perfect, but... that's different to knowing you'd rather *make* it more imperfect."

Six Taskforce police ran along the boulevard, activating energy shields in the process. Kaiya held Kormac tight, and he traced patterns on her arm with his fingertip.

"I want Leth to be perfect, too," she said. "And for us to be perfect. That's why all of this is so important, Kormac. It's the only way to make everything perfect again."

"Kaiya," he said, grinning lightly, "I can live without perfection. I'd settle for one night of peace."

She kissed him on the temple and he slipped his arm around her back. They faced each other, Kaiya resting her fingers on his neck, diving into his weary eyes, and they kissed for the first time since his return. A gentle but awkward gesture, without any all-consuming passion or depth, but light and exploratory, simply another step in their gradual reconnection.

The significance of Kormac's presence struck deep inside her as she kissed him again, clenching his skin and maintaining the physical link between them as long as she could. When they pulled away with unspoken, mutual understanding, he grazed his lips on her forehead, and she let herself be encompassed by his embrace as the chilly breeze blew the neighbour's wind chimes.

"Do you think we would have met?" he whispered. "If they'd never come?"

"Shh," she said. "A night of peace, didn't you say?"

Frequency rifles punctuated the air, and the Taskforce police who had earlier ran towards the river now fled the other way, energy shields raised against invisible bullets of sound. Amelia's force had come to southern boulevard, bringing righteous justice in their wake.

Still in Kormac's arms, Kaiya watched as angry victims broke down doors and stormed two of the buildings opposite. Not much later, two men dragged a woman onto the boulevard. She howled, kicking and struggling, until they threw her down onto the glossy road tiles. A collective roar of victory emanated from the oncoming crowd, and a circle of two dozen formed around the woman, who raised her arms to protect herself as another man stepped forward and cracked a whip against her back.

The woman convulsed as sparks flew.

Kaiya stiffened, heart beating hard. Where trickles of reemerged passion had just flowed, now there arose an unwanted trace of sympathy for the whore collaborator. She steeled herself against such a corruption of thought, staring at the scene below.

Another man stepped forward from the circle and gestured dramatically to the crowd, which applauded. He kicked the woman in her stomach, and she curled into a ball. He kicked her again, this time in the face, before pulling her up by the hair so she dangled like a rag doll, blood spattered from her nose and down her mouth. Someone else stepped forward holding a pair of hair clippers, and ripped off the woman's nightgown.

The crowd laughed.

The woman gave a final, pathetic struggle against her deserved humiliation, and the man began to shave her head.

"No Tarkinian'll want her now!" yelled someone from the crowd to great laughter.

Kormac glanced down at her with a frown. "We don't have to watch this."

Kaiya swallowed and kept her eyes on the scene, shaking in Kormac's arms. "She was a collaborator," she said. "A Tarkinian whore."

The ritual had been completed. The woman, shaven head now marking her for what she was, quivered on the ground, covering her naked body as best she could. She clutched at her hair that littered the ground, the crowd spitting on her. A boy who looked Masuma's age stepped forward and kicked the woman in the face, smiling back at the encouragements he received.

The crowd began to move on.

Kaiya tapped a combination on the window, still staring at the woman who now struggled to stand. She faded from sight as the window darkened, and slowly the sounds of punishment dulled. Kaiya was left in the quietude of her room, unsure how to feel.

"She slept with a Tarkinian," she explained. She could feel Kormac's disapproval, his ignorance of how treacherous such an act was.

He frowned but stayed silent.

"How could someone do that?" Kaiya continued. She had to make Kormac understand the gravity of the woman's crime. "It's a complete betrayal of everything that people like us believe in. The sacrifices that good people made. It's like saying to the Tarkinians that they're welcome. How could any of us tell them we didn't want them here when those sluts were saying the exact opposite? They didn't just do nothing, they actively worked against us. I don't care if they did it for money, or if some of them think they were in love, it's just disgusting."

This time Kormac shushed her, planting another kiss on her forehead. "A night of peace," he reminded her.

She smiled despite the rush of loathing in her veins, and looked up at his face. "Sorry," she murmured, and traced the thin lines creasing his eyes, examining the years she had lost. She couldn't feel guilty about not being out there. Amelia had specifically not wanted her involved in it. She had to allow herself to be with Kormac, to move closer towards his dream of perfection.

Kaiya took his hand and led him back to the bed.

Apprehension teased her as she eased herself onto the mattress, bringing Kormac's weight along with her. He was definitely weaker, she could tell that much. Time had faded her recollections of their passion, but she remembered the fact of his strength. His lusting power that had glorified her, leading to a mutual exaltation of one another, a feedback loop of commitment to the higher levels of fervour.

Now their lips touched more hesitantly. Their hands crept as if afraid. Kaiya pulsed with an intermingling of old desire and new trepidation. Kormac touched the skin on her lower back, pulling her closer to him.

Somewhere in her brain a signal fired, and her body tightened against her will. She railed against the imposition, clutching suddenly to Kormac and attacking him with her desire to desire. If she just pushed forward and broke through the barrier of her mind's fear, she could rewire the ruptured connection.

Her fingers moved underneath his t-shirt, splaying against his back, pressing against small horizontal ridges.

"What's that?" she breathed, stopping in alarm.

Kormac pulled away. "Nothing," he said.

"What do you mean nothing?" She moved back closer to him. "Show me."

"No," he said.

Kaiya looked at the wavering eyes that didn't want to connect to her own. "Kormac. Please."

He remained still.

Had there been only one ridge of limited length, she might have passed it off as a new curiosity, but something so consistent and severe demanded her recognition.

"Kormac," she whispered again, and he relented, pulling off his t-shirt as he shifted onto his stomach.

The soft lighting of the bedside lamp illuminated an array of scars from shoulders to waist. A momentary wave of dizziness caught her as she surveyed the injuries, and she reached forward gently, tracing a slow line down his back. He jolted at her first touch, then stilled.

"What happened?" she asked, though the question sounded weak in her mouth.

Kormac remained silent.

She had thought the scars perfectly horizontal, but closer inspection revealed they each had a different angle, ever so slight. Some places had been struck multiple times, ridging higher than their neighbours in a horrific shade of pink. The flesh had been twisted in one spot, a circular mess of scarring completely distinct from the neatness of the lines.

"Kormac?" she probed, picturing different circumstances that would warrant such punishment. Perhaps Kormac had been a rebellious captive – someone like Amelia. The thought gave her some satisfaction.

"Disciplinary measure," he said, head turned on the pillow.

"With *what*?" She had seen the floggings in town square, but these lines were too straight for a human to have inflicted them.

"Does it really matter?" he asked, eyes flicking up towards hers for the first time. "Do you really have to know?"

Kaiya frowned. Surely he could tell her. "I just thought that... you know you can trust me, don't you?"

"It's not about trust," Kormac said, turning over onto his back. "Some things are better left to ourselves. Secret. Maybe that's a stronger type of love. To never let the other person know."

Kormac's words struck deep inside her, and she realised then that they applied equally to him. He could have his secret, and she could have her own. Never to question and never to judge.

"I'm just worried," she said. "Your back—"

"It's not my back I'm worried about," he said, taking Kaiya's hand in his own.

She smiled, unsure what to make of the statement, and rested herself down beside him, half-draped over his body. His eyes, once so clear with honesty, hid things now, but then so did hers. The gaze they shared became too intense, too probing, and she pulled herself up to kiss him, breaking away from that invasion of defences she'd built over the previous year.

His desire had lost the hindrance of previous hesitation, and Kaiya realised that he had been afraid of the moment she would discover his secret. What reaction had he expected? Why would he hold back from revealing the suffering that could only give her greater understanding of his experience?

Now his too-thin arms held her with the kind of vigour she remembered, and the reality of the moment she had thought about for so long began to approach. His touches thrilled her skin, and she pulled off her own t-shirt, heightening the flurry of sensations that shot through her body as they pressed together.

Her brain sent off the same signal as earlier, tightening her against her will. The feeling was almost imperceptible, but she could sense it as keenly as if she had been branded by an iron. She pushed against her mind again, knowing that she could force it to change.

That she could rewrite the consequences of history.

She grabbed at Kormac, kneading his body with violent eagerness, telling herself to trust the direction of their lovemaking. Two people battled inside her, one a woman with no desire greater than to connect in that most primal way, a way to which she had every right, the other a shadow of frightened experience that cared only for remembrance of impuissance.

They writhed with hunger, shedding the armour that hid their souls from each other, while Kaiya battled against that urge to slam another shield between them.

Kaiya rolled onto her back, pulling Kormac into her open legs.

Pain shot through her body before he even entered, and she lost the battle against the shadow woman inside. She clamped her legs shut, pushing Kormac away as she cried out, face scrunched. The world went hazy in her eyes, but she refused to surrender, and drew him back towards her.

The clenching came again.

Kaiya curled onto her side, doing her best to hold back tears. Kormac knelt by her legs, primed and obviously lost in confusion.

He touched her waist tenderly, and Kaiya cursed the unwanted mechanism that disallowed her from experiencing that to which she was entitled and had longed for. He whispered her name, cautious and innocent, reminding her of what price she had paid for resisting Occupation.

Kaiya touched Kormac's face and began to cry.

11

KAIYA SAT ON AN ALCOVE IN THE DINING ROOM, HEART THUMPING. No matter how hard she tried, Tilda refused to understand. There wasn't much time left – night had almost fallen, and there was a fair walk to the town centre, where Amelia's protest would begin. If Tilda was to be convinced, it had to be now.

Kormac watched from the dining table. She avoided his searching eyes. He didn't want to go, either, nor wanted her to go, but she could forgive him that. He had paid his price in a Tarkinian camp, and whatever horrible things had happened in there, whatever had given him the scars on his back, he still had not experienced the whole horror of Bennett's rule.

Tilda had. She had no excuse for staying home.

Kaiya stood up and stared into the dining room where Tilda had gone to sulk. "I'm going now," she said. There was no response, and Kaiya could already feel her ears burning. "Tilda—"

"Stop asking me," Tilda said.

"Why not?" Kaiya asked. "Why won't you come?"

"Because I don't want to. Why does there have to be a reason?"

"You can't just say no without a reason."

"Yes, I can," Tilda said, standing up. "I can say whatever the hell I want. The Tarkinians aren't here anymore. Bennet's gone. It's over, Kaiya."

"Are you kidding me?" Kaiya yelled. "Have you had a look around lately? Seen the state of this town? You haven't, I don't know, noticed anyone missing?"

"Do you really think that going out and screaming about shit is going to help find your parents?" Tilda asked. "Are you that stupid, Kaiya?"

"So now I'm stupid."

"Oh, shut up!" Tilda stared at her, eyes flashing in a way Kaiya hadn't seen in a long time. "You can't shout them back into existence."

A silence fell in the apartment, and Kaiya shifted her gaze away. The premise of Tilda's words stung. "How could you say that?" she said, softer.

"You have to deal with it eventually," Tilda said.

Kaiya shook her head. "No," she said. "I don't have to deal with anything. You're wrong. I know you are. You should be helping me do something about it. Helping me fix this place before they get back." She pointed at Kormac. "You see Kormac, Tilda? He's back. He's alive. Just like everyone else. You've given up cause you don't think it matters anymore, but it *does* matter. You hide in here cause you don't think you have the power to do anything, but you *do*. We all do. Don't you want to make things better?"

Tilda folded her arms and set her jaw.

"Kaiya," Kormac said from the table.

"What?" she snapped.

"Maybe Tilda's right," he said. "Maybe you shouldn't go to this thing. I... don't like the sound of this Amelia person."

"You don't know anything about her!" Kaiya said. "Amelia's

done more for Leth than anyone. She was the one who organised the resistance, and she's the one who's—"

"The resistance was a complete failure," Tilda said.

"It was not!" Kaiya spat. "We did something important. We paved the way for *Allied Atlantica*. And now we're going to bring Bennett and the rest of his collaborators to justice!"

"You have no idea what you're talking about," Tilda said. "You don't give a shit about justice."

Kaiya advanced into the hallway, expecting Tilda to back down, but she didn't.

"I don't give a shit about justice?" Kaiya said. "Are you kidding? Me?"

"That's exactly what I said."

Kaiya stepped forward and pointed at Tilda. "You're a traitor!

Tilda glared back at her and took a step forward. "Don't call me that."

"You are, you're a traitor."

"Don't call me that, you bitch!" Tilda took a swing and Kaiya dodged it. Before she could respond, Kormac had inserted himself between them. "Why can't you leave me alone?" Tilda said. "You think I don't want to see my parents again? You have to face reality, Kaiya. They're gone, just like yours. They're not coming back."

"You're wrong."

"What are you trying to achieve?" Tilda continued. "What are any of you trying to achieve? Going around burning people's houses down, beating them in the streets, what's all that about?"

"I haven't done any of that."

"Oh, please, it's not like you don't sit there and watch them and wish it was you. What kind of people do you think are going to be there tonight?"

"What does that have to do with it?"

"It has everything to do with it."

Kaiya stepped back. Kormac's presence wouldn't allow the punishment Tilda deserved.

"You think it's fine that they just get to go back to normal?" Kaiya asked. "The collaborators? As if nothing's changed, everything's the same as it used to be? They're the ones who made this happen, Tilda."

"No," Tilda said. "They're not the ones who made anything happen, that was the Tarkinians. And Bennett. And only him because of the Tarkinians."

"Just because you did nothing! At least I can say I helped, what did you do the whole war?"

"Did you ever talk to a Tarkinian, Kaiya? Did you?"

"Why would I? What does that have to do with anything?"

Tilda gave an angrily dismissive wave of her hands. "Nothing. Forget about it. You just don't get it."

"Yeah, I forgot, I'm stupid."

"Oh, give me a break. You really think you're the only one hurting—"

"That's bullshit."

"No, it's not. You say that, but that's not how you act. It's like you wish the war were still going. So you can just wallow in your self-pity."

"And your strategy is so much better? Just forget it ever happened, pretend everything's all fine."

"You have no idea," Tilda said. "You have no clue." She shoved past into the dining room and stared out the window, back rising and falling in bursts of raging breath. She would never admit she was wrong, Kaiya knew that, but she had at least expected her best friend to understand and support a movement for justice. Now all she was left with was a bitter, reluctant acceptance that tonight Tilda would be just another coward letting everyone else do the fighting for her.

"You disgust me," she said. Tilda ignored her, eyes fixed outside, and she walked out of the apartment, slamming the door as she left, frustrated her comment had received no reaction. The silence of the corridor pressed against her ears, drawing attention to her accelerated heartbeat, the galloping stampede of blood in her veins. Part of her wanted to march right back in there and give Tilda a few more pieces of her mind. Force her to understand the consequences of a failure to act.

The door opened behind her, and Kormac stepped out quietly, reaching out to touch her arm.

She shook him off, annoyed that he, too, refused to see the need for Amelia's actions.

"Don't go," he said. "Please. There are Taskforce police, Kaiya. They don't mess around."

"If they wanted civil order," she said, "they'd give us Bennett. But the Taskforce has never been about civil order, no matter how much they call themselves that. It's about Nymian control. About keeping the people away from what we want."

Kormac frowned. "But who are the people, Kaiya? I don't understand. I—"

"Stop worrying," Kaiya said, and cupped his cheek in her hand, forcing a smile to her face. "You don't know Amelia. Everything is going to be fine."

She let him take her hand and kiss it, then walked away down the corridor with a final glance.

Tonight the people would make a stand, and Bennett would be punished.

———

Smoke still lingered from shells of buildings gutted in the previous night's uprising. Chunks were missing from the balustrades on both sides of the central bridge. Kaiya stopped in the middle to look around at the devastation the collaborators had wrought upon themselves. Three riverside buildings had collapsed, their centuries-old stonework littering the ground, along with glass and charred pieces of furniture. Under her feet the road tiles had been injured so badly she wondered if they could ever be healed. Someone had shot right at them, to create that kind of damage. Maybe even used a force projector.

Kaiya walked on into the centre square of Leth, that area that no quadrant claimed. She kept her arms folded, eyeing the other people walking towards the town square, other people just like her. How many of them had been out there the previous night, doing what she should have done?

Much of the glowstone nearby was malfunctioning, plunging the boulevard into uncharacteristic shadow. But there were lights ahead, bright lights, and even from this distance Kaiya could tell that the turnout for this event would be memorable.

She passed a little park and glanced at the ancient tree inside, stopping to do a double take. Seven noosed bodies hung from the branches, looking down at the darkness of death. Five men, a shaved collaborator whore, and a woman whose crimes had obviously been something other than that. She stared at them alongside others who walked in her direction, and wondered who had suffered because of their treachery.

Who had betrayed the Parker family?

The frustration of not knowing spurred her to continue, and she allowed it to fester in her mind. More fuel for the fight ahead.

A crowd came into view as she approached, stretching at least a hundred metres from the town square fountain. The foot-paths glowed strong in some sections, faltering in others, and two towering floodlights stood on either side of an energy field, illuminating the entire area in a blazing spectacle. Kaiya had to squint to see the podium that had been erected on the stairs to the town hall, surrounded with Taskforce police dressed in complete riot gear. She squeezed through the crowd, searching, and giving people here and there a piece of her mind as placards and banners threatened to smack her in the face or defraud her of an eye.

Amelia had planned to be near the fountain, and Kaiya cursed herself for not coming earlier. Still, this was a good sign. The people were waking up. The people were demanding answers, demanding justice. She was no mere spectator, but an active participant in the defence of Leth, a touchstone of strength for the disenfranchised, an example of good and proud citizenship. All around her the people chatted to each other, sharing stories and anger, making introductions and, here and there, showing each other weapons. Amelia had said there would be no repeat of their previous defencelessness, and Kaiya believed her.

She wished Tilda were there.

"Kaiya," came Amelia's voice from a circle of space near the fountain.

She turned and hugged the woman who deserved all the credit for three years of secrecy and rebellion.

"I was getting worried you'd backed out on me again," Amelia said.

Kaiya flushed with shame. "Never," she said.

"Come with me," Amelia said, leading her to a watching group of five. "Everyone, this is Kaiya."

The three men and two women nodded, all considerably older than either her or Amelia.

"Good to meet you finally," said one of the men. "You hosted the south gate bomber, didn't you?"

Kaiya let out a sound of surprise. Amelia had always made a point of not telling her who the other hosts were. She'd had enough trouble getting Amelia to tell her who would be coming to her *own* place, let alone what anyone else was doing. Back in the days before she realised the truth about the Nymians.

"Amongst others," Kaiya said modestly, unsure what her

position was amongst people who seemed to know more than she did.

"What was it?" the man said. "A hundred and fifty-two Tarkinians? Impressive."

Amelia smiled. "Kaiya, this is Jerome. He ran surveillance in southeast quadrant. Coordinated placements. He's the one who convinced those two families in William Street to rig their houses with explosives."

Kaiya looked at Jerome, who seemed pleased with himself. "I never understood that," she said. "All that for a patrol of three?"

"No," Jerome said, shaking his head. "The General, a Lieutenant-General, and some Colonel."

"Worst breach in Tarkinian security for the whole war, at least in Leth," Amelia said, then indicated one of the women. "Charlotte had northeast quadrant. Took her over a year to bug the HQ. Found out the Tarkinians were running a code relay in a house in southeast, so Jerome managed to figure out the General's visitation pattern. Took him and the relay out in one attack. Without that, we wouldn't have been able to do the east gate blockade, the HQ bombing, the police assassinations, or the jail fires. One of our more successful strategies, I think."

Amelia shared a smug look with Jerome. Kaiya glanced at them, feeling an immediate sense of ignorance. Amelia had never mentioned anything about delegating her responsibilities. She had always just assumed Amelia was the only point of contact for those like her hosting Nymian soldiers.

"What was he like?" Jerome asked. "The south gate bomber."

All eyes turned to Kaiya, who licked her lips in hesitation. "Quiet," she said. "Almost never spoke. Just smiled. Nodded. He was very polite, like that. But he spent all his time looking at maps, making bombs, that kind of thing. Sometimes I'd wake up early in the morning, and he'd be there at the dining table. I used to watch. He would just smile and go right back to it. And then he disappeared. I didn't realise he hadn't planned on coming back."

She frowned at the memory. She had woken up one morning to find him gone. By midday, the ground had shook with the force of the south gate explosion. The rumours had started by the evening, and he was a myth by the next day. Someone had told her with certainty that after he blew himself up, he had reappeared in the middle of the destruction unharmed, as if risen from the dead.

"After that," Amelia said, "I knew Kaiya was our best. Seven weeks he was there, longer than any other stay, and every four days I had to find a way to deliver materials undetected. I've never seen anyone make what he made. Maximum damage, tiny charge. He lined the Levway with bombs at night. No one ever saw him. I told Kaiya that five troop convoys were heading to the southern front, and that was the end of his stay. All I've been able to piece together is that he went to south gate as the convoys were leaving, walked straight up to the sentries, and boom. Destroyed the gate and the last convoy truck by himself, and set off a chain reaction up the Levway. It still hasn't been fixed."

Kaiya had quite enjoyed his unassuming company. She had passed on Amelia's message the afternoon before he disappeared, wondering how much longer he'd stay after completion. Some memento of his existence in her life would have been nice, something to remember him by, but he had removed every trace of him ever having been in her apartment.

"We should take positions," Amelia said to the five older companions. "Remember, whatever it takes. We have to think about the long term." The companions nodded and, except for Jerome, scattered into the crowd. Kaiya saw the ease at which they followed Amelia's orders, and imagined herself commanding such respect and devotion. Surely she could culti-

vate that. If she just became braver. More unrelenting. More...
just more like Amelia in every way.

"I want you with Jerome tonight," Amelia said to her. "Whatever happens, stick with Jerome."

Kaiya nodded, and Amelia walked over to the fountain, where the same makeshift podium from the last protest was waiting. The striding, female figure of a faceless Emancipator stood immortalised in the middle of the fountain.

"Police are closing in," Jerome said.

Kaiya turned her gaze in the same direction as the older man. The police had crept further towards the crowd, boxing it in so there was no space between it and the boulevard beyond.

"You have to hand it to the Nymians," Jerome said. "They're brilliant. They have the people brainwashed, but they know we're getting through. That the people are waking up. That's why they sent this guy." Jerome nodded up at a well-dressed man who had appeared on the steps of the town hall. "He was the media advisor for the former president before taking on this job with Taskforce. It's all political. The Nymians want everyone watching tonight to think we're some sort of disease they need to be protected from. Contained. As if we're the criminals."

Kaiya looked up at the propaganda man and clenched her jaw. The whole concept that she could possibly be presented as some kind of aberration from the community grated her. She *was* the community! Part of the community. Speaking out against those who themselves had failed the people of Leth.

Amelia and Jerome, even herself – they were the beacons of truth that needed to be heard.

"Has she spoken to you, yet?" Jerome asked. "About... the organisation?"

Kaiya peered at him. "No?"

Jerome looked surprised. "Another time, perhaps. Let's just say that that Amelia really believes in you. That's why she didn't want you involved in last night. She wants your hands as clean as possible."

"For what?"

"For public support," Jerome said. "We can't get rid of the Nymians and offer nothing to the people of Leth. We need to give them a new vision, with new people. Loyal people we can trust to help us."

He grinned as he gazed at her, and Kaiya nodded her understanding, thrilled by the notion that Amelia thought her worthy enough of such an honour.

"I'll do anything Amelia wants," Kaiya said. "She knows that."

Jerome clapped her on the back. "I like you already," he said. "Just who we need."

Kaiya smiled. She was a voice of the people and, one day, when they had won, Amelia would bring peace, and all the true people of Leth would rally behind her in solidarity for liberating them from the traitors. There could be no doubt.

She looked back towards the fountain, and saw Amelia stepping up onto the makeshift platform, a ripple of cheers and whispers racing through the crowd. Amelia began to speak, but the words were inaudible, and she motioned for quiet. The noise died to a restrained murmur, a box of fireworks with too short a fuse.

"Thank you," Amelia said, her voice emanating from wireless receivers throughout the crowd. "Thank you for your attention. For those who don't know, my name is Amelia—"

Pockets of the crowd cheered and whistled.

"Thank you, please," she continued, voice reverberating against the walls of the residential buildings each side of the boulevard. She stared out into the crowd, a mask of seriousness forming on her face, as she began to glow with the intensity Kaiya longed to experience. "We are here tonight... to demand justice," Amelia said, and the crowd cheered. "We are here tonight to demand that Commissioner Benjamin put us, the citizens of Leth, first. We are here tonight to demand a flame... A flame for a dream that so many thought dead over two hundred years ago. A flame to ignite a passion that has hidden inside us for so long, since a time of darkness eight hundred years ago. We are here tonight... to demand our independence."

Kaiya shouted her assent in solidarity with the crowd, and Amelia stared out at the masses, raising her arm to quell the ever-present surge.

"Too long have we been subject to the whims and fancies of our oppressors. Too long have we sat idly by and allowed our lives to be ruled by those who have no affinity with our values. Too long have we dreamed with no action. Well tonight I say to you – we shall wait no longer!"

Amelia raised her fist in the air, and Kaiya mimicked her along with hundreds.

"People of Leth, tonight I give you this hope. That we shall be free from all those who would destroy our way of life, whether they be Tarkinian, Nymian, or those who have corrupted themselves to make union with our enemies. I have heard people say to me that the Nymians are our friends, that they came here to fight the Tarkinians," the crowd began to boo, "and I say this is true! My friends, hear me – this is true. Let us not say that we despise all Nymians, for there are those of us here tonight who know only so well the bravery of those soldiers who risked their lives to assist us in ridding ourselves of the Tarkinian menace. But we speak not of those... fearless Nymians who came to our aid. We speak not of the Nymian villager living his life in peace in a home that has always been Nymian. No! We speak of Nymosen. Nymosen as an idea. We speak of its capital's tendrils – Akheron's tendrils – creeping out across the nation and into the hearts of those of us who have never been subject in our souls to Nymian ideals. I have heard it said that the people are tired. That the people are weary. That the years of oppression are behind us, and now we must return placid to the lives we led before, content in the protective embrace of the overlords who sit in Akheron. And I do not disagree."

The crowd rumbled along with bursts of supportive noise here and there, all over a sea of wariness for what Amelia seemed to be saying.

"Because we *are* tired, my friends... but we have been tired for eight hundred years."

The sea boiled with shared indignation.

"I ask you this tonight, my friends, are we a cowardly people?"

"No!" came the response.

"Are we a people ashamed of our history?"

"No!"

"Are we a people to be told that our values may be super-seded by those of our oppressors?"

"No!"

"Then it is clear, my friends, that we are a people who must act! We know who we are. I know who we are. I see it in your eyes. I hear it in your voices. I feel it in my body, the very aura of your righteous presence here tonight. You stand here for the same reason as I – to declare to the butchers of our spirit that we will no longer be afraid! We will stand together and declare to all those who would oppose our purification that they are either oppressor... or collaborator."

The crowd roared and began to chant in the same manner as their previous protest: "Death to traitors! Traitors hanged!" The sound hammered through Kaiya's body, and she felt herself as one in a multitude of shining truths, a single flame in the fire of those awakened souls who stood beside her.

"This government," Amelia continued, "thinks us children to be corrected. To be punished for fulfilling our most basic duty to one another – the righting of wrongs. They say they bring justice, that they shall have trials, that there shall be 'due process,' but let us not be blind to the reality of what they mean. People of Leth, we are being deceived! They play us for fools! This government thinks to tell us that a traitor is as deserving of life as you or I, but you and I know this is false. You and I know this, together, for it is a knowledge that beats as strongly in your heart as it does in mine. The lives of the traitors were forfeit the day they sold their souls to the Tarkinians."

"Death to traitors!" Kaiya screamed, eyes fixed on Amelia, who glowed with a floodlight halo.

"This is the truth they seek to keep from you! And I tell you one more truth, my friends, and be not blind to it. As sure as Bennett belonged to Tarkinia, Benjamin belongs to *them*. Why else would our own Commissioner betray us, the true people of Leth, were it not that he himself is a traitor to Leth? There can be no question of this, my friends. The treacherous influence of Bennett has not disappeared. It has only shifted in form, and I say that it is time we take back what is ours.

"I say that we are the arbiters of what we will accept – no one else! We will determine when we are ready to forget. We will be the ones to decide the fate of the collaborators. Make no mistake, the tendrils of Akheron stand here tonight with one message – that we will be denied the justice that belongs to us. That the whores and collaborators will be spared for their crimes. That we, the people, those who Akheron purport to represent, are not to be trusted. I say they are the ones who cannot be trusted!

"They do not know us!" Amelia said, her arms wide with fists clenched, the weight of righteous fury a thundercloud on her face. "They do not know the depth of our agony! They come and they speak of justice, but we all know that their justice is false. We refuse to swallow the lies of Akheron.

"This government tells us that the collaborators will be dealt with, but this government lies! This government tells us that once more the police are our friends, but I say they are as corrupt as ever! This government sends its advocates from Akheron to hear our petty complaints, but tell us there is nothing they can do! Who here has experienced the loving hand of our leaders? Have you?"

"No!" came the crowd.

"None of us! And do you know why? It is not because Akheron has forgotten us. Akheron does not forget. It is because Akheron has never cared for those it knows are not truly Nymian. But we are the people of Leth, and the people of Leth stand together in the face of our oppression! We will stand together as one, as we did during the Occupation, because I tell you now, my friends, we are still occupied. Look around you!" she shouted, arms wide and all-encompassing as she turned on the spot. "What do you see? I see the same face that has stared at us not for six years, but for eight hundred. The face of a Nymian is no different to the face of a Tarkinian. They tell us that we are free now that the Tarkinians are gone, but my friends, the Tarkinians are not gone. They are merely replaced, and we are still occupied!"

Kaiya felt herself swaying in the humid sea of restless bodies. Beside her, spittle sprayed as Jerome shouted.

"People of Leth, we will be victim no longer. Tonight we stand together in solidarity, our voices clear and righteous. We are here to take back who we are. To take back the identity that has been stolen from us. To stand up and say that we will no longer allow our lives to be a choice between one oppression and another. The bureaucrats of Akheron have told us that they care more for the life of a collaborator than the lives of your children, your mothers, your fathers, your brothers and sisters, all the loved ones we have lost.

"Do not allow them to deceive you! I speak to you as well, those of you who hide inside your homes, those who have been frightened into submission. We know, all of us, the truth, and we must stand together in a shared hope, a shared commitment, a shared sacrifice, and only then shall we make the mountains tremble with our shared voice. Join me, people of Leth, join me and speak as one," she commanded, turning to face the town hall. "Give us back our home!"

The air exploded with fervour, the natural reaction of impassioned anger combined with a divine command of inflection and zeal. Kaiya saw with a new, deeper clarity. The voices of hundreds engulfed the town square, her own playing its small part, the part of no one yet everyone. A great justice was to fall upon Leth, she the arbiter of the guilty, standing with her fellow righteous to defend the honour of the people. She thrust her fist into the air, howling with the choir of mourning and aggrieved.

Above her, the windows of the terrace houses had all turned black, and she grew more committed. She carried upon her shoulders the weight not only of her own grievances, but the weight of those too fearful to step forward. She marched with a new army, an army of purification and hope, that would provide a beacon to the disaffected, and shine a light on the path to victory. She stood not just for herself, but for Tilda, and what Tilda had lost at the hands of the enemy – her liberty, her passion, her fearless heart. She stood for Kormac and the time stolen from them both. She stood for Masuma, who carried within her the abomination of collaboration. She stood even for Cecilie, and those people who saw in Leth what it could be were it freed of ties to the subjugators of the people. Only she, Kaiya, and the legion of hope surrounding her, could return dignity and honour and pride to Leth.

A wave of anger burst from the front of the crowd. The well-dressed man, the Taskforce spokesperson, stood on a podium behind the protective energy field, surveying them. "Death to traitors! Traitors hanged!" came the chant, but he remained unperturbed, almost aloof.

"People of Leth, of Nymosen," he said, his measured voice echoing through the buildings and met with a cacophony of hatred, "thank you. Thank you all for coming tonight and sharing with us your passion and your dedication to a just and noble cause."

His voice slipped into Kaiya's mind, almost unnoticed, so well-articulated, with such clarity, such a rhythm of... reassurance. Every word was cultured and rich, promising affection and peace and security and...

No.

She shook her head, and jeered along with the crowd. It didn't seem to touch him, and he remained standing, ever so patient, until a momentary lapse in the wave of sound allowed him to continue.

"I am here tonight for *you*," he said, and honey coated Kaiya's mind, slowing the urge to shout him down. "To speak with you and, above all, to listen. Only together can we rebuild our proud nation and move forward into a new and prosperous future."

"Liar!" yelled Jerome, and the accusation was repeated by others nearby, accompanied by a string of expletives.

"We know the terrible tragedy that has befallen you. It is the same tragedy that has befallen so many across this great nation of ours, and I give you every assurance that we have not forgotten you. This is why we have acted so quickly to provide you with recourse to the court of priority. Know this, people of Leth, of Nymosen, we do this for you."

A flash of light erupted from the energy field, and a thrown glass bottle smashed down onto the ground.

"We have heard your voices. This government is committed to pursuing every avenue of investigation and prosecution into crimes of treason. The court of priority has begun already to dedicate itself to these ends. We ask only that you assist us. In such dark times, more than ever we need unity."

Another flash of light erupted from the energy field, and Kaiya cheered along with those around her.

Behind the energy field, Taskforce police shifted, hands creeping closer to stun batons.

"For centuries we have lived together, enriched and supported by the legal institutions that guarantee us liberty. It is for this reason that I say to you, let us put this madness behind us. Let us return this town to peace and allow the traitors to be dealt with in due course, under the light of public scrutiny. Let us put away our weapons and join together to support the work of those who endeavour to bring peace back to Leth."

"We want Bennett!" came a voice from behind Kaiya, and soon more voices pierced the evening, demanding the former Commissioner.

"And have him you shall!" the speaker said. "He shall be tried in accordance with all—"

"That's not good enough," Amelia yelled, and her voice reverberated through the speaker system, her message carried along with cheering.

"We must not let chaos threaten our communities," the speaker said. "We must... approach these issues with sober minds and—"

"Give us Bennett!" Amelia shouted, and the energy field shimmered.

"We must stand together and show full support to the institutions that give us liberty. This violence must stop. We can no longer accept the turmoil of—"

"He is a traitor!" Amelia said amidst an eruption of fury. "He means to deny us Bennett! He means to let the collaborators go!"

The Taskforce spokesperson stared at Amelia for the first time, then lifted his head towards the upper levels of the buildings surrounding them. "Listen carefully, people of Leth, to the words of hatred this woman speaks, and ask yourself – is this who you are? Will you be represented by the bloodthirsty and tyrannical, or do you reject her as you rejected the barbarous Tarkinians? I ask you all to direct your energies into helping us reunite this great nation and bring justice to those who would seek to harm it."

He stared back to Amelia as he delivered his final line, and there could be no doubting the intent of his words.

Amelia had been right. The man was a traitor.

The volcano of shouting became a writhing mass of bodies. The energy field flashed every few seconds as projectiles smashed against it, and Kaiya joined the chorus of "Death to traitors!" once more. A nearby man stared like an enraged bull, his mouth open in a cry of passion that blended like soup into the clammy atmosphere.

"People of Leth!" came Amelia's voice, and Kaiya looked up to see her on the makeshift platform again, her eyes wild and fist raised. As she stared up, the floodlights intensified until looking in Amelia's direction was painful. Kaiya squinted and raised her hand as if she were blotting out the sun.

Behind the energy field, the Taskforce spokesperson watched.

"People of Leth, hear these words of betrayal!" Amelia said.

"Charging!" someone yelled from the front nearby, and wrath washed over the crowd at the sight of unholstered stun batons. Kaiya watched the regular police hold their line, but then an officer fell to the ground, struck by some projectile – a rock or a bottle, she couldn't tell.

Within seconds, a line of energy shields ascended.

"See their treachery!" Amelia yelled.

Kaiya's heart began to race.

The Taskforce spokesperson turned his back on the crowd and motioned to the Taskforce police.

And on the other side, at the rear of the crowd, Kaiya could just see the wall of Leth police blocking the southern boulevard, shoulder to shoulder with shields and stun batons ready.

Amelia began to speak again, her voice muddied within the discord. "People of Leth, I speak to you all! Look outside your windows! See the lengths the traitors will go to deny us justice and our independence! I know you are frightened. I know you are tired. I know you may not trust your own heart to stand strong in the moment of need after all we have suffered, but if you believe in nothing else, believe in the strength of our unity! Believe in a future free from subjugation, free from—"

"Kaiya," came Jerome's voice. "We need to get her down."

Amelia stood on the platform, burning with a devotion Kaiya had never seen. She loomed titanic, a sister to the statue of the faceless Emancipator silhouetted against the too-strong flood-lights, her hair sweaty and sticking to her face as her voice rang through the centre of Leth. A crackling sound near the front of the crowd grew louder, and Kaiya looked over as a barrage of bric-a-brac missiles smashed into Taskforce energy shields.

Something shot into the crowd, and gas began to rise.

"I will never surrender for as long as the people of Leth—"

"That way," Jerome said, pointing towards the fountain.

They moved towards Amelia, trying to avoid the gas. Kaiya stopped just short of a man who held up a frequency rifle and shot towards the energy field. The police were still holding their lines.

"Amelia!" Jerome called as they reached the fountain.

She ignored them, still lost in her own whirlwind of passion.

"Amelia!" he called again.

"I promise you that day will come!" Amelia told the crowd. "That day will come, and when it does, we shall all stand together—"

She fell silent, a canister of tear gas slamming into her head.

Kaiya watched in a frozen moment as Amelia stumbled on the platform, eyes wide in surprise, then fell. Her head smashed against the side of the fountain, and she lay still beside it, blood beginning to coat her face. Kaiya rushed forward, pushing past stunned onlookers, Jerome by her side, and she knelt beside Amelia's body, trying in vain to wake Amelia from her final rest.

Kaiya gazed into the martyr, and the martyr gazed into her.

Any semblance of restraint fled the town square.

The crowd charged in multiple directions. Protestors threw themselves at police. More canisters fell, and Kaiya coughed as a cloud of gas erupted nearby, gleaming in the floodlights and shrouding dark figures. Shots rang out, but they reverberated against the walls, and she couldn't place them.

"Come on," Jerome said, and Kaiya stared a little longer at Amelia before finally following.

They ran away from the encroaching gas cloud, towards the western side of the town square. Straight towards lines of waiting police.

Protestors clashed with the first line. Stun batons found their marks, and protestors fell, but the first line soon retreated, three of its members dead on the ground. A fourth screamed as his own stun baton was turned against him, burning a hole through his face.

Kaiya found her way to the building walls, eyes swimming, and gasped for fresh air.

Above her, one of the giant floodlights exploded, and she flinched. She covered her head as shards of glass rained into the town square. Within seconds, the structure had collapsed, its metal base splintering. Her comrades swarmed over the area, and Kaiya watched as a man emerged from the wreckage holding a javelin-length shard of metal. He ran a few steps and unloaded the weapon, which smashed against a police energy shield. Sparks flew as the shield broke. The officer reached down to find a replacement bulb, but couldn't compete for speed. Another javelin tore through his chest and he fell to the ground, a metre of metal protruding from either side of his body.

Another explosion flowed through Kaiya's body, and the town square fell into darkness. Frequency rifles sounded from somewhere behind her. She looked back and watched the second floodlight crash down into the energy field guarding the town hall. Already under fire from the frequency rifles, the energy field shimmered and sparked as the weight of the flood-light bore inexorably down.

At first it sparked.

Then it snapped.

All over her body, Kaiya's hair shocked to attention as a wave of invisible energy erupted from the dying energy field. Closer to the source, protestors and police alike fell to the ground, clutching their heads. Metal splintered and crashed onto the town hall steps, and Taskforce police reformed on the entrance landing, backing into a tight two-rowed semicircle, energy shields lifted in phalanx formation. One of their number lay still on the ground, surrounded by six protestors.

Now the only light to be found emanated from sometimes-broken footpaths, an odd lantern hanging from a building, and the faint glow of energy shields. "Fall back!" came a voice from the protestor side. "Fall back!" he repeated as he emerged near Kaiya holding a frequency rifle. Four others joined him, falling to single knees and taking aim as their comrades followed the order.

"Full strength!" shouted one of the Leth police, and the enemy lines stepped back to brace themselves, turning shields to maximum. Sparks flew as the shields shook, and Kaiya covered her ears as the protestors discharged their weapons. The sonic blast crashed into the first line, sending two officers sprawling and smashing another's shield, which exploded in a concentrated beam to the front. One of their inherent features, she remembered. Designed as a final weapon if it were somehow overloaded.

She cursed herself for not thinking to warn her comrades.

Officers helped each other to their feet, and their commander ordered a major fallback. The protestors jeered as the five with frequency rifles recharged. Their second round had much less effect, the targets further away and locked in phalanx formation.

There was celebration, but Kaiya could already see what would happen. With Leth and Taskforce police, a backdown could not be expected.

Jerome stood near the mouth of the town square into the western boulevard, tending to an injured woman. Kaiya rushed back towards the fountain, holding her arm against her nose, and began to drag people away towards the walls. She had to do more. She had to pull her weight, give everything to the cause, instead of cowering as people braver than her risked their lives.

Men and women cried or stared in shock, their eyes and skin burnt. Sometimes they screamed in silence, the gas having stripped away the ability to create any sound. Kaiya rubbed her inflamed eyes, the image of Amelia's broken body flaring in pinpricked darkness.

Kaiya placed her hands under a semi-conscious man's arms and heaved him backwards towards the open air. He groaned in recognition of the assistance, but didn't seem to fully comprehend what was happening. Kaiya let him down on the footpath and wiped away the sweat on her brow.

"Jerome!" she called across, watching him tend to a protestor, emergency kit beside him. "Do you have a lightning heal?"

He looked back and fumbled through his kit, throwing a lightning heal across to her. She picked it up and stopped as she began to unwrap it, staring at the flecks of blood all over her hands. How did that get there? She pushed aside the thought and tried to look as though she knew what she was doing. She opened the package and removed the soft dressing and leaned over the semi-conscious man she'd pulled out from the gas. "Just relax," she said to the man, who could barely move and only made a low moaning sound. Kaiya took his head in one hand and pressed the dressing onto his cheek, where a stun baton had opened a deep, imprecise gash. The man arched his back impulsively and tried to defend himself with barely-moving hands.

Kaiya pressed down on the wound as the dressing gripped onto the man's skin, seeking the best position from which to begin its work. The dressing sank into the wound, excreting dried blood and other foreign matter, pulling the skin back together ever so slightly.

The injured man's face relaxed, and he closed his eyes.

"Grab his legs," came Jerome's voice from behind her. She complied with the request, and they carried him the remaining distance to the wall, where they propped him up against it.

"We can't go back in," Jerome said. "We need to reorganise."

"They'll come with reinforcements," Kaiya said.

Jerome grunted agreement. "We're prepared for that."

Protestors were beginning to gather around them, and Kaiya stood up. "What weapons do we have?"

Several men stepped forward and held up frequency rifles, but Kaiya's attention was focused on a single force projector. That kind of lethality could change everything.

"I told you we came prepared," Jerome said as he stood up. "Does anyone know where Aaron is?"

"He's on southern boulevard," came one response.

Kaiya glanced over at the shrouded town square centre, the fountain barely visible. The century-and-a-half statue of the Emancipator stood cracked and broken. There was no way to get to southern or eastern boulevard without going blind. "It's lingering gas," she said. "We're trapped on west. Do you have a plan for that?"

Jerome looked around. More protestors were coalescing around them, like flies to a rotting carcass. Dozens became over a hundred, then that number doubled as people emerged from alleyways and places made invisible by the gas.

"We can't win on numbers," Jerome said. "They have better weapons."

"They have Obsidian Tanks," Kaiya pointed out.

"Then it's a good thing we have a force projector. Besides… if they can manoeuvre an Obsidian Tank through the streets they deserve a victory. We took care of that last night."

Of course. The damage to the central bridge would have been repeated in a multitude of strategic locations. Amelia never let anything past her…

Kaiya looked back towards the fountain, unable to see Amelia's body, and her mouth soured.

"Have you…" she began, and peered towards Jerome before lowering her voice. "Have you laid any explosives?"

Jerome smirked.

"We need height," he said to the crowd. "And we need invisibility. We need them to not know where our shots are coming from. If we can break their phalanx, we can pick them off. As long as it's two lines with one front, we'll come off second best." Jerome pointed to one of the men with the frequency rifles. "I want you to go through as planned. Go now. You need to be in positions before they come."

The armed man nodded and walked towards the entrance to western boulevard. Others with weapons followed him, people who obviously knew their role, but the man also called for volunteers, explaining their objective.

Everyone stopped as the sound of rifle fire pierced the evening. Kaiya's ears pricked up and she moved her head, listening. Eastern boulevard, she was certain of it.

"We're wasting time," she said to Jerome.

"Let me think," he said. "We didn't count on lingering gas."

"You didn't count on it?"

"The plan relied on keeping a hold of town square. Maintaining access between east, south, and west."

"And you didn't think they would use lingering gas?" she said. "What did you think they were going to do? It's the first thing I would have done, if I were them. They're not idiots, Jerome. I know how well-trained these people are."

"So tell me what we should do, if you're so smart?"

Jerome stared at her half-mockingly, containing an obvious fury underneath. She kept her gaze steady, refusing to give in to his threatening facade, but found her eyes slipping ever so slowly towards the balconies of western boulevard.

Kaiya felt her face rise in realisation.

"Height, you said. We attack from above."

Jerome frowned and looked into the boulevard. "The question is how, though."

"We walk in and do it."

It seemed quite obvious to her.

"Right," Jerome almost laughed, and began speaking to the crowd, his message relayed by one of the armed men whose voice was like a sledgehammer on stone, all force and no finesse. "You need to make a choice right now. You can stay, or you can go. If you stay, we need to go into the buildings. We need to get the people on our side, convince them—"

"Hang on," Kaiya said, "that's not what I said."

Jerome peered at her, and the eyes of the people turned in her direction.

"I said we go in there. I didn't mean we ask to go in."

"You want us to force our way in?"

"It's the one thing we have that the police don't," she said. "They can't come here with height. They're stuck on the ground. And they're not about to start blowing up buildings. I think that would be enough for *Allied Atlantica* to get involved."

"So you want us to just blast our way in and—"

"Yes!" Kaiya said, her conviction met with murmurs of agreement.

"We need them, Kaiya. We need them to know we're on the same side."

"But we aren't on the same side," Kaiya said, turning her

voice to the crowd and pointing. "Those people up there – they are not on the same side as us. If they were on our side, they would be out here. But they're not. And if they're not, then they're a collaborator. It's as simple as that."

The murmurs turned to shouts of approval.

"By all means, knock and ask first. Any person loyal to Leth will assist you. But if they don't, that tells you everything you need to know about where their loyalty lies."

The crowd gave overwhelming assent to her message.

"We can't fit them all up there," Jerome whispered to her.

"Then tell me what else you want to do."

Jerome searched her eyes, nodded, and told her.

Kaiya was smiling by the time he finished.

"Excellent," she said.

"I want half of you to stay here," Jerome announced to the crowd. "Anyone who can hold their own in a fight – a real fight – you stay. The rest of you, get the height. Three blocks should be enough. Whatever it takes, you get the height, and remember – everything is a weapon, if you use it that way."

The crowd began to disperse, and shouting overtook the sound of distant rifle fire. Already fists banged on the doors nearest the town square, and protestors demanded the assistance they deserved. Kaiya grimaced at the dawning realisation that there would be many collaborators tonight who would stand in the way of victory against the oppressors.

She hoped the rest of their movement maintained their strength of character, and brought an end to any such resistance.

Kaiya gazed back into the town square, where dozens of bodies lay motionless on the ground, and the lingering gas shrouded even more. The stairs to the town hall were semi-hidden in haze, but she could see more bodies there, crushed by the first falling floodlight, pools of red coagulating on the glossy black road tiles or soaking into discarded banners. The second floodlight lay cracked across the steps of the town hall, jagged protrusions of metal forming a further line of defence to the bureaucrats hidden inside.

"It's time to go," Jerome said.

They looked at each other and Kaiya clasped his forearms, wishing him luck.

She watched him depart into the western boulevard, then felt the ground shake with an explosion from somewhere in the east. Rifle fire pierced the night, and tendrils of distant fire put the stars to shame.

Time to move on.

Kaiya jogged down the western boulevard, watching as protestors argued with intercoms. They were surrounded by collaborators, and they were moving too slow – letting the collaborators delay. If they wanted to succeed tonight, they needed to take control of the situation.

Ahead of her stood a man with a frequency rifle, trying to reason with whoever lived at that house. The sight of it sickened her, and she changed direction, heading towards him. "You," she said as she approached. The armed man failed to respond, and she repeated herself to gain his attention. "Give me that," she said, pointing to his frequency rifle.

"What?"

"I told you to give me the gun," she said. "Now." The man looked down at her, a good few inches taller, and she attempted to cloak herself in as much of her father's authority as she could muster. After a few moments of consideration, the man complied.

Kaiya stepped forward to the intercom. "Can you hear me?"

"Who is this?" came a man's voice. "I tell you what, I'm looking forward to seeing those cops beat the shit out of you."

Kaiya raised the frequency rifle and fired it into the man's top window, a shower of glass shattering from the force of the sound waves. After everything they had already done to protect the people from the oppressors, still these collaborators denigrated their sacrifice.

A child's cry emerged from within the house, and Kaiya recharged the weapon.

"You bitch!" came the voice from the intercom. "You little bitch! What the fuck do you think you're doing?"

Kaiya raised the frequency rifle again and fired, this time into the next window down, obliterating the glass into tiny fragments and cracking the surrounding stone. The man at her side looked at her as she recharged the rifle, then held up his hand in a waiting motion.

"Do you still refuse to let us in?" the man said to the intercom.

Silence greeted his question, and Kaiya raised her weapon.

"Wait," her companion said.

"We don't have time to wait," she said, then directed her voice at the intercom. "We are coming in whether you open the door or not. Five seconds."

She pointed the frequency rifle at the door, and three seconds later it slid up, revealing a vestibule void of human life. Kaiya and her fellow demonstrator stepped inside, staring at two bronze statues towering by the polished stone imperial staircase. Their footsteps echoed on intricate parquet, crunching occasionally on slivers of glass from the floors above. Kaiya looked up. The terrace house was divided into six levels, each one visible from the ground, with a chandelier hanging from the top ceiling. It reached all the way down to where the ceiling for the first floor would have been, had it existed.

Kaiya had never seen anything like it.

She hated whoever lived there.

"You should take this," she said, and returned the frequency rifle.

The man considered her. "You don't want to stay here?"

"No. I have other plans. Good luck."

Kaiya stepped outside and looked up and down the boulevard. The atmosphere had changed, as more protestors accepted they would need to resort to what she had just done. Glass littered the road, and finally doors were opening rather than being forced open. The collaborators had begun to understand their position, and were ceding, albeit reluctantly.

They could be punished another time.

"Kaiya," came Jerome's voice. He stood on a balcony, holding a kitchen knife. "Hurry up. Listen."

She closed her eyes and listened. The sounds of the boulevard were difficult to penetrate, but after a few seconds she could make out distant gunfire. Coming from the southwest...

The police had reentered northwest quadrant.

Somewhere out there, her allies were hiding, trying to goad the police into breaking formation.

Kaiya jogged again. Anyone who hadn't found a position yet only had themselves to blame if they were killed, and she didn't want to join that list. She passed through the first intersection and looked south. Police in phalanx formation were visible in the distance, too far away to make an accurate shot, and moving slowly as they dodged lethal sound waves.

They weren't rising to the planned provocation.

Kaiya continued to the second intersection. Two more phalanxes approached, closer than the one in the previous street. She went forward onto the third block and stopped.

She knew this tactic...

Her father had used it years ago...

"Stop!" she called behind her.

Some of the fake surrender group had already made it to the third block, but the majority were still behind her, waiting for a signal. They followed her order, and she jogged over to the third intersection, stopping before she stumbled straight into visibility.

The western boulevard had fallen silent.

Kaiya pressed herself against the wall of the corner building. The outer kettling phalanxes would be closer to this intersection than the other phalanxes were to theirs. The attack would come from here – possibly from intersections further along as well – and push them back towards the town square, every phalanx from the adjoining streets ensuring there was no escape.

Good. She could deal with that.

Kaiya glanced around the corner, and whipped her head back when she saw how close the police were. "Help me!" she screamed, and ran back to the centre of the block as the majority of the surrender group came in her direction, raising their voices at her signal. Some stayed back, and those already in the third block stood on high alert. As best they could, the surrender group needed an even dispersal of people between the three blocks.

Kaiya glanced across at a woman a decade her senior, who gave her a grin.

Then everyone waiting at the third block began to move.

Police emerged onto the boulevard, rearranging their phalanx into a broader one that would allow no one to pass. Demonstrators shouted, creating as much noise as they could, and ran towards the police, then back. Some fell to the ground close to the police, then crawled backwards, pleading for mercy.

Kaiya ran back to the second intersection and fell to her knees at the sight of police closing in from the side streets.

"I'm unarmed!" she yelled.

All around her protestors either tripped over, or fell to their knees, or stood standing with arms above head. "We surrender!" some yelled, while others spoke about how they had children or had never meant to go this far.

"On the ground!" police yelled, their stun batons primed for action.

Kaiya watched closely as the demonstrators complied, those closer to the police giving more resistance. The police remained still, however, maintaining their phalanx formations and taking no steps into the boulevard. The kettling manoeuvre was complete.

Now she just had to break it.

"On the ground!" police continued to yell.

Kaiya lay down on her stomach, cheek pressed on the divide between two road tiles. She watched her comrades do the same, gaze shifting between them and the windows above.

"My reports said there were more," came an officer's voice from behind Kaiya's vision.

"Killed a bunch in town square," another said. "Others would've gone east or south."

"Taskforce and division six have them," a third voice said. "Just focus on this lot."

None of the protestors made any more sound, and Kaiya listened to distant rifle fire. She could feel her heart thumping against the road, pumping blood through her body. Hyper-awareness. The sharp point of a tiny shard of glass under her thigh. The scent of smoke. The tensity of shielded bodies, like a spring stretching to the point of breaking.

And all around her a cocoon of expectation.

"Forward and tighten kettle," came a voice from the third intersection. "Maintain formation. Eyes above."

Damn.

Kaiya could hear the police rear force beginning a slow approach down the boulevard. The plan couldn't succeed if they kept such tight discipline.

"You will stand as we approach," the same voice called down the boulevard, "and make an orderly procession towards town square. Any attempt to evade capture will be met with decisive and incapacitating action. You have been warned. You will comply."

Something about the voice niggled at her. Probably someone she had heard years ago, someone who had betrayed her father.

Kaiya managed to peek down towards the approaching phalanx. Demonstrators stood slowly before they could be crushed by heavy boots, and began their procession towards her. Her mind raced as she tried to figure out a response before the police reached the second block. If the police gained too much ground, the effectiveness of those in the windows would be diminished.

Jerome needed to act. He had that capacity.

A small commotion arose outside of Kaiya's vision. Someone cried out – she couldn't tell if man or woman – and fell over, halting the phalanx. A scream rose, the kind that could only indicate the use of a stun baton, and then the commanding voice of the previous police officer returned. "Stop," it came.

Kaiya's ears pricked at the tone, and the almost imperceptible murmur that came from other police nearby. The command had been delivered too quickly, as if he were trying too hard to assert authority.

Now the answer burst into her mind.

"This way!" she yelled, jumping up from her position and indicating to the demonstrators around her. "This way!"

Kaiya ran into the middle of the second intersection, a few seconds passing before her allies realised what she was doing. When the realisation came, however, bodies lifted from the road all over the boulevard, along with dozens of voices lifted in an assortment of fear and anger.

"Hold positions!" came the police officer's voice, but Kaiya could see just how many were itching to step forward and put an end to their renewed insurrection.

The officer's orders were useless, and a trickle of police officers rushed into the fray, swinging stun batons indiscriminately. They were followed by most of their colleagues.

The phalanx formations had broken.

"Get down!" Kaiya yelled, falling back down to the road.

Around her protestors fell, but the attack had already begun, and Kaiya watched as stun batons began their work, cracking into nearby skulls.

A police officer unlatched a frequency rifle and took aim into the crowd.

"No rifles!" the commanding officer said, his voice helpless in the din.

He was ignored.

Finally, Jerome's group responded.

A barrage of frequency fire rained down over the boulevard.

All around Kaiya police officers raised their energy shields, or fell to the ground clutching the parts of their body the frequencies had hit. Full body armour would be enough to stop penetration at those ranges, but not enough to stop pain.

The momentary confusion was enough for Kaiya to act.

She launched herself up from the ground at the same moment as her comrades nearby, tackling a police officer whose attention was fixed on stopping anything hitting him from above. Kaiya brought him to the ground and tried to pin him down, but the officer was too quick. He swung his energy shield and knocked Kaiya away, lifting his stun baton.

Kaiya rolled to the side as the stun baton rebounded against the road, sparking wildly. She kicked the officer's wrist as her eyes were flooded with the chaotic dance of feet surrounding her. Shouts from both sides mixed with wounded screaming and the sound of shattering glass.

The officer swung his stun baton again, and Kaiya yelped as it grazed her thigh, sending a shock through her entire body. She reacted out of instinct, aiming a kick at the officer's head. He dodged the attack, but it gave her enough time to crawl a little further away from her assailant.

Another officer nearby held up his frequency rifle and shot a protestor in the chest.

Within seconds three other protestors were pulling him down to the ground and smashing his head into the road. One grabbed the frequency rifle and charged it, but he was shot down before he could fire, blood erupting from his stomach and spraying in front of him.

Kaiya felt a hand on her foot, and tried to shake off the grip of the officer she had been struggling with.

He jabbed at her with his stun baton, pressing it into her leg, and she screamed as fire scored through her nerves.

Her vision swam.

Bright colours bled through her eyelids. Sound penetrated as if through water, a gurgle of turmoil.

And then the pain stopped, leaving her with a throbbing aftershock.

She gasped as clarity returned, staring up as a protestor fell down from a balcony and smashed against the boulevard.

Kaiya gazed down her legs. Her attacker lay still on the ground, helmet forcibly removed. Crimson darkness oozed from his baton-seared head onto the road. A woman stood by his body, holding the stun baton she had obviously taken from it, and jabbed wildly at an officer missing his shield.

The officer swung his own stun baton, and the two met, emitting such a bright intensity of sparks that they both lost their charges momentarily.

Kaiya clutched her leg as sensation returned, hobbling to her feet.

A protestor fell, frequency concentration tearing through his chest.

An energy shield exploded, setting fire to protestors in front of it.

Another officer turned his attention to her, and Kaiya stepped backwards as he approached. The glint of a knife spun through the air, embedding itself into the officer's armour. He hesitated before taking another step, then another knife thumped into his chest.

He fell to his knees and pulled out the two knives, both tips wet with a trickle of blood. His moment of weakness ended him, demonstrators rushing forward and pinning him to the ground. They removed his helmet and took the knives, thrusting them down into his neck once, twice, three times, four times, five... until his face and their hands were covered in crimson.

Kaiya looked back towards the woman who had saved her. She still sparred with the officer, but suffered from a lack of armour and training, and was quickly losing ground. Kaiya pressed forward, stumbling a little, and screamed at the officer. It was enough to distract him long enough for the other woman to land a blow on his ungloved hand.

He stepped back, flexing the now-wounded hand, face invisible behind helmet.

"Tank!" came a voice from somewhere Kaiya couldn't tell.

She looked behind her, and saw the rippling, semi-transparent midnight shell of an Obsidian Tank entering the third intersection. A lull flooded the boulevard, attention turning towards the machine.

Then it fired.

The force of the explosion against a nearby building sent Kaiya sprawling to the ground. She watched as centuries-old stone from the fourth story and up began to crack, disintegrating in the face of a frequency canon designed for that purpose.

Slowly fragments of the building began to fall, crashing to the boulevard below as people ran away. Bodies tumbled from balconies, along with furniture and glass. Dust billowed into the air and Kaiya crawled away, back towards the town square. This was a fight she couldn't win, and the nearby police had been emboldened. The woman who had saved her took a blow to the face and fell to the ground.

The officer brought down the stun baton again.

Kaiya stepped forward—

And the sky shattered...

The world inverted.

Her head pounded, ears ringing.

Time moved so slow she could touch it. Manipulate it.

She watched the atoms of existence birthed and die.

If she could just reach out... control her body...

She kneeled against the wall... why was she against a wall?

Clutched her head.

Lightning scoured her brain and refused to dissipate, shattering along inside her, gnawing.

She tried to stand, and fell back down, flecks of light bouncing up and down across her vision.

Smoke curled around her body, snatching away the precious air she tried so hard to breathe. There was no glow from the footpath. She was surrounded by near-darkness, punctuated only by that light that managed to dance through vapours, misty and formless, pretending at solidity and revealed always as deceiver.

The shroud began to clear, if only in her head and not in sight. Loud cracks reverberated from all around. Frequency rifles...

The pieces of what had happened fell together. Those had been Jerome's explosives...

But they were still on the boulevard... it must have been a mistake.

Kaiya tried to stand, and failed. But she felt stronger, as if the returning realisation of where she was endowed her with a new vigour. Beams of light pierced the veiling tendrils. Kaiya crawled forward, whichever way that was, groaning at the effort, her determination to escape overpowering any incapacity to move.

One hand, one knee, one pair after the other, passing over splinters of wood and shards of glass.

A voice flooded her ears, murky at first, but gaining in clarity, booming over the area and commanding the protestors to surrender.

If the sounds of continued battle were anything to go by, no one was listening.

She managed at last to stand, holding on to a door frame for support. A new wave of dizziness assaulted her, threatening to undo her progress. Kaiya held tight to the doorframe. More beams of light approached, ever closer. All over the boulevard she could see figures darting through smoke, whipping it into a frenzy that fast returned to a near stasis.

Kaiya flexed her hands, one by one, strength returning. Soon she didn't need to hold on to the door frame, and began to notice the door itself. The explosion had splintered the wood and disintegrated most of the metal, leaving it ajar. Kaiya reached forward and touched the handle, concerned it may collapse, but it remained. With a new confidence she pushed the door open and stepped through into darkness.

Still teary from the smoke, her eyes adjusted just enough for her to recognise a modest vestibule nowhere near as extravagant as the one she had been in earlier. She closed the door behind her, as far as it would go, until a trickle of light peeked in through the resultant crack. The gentle illumination revealed motes of dust floating above a plain, polished floor, and a set of humble stairs set neatly into the undecorated walls of impressionist patterning.

"Who's there?" came a man's voice from the stairs.

Kaiya crept back against the wall and stared in the voice's direction. The man was invisible.

"I can see you," he said wryly.

Kaiya sifted through her various options and chose silence.

"Who are you?" the man asked.

Outside there were shouts and the sound of rifle fire. She had no idea if the protestors or the police were winning, and here she was stuck inside with some vicious collaborator. If she had to, she could defend herself.

"Should you be here?" the man asked, and his voice annoyed

her, condescending by virtue of its lack of condescension. "Why are you here? Answer me. I'd rather not have the police coming into my house. It's already been damaged enough, don't you think?"

"So you're on their side," Kaiya said.

The invisible man paused. "I reject your distinction. But if you insist on it, then I must answer yes."

"So you admit it," Kaiya said. "You're a collaborator."

The man stayed silent, and Kaiya seethed. The man was completely unabashed with his shameless recognition of his own criminality, as if he were somehow above justice!

"I'm as much a collaborator as you are a guest," the man said. "I think you should leave."

There was a gentle threat beneath the words, and Kaiya weighed it up against the sound of fighting from outside.

"No," she said.

The man gave a thoughtful sigh in response, stepping into the crack of light that reached towards the stairs. Kaiya couldn't properly make out his features, but he looked fit for his age. He stared at her, and she prepared herself for an attack.

"You refuse to leave?" he asked.

She ignored the question. He should have realised by now that she wouldn't be going anywhere. They stared at each other, and Kaiya wondered how visible she was to him in contrast to how little she could see him.

The man took a single step towards her, and she realised the time for action had come.

She charged forward and the man's eyes widened in brief shock as he yelled for the police. Hopefully the sound would be lost in the outside din.

Kaiya punched the man in the face before he had time to lift his hands in defence. He fell back against the railing of the stairs and Kaiya advanced, landing a blow to his stomach. "Police!" he yelled again, but with nowhere near the same strength as his earlier call, and Kaiya landed another blow on his face.

And another.

"Stop it!" came a girl's voice from the top of the stairs.

Kaiya looked up.

A teenager. She screamed for the police and Kaiya tried to extricate herself from her conflict with the man. She lunged up the stairs, determined to silence the girl, but felt herself pulled back down. Her face slammed into the railing and she screamed, kicking back at the man and connecting with his knee.

"Shut up!" she yelled up at the girl, who was still calling for the police.

Kaiya pounded away at the shadowed man, unloading her rage and denouncing his collaboration. He lifted his arms to protect himself as best he could, but her fists came again, and again, and again, and again, raining justice until blood spattered a third of his face and his swollen eyes could only gaze up in defenceless pleading.

Somebody shouted from the door, but Kaiya continued punishing the man. The voice came again and Kaiya looked up in time to dodge an officer's swinging stun baton. It scraped the side of her arm and she stumbled backwards, yelling as the shock passed through her body. The officer swung again, but Kaiya jumped at him, grabbing his baton-wielding arm. They fell to the ground together and wrestled, Kaiya flailing about as she attempted to extricate herself from his grip and avoid the stun baton. Landing any kind of effective blow proved difficult on a man in full riot gear, but try she did, and somehow managed to roll away and stand up, scrambling for the half-open door. She kicked it off its weakened hinges and ran outside.

Smoke obscured her vision of the boulevard. Back in the direction of town square a line of police advanced methodically, holding torches and stun batons. Kaiya left in the opposite direction, further west, senses alert. Behind her, the officer who had protected the collaborator followed.

Bodies and rubble littered the too-quiet boulevard. Rifle fire and explosions arose from side streets, but if anyone directly ahead of her was still alive, she couldn't tell. The remains of the top half of the building obliterated by the Obsidian Tank rose in front of her, great chunks of stone standing in a beachfront of dust. The Obsidian Tank itself stood almost invisible in the distance, hidden both by the smoke and its naturally transparent material. A gaping hole had incapacitated it. The only weapon that could do that was a force projector. Kaiya scurried into a crevice formed by fallen stone and watched as the officer pursuing her ran forward into the smoke and disappeared.

The sound of fighting dimmed within her semi-cocoon.

She looked down and stared at a woman whose detached legs had found themselves resting beside their owner.

The doors of the nearby buildings had been smashed to pieces, as were the majority of windows. Jerome's explosives had done their job perhaps a little too well. Why hadn't he waited until only police were left?

Kaiya stared down at her hands. They were covered in blood. How had that gotten there? Her arm still throbbed.

Lethargy threatened to overwhelm her, legs and hands shaking. She had to keep going. The bridges would have been secured by now, so no chance of getting home. Maybe if she went as far into the northwest as she could, they wouldn't be looking.

No, of course. Nine blocks and she would be at Tilda's house.

Plan of action decided, she ran forward to the next intersection and peered around the corner. The side street was empty, for the most part, except for rubble from the half-destroyed building and a few bodies. She moved forward, the smoke beginning to clear, and noticed a frequency rifle.

She hesitated, but resisted the urge to pick it up. Any traitor who saw her with that would ask no questions, and tonight was not a time to die.

A little thoroughfare park stood ahead, half-destroyed, its playground reduced to a mess of twisted metal. Kaiya jogged through the park and hid behind some of the untouched shrubbery on the other side. A few canisters of tear gas lay on the tiles, used and dejected. Two police officers shock-cuffed a man in the middle of the street, while smoke rose from a doused townhouse fire. Kaiya waited until the officers had removed their prisoner from the scene, then left in the opposite direction, further north. The northwest quadrant had come out fairly well after the previous night's uprising, and she ran so fast that the glowstone footpath had trouble keeping up with her.

Every second or third street she passed offered some spectacle of protest. Police chased their victims down one, and on the next fire spewed from the windows of several houses while a small crowd chanted below. Two streets further another group banged on a door, threatening to break it down, and three streets beyond that one of the whore collaborators had been stripped naked and was in the process of having her head shaved. Here a fire, there a gutted and black shell.

Surely the message was getting through to the collaborators. Their days were numbered.

Kaiya slowed, unable to maintain such a furious pace, and collapsed against a wall, gasping for air. The world struggled to stay straight, her heart threatening to break loose of its prison, lethargy and adrenaline battling inside her veins in a war of ever-changing dominance. The shaking recommenced. Her teeth chattered as if she were cold, yet her clothes were damp with sweat, her feet a pair of trapped flames.

A wave of shouting emerged from a nearby street, and frequency rifles blared. Kaiya searched the space around her, eyes struggling to stay straight. Around twenty police emerged from a nearby street corner, and she wheezed as she forced herself back onto her feet. The brief rest had done little to satisfy her, but she jogged ever onwards, legs heavy and full of protest. Protestors stopped what they were doing and turned to face the new threat, but Kaiya was satisfied with the damage they had done that night.

Just one more corner.

She came to it and turned onto Tilda's street. Perhaps she wouldn't be able to go inside, but Tilda's house was one of the rare freestanding homes still left in Leth, and if she could just find a small crevice of darkness...

Kaiya slowed.

The blackened corpse of Tilda's family home greeted her.

"You there! Stop!" came a voice from behind.

Kaiya complied, panting as she stared at the gutted remains.

"Hands behind your head," the officer said.

Kaiya hesitated. If she could just make it a little further, outrun him... but the exhaustion was too great. There had to be a way out...

She put her hands up slowly and rested her head against interlocked fingers, turning to face the traitor.

He strode towards her, ready to use his stun baton, while the sounds of skirmish rose from behind him.

"On your knees," he said, stopping several metres in front of her and fingering the shock-cuffs at his side.

Kaiya delayed, eyes flicking between the officer's helmet and the fighting that had become visible behind him.

"Now," the officer said, stepping forward and gripping his stun baton tighter.

A man approached from the intersection, holding his own stun baton, and Kaiya stepped backwards. The officer stepped forwards in response, and Kaiya tried to determine how much time she had before the fellow protestor came to save her.

When the silent assailant had almost closed the distance, Kaiya turned to run in the opposite direction. The sound of a stun baton thwacking down onto armour sizzled through the air, and Kaiya glanced behind as if her thankful intent could be read by her saviour in such a minor move.

The police officer slumped to his knees, and the assailant thumped him again with the stun baton.

"Stop!" came a voice from directly in front of her.

Apprehension flooded Kaiya's body. She turned her head as she stopped, but crashed straight into another police officer, who grabbed ahold of her and threw her to the ground. She broke the fall with her arm, a sharp needle of pain radiating up into her shoulder.

The protestor who had incapacitated the previous officer made to run, but a frequency rifle blared not two metres away, opening a hole in his body. He slumped to the ground and lay still.

Still panicked, Kaiya lifted herself up from the ground and charged at the officer who had assaulted her. She grunted as her shoulder connected with his chest, and suddenly she found herself surrounded by three other officers yelling orders and brandishing either stun batons or a frequency rifle.

The world went hazy as she screamed and struggled against firming grips, kicking out until she found herself no longer in contact with the ground. The traitors lifted her up and threw her backwards.

Pain shot through her back as she slammed onto the road.

Way out... had to be...

She crawled to her legs and made to sprint away, but found herself pulled back down again.

The sky was so clear.

The stars...

Smoke...

Helmets...

Stun baton swinging towards her fa—

12

EVERYTHING FELT SOFT AND SHARP. SHE LAY ON NEEDLED feathers, while feathered needles pierced her brain. A great cloud enveloped her thoughts so that all existence was pain, and comfort, and horror, and bliss...

Muted nothingness. She screamed in darkness, floating on calm clouds.

Her eyes drifted open, body aching. She could see light. Blurry.

White light. Warm light.

The room and the sun.

Yes... morning...

White. The room, that was white. Or the ceiling, at least.

Distant chattering drifted, machines beeping.

Murky.

She wanted to move her head, but could hardly move her eyes.

Fingers. They were beside her, resting... on something soft but firm. A bed?

Yes... she was on a bed.

She tried to move her fingers. Nothing.

Images flashed through her mind, of birthdays, sleeping, parents, tears, parties, dinnertimes, laughter, running, falling, pain, jumping, Kormac, joy, explosions, flesh, concrete, doors, soldiers, Tilda. They appeared and disappeared, then returned, and went, and returned, too fast for her to grasp. She tried to comprehend some context, desperate to hold on to at least one of the images. There were feelings attached to them, things that were important to her, but it was all just knowledge... and how had she come by that knowledge?

Kaiya focused her energy on restraining her mind, but the effort was worthless. Her brain was as unresponsive as the rest of her body.

What if she never moved again? A feeling of dread settled inside her.

Timelessness.

Nothingness.

How had she come to be here? Where was 'here?'

Slowly she began to reclaim her body, unsure if such a feat took minutes, or hours, or seconds, or days. She wriggled her fingers and toes, opened her mouth, looked at different points in the ceiling. Sounds became clearer...

Chattering...

Beeping...

A laugh...

Someone approached, shoes clicking against tile.

A woman appeared, dressed in nurse's blue.

"You're awake," she said, though her voice rang like echoing metal. She had a glow about her body, throbbing, that lanced through Kaiya's brain.

Kaiya closed her eyes, the afterimage still burnt into her hazy vision.

"Can you hear me?" came the nurse's voice.

"Yes," Kaiya said. At least her voice still worked.

The nurse stayed silent.

Kaiya didn't want to open her eyes, the pain of vision still subsiding, but she could feel that the nurse still stood beside her.

"Can you hear me?" the nurse said again, this time louder with a gentle push on the arm.

"Yes," Kaiya repeated, annoyed.

The nurse's fingers remained on her arm, an oddly warm sensation. Lethargy was descending, as though sleep were an inevitable, crashing wave that could not be escaped, no matter how hard she tried. The nurse removed her fingers and placed them in the bend of Kaiya's.

"If you can hear me, squeeze my fingers."

If only she could scream. The nurse refused to listen!

"I can hear you!" Kaiya said, waiting for the nurse to realise her mistake.

No reaction followed, and the nurse's fingers remained touching her own. Kaiya realised her predicament. She focused on squeezing the fingers with a sense of urgency, lest the nurse leave before an answer was adequately given.

Kaiya struggled against the invading lethargy, forcing her fingers to respond to continued instruction, each refusal to cooperate sending her into a further state of panic. She visualised her hand, tried to see her fingers wrapping around the nurse's, and managed the barest movement of one. If the nurse thought it a reflex motion, Kaiya would not have blamed her.

But the nurse squeezed her hand. "Wonderful," she said.

Kaiya could have cried, but the effort of moving her finger had drained her so completely that she fell straight back into darkness.

The first thing she heard was the hum of low chattering, soon superseded by the slow, steady beep of a machine. Kaiya opened her eyes and stared at the ceiling. Where was she? She had a vague sense that she had been here once before, in a dream... or perhaps it was just a mild déjà vu. The ceiling looked familiar, but only insofar that it was white. Though it wasn't simply white. There were patterns, like swirls, plastered into the ceiling, giving it a texture she hadn't noticed before.

Though she hadn't been here before...

She flexed her fingers, slow at first. They had great trouble keeping up with what she asked of them. She followed with her toes, and was soon flexing and stretching her feet while wiggling fingers and even twisting her wrists. She didn't know why these actions brought her so much joy, but she smiled with relief.

Her body felt stiff. Best thing for that would be to walk it off, and she tried to swing off her bed. Instead, she managed to bend her knee a little and grabbed the edge of the bed with one hand, grip weak.

Kaiya stretched her neck to survey her position, and a flood of discomfort descended. She returned her head to the pillow. The walking would not occur, but she contented herself with turning her neck slowly to each side and observing her surroundings. Beds stretched to either side of her, but she could tell there were more hidden behind drawn curtains. The doorless entry led to a corridor with a built-in desk. A woman sat behind it, looking busy, then glanced up and stared straight at her.

Kaiya didn't have the energy to turn away, and the woman rolled in her chair over to another part of the desk and began to speak into some hidden device.

A nurse pushed a stretcher down the corridor.

A hospital. That's where she was. Why hadn't she made that connection sooner?

How had she...

There she was, down there on the bed...

But...

Panic gripped her, throat tightening.

Memories flooded, a deluge of solid images. A hanging man, Bennett leading a procession, a concrete room with EVC technology, a little girl with rounded belly... what was her name?

Kaiya's heart raced as her breathing became shallow, and she began to shake.

There she was, again, on the bed... is that what she looked like?

Then inside herself again, without an inch of control, convulsing.

She saw faces, and light, the ward, the darkness of a room with a bloodied man cringing against a staircase, a sunrise over fields of lavender, Amelia's cracked head, a deserted beach, a soldier pressing down, invading her...

Kaiya thrashed against some invisible restraint, mouth forced open in a silent scream.

Some foreign power had her in a cage, deep in the recesses of her mind, circled by terror and flowers and sunlight and blood. All of existence splintered, fragments of her life rearranged into mosaics of nonsensical narratives. Everything faded, and even the cage of her entrapment disappeared into the expanse of nothing.

Light flooded her consciousness.

Pressure.

Her eyelids were being held open.

Instinct took over and she pulled away from the hand. The light disappeared, leaving a halo on her vision. She squeezed her eyes, as though she could expunge her headache through sheer will. A light dizziness filled her, the afterimage of wild spinning. Galaxies and sunlight raced behind her eyelids and she pressed her hands to her temples, attempting to squash the pain.

She wanted to ask what was happening, but all she could manage was a jumble of meaningless sound. She kicked off her sheets, frustrated by their oppressive warmth, then tried to speak again, with no better result. The halo of light faded from her vision, and Kaiya opened her eyes to stare at the ceiling.

The patterns danced.

"Can you hear me?" came a woman's voice. The nurse who had held the light.

"Yes," Kaiya said, though the sound that came out of her mouth was more a grunt than anything.

"I understand," the nurse said. "That's an improvement."

As though that should make her feel better.

Kaiya focused her mind and opened her mouth to speak. A string of sounds escaped, though they possessed a greater sense of form, now. The nurse waited with great patience as she practised.

"Hi," Kaiya said at last, somewhat slowly and overemphasised.

"Hi," the nurse said. "That's good work. You'll get it back in no time. I just have a few questions. Do you know where you are?"

"Hospital," Kaiya said, though she had great trouble pronouncing the consonants.

"Very good," the nurse said. "Do you know what day it is?"

Kaiya thought about the question. "Wednesday," she said with great difficulty.

"I see." The nurse wrote on her tablet. "Not to worry," she said.

What did that mean?

"Now," the nurse continued, "can you tell me your name?"

Kaiya stared away from the nurse and clenched her jaw. The memories were beginning to find their right places in her mind.

If it had been the police who captured her, then the police had brought her here... they would already know who she was. Resisting would be worthless.

"Kaiya," she said, leaving out her last name in defiance. She could at least put a small roadblock in the way of the nurse's questions.

The nurse scribbled on her writing tablet, eyes weighing.

"Alright," the nurse said, "and can you tell me how you're feeling? Any particular sensations?"

Kaiya took a few moments to search her body. Her headache remained, throbbing and dull, and it took great effort to stop herself sinking back into dizziness. The rest of her felt stiff, though she wished she could move. The thought of having to describe all of that frightened her, so she opted simply for, "Tired."

The nurse gave a curt smile. "I'm not surprised. You should get some more rest."

Kaiya watched the nurse walk away and drifted back to oblivion.

———

She woke to the sound of gentle hustle and bustle. A soft conversation somewhere in the room, with a touch of laughter, and cutlery clinking against bowls, or plates, or something. She opened her eyes to streaming mid-morning sun that illuminated each strange, textured pattern on the ceiling. She remembered a conversation... when had that been? She could have sworn it was nighttime not so long ago.

Two empty chairs waited by her bed. People had been watching her. The idea of it sent a chill through her body.

Kaiya looked around the ward. Other patients were eating, some of them with guests nearby. The man near the entranceway guffawed as his friends made jokes, the side of his healing burnt face shining in the sunlight. A black skull-and-crossbones eyepatch gave him a comical look. Kaiya stared at the plate of food sitting on the patient's tray, and noticed a tightness in her own stomach.

How long since she had eaten?

The old lady in the bed beside her gave a placid grin. "Morning, dear," she said. "Good to see you awake."

Kaiya nodded politely at the stranger.

"I like to hear people laughing," the old lady said. "Especially in here. How are you feeling?"

"Fine," Kaiya said automatically, voice stronger. "Hungry, actually."

The admission caused the feeling to grow. Her stomach twisted in protest, demanding attention.

"Yes, I'm not surprised. You've been here since before I arrived, and that was two days ago."

Kaiya sat herself up further on the bed. "Do you know how long I've been here?"

"I think three days... three and a half," the old lady said, then grinned. "I try not to eavesdrop, but that's what the nurse said to that friend of yours. Tilla?"

"Tilda," Kaiya said. "She knows I'm here?"

"She came this morning," the old lady said. "With a boy."

"Kormac?"

"I don't know," the old lady said. "But they never found out you were here until this morning, apparently."

"Where are they now?"

"Breakfast," the old lady said. "But they'll be back. You should relax until then. You're so tense all of a sudden. That's not healthy."

Kaiya explored the sensations in her own body and realised the old lady was right. She lay back on the bed and stared once more at the two empty chairs.

"I hoped you'd wake up before I had to leave," the old lady said. "I'm going today, once the doctor signs me off."

"Nothing serious?" Kaiya asked. There was something different about the old lady. Something charming. Something that didn't make Kaiya want to cut off her own ears to escape.

"Just what happens when you get to my age," the old lady said cheerfully. "It happens to everyone. It'll happen to you one day... if you can manage to get there."

The old lady grinned at Kaiya, eyes probing.

"You were at the riot, weren't you? That's how you got... those scars."

"What scars?" Kaiya said. She ran her fingers down her face, stopping on one cheek at a tiny bump that she explored further.

"It's nothing to worry about," the old lady said. "You can barely see them."

Kaiya ignored the old lady and traced a series of lines and distortions down her face and across her mouth. Her stomach kicked again, reminding her that she hadn't fulfilled her promise to look after it, and a few tears began to form. She let them slide down her cheek onto the rivulets of ruin before wiping them away.

"What's the matter?" the old lady said. "The doctors did a wonderful job. There's almost nothing left to see."

"But you can still see it, can't you?" Kaiya said. "It's still there."

"Of course it's still there, but it's nothing to be upset about. What will that achieve?"

Kaiya sniffed and stared up at the ceiling. "Maybe..."

Maybe that's why Kormac wasn't there. Maybe he'd already decided to leave when he saw her that morning.

"My daughter had an accident when she was in high school," the old lady said. "That was a long time ago. She was in chemistry, playing with... nitrates, I think. I don't understand the science. But something happened, some kind of fume built up, and the fumes caught fire. They exploded. Set fire to her arm and neck. The teacher tried to put the fire out but by the time she did, all my daughter's skin from her upper arm to the bottom of her cheek was melting.

"I didn't see her until the hospital. She was screaming and screaming – I'll never forget that sound. The doctors anaesthetised her, and I waited until they'd finished surgery. Felt like ages, at the time. After a few days you could only see a bit here and there where the fire had hurt her, but everything was different after that.

"She didn't want to see her friends anymore. Wouldn't go out. It didn't matter how much I encouraged or tried to reason with her, the answer was always the same – no. She was totally convinced that nobody would want to see her, that everyone would think she was ugly."

Kaiya looked back towards the old lady, whose sagging skin wrinkled up in a wistful smile.

"It was two months before I could get her to go to school again. She covered herself up completely so nobody could see, but then when she got there everyone wanted to. They kept asking her to show them. She came home crying for a whole week, but then when she went back the second week, she decided she'd let everyone see them. After that, nobody bothered her again. They lost interest."

"Why did she give in?" Kaiya asked. "It wasn't their business."

"No, it wasn't," the old lady said, "but I don't think that matters. All that matters is what she got out of it, and after her second week back, everything went back to normal. She grew up, studied, had boyfriends, had a career, got married, had children."

"Just the same as if she didn't have the scars," Kaiya said testily. The old lady was just like Tilda. "I know what you're trying to tell me. You want me to focus on all the good parts. The stuff that's not injured."

"Not at all," the old lady said. "It wasn't just the same as if the accident had never happened. Nothing can ever be just the same after that. It doesn't help to deny it. She didn't have her life because of what happened, or in spite of it. For a few months, the accident meant everything to her. But after that? It was just another thing that happened, like breaking up, or... walking the dog. A part of who she was."

Kaiya grimaced. "Sounds nice in theory."

The old lady laughed huskily. "You're still feeling your face," she said.

Kaiya realised she was doing just that, and quickly dropped her hands. "You really think they're not that noticeable?"

"I do," the old lady said, "but that's not the point."

Kaiya scratched her cheek where the tears had dried. Some people could never give a straight answer. "I *was* at the riot," she said. "I can't remember how I got here, though."

The old lady gave a murmur of recognition. "So you were part of *that* crowd."

"That crowd," Kaiya bristled automatically at the judgmental tone. Old lady was probably a collab— "You must think I'm stupid," Kaiya said, pushing aside the unwanted thought.

"Stupid? No, my dear, I don't think stupidity has anything to do with it. Even the smartest people make bad decisions. But you probably don't think it was a bad decision, do you?"

Kaiya gazed at the old lady and frowned. "No. I don't. We did the right thing. You don't think the... collaborators should be able to get away with what they did, do you?"

The old lady smiled. "I'm not so sure that's the right question."

A movement at the entranceway distracted Kaiya.

Tilda walked into the ward, arms folded and shoulders hunched, followed closely by Kormac.

The air surrounding Kaiya lightened, and she sat up straighter in her bed again, ignoring the old lady, who followed her gaze.

"I fucking hate you," Tilda said with tears as she bent down and squeezed Kaiya tightly.

"Same to you," Kaiya said, her own emotion bubbling to the surface.

She looked over to Kormac as Tilda pulled away, standing at the far corner of the bed. His eyes flickered back and forth between her and the rest of the ward, body stiff.

He didn't want to look at her or touch her.

She was ugly.

"How did you find out I was here?" she asked Tilda, trying to mask the horror of her realisation.

"Benjamin," Tilda said. "He came by this morning, really early. Said he would have come sooner if he'd known, but he didn't find out until last night. He seemed really... on edge."

"Did he say why?" Kaiya asked.

"No," Tilda said, "but the last couple of days have been really bad. It's... like Bennett all over again. There are Taskforce police everywhere. Seven new units from Akheron, another five coming in the next few days. I've seen Leth police fighting each other in the boulevard. There's still fires every night, more hangings."

"People are too afraid to go out," Kormac added, still scanning the room. "I've seen this before. It happened at the... place I was in."

Kaiya stared at Kormac along with Tilda, waiting for him to say more, but no further explanations came.

His presence made her uneasy.

"So what's Benjamin doing about it?" Kaiya asked.

"I don't know!" Tilda said. "I'm not friends with him – I didn't ask. Why would he tell me anyway?"

"Probably the reason there are more Taskforce police," Kaiya said. No matter how hard good people like her pushed, the traitors always pushed back harder. The only consolation was that maybe, somewhere in Leth, those suffering the evils of the collaborators would have that suffering eased by the knowledge that there were still people who would punish the wrongdoers.

"Well, whatever happens, I think you made your point the other night," Tilda said, unable to hide her disapproval.

"What kind of numbers?" Kaiya asked.

Tilda sighed. "Hundreds. Mostly protestors, but there were police, and just random people."

"You mean the collaborators."

"I'm not going to argue with you about this," Tilda said. "I don't care anymore. I'm sick of hearing you go on and on and on about it."

"You can't—"

"Stop it!" Tilda said. "If you mention collaborators or traitors or Bennett one more time, I swear I will put you under for another two days."

Kaiya examined the hurt on Tilda's face, trying to understand why she would still be so supportive of the enemy.

"They killed Amelia," Kaiya said.

Tilda bit back whatever it was she really wanted to say. "I know."

"They burnt your house down," Kaiya said. "The police. They're not good people."

Something flickered across Tilda's face. "Oh?"

"Don't you understand?" Kaiya said. "This is why we have to—"

"Kaiya, I warned you." Tilda stepped back from the bed, and Kaiya shut her mouth. No matter how hard she tried... Tilda stared out the windows opposite and shook her head. She looked so resigned.

Kaiya glanced across at the old lady, who lay still in her bed, eyes closed and grinning at the ceiling.

"Do you want food?" Kormac asked all of a sudden, turning a gaze of rigid intensity towards Kaiya.

His eyes pinned her to the bed, and she struggled to make sound as her stomach grumbled. "Yes," she said at last, and watched Kormac turn to leave. He scratched his arm idly while he scanned his surroundings.

"Tilda," Kaiya whispered when Kormac had left. She didn't want the old lady to overhear her next question. Tilda took a few moments to respond, but came and sat beside her on the bed. "Am I... what does my face look like?"

"What does your face look like?" Tilda cocked her head. "It looks like your face..."

"No, but... the scars," Kaiya said. "Kormac's acting weird. Won't look at me properly."

"I wouldn't worry about that," Tilda said. "Kormac's... I told you what I think Kormac needs, but you won't listen to me."

"But don't you think—"

"Kaiya, your face is fine," Tilda said.

"Has Kormac been taking the supplements?"

"Yes," Tilda said with a stern expression. "Much more consistently when I'm the one doing it, I might add. We need to talk about this, Kaiya. Kormac keeps... talking about weird things. Saying everything's a trap, that people are watching the house. The whole first night you didn't come back he was pacing up and down the hallway, shouting about how you were a Tarkinian spy. I had to lock myself in my room, he just... last night he wouldn't take the supplements. He's been going on about how I'm trying to poison him."

"How do you know he's not right?" Kaiya asked. "Not about you, but the doctor. I met that doctor—"

"Kaiya, stop it," Tilda said. "Listen to me – take it seriously. He *needs* help. He *needs* to go somewhere, to see someone."

"You're wrong," Kaiya said, shaking her head. "We don't need anyone else, we just—"

"I can't talk to you when you're like this." Tilda stood up, voice lowered. "I can't deal with this... self-delusion anymore. The selfishness. Do you have any idea what the last two days have been like? I had no idea what happened to you. Kormac's been off the rails. I came to stay with you because I thought I could..."

Tilda began to cry, face quivering, and took a deep, ragged breath.

"Just... do what you need to do. I don't want to be around you anymore."

Tilda turned her back and walked out into the corridor.

The ward turned quiet. Kaiya tried to hide her face as she glanced around at all the patients doing their best to ignore what had just happened. Tilda had been completely unfair! Making it out as if everything were her fault... she was the one who was standing up for her!

The old lady in the next bed didn't bother to hide her interest.

Kaiya packed away the tendrils of rage and disappointment into a little ball, shoving it deep into some secret compartment of her soul. Tilda would come around, in time. She would see how important Amelia's work had been.

When Kormac arrived with the food, Kaiya's stomach knotted itself in excitement.

"They said they could bring it, but I wanted to do it myself," Kormac said, his face changed from when she last saw him. He smiled down at her as he placed the tray onto her lap, and planted a kiss on her forehead before dragging one of the chairs closer.

"Thank you," she said, trying to penetrate the depths of his eyes. Whatever he hid there, she would break down that wall little by little. She knew him better than anyone. Tilda would never understand Kormac, not like she did.

The omelette on her plate smelt delicious. Bacon, cheese,

olives, semi-dried tomatoes, red onion, chives, assorted herbs... real food! Her mother had always said the hospital had its own farm in the basements.

By the end of the dish – three minutes, at most – Kaiya was forcing the last of it down her throat. Her body struggled, insisting that it wanted no more, but she refused to listen. *She* would be master. She groaned to herself after the final, tiniest scraps had been consumed, and sank down into her bed. She stared out the windows, sprawled and replete, breathing heavier after such a great expense of effort.

Kormac took the plate and placed it on the bedside table.

"I saw Tilda," he said. "When I was coming back. She looked upset."

Kaiya watched workers milling about on the roof of a nearby building. "She's different," Kaiya said. "I'm surprised she even came. She never leaves the house."

Kormac rested his head on Kaiya's sheet-covered leg, gazing up at her face. "Do you ever ask her why?"

"Of course I do," Kaiya said, "but she won't tell me. She's a hypocrite. Always telling me how I should feel and act, that I should talk to someone – maybe she should take her own advice."

Kormac stayed silent, but took her hand in his and placed it against his lips.

The gesture melted a little of the frost that Tilda's unfairness had wrought, and Kaiya closed her eyes, heavy in the aftermath of her eating.

"Everything's going to be fine," she whispered to Kormac. "You'll see."

His lips pressed into her skin once more, and soon Kaiya danced by herself in a field of endless lavender.

Somewhere in the distance, a woman was speaking.

"I just want to check how the cornea is recovering," she said. "There we go."

Kaiya opened her eyes. The world was hazy for a few moments, but soon she could see clearly out the windows again, and rubbed away the accumulation of half a day's rheum. The southern sky had turned a pale crimson, and deep shadows fell from the tops of the buildings visible from her position.

"Now, just look straight at this," the woman's voice came from nearby.

Kaiya glanced across towards the man with the skull-and-crossbones eyepatch. He had taken it off, and complied with the doctor's orders.

"This is good," the doctor said, "for what it is, of course. How does it feel?"

The patient struggled to form an answer. "Still a bit weird. Uncomfortable."

"Blurry?" the doctor asked.

"Yeah, definitely."

"That's to be expected," the doctor said. "There's not a lot more we can do, at this stage, to repair the damage to the optic nerve, but hopefully the new components will settle in and we can do some digital modifications to get your vision as close as possible to before."

The man grunted in response and put his eyepatch back on.

"I'm going to visit you again in the morning, and then I think we'll be ready to discharge you. It'll probably take a few days for us to grow the new lens, so we'll have to organise a time for you to come in and replace the temporary one. In the meantime, I want a guarantee you won't be jumping in the way of any more stun batons. Sound good?"

The man grinned and promised he would be more careful.

Kaiya's gaze shifted to the old lady's bed beside her, neat and fresh. Ready for a new patient.

The two chairs Kormac and Tilda had used remained by her own bed, empty.

"So you're awake," the doctor said as she approached.

Kaiya murmured agreement. What was she supposed to say to that? The doctor could see for herself.

"How are you feeling?"

"Fine," Kaiya said, and realised that was largely true. She repositioned herself on the bed, flexing her fingers and toes and finding them all perfectly responsive.

"You certainly look a lot better than you did when you first got here. I operated on you," she explained.

"I guess I should thank you, then," Kaiya said before touching the faint lines on her face again.

"That's my job," the doctor said. "Wouldn't trade it for any other. I've treated a lot of people like you over the last few days. A lot of your victims, as well. Frankly, I find it disgusting, but that's irrelevant to me doing what I'm here to do. So if you want to thank me for anything, thank me for keeping my personal feelings outside of the operating theatre. Don't look so shocked. You're just like the rest of them. Maybe this'll teach you a lesson."

Kaiya stared dumbfounded at the doctor, who went about reading from a tablet as if she hadn't said anything. Her face was a blank slate.

"You feel ready for visitors?" she asked, staring straight down at her without a skerrick of shame.

"I had some this morning," Kaiya said, trying to sound unaffected by the doctor's unabashed demeanour. "They must have gone."

"Well, you've had another patient asking for you. No idea why – I certainly wouldn't be around you if I didn't have to be. I'll send her down."

The doctor turned and strode confidently out of the ward,

leaving Kaiya with a thumping heart and a taste of acid in the mouth.

Anyone who had opinions like that had no qualms about broadcasting where their true loyalties lay. Amelia would want to know—

Kaiya glared at the ceiling, straight into the memory of Amelia's blood-soaked face.

When she left the hospital, she would have to find Jerome. They must have decided on a course of action in the event of Amelia's assassination.

Ten minutes passed with nothing but the occasional outburst of chatter from the corridor, and the incessant beep of a machine from the end of the ward. The ten minutes seemed like an hour, and Kaiya prepared herself to give up her curiosity as to who wanted to visit, until a diminutive figure stopped at the entranceway.

Dressed in a loose frock, Masuma stood hesitant, staring not quite at Kaiya, but near enough for Kaiya to know her intent. The presence of the girl forced a smile on Kaiya's face, and she sat up in her bed, heart growing lighter.

She beckoned Masuma closer, and the girl crept forward with soundless footsteps until she was at the side of the bed.

"Sit with me," Kaiya said, making room, and Masuma lifted herself awkwardly onto the bed.

Kaiya stared at the swollen stomach no frock could hide.

"You look... radiant," she said, and meant it. Masuma's skin glowed, far healthier than it had been when they met.

"Thanks," Masuma said, as if she were afraid of using her voice.

"I'm happy to see you," Kaiya said.

Masuma gave an embarrassed titter and stared at the sheets.

"How did you know I was here?" Kaiya asked.

Masuma shrugged and started to trace patterns on the bed. Kaiya waited patiently for a solid minute, allowing the girl space to answer. "I asked," Masuma said, almost as if she were questioning herself.

What did that even mean – she asked? Asked who? How did she know to ask? What did she ask? Kaiya watched her, waiting for more information, but none was forthcoming.

"Why did you think I'd be here? Are you a psychic?"

Masuma grinned. "No, I... thought maybe you came again, but the nurse said no one had come, but I told her your name cause I've never heard anyone called that before and she said she'd tell me if you came and then she said you were here and she said what you looked like and I said it was you and she said I could see you if I wanted to she was very nice she's the nicest one and then I came here but..."

Whatever else the girl had wanted to say in her near-breathless answer, it faded away as she continued playing with the sheets. She didn't seem aware of what she was doing.

Kaiya watched the unconscious pattern-making, a curious feeling growing inside her.

Was that... shame?

She had promised Masuma she'd visit again. She had *wanted* to see her again. But Masuma had waited... and waited... and she had never come.

Kaiya steeled herself against overwhelming guilt. Masuma had come to see her without even knowing if the desire was reciprocated. That's why she had been so afraid.

"I'm sorry," Kaiya said.

At first Masuma didn't seem to register what she had said, but slowly the pattern-making stopped, and Masuma sat still on the bed. Her gaze shifted towards Kaiya ever so slightly, but the ability to make it all the way hadn't yet come.

"It's ok," Masuma whispered.

"No," Kaiya said, "it's not. Come here."

Masuma hesitated for a few moments before crawling into the space Kaiya had indicated with an open arm. The girl lost her stiffness as she rolled in towards Kaiya, resting her face against her breast. Kaiya wrapped her arm around Masuma and held tight, while the girl's stomach pressed against her side.

Kaiya wondered what she was even doing.

Whatever it was, trickles of... something... flowed through her. The trickles felt familiar, like something she had felt with Kormac, but they weren't the same. They burnt through her in a different way, as though they bound her to some divine duty she didn't yet understand, one she had no fear of.

"Have you been reading?" Kaiya asked.

"Sometimes," Masuma said. "Reading's hard."

"I guess it would be," Kaiya said, and as her fury at the Tarkinians grew, so too did the burning duty inside her. "If you bring me a book I can read it to you, if you like. Or maybe we can learn how to read, again?"

Masuma gave a half smile.

"I'll come in every day and see you, I promise. I'll read you more fairytales, if you like, or maybe there's other books you'd enjoy. Would you like that?"

Masuma nodded, face still pressed against Kaiya, but she didn't look all that convinced.

Another knife of shame sliced through Kaiya, and she lowered her head just enough to place a lingering kiss on the girl's hair.

"I'm sorry," she whispered again.

Masuma didn't say anything, but Kaiya felt the girl's weight fall further into her.

Outside, the sky of pale crimson faded inch by inch to ink.

Kaiya thought briefly of how truly odd the situation was. Stripping away all else but fact, she barely knew the girl, nor did the girl really know her. There had been no familial tie, no previous acquaintance or preconceived desire to find someone like her. It had simply... happened. A moment of connection through the knowledge of shared experience, if different by degree.

But what was the point of stripping away all else but fact? Those tendrils of warmth and lashings of guilt cocooned the pair of them, no matter how illogical such a reality seemed to her brain. There were times for sober reflection, and times for passion. The trick was to *know* the time for each.

Masuma's barely-developed chest rose and fell with deep breaths.

What had life shown her in three years? Where had she slept? What had she worn? What had she eaten? Who did she talk to? Who was looking for her now? What would happen when the time came for her to bring forth new life – life she could barely be expected to care for or even want? Did she even understand?

Kaiya palmed away stray tears, making sure Masuma's eyes were closed. The girl didn't need to see her weakness. Not when she was relying on her in... whatever way this was. And whatever happened, Kaiya knew she had to keep her promise.

If she'd never gone out to support Amelia, she could have kept the first one...

"Are you awake?" Kaiya whispered.

Masuma's head moved slightly to indicate assent. Her arm now draped across Kaiya's body, and Kaiya held the languid hand, making circles on the back of it with her thumb.

"Have the nurses told you anything about what's happening?" Kaiya asked. "Have they notified your parents?"

Masuma didn't answer, but she did open her eyes.

Kaiya waited for half a minute before asking again, this time a little more forcefully.

"They had the *Rapture*," Masuma said flatly.

The news didn't even come as a surprise. After everything else Masuma had been through, what was another disappointment? That was the problem with Leth. If it wasn't full of collaborators, then it was full of cowards. The confrontation with Kormac's mother replayed itself in her mind, but so too did desire return...

The thought of *Rapture* brought with it that familiar longing. If she could just remember what she had seen... maybe she wouldn't need to go again.

Maybe next time she *would* remember...

At least if she had the full *Rapture*, she wouldn't be abdicating any responsibilities.

No, it wasn't so bad. In fact, she understood why Masuma's parents had opted for perfection, but she couldn't bear to tell that to the girl.

"Couldn't you get the *Rapture*, too?" Kaiya asked. "Because you've been in Tarkinia. That's what I heard."

"I don't want it," Masuma said, and Kaiya had to restrain herself from launching immediately into a list of reasons *Rapture* was worthwhile.

If Masuma had the treatment, would she still be there in the girl's mind?

The idea seemed less appealing, now.

Kaiya squeezed Masuma's shoulder affectionately. "So what happens now?"

"Don't know," Masuma said. "It's my birthday next week."

The change of subject told Kaiya all she needed to know about the direction of that conversation. "How exciting," she said, trying to inject some level of enthusiasm into the girl. There had been a spark of it before, stuck within the traces of a smile, and Kaiya didn't want herself to become associated in Masuma's mind with people who still had an emotionally deleterious effect.

"I'm turning thirteen," Masuma continued.

"Really?" Kaiya said. "We'll have to have a big party, then."

Masuma gave another titter of embarrassment, lips curving gently.

Kaiya looked up to the ceiling, with its odd-patterned texture, and visualised the children's wards decorated with balloons and streamers and vibrant colours. Laughter rang, and crumbs littered the floor as children stuffed food into their mouths.

She dismissed the idea. This was a hospital, not a party house.

Still... she would have to do something.

An old man approached Kaiya, wearing the volunteer shirt of a hospital orderly. Dinnertime had arrived, and Kaiya made her selection.

"And will you be eating too, missy?" the orderly asked Masuma.

She froze, averting her eyes towards Kaiya, who answered, "Yes" for her.

Kaiya felt Masuma relax again, and watched the orderly move around the ward taking orders. The man with the eyepatch near the entrance waved over at her with a grin, and Kaiya lifted her hand in response. He must have fought on her side, with injuries like that. She needed no more information to know he was worthy of recognition.

Through the entranceway, the receptionist's attention was caught by someone Kaiya couldn't see. The receptionist looked straight in towards her and pointed, speaking to the hidden stranger, and Kaiya felt her hold on Masuma tighten without thought.

A Chief Inspector walked through the entranceway and looked straight at her. He had that unbreakable expression certain officers developed after so many years in the force, the one she'd been afraid of when she was a child and her father introduced her to colleagues. She knew that face...

Joseph. Benjamin's lapdog.

The dull throb of his kick impressed its memory on her shin, if not in reality, at least in her mind. She'd done nothing to deserve that!

"Hello," he said to Masuma as he approached Kaiya's bed.

"What do you want?" Kaiya asked, sitting up as best she could without disturbing Masuma too much.

Joseph looked straight into her eyes, his own flashing with anger.

"I'm going to need to speak to you alone, Kaiya."

She weighed the situation in her mind. Joseph was not a man to be crossed. She planted another kiss on Masuma's hair, and told the girl to wait until Joseph left. The girl lingered before making her way out into the corridor and looking back in with a blank expression.

"Who's the girl?" Joseph asked.

"None of your business," Kaiya said.

Joseph shook his head in frustration. "If that's the way you want to play this, then I won't bat an eyelid when they throw you in jail. So if you know what's good for you, you'll cooperate. I'm sick of your nonsense. Understand?"

Kaiya set her jaw firm and stared past Joseph. She gave a curt nod.

"I'll ask you one more time. Who's the girl?"

Kaiya held out for a few drawn-out seconds, but relented as she wondered how serious Joseph had been about jail. "From the camps," she said.

"And how do you know her?"

"I don't, really."

Joseph peered at her and took one of the seats. Kaiya knew exactly what he was doing – setting himself back down to her level after asserting his control over the situation. As if that would work on her! She knew all their tricks.

Though he did look more relaxed, now.

"What's her name?" Joseph asked.

"Masuma."

He sighed thoughtfully. "Thank you. I'm going to be your biggest ally from now on, so you're going to need to be able to tell me anything. Understand?"

"My biggest ally?" Kaiya scoffed. "You think I'm going to let some collaborator—"

"Be quiet," Joseph said, and Kaiya closed her mouth straight away. "The only reason I'm here is because of Benjamin. If it weren't for him, this would be going down very differently. So be grateful. Benjamin wants you to know that Bennett is gone."

Kaiya sat up straighter in her bed. "He sent him to Akheron?"

"No, Kaiya. Gone. Freed by loyalists."

Kaiya punched the bed and swore loud enough that every other head in the ward turned towards her. "When did this happen? This is your fault – you! Benjamin put *you* in charge of keeping Bennett there."

Fury crossed Joseph's eyes, but his voice remained measured. "It's a pity I was called out the night it happened, then, isn't it? From memory, a bunch of vigilante idiots decided it would be a good idea to go out and ransack the town. You wouldn't know anything about that, would you?"

"We were *doing* something," Kaiya said, "unlike you!"

"No, of course not," Joseph said. "Cause we just sit around all day and play cards, correct? Or talk to Tarkinians."

"And what are you doing about it right now? What are you doing about Bennett?"

"We will deal with Bennett," Joseph said. "We have multiple leads, and I will be making sure he is captured."

"But—"

"You don't understand the gravity of your situation, do you?" Joseph said. "Nor the gravity of what you've done. So let me make this clear for you. Right now, you are responsible for Bennett's disappearance, along with all those other fools from your escapade. Furthermore, you are under arrest for attempted murder. Is that clear enough for you?"

Kaiya rolled her eyes, but Joseph's gaze didn't falter.

"You're kidding," Kaiya said.

"I'm not."

Her stomach churned with the sudden weight of an ancient cannonball. "You're lying," she said, throat constricted.

"When you are well enough recovered, tomorrow likely, you will be taken into custody. You will be arraigned under emergency provisions of the Civil Order Defence Act and face court. What you do in that visit is what I am here to discuss."

Kaiya struggled to speak, heart thumping. "What... I want to see Benjamin. I need to talk to Benjamin."

"I am here in Benjamin's place," Joseph said. "This is what he wanted."

"This is a joke," Kaiya said. "You can't be serious. I haven't done anything wrong!"

Joseph raised his eyebrows. "I don't have time to argue irrelevant points with you, Kaiya. You need to ask yourself one question – do you want to go to jail or not?"

"I shouldn't have to be answering that question. I haven't—"

"You don't have any other option," Joseph said. "There are two possible answers to that question, and you have to pick one. There is no way out of this."

Kaiya licked her lips and stared at Joseph, trying to find any trace of a lie. The entire situation was ludicrous! No one would send *her* to jail. He had to be bluffing.

"I want proof," she said. "I want to talk to Benjamin."

Joseph pulled a holo projector out of his uniform and handed it to Kaiya. She turned it on and read the warrant for her arrest.

"But I didn't..." she said, voice fading. "I didn't want to kill anyone. I didn't mean... I just..."

"This is your last chance to answer my question," Joseph

said. "If the next word out of your mouth isn't yes or no, I'm walking out and you're on your own."

Kaiya's thoughts turned to the train station. She could make a run for it after Joseph left. Would anyone be watching for her? She could go back home, grab a few things... bring Kormac and Tilda with her. They would come, surely. So would Masuma – there was nothing keeping her there. They would all go together, maybe to the north. Somewhere—

"No," Kaiya whispered in defeat. "I don't want to go to jail."

Joseph nodded. "Good. Listen to me, then, because you know that neither Benjamin nor I have the power to decide what the judge will do. Benjamin is willing to help you if you cooperate with me, and his testimony will have some weight, but nothing is guaranteed. Understand?"

"Yes," she muttered.

"Get rid of that attitude," Joseph said. "That's the first thing. I don't care how much it kills your pride, when you walk into that room tomorrow, you will be the most contrite girl who's ever walked the face of this planet. I'm the investigating officer, so you have everything in your favour, you understand? When the charge is read, there's going to be some formalities you don't have to worry about. I'm going to say that you've elected to plead guilty to assault occasioning grievous bodily harm. When the judge turns to you, that's all you're going to say. Don't try to justify yourself, just don't say anything. You plead guilty, and that's it."

"No!" Kaiya said. "I'm not going to plead guilty for something I didn't do. I was defending myself!"

"From what?" Joseph said. "From a man inside his own home?"

"He's a—"

"I don't care what he is or isn't," Joseph said, "and neither does the judge."

"I won't plead guilty," Kaiya said. "It's not right. You're pressuring me. You're not allowed to do that, I know it. You're supposed to give me legal representation. You—"

Joseph burst out laughing, a harsh and bitter sound.

Kaiya glared at him.

"Hypocrisy is my favourite form of humour," Joseph said.

"What's that supposed to mean?"

He shook his head. "If you want to fight, then go ahead. But don't expect to see the outside world any time soon. We have the victim's testimony and his injuries, we have the daughter's testimony, we have the testimony of a police officer, and we already have your DNA thanks to your being here. There's nothing in the world that could break the case we have against you, so why don't you step up and start taking responsibility for yourself?"

Kaiya slammed her fist on the bed, wishing the action would bring more sound. Every possibility she perceived revealed itself as a hollow promise. There was nothing she could do but dance to Joseph's tune, and to Benjamin's by extension.

"Fine," she said. "Whatever you want."

Joseph stood with a curt nod. "Then I'll see you tomorrow, if the doctor is accurate."

Kaiya ignored him, but he lingered, studying her face as if he wanted to etch it in his memory. She couldn't help but glance at him and notice the secretive, melancholy eyes. He dropped his gaze and turned to walk away.

"It was you, wasn't it?" Kaiya said, fragments of her memory sparking off each other to create understanding. "I remember your voice. You were the one giving orders on western boulevard."

Joseph pierced her with his eyes. "Yes. I was. But giving orders is different to having them followed."

They stared at each other. As much as she hated the sensation, Kaiya couldn't deny a certain level of... curiosity for the Chief Inspector.

"Why are you helping me?" she asked. "What are you getting out of this? A promotion?"

Joseph smirked wearily. "I don't know. I ask myself the same question every time I have to speak to you."

With that passing barb, he left, and Kaiya stared through to the corridor. All the murmurings and beeps of hospital boredom returned to her attention.

Masuma appeared, looking cautiously into the ward, and Kaiya indicated for her to come closer. The girl climbed back onto the bed, and Kaiya did her best not to show the terror erupting inside herself. She sang softly, barely more than breath against Masuma's hair, more to distract herself than anything else, though Masuma closed her eyes and smiled at the sound:

> *Will you pick the lavender,*
> *the young and blooming lavender...*

When dinner came, Masuma devoured both of the meals. Kaiya was too sick to eat.

13

KAIYA SAT NUMB OUTSIDE JOSEPH'S OFFICE, HOLDING KORMAC'S hand.

The entire hearing had been surreal, almost as if she didn't even exist. The judge spoke, Joseph spoke, some stranger who was supposedly her counsel spoke, other people spoke. Endless words about her and rarely ever to her, a letter from Benjamin the judge said she took into consideration but never revealed the contents of, and always the looks from everyone in the room. Glances here and there, penetrating and judgmental, appraising her, weighing her. Everyone so civilised.

"Why didn't Tilda come?" she asked.

"I don't know," Kormac said. "That's the fifth time you've asked me."

"She should have been here. If she doesn't want to see me anymore, then she should go. But if she's still at my place, then she could at least come here and support me... see what kind of farce we're up against."

Kormac sighed and closed his eyes.

"What's wrong?" Kaiya asked.

"Nothing," he said.

Kaiya squeezed his hand tighter. "Tell me. Please."

"Another time," he said. "But you're lucky, Kaiya. Do you realise that?"

She let go of Kormac's hand and folded her arms. "He deserved it."

They sat in silence until Joseph appeared.

"Just you," he said to Kaiya, and shared a brief nod with Kormac.

She walked into the Chief Inspector's office and sat quietly, unsure of her position. The court had appointed him as her mentor, whatever that meant. She just knew that if he stayed happy with her progress – what she was supposed to be making progress on, she didn't know – then she wouldn't face a custodial sentence. If that's the way they wanted to play the game, then so be it.

He already acted like they were old friends. An odd part of her understood the feeling, but she didn't know why it existed. Perhaps an unwanted association with Benjamin.

"You did well," Joseph said from across his desk.

Kaiya avoided his gaze and looked at the line of his holos. Most contained a woman she assumed must be his wife, and multiple shots of a boy as both baby and toddler. A few old digital photo frames displayed flat representations of people who must have all been dead by now, or at least *well* into their old age.

"So that is your fiancé?" Joseph asked.

"Yeah. Kormac."

"He came back from the camps, correct?"

"Yes," Kaiya said.

"And your parents?"

"Why are you asking me these questions?" Kaiya asked.

"Because you're going to be seeing a lot of me, from now on." Joseph reclined in his chair. "I could ask Benjamin anything I need to know, but I figure it's better to go to the source. Sometimes information becomes... outdated, if you know what I mean."

She peered at him from the corner of her eye. He was holding something back.

"I'm still waiting for my parents," Kaiya said at last.

"What do you think they'd say about today?"

"They don't need to know."

"That's always an option," Joseph said. "Though I'm not sure you've thought that one through very thoroughly, given who your father is."

Kaiya frowned at a sudden thought. "Benjamin said something the other day, when he told me why he had pointed me out to you. Something about respect for my father. Did you ever meet him?"

Joseph's eyes flickered over towards the holos on the side of his desk. "I did. You should be very proud of him. I thought he was a great man."

Pride seeped through her body, but she couldn't help notice the Chief Inspector's use of past tense.

"He's coming back," she said. "I know it."

"I believe you," Joseph said with a smile. "And I look forward to that day."

There was something faraway about his eyes. His voice gave away more than idle curiosity.

"Do you understand the sentence you have been given?"

"I didn't think there would be one so quickly," Kaiya said.

"Justice on steroids, I like to call it. All the rage in this country at the moment." Joseph's distaste was plain to see. "Spurred on by people like you, I might add. You should congratulate yourself. Your government is giving you what you want."

"I'll believe that when I see Bennett's body in mid-air," Kaiya said, "along with all the other ones like him in this town."

Joseph studied her. "Do you think Bennett is relevant to your case?"

"Of course he is," Kaiya said. "What kind of a question is that? That's like asking if the sun is relevant to a tree growing."

"At least the tree grows," Joseph said. "It's not stubborn like you."

"Don't pretend you know me. Just cause you and Benjamin have little chats from time to time."

Joseph gave a small smile and called up a holoscreen from his desk. He swiped his hand through the air, exploring the file tree until he came across a folder and pinched it open. Kaiya had to interpret its contents from back to front position, but everything inside pertained to her.

"I can read you everything you and your friend Tilda have sent each other since childhood, if you like? Or maybe we can look through some of your high school holos? In fact, I quite like this dress. You must be about seven, correct?"

Joseph reached within the holoscreen field and turned the image of Kaiya around so she could see.

"How did you get these?" she said, beginning to feel queasy. The thought of him reading her private correspondence stripped her bare.

"Data capture unit," Joseph said. "All data in or out of Leth was stored in a localweb only semi-connected to the Network. The link closed when the virus was injected, so it's more like an archive these days. No new information since that point in time. There are strict rules around accessing the unit, but... you're fine with me having all this, correct? There are times when action must come before thought, wouldn't you agree?"

Kaiya frowned. She felt like Joseph was making a point, but she couldn't see what it was. She stayed silent.

"I haven't read through your letters," Joseph said. "I promise you I have better things to do with my time than subject myself to that, but let's make this clear – if there's something I don't know about you, you have two options – tell me, or let me find out for myself. You can decide which is the less invasive."

"This isn't fair," Kaiya said.

"Fair would be putting you in jail," Joseph said. "Instead, you get a lucky break – me. You have Benjamin to thank for that."

Kaiya wished she could find the words to express the outrage building inside her, but no thoughts seemed capable of coalescing into a coherent sentence.

Joseph flicked off the holoscreen. "Let's talk about the riot."

"It wasn't supposed to be a riot," Kaiya said. "We were demonstrating, that's all. You made it a riot."

"I see," Joseph said. "And how did we do that?"

"Are you kidding me? I was there – you killed Amelia!"

Joseph frowned. "So you're saying that, before then, the crowd was entirely peaceful? No one assaulted police officers?"

"That doesn't mean you have to start killing people," Kaiya said.

"That girl wasn't targeted, Kaiya. That was an accident."

"Her name's Amelia," Kaiya said.

"I know that."

"And what a convenient accident." Kaiya sneered. "You want me to be honest with you? Then don't lie to me. I hate people lying to me. I know what kind of training you have to do before you get to use anti-riot gear. There is no way someone could have *accidentally* hit Amelia. No way."

"You're absolutely sure of that?"

"Yes!" Kaiya said, banging her hand on the table.

"A lot has changed here since your father left," Joseph said. "You should know that."

"Really? I never would have guessed you were working with the Tarkinians for the last six years."

"It's not as simple as that," Joseph said.

"I think it is. I think it's *very* simple."

Kaiya lifted her chin and stared at Joseph's nose. She couldn't quite bring herself to meet his eyes.

"There is an alternative explanation," Joseph said, "an even simpler one. Training regimes changed significantly upon Bennett's rise."

"So now you're blaming Bennett?"

"I'm not blaming anyone, Kaiya. You are. I'm just stating facts."

Kaiya leaned back and folded her arms. "I don't believe you." There was no use arguing with the Chief Inspector. He was as deeply ingrained in the culture of collaboration as anyone else in the building.

Infected.

She stared at the holos on his desk, eyes lingering over a particular one of the woman she assumed to be his wife with a much younger version of the Chief Inspector. Now that she gave more attention to the holos, she could see they were all from before the war. The younger Joseph smiled with larrikin sensibility, face unlined, hair without grey, his demeanour mischievous. Did the man in that holo hold any regret for the path he had taken? He could have fought until the end, had he wanted to. Returning to the force betrayed a weakness of character. Such a man could not be expected to be honest with himself or others about his own actions or those of his fellow officers.

She looked up. Joseph was staring at the same holo.

"He's been disciplined," he said, almost like an afterthought. "The officer who fired the canister that hit Amelia. Leave without pay."

Kaiya scoffed. "Of course. You have to look after your own, right? Can't fire him. Can't charge him. Can't admit that anything's wrong with the force, can you?"

Joseph gave a heavy sigh. "What would that achieve, firing him?"

"Justice," she said. "Isn't that what you're supposed to be

all about?"

"That depends who you ask," Joseph said. "But yes. Ideally. As long as you believe that officer did it on purpose, though, and as long as I believe he didn't, we will have different ideas of what is just."

What a typical answer. It wasn't really an answer at all. The Chief Inspector *knew* the officer was guilty, whether or not he would admit it.

Joseph leaned back in his chair, brow furrowed. "Do you think he should die, Kaiya?"

She thought about the question. "I don't think it should be up to us to decide. It should be Amelia's choice."

"Amelia is dead," Joseph said.

"I know that. So... her family should get to decide. Her sister when she comes back."

"And if her sister decided the officer should die?" Joseph asked. "Would that be an acceptable outcome?"

"Yes." Kaiya leaned forward, trying to explain. "You don't get it. He doesn't matter anymore. He... *wronged* Amelia, and the people that knew Amelia. He needs to pay the price for that. Whatever makes it better for the people left behind, that's how it should be. Whatever will bring peace to Amelia's sister."

"Is that what you would do, if you were Amelia's sister?" Joseph asked.

"Absolutely."

They stared at each other for a moment. Kaiya felt emboldened enough to glance him in the eyes, but the intensity of his gaze deflected her own.

"And that would be just," Joseph said.

"Yes. It's the only way that anyone who cared about Amelia could move on."

"Then by that logic," Joseph said, "you should pay a penalty set by Stephen. You almost beat him to death, after all."

Kaiya shook her head. "No, you've got it the wrong way

around," she said. "This is why my whole case is a farce. That man was a collaborator, and on that night, he received his judgment. I don't have to pay a price for being the person who carries out justice, just like you don't have to. It's like saying that Amelia's sister would be punished for making a judgment against the officer who killed her. *We're* the victims. The people. We all have the right to determine the price a collaborator pays. They forfeited their right to be members of the community the moment they worked with the Tarkinians."

"So you must feel better," Joseph said, "having been involved in the dispensation of justice."

"Better?" Kaiya said. "Have you looked around? This whole building is full of collaborators just like you. The whole town. I don't feel better because one man got what he deserved. There's are whole cities of men just like him. You see them everywhere, but you can't tell. We should pay more attention to them, but we don't."

Why did she bother? Trying to convince someone like Joseph was like trying to smother a burning building with a blanket. The Chief Inspector could be readied for execution and still deny he had any price to pay.

"By what evidence did you decide that Stephen was a collaborator?" Joseph asked.

"This is ridiculous."

"I quite agree," Joseph said. "I don't particularly care whether or not Stephen was a collaborator, but let us assume that he was. Were you or were you not privy to the knowledge that Akheron had instituted a court of priority to try—"

"A court!" Kaiya said. "What are they going to do? Put a few officials up there and give them suspended sentences? What a joke."

"That... court, as much as I don't want to call it that, has barely existed for two weeks, and already twenty-seven people have been sentenced to death. Over a hundred have been stripped of the rights to vote and own a business or property. Don't tell me that's a joke."

Kaiya shifted in her seat. He had to be lying. This was some sort of propaganda. A ruse. "Even if that's true," she said, "they won't get everyone."

"You're correct about that," he said, and looked back at the holos on his desk.

The admission came as a surprise to Kaiya. "So you agree with me..."

"Of course I don't," Joseph said. "But that doesn't mean I agree with Akheron. I may have less opposition to the way they're going about this than the way you are, but they're still wrong. No one has yet convinced me that the abandonment of this country's principles will lead to a better outcome. No one has proved that the disintegration of civilisation back to its primitive form is a magical path back to prosperity. Do you ever think about that when you're out there, Kaiya? About what you're fighting to defend? Or does it just feel good, and that's all that matters?"

Kaiya stayed silent. Joseph was right about the last part. It did feel good. But the rest of it should have been obvious to him. She fought to defend... well, she could articulate that another time. A person either possessed the innate knowledge or they didn't. The Chief Inspector would never understand.

"Why are you so angry?" he asked. "If I gave you a frequency rifle and let you walk out of here to kill every single collaborator in Leth, would that make you happy?"

She wanted to say 'yes,' but held back. He wouldn't accept such a quick response, and she didn't want to lose the more peaceful disposition he had begun to display, so she pictured herself achieving the hypothetical. Before her, waves of faceless men died... no, men and women... or perhaps there were only men inside the imagination... They suffered beneath her, but their deaths gave no satisfaction.

And every so often her mind returned to her bed, and the early morning, the weight, the—

No, that was irrelevant.

"I don't know," Kaiya said, and shifted in her seat.

Joseph made a sound that indicated he didn't believe her, but would let the matter go.

Silence descended, and Kaiya returned her gaze to the toddler boy in Joseph's holos.

"When Benjamin first raised the idea of me getting to know you," Joseph said, "I said I didn't want to. It took him a week to convince me. He told me how smart you were, how you had inherited your father's sense of... moral duty. He also told me you were argumentative."

"He told you I'm argumentative?"

Joseph smiled. "You haven't disappointed on that one, yet. But frankly, you're a disappointment on the first quality. The worst part is I can tell when a person is naturally stupid, and that's not you. You're what I like to call wilfully stupid. You try to convince yourself that your behaviour is because of this, that, or the other, but all you're doing is hiding the fact that, deep down, you know it's about something else."

"What makes you so certain?" Kaiya asked.

"Experience," Joseph said.

Kaiya folded her arms and stared at the desk. He sounded like Tilda, but... more authoritative. And why hadn't Tilda come? She should have been there to support her.

"I want you to think about that," Joseph said, "because you're going to need to make a decision. Do you understand the conditions of your sentence?"

Kaiya shrugged. "I have to follow your orders and if I don't you'll send me to jail."

"Not quite how it works," Joseph said, "but close enough. As your mentor, it is my job to help you... see the errors you've made. You are to accompany me to Akheron in two days' time."

"What?" Kaiya said. "I don't want to go to Akheron!"

"You don't get a say in the matter," Joseph said. "If you don't like it, there's a cell with your name on it. Besides, I thought you'd like an opportunity to chase after Bennett."

The tidbit of information piqued her interest, and she stayed silent, waiting for more.

Joseph grinned.

"I told you that I had leads," he said. "Those leads go to Akheron. You will come with me, and you will assist me in locating Bennett. I will also be providing evidence in the trial of the Ambassador to the Occupied Territories. Or the pre-trial, whatever it really is. Those two stages look curiously similar in this court. You will not be required on that day, and you will have your evenings and mornings to yourself, bearing in mind that if you leave the agreed upon area you will be apprehended by the Akheron Police Force and put into custody. You have an uncle in Akheron, correct?"

"Kytos?" Kaiya said, dazed by the Chief Inspector's whirl-wind explanation. "I barely remember him."

"Then perhaps it's time to reconnect," Joseph said. "Take a friend with you. Kormac, if you like."

"Isn't this supposed to be punishment?"

"Would you prefer that?" Joseph asked. "Do you feel you would benefit from something harsher? Perhaps a public flog-ging? Don't answer that. This is what I have decided. You will meet me back here at eleven a.m. in two days' time. Understood?"

Kaiya frowned, stomach already turning with apprehension. "But Masuma," she said, "I promised I'd see her..."

"The girl?" Joseph said. He reclined and studied Kaiya. "You still have today and tomorrow. That is enough to explain your situation, is it not?"

"But I promised," Kaiya repeated. "It's... I don't want to let her down."

She tried to meet Joseph's eyes, but they were like truth-seeking drills boring into her skull. "You feel... responsible for her?" he asked.

"Obviously I'm not—"

"I didn't ask if you *are*," Joseph interrupted. "I asked if you *feel* you are."

The peculiar tendrils of warmth she experienced with Masuma began to flow once more along with her memory of the girl. What they were or where they came from, she still could not tell, but they bore with them precisely Joseph's description.

"Yes," she said. "I don't know why. I just... do."

Joseph nodded slowly as his face brightened. "That could be the most honest thing you've said to me so far. I hope you keep it up, and I expect you to think about what I said before. Next time I see you, I want the real reason for the way you feel. Otherwise I can't help you."

A sense of quiet trust had begun encroaching on Kaiya's mind, and she pushed it away vehemently. She had to remember that Joseph was the enemy. The only way she could come through the humiliation of being tied to him was to be ever-vigilant against his seeds of propaganda.

"Can I go now?" she said.

"Not just yet." Joseph pulled up his holoscreen again and swiped through the air to pluck out a folder. "Do you have a holodisc on you? Or a data card?"

"I have some space on my identity card," Kaiya said, and hesitated before handing it over.

"Do you know what Amelia was doing before the Tarkinians came?" Joseph asked as he formed a link between the holoscreen and identity card. "She was at the university here. Third year political science and history." He pinched a holo from the holoscreen and placed it against the tiny strand of light linked to the identity card, and the holo made a copy of itself and began to travel down the line into the identity card. "I thought you might like a... memento. I know you didn't know her back then, but it's the best I could find." Joseph turned the original holo around and pushed it deeper into the holoscreen towards Kaiya. "Annual debate of the Nymian National University. Third year students compete for one of the six spots. The highest-placed competitor coming into the final debate gets to set the motion and choose which side they will appear on. You know what motion Amelia selected?"

Kaiya waited for an answer, eyes locked on the holo of a younger Amelia in passionate speech.

"That the border territories enjoy greater freedom through their inclusion in Nymosen," Joseph said.

Kaiya tittered. "So she spoke for the negative?"

"No," Joseph said. "She chose the affirmative."

He stared at her with a boyish grin.

"What?" Kaiya said. "That doesn't make sense."

"I think it makes perfect sense," Joseph said.

Kaiya peered suspiciously at the Chief Inspector. "Why are you telling me this?"

"Because she was young, and so are you. Figure it out."

The data transfer had ended, and Joseph handed back the identity card.

"Thanks," Kaiya said absentmindedly.

"It's a pity what happened to her," Joseph said. "She would've made a hell of a politician."

Kaiya searched for the words to express the conflict raging within. Amelia's voice was etched inside her memory. So, too, the humid camaraderie of buoyant crowds united beneath her zeal. All of that passion should have led somewhere... given them something...

"It was so... meaningless," Kaiya said. "She was there and then..."

She lifted her hands to indicate nothingness.

"I know," Joseph murmured. His eyes seemed distant for a

few moments before returning to the present. "Why did you like her? What qualities did she possess that meant so much to you?"

Kaiya thought back to all the times she had sat across Amelia's table, with the infamous teapot in the centre. The coded messages sent through a network of associates informing Kaiya when the next saboteurs would arrive, when the next delivery of materials would be there. Amelia's head smacking against the fountain...

Kaiya glanced at the Chief Inspector. He was trying to disarm her. She couldn't let him creep through her defences with his false demeanour and begin extracting information, but...

What if she was wrong?

Dizzying heat rushed through her head, and she closed her eyes, trying to assuage the sensation of swaying.

"She was always in control," Kaiya said. "Always strong."

"Even when you couldn't see her?"

"Well... I don't know," Kaiya said. She barely knew anything about Amelia, she had to keep reminding herself of that.

"What do you think it says about you?" Joseph asked.

Kaiya frowned, not understanding.

"What you saw in Amelia says more about you than it does about her," Joseph said. "What I want you to think about is whether what you saw in her was the same when you met her as it was when she died. No, not now. Go home and think about it there. I'll see you in two days."

Kaiya remained in her seat for a few moments, unsure what to do. Joseph pulled the holoscreen back up and began flicking through folders as though she had disappeared. Why the curt dismissal bothered her, she couldn't tell, but it did. Almost like a betrayal.

She walked over and opened the door, giving a final glance behind her as she exited.

Their eyes connected for a lingering moment, and Kaiya

couldn't help but smile.

Kaiya trudged up the boulevard, face locked in consternation with the memory of Masuma's heartbroken expression.

"This one," Masuma had said, pointing to a thick book with green binding.

"That shouldn't be here," Kaiya had said, flicking through the pages. The book was one she remembered reading over a year prior. She hadn't even made it near the end of the first third before she aborted the attempt in disgust at the protagonist's behaviour. "I think you're a bit young for this."

"I still want to try it," Masuma had said.

"But why? There are so many other things you could do. Why spend all that time struggling through something that's too difficult for your age?"

"Because I don't have a choice," Masuma had said. "I have to be able to read it."

Masuma had looked up, then, her eyes shining with vulnerable clarity, and gazed right into the innermost part of Kaiya's soul. The girl's voice carried a desperate but gentle plea.

"Will you help me?"

And so she did.

After the first chapter Kaiya had looked out at the sky and saw encroaching darkness. Masuma had made great effort to understand not just the words of the story but also their meaning, and though she had struggled, her face shone with pride at the achievement.

"We'll read some more tomorrow," Kaiya had said, and Masuma embraced her from the side. "But there's something I need to tell you."

The girl had said she understood... that she didn't mind... that she would be fine... but every word stabbed Kaiya with guilt. No level of prodding or apology or optimistic persuasion could break the protective wall that the girl had slammed up between them.

The eyes with all their vulnerable clarity faded into some distant, unreachable void.

Now near the front door of her own building, Kaiya focused on the last she had seen of Masuma. A girl sitting by herself with a book in her lap far too advanced for her age. If there only had been something she could have said to her, a key to unlock whatever secret cells of suffering lay within the girl's heart, then perhaps Masuma's gaze could have been lifted from the forbidding tome and onto some vision of the future.

Her mother would have known just what to say, and the memory of that did nothing to lift her spirits.

"Who are they?" Kormac asked as they approached the front door.

Kaiya hadn't noticed the four people milling about together on the opposite side of the street. They looked completely average.

"How am I supposed to know?" she said, and they entered the building.

Kormac glanced back as the door closed behind him.

Inside her apartment, Kaiya turned her attention straight to Tilda, who stood by the dining room windows. "You didn't come today," she said.

Tilda didn't respond straight away, but continued staring out the window looking distracted.

"I'm sorry," she said, but the words sounded hollow and distant.

"What's happening out there?" Kaiya asked.

"More fighting," Tilda said. "Didn't you hear it?"

"I wasn't paying attention," Kaiya said. "Stop looking so worried. All your police friends are swarming this city, nothing's going to happen."

Tilda began to cry, covering her scrunched-up face with her hands.

"What on earth is your problem?" Kaiya asked. She didn't have time for Tilda's antics, trying to turn around the fact that she hadn't shown up at court for her when she needed it.

"Do you remember when we went to the Sticks Waterfall?" Tilda said.

Kaiya's eyes widened at the abrupt change in direction. They had followed the river all the way up into the mountains and camped there for seven days at the end of high school. "Of course I do."

"We made the stupid little toy boats and put the stick people inside them, and watched them float to the edge." Tilda half spoke to Kormac, as if he cared about silly things they had done over six years ago. "And we went all the way down to the bottom of the waterfall, and they were still intact. And we said that we'd always be like that. Do you remember?"

"Yes," Kaiya said, softening. "I remember."

"Please don't let them take me," Tilda said, gurgling her words and leaning desperately against the wall for support.

"What are you talking about?" Kaiya said. She looked out of the window, wondering if Tilda meant someone specific, but the boulevard had emptied itself except for the sound of new fighting from the direction of the river. Even the quartet who Kormac had mentioned were gone.

"They've been there all day," Tilda said. "That's why I didn't come. They've been waiting. I'm sorry, Kaiya. Please don't let them take me."

Kaiya turned her attention from the darkness outside to Tilda's splotchy, red face.

"It's ok," Kormac said, stepping forward and placing a hesitant hand on Tilda's shoulder.

Four heavy knocks came from the front door, and Tilda choked on her tears.

"Let me do this," Kormac said, and walked to the front door.

"Who is it?" Kaiya asked. Tilda's state put them in a horrible position to receive any visitors. People always had the worst timing.

"We know you're in there," came a man's voice from outside.

Kormac stood still, watching the viewpanel, then cast an ashen glance back to Kaiya.

"We're coming in whether you open the door or not," the outside voice said. "Five seconds."

Kormac bowed his head and stepped forward to open the door.

"I'm sorry," he whispered, and Tilda let out another gasp as she lost the ability to stand. Kaiya grabbed her in time to stop the fall, and Tilda's weight threatened to drag her down to the floor.

"Come on, it's ok," Kaiya said, pulling her friend back up.

Tilda stared at her with drowning eyes.

She could feel Tilda's breath on her face.

"You don't have to do this," Kormac said from the hallway.

Hot adrenaline sliced through Kaiya's body as she looked up and saw three men and a woman standing at the doorway; the four from outside. One of the men held up a frequency rifle at Kormac's face.

"Get out of the way, you fucking traitor," the man said.

Kormac hesitated but gave way, stepping back into the dining room.

"What are you doing here?" Kaiya said. "You're fighting the police, right?"

The situation began making sense to her. They were too exposed in the open. They needed somewhere to lay low for a while.

"It's ok," she said. "You can trust us. You need a place to hide?

The quartet glanced at each other.

"You were there the other night," the armed man said.

"With us."

"Yes," she said, stepping closer towards them. Tilda sobbed as the space between them grew.

"She's lying," one of the other men said.

"No," the armed one said. "I saw her. She was there, right in the thick of it. This doesn't make sense."

"I don't think she knows," the woman said.

"How could she not know?" the armed man said. "It doesn't matter. Let's get this done with."

Outside, the sound of a chanting crowd grew larger. The quartet of strangers stepped down into the dining room, and Tilda sank back against the wall.

"Don't let them take me," she whimpered, voice drained to a thin thread. "Please."

"Thought you could run away, you slut..." the armed man said.

"What did you just call her?" Kaiya said.

"Stop playing stupid," the man said. "I saw you the other night, so I know you're one of us. I don't want to hurt you, but if you get in our way, I won't have a choice. You're harbouring a collaborator. That's enough for you to get the same treatment as her."

An overload of thoughts flooded her brain and she struggled to think. What kind of an accusation was that?

"Tilda?" was all she could think to say, and she wasn't even sure if she sought clarification from her or the stranger, but there was an unmistakeable dread forming in the pit of her stomach that told her there were either one or four unwelcome people in her presence.

Perhaps five.

"It's not true," Tilda sobbed.

"Shut up, slut," the unknown woman said. "Liar."

Tilda gasped and grabbed Kaiya's shoulder. Kaiya shook herself free and slapped Tilda's hand away before half turning to face her. "What is he talking about?" she asked. Slowly the bottleneck to her brain was clearing. Tilda had been upset before they even came... she'd been strange ever since she first arrived, never going out...

The house. The house had been burnt down. But that had been the police, surely...

"Tell me!" Kaiya said.

"I don't know what they're talking about," Tilda said.

"Don't lie to me!"

"It's not true," Tilda said, stepping back and clasping her hands in front of her. "It was just a rumour."

"It's more than just a rumour," the armed man said. "We know for a fact she was sleeping with a Tarkinian officer."

"For a fact?" Kaiya asked. "How do you know that?"

"I don't need to justify myself to you," the stranger said. "Everyone in northwest quarter knew. We thought maybe the Tarkinians took her with them when they left – good riddance if they had – but she was spotted yesterday. Coming out of the hospital."

"You don't understand," Tilda whispered to Kaiya, eyes panicked and pleading. "You don't understand."

"What don't I understand?"

"I hated them too," Tilda said, "but they're not all the same. I wish you could have met him. Please, I know you'd understand if you had met him."

The gentle force of Tilda's admission set fire to the brittle ice coursing through Kaiya's veins.

"We loved each other," Tilda said. "Just like you and Kormac."

On the other side of the table, Kormac gazed at her with some impenetrable despondency Kaiya could not comprehend. The reality of Tilda's betrayal crashed home inside Kaiya.

"You slut!" she said, and slapped Tilda hard across the face.

The shock stopped Tilda's tears for a few seconds. There

would be no sympathy for her treachery.

"Kaiya..." came Kormac's voice, and he stared at her with lips parted in shock, eyes drooping as though betrayed. So he felt it too! He felt the hot sting of Tilda's whore behaviour!

The armed man stepped forward and grabbed hold of Tilda, who put up a measly struggle as she cried and screamed in vain. Kaiya stared at the table, listening as Tilda shouted for her, pleading, "Kaiya! Kaiya!" She didn't want to see her, and refused to watch, limiting herself to the peripheral image of Tilda kicking as the quartet pulled her towards the front door.

"Kaiya!" she screamed.

In the corridor the sound of doors opening came, but they soon closed again. Everyone knew what had just happened. Still Tilda screamed, voice growing distant down the outside hallway then the stairs, and still Kaiya stayed resolute in the deafening anger that protected her from Tilda's pleas. Her body shook, a volcano of cracked belief and betrayed emotion.

If only she could rescue Tilda from the quartet, just to be the one who punished her.

On the other side of the table, Kormac's face split open with grief.

The street below erupted in a series of shouts and jeers as Kaiya picked up a chair and smashed it against the wall. She bashed the window with her fist and doubled over, emitting a whine of restrained wrath as she squeezed every muscle in her body, trying to crush the quiet rage into some unyielding black hole.

She forced herself to listen as the crowd cursed, hurling the most atrocious – and fitting – abuse. Tilda could still be heard within the crowd's vengeance, her voice hoarse and distant. Only once more did she cry out for Kaiya, then her voice disappeared amongst the laughter and chanting.

Kaiya turned the windows to full night mode, and faced the resounding emptiness of her home.

14

SOMEONE ALONG HER CORRIDOR WAS HAVING A PARTY. A FAMILY celebration, she guessed, thrown by the woman three doors down on the other side. Such celebrations had been regular events as far back as she could remember. Even during the Occupation they had continued them, swearing her to secrecy when she had stumbled upon them one evening. She had admired them for that resistance, however small and inconsequential, but tonight she found the sound of their cheer offensive.

No one had a right to such joy. Not until she forced her own to return.

Another convoy had come that morning, and off she had rushed to the hospital, searching and searching and finding no one. They came less frequently now, but that meant nothing. There always had to be those who came last. No doubt her parents would be staying back and assisting. They would let other people go first, that's what they would be doing.

Kaiya stared at the Vision Caster, which could now play a single channel, reviewing the details of her morning. Had

Kormac taken his supplements? She'd left without even thinking about it. No matter. Missing a round here and there wasn't an issue. As long as she remembered at their meal tonight, everything would be fine. They hadn't spoken all morning before she left, but tonight they could reconnect. They could move forward without the poisonous influence of that traitor.

The Vision Caster played through commercials, and a familiar scent greeted Kaiya's nose. Salty air with the distant tinge of frangipanis, and... no, she couldn't do this again. She turned off the Vision Caster, ending the *Rapture* advertisement, and walked back to her bedroom. By the time she could next have a basic treatment, she would be in Akheron with that damned Chief Inspector. Maybe the clinic would let her have an early one, if she explained...

Kormac was still in the bathroom, singing in a low, pleasant voice.

> *Will you pick the lavender,*
> *the young and blooming lavender,*
> *will you pick the lavender,*
> *before its time has come?*

The sound of the old folk song gave Kaiya some comfort as she looked at herself in the mirror, wearing a dress Kormac had never seen by virtue of not having known her before the war. It had been so long since she last touched it, with all its attachments to memories of her mother. Bittersweet nostalgia, to wear it again. Her body had changed so little in six years. She compared herself in the mirror with a holo of her and her mother. She did look older, now, but anyone who had known her in both times would recognise the same person.

What would the Kaiya of six years prior see, if she stood beside her? And what would she say to the Kaiya of her past?

Naïveté echoed through the holo, both she and her mother looking forward to some future that would never be lived.

Kormac entered the bedroom, naked. Kaiya watched as he dressed himself slowly, noticing the slightest of limps. Why had she not seen that before? There was no sense of awkwardness, despite the oscillating distance between them. Sometimes he seemed lost in a completely different world, oblivious to her presence, and other times he stared at her as though he may never see her again.

Perhaps all he needed was more proof of her dedication to him. Tonight she would do nothing but focus on him. And after dinner, then... they would try again. She would succeed. And she would prove to herself that *she* was in control of her body, and maybe when they returned to that place – the place where individuals vanished in the forging of greater union – maybe then the perfected future would slip closer to the present.

Kaiya took a jacket out of her closet. There was little chance she would need it, but one could never know. She stared at the scars on Kormac's back. Their presence gave her a physical reminder that something had happened she didn't understand, something real and tangible. She touched the undulating skin, running her fingers slowly down then out until she reached around and embraced him from behind.

He stood still, and placed his hand gently on her own.

She had to remember, always, that this was the reason she fought.

Kormac finished dressing, and Kaiya tried to straighten the curvature of his collar. He gave a tiny spasm as her fingers brushed his neck, but covered it with the hint of a smile in response to her own. How much of him had been stolen from her? How much could she recover from the ruins of whatever the enemy had done to him? Did a desecrated temple remember its desecration, no matter the skill of its restoration?

Or could there be no restoration, for either of them?

By the time they arrived at the restaurant, tucked away on a side street of southern boulevard, Kaiya had counted seventy-six smashed windows and nineteen completely gutted apartments. Taskforce police patrolled in clumps of six, eyes always suspicious and searching. Kaiya could feel the eyes as she stepped into the restaurant's chilled ambience.

The waiter seated them near the centre of the room, and she tried to ignore the fact she had taken Jonathan there.

Kormac glanced around the room. Whether in curiosity or anxiety, Kaiya couldn't tell.

"Are you unhappy?" she asked.

He grinned and looked her in the eyes. "No. Just... restless."

As the moments passed Kaiya became convinced his endless spatial survey came not from a place of curiosity. "What is it?" she asked.

"I just..." he began, swallowing. His eyes danced furtively and he twisted his neck to look behind him. "The people. I can't see them."

There were only a handful of others in the restaurant, but whatever threat Kormac perceived seemed enough to make his breathing shallow.

"Do you want to move?" Kaiya asked.

"Mm," he breathed, closing his eyes.

Kaiya spoke to the waiter, who offered them another table where Kormac could sit with his back to the wall. His breathing became deeper immediately, and his eyes lost the urgency of their movement, reverting to their usual uneasy suspicion.

The waiter placed a chill bottle on the table. Kaiya stared at the tiny circuits buried within the bottle before picking it up and pouring herself a glass of water. As she drank, she became conscious of Kormac watching her. For some reason the attention annoyed her, and she glanced up at the mirror on the wall to scrutinise whoever else was in their company tonight.

After a few moments, Kormac picked up the chill bottle and poured his own glass of water.

Kaiya fiddled with her glass as she listened to the soft chatter and mood music. An over-smiling couple sat nearby, exhibiting all the signs of fresh affection – the woman's lowered chin and upturned eyes, the laugh just a touch higher than it otherwise would have been, the man's gregarious and expansive demeanour, the gentle push and pull of attracting bodies and hesitant minds cautious to avoid signalling too much interest.

Behind her sat a family of four, silent as they ate with pristine propriety. Straight-backed and dressed in matching colours, the boy and girl ate without smiling, eyes locked onto their plates without travelling anywhere else. Kaiya stared at the mother and father within the mirror, wishing one of them would say something – anything – either to each other or the children.

"Kaiya?" came Kormac's voice, obviously a repeated attempt at gaining her attention.

"What?" she said, focus returning.

"I asked how Masuma was today," Kormac said.

"Oh," Kaiya said. "Better than yesterday. We read some more of that book."

"Is she managing it ok?"

"She struggles," Kaiya said, "but she manages to read the easier words by herself."

"I don't know why she bothers," Kormac said. "It won't actually mean anything if she finishes it. Just a lot of hard work for nothing."

"Maybe," Kaiya said, "but she has to be able to read properly. It would have been better if she had other stuff, but there's nothing age-appropriate there for her. It's all either too young or too old."

"Have you read the book?" Kormac asked.

Kaiya glanced back to the early-flame couple. "No..."

"So how do you know she can't handle it?"

"I didn't say she *can't* handle it," Kaiya said. "I just said it's not age-appropriate."

"Fair enough," Kormac said. "I'm surprised her reading isn't better, though. There was a school in my camp. I used to see kids there all the time, but I didn't really ever pay attention to them, so I don't know if I ever saw Masuma."

"They had schools?" Kaiya said. "Maybe they didn't where Masuma was."

"We were in the same load, weren't we?" Kormac said. "We must have come from the same camp. She must have had some kind of education in there."

Kaiya glared at the mirror. "Oh, she had an education, that's for sure..."

Kormac took his glass of water, studied it for an uncomfortably long time, then drained it, and neither of them spoke again until the waiter arrived.

He gave them an unctuous smile, ready to take their orders.

"I'll have the sweet and sour pork, please," Kormac said.

"Eastern cheeses," Kaiya added.

The waiter commended them on their choices, and Kormac traced his finger around the menu circle on his side, making the menu disappear.

"At least that's one thing about you that doesn't change," he said.

Kaiya grinned. "What do you mean?"

"Eastern cheeses," Kormac said. "You should try something different every now and then."

"What's wrong with eastern cheeses?" Kaiya asked.

"Nothing," Kormac said, "but that wasn't my point."

Kaiya gave her best impression of a smile and reached across the table to take Kormac's hand. He seemed tentative in response, staring at the point of physical connection.

"How exciting," she said. "Get to have *marashta* again."

Kormac's eyes brightened. "It *is* exciting. I can't tell you how many times I wished I could just have *marashta*. It's like... you fixate. Everyone had some kind of food they talked about all the time. Chocolate, or sausages, or *marashta* for me... there was one guy who would have done anything for a banana. We used to talk about what it would be like to eat properly again. I don't know why – it always hurt to talk about it, even if we were able to laugh about it. I guess we just wanted to... remember the things we wanted to have again. The people we wanted to see..."

Kaiya watched the memories unfurl within his eyes, and thought back to the odd jokes those men who had been in Kormac's hospital ward had made. Kormac gazed at her almost inscrutably, some mixture of deep connection yet estrangement. Those eyes saw her differently, now, as though a filter had been placed over them that altered a reality that hadn't changed.

All she needed to do was take away the filter.

"You know, the Tarkinians have their own *marashta*," Kormac said, "but it's different. Like a dessert."

"I know," she said with genuine amazement, thinking back to the menu at *Cecilie's Coffeepot*. "Typical, though, stealing all our stuff."

Kormac chuckled and squeezed her hand. "It was the most atrocious thing I have *ever* tasted in my *life*. They gave it to us every Christmas – at least, they told us it was Christmas. You've never had anything so sickly sweet. But I ate it. It was terrible, but at least it was something other than the usual rations."

Kaiya smiled, studying the shadowed features of Kormac's face. Truthfully, this was the kind of hero that needed celebration – the survivor. In a sea of traitors, he still glowed bright with purity.

"Where were you?" she whispered, dragging her chair further under the table to bring herself closer to him. "What did you do?"

She watched him as he thought on his response, cautiously

optimistic that her strategy was beginning to work. Time, she had said – he just needed time. Well... time was passing, and here Kormac was, finally letting her into a secret world she was both curious about and frightened of.

"I don't know exactly where I was," Kormac said. "Somewhere in southwest Tarkinia, though – we were close to the border. We repaired machines. Tested frequency weapons. Menial stuff, but... important. To them, at least." He didn't seem to know how to feel about that fact, but soon a small grin replaced the confusion. "I helped make road tiles."

"So you worked for the enemy," Kaiya quipped gently.

Kormac laughed. "Yes, you could say that."

The joyful expression stayed on his face for a few seconds but began inexorably to slip.

"That's exactly what I did, isn't it," Kormac said. "I'm just as bad as any collaborator here. Worse, even."

"That's ridiculous," Kaiya said.

"Is it, though?" Kormac said. "We tested weapons. We repaired Obsidian Tanks, lightning drones, surveillance pods. Everything we did supported the war effort. I may as well have been one of them."

"You had no choice," Kaiya said.

Kormac shook his head. "I did, though. We all did. People didn't talk much about it – I don't think we were supposed to know – but there were other camps. Not all of them were for work. I think the others were more... correctional. But sometimes people refused to work. I thought about it once but... I just couldn't. I thought I was strong when I went there, but these men, Kaiya – you should have seen them. When we arrived, the guards... showed us what they could do to us if we disobeyed. They didn't just have stun batons or things like that, they... they had the boards."

He mumbled the final words and stared beyond Kaiya into something impenetrable.

"They told us at the very beginning that we had a choice – cooperate or suffer. I never wanted to feel that... machine... again, so I did as they said. But not everyone did. Some people were tough like that – not me. I wasn't prepared to go through what they went through. Eventually they disappeared. Towards the end, for the last half a year, we would have to watch every day. The guards would hook people up to the boards as examples. And every day, there were less and less of us around. No one ever told us where the others went, but... we all knew."

Kaiya listened, waiting to see if he would add more. What kind of details had he omitted? What were these boards he never seemed capable of mentioning properly? "You were a slave," she said. "That's not the same as being one of them."

"Perhaps," he said, gaze still vacant. "But at least I wasn't in the women's section."

All of a sudden Kaiya's appetite didn't seem so large.

She could see the memories playing out within Kormac's eyes, and her own mind provided an unwanted soundtrack to its vivid depictions of all he had described and – more importantly – not described. Not content to provide only an abstract construction, her mind brought forth the image of Masuma, whose existence was the fact that moved the abstract into the real.

Nauseating rage roiled through her body.

"What's wrong?" Kormac asked.

"Nothing," she said automatically, but Kormac's resigned reaction made it clear he didn't believe her.

The solution to Kormac and Masuma's experiences was clear to her. It had been there all along, no matter how much its effect on Kormac's mother had impacted her at the time.

"Don't you think that having *Rapture* wouldn't be so bad?" Kaiya asked.

Kormac's face tightened. "I don't want to think about it."

"Please," Kaiya said, "just listen to me. Can't you see how

much better it would be never to have to think about those things again? I know you were angry because of your mum, but think of it from her perspective – she doesn't even know that she doesn't remember."

"That's not—"

"So what if you forget someone?" Kaiya continued. "You won't know it. You won't regret it."

She had worried that the *Rapture* might take her from his mind as well, but the more she thought about it, the more it made sense that she would stay. Why would the treatment decide that she didn't belong there?

"I don't want a life like that," Kormac said.

"Like what? Perfect?"

"Pointless," Kormac said.

Kaiya frowned. *Rapture* did many things, but making life pointless was not one of them. If life was pointless, then surely the pointlessness came from living with the mundane, and *Rapture* provided something more than that.

"You know those times," Kaiya said, "when everything's just... amazing?"

She tried to articulate the memory that had come into her mind, but how did one express something like that? It was an old memory, from at least a decade ago. Her parents had been standing in the kitchen, cooking together, the sound of their laughter filling the apartment. Everything about that image infused her with a magical sense of wonder. She remembered feeling that with Kormac, long ago, but those feelings always faded. *Rapture* would be different. The wonder would be complete through its permanence.

"What's the point of anything good if it doesn't last forever?" Kaiya said.

Kormac leaned back in his chair. "I'm not having it."

"Well, I am," Kaiya said, folding her arms.

Kormac didn't say anything for an uncomfortable amount of time, and simply stared away from Kaiya.

"You want it," he said at last, "then go get it. I won't be around when you're done."

The threat stung deep.

"What are you so afraid of?" Kaiya said. "You'll still remember me after—"

"It's not about you!" Kormac said, looking at her as if he couldn't believe what she was saying. "Tilda was right. Everything's always about you."

"Don't talk about her," Kaiya said.

"I'll talk about whoever I want."

His eyes burnt with an ugly malevolence she'd never seen him display before, and Kaiya turned her attention back to the couple nearby.

They laughed.

Over the next few silent minutes Kaiya glanced at Kormac, watching his face morph to a mask of reserved agitation. He'd gone back to scanning the room, eyes flicking back and forth towards the door.

The waiter approached, holding a tray with both dishes.

"The eastern cheeses," he said as he placed Kaiya's plate in front of her, "and the sweet and sour pork."

Kaiya thanked the waiter and watched as Kormac stared at his plate. She flashed him a smile, but he either ignored it or didn't see, and remained motionless.

Whatever. His problem.

She picked up the fork and prodded the luxuriously-presented *marashta*, playing with the gooey cheese and twirling up strands ready to eat. Kormac's eyes rose as she lifted the fork to her mouth.

"Don't," he said.

Kaiya stopped with her mouth open, fork in mid-air.

"What?" she said.

Kormac bent over his plate and poked the *marashta* with his fork, sniffing.

"Something's not right," he said, and his eyes widened. "Put it down. Quick, put it down."

Kaiya hesitated and placed the fork back onto her plate, tendrils of steam fading into the air.

"It's been poisoned," Kormac whispered. "They're trying to kill us."

"What?" Kaiya said, astounded at the accusation.

"I knew it," Kormac said. "I knew something wasn't right. Not enough people. You see them? They're plants. It's what they do, it's how they trick you. They put them here just to get us."

"Kormac, who is 'they?'"

"The Tarkinians!" Kormac said. "They've been watching me. I knew it."

He looked around the room, movements sharp and frantic.

"What do you want?" he yelled at the couple nearby. "How much are they paying you?"

The couple stared at him, eyes flicking back to each other, holding stunned smiles as though they weren't sure if this were a joke or not.

"Kormac, what are you doing?" Kaiya's heart began to race.

"I can fight back!" Kormac said. "You won't take me this— what are you looking at?"

He stood up and hurled his plate of *marashta* at the couple. The woman screamed and held her arms up in defence while the plate smashed onto the table, food splattering both of them.

"You think I don't know?" Kormac screamed, holding his fork like a knife. "I know who you are. I know what you're doing here."

The man stood up.

"Don't you come near me!" Kormac continued. "I'll fucking kill you, fucking traitor! How long have you been working for them? What— sit down!"

Kormac pointed at the family.

Mother and father assessed the situation, then slowly returned to their seats. Kaiya watched the little girl's face scrunch up in tearful fear. The mother placed her arm slowly around the girl.

"Kormac..." Kaiya said.

He turned his head, eyes blazing with distress.

"No..." he said. "You're in on it, too, aren't you? I knew it! I knew you were working with them! That's why you brought me here, isn't it? That's..."

He stepped back against the wall, gripping the fork tighter.

"No one's working with anyone," Kaiya soothed. "Everyone here is—"

"Shut up!" he yelled. "You're trying to poison me. You're... it's all fake, all of it. I knew it, I knew it. You did it to my mother, didn't you. It was you. You and—"

The restaurant doors burst open, and three Taskforce police entered, stun batons primed.

"Where are you taking me?" Kormac yelled at them. "I won't let you take me, I'll fucking kill myself. You're not taking me back there."

"He doesn't know what he's talking about," Kaiya said to the police, who approached with hesitation.

"Working together the whole time," Kormac was mumbling to no one in particular. "I knew it, knew they were. What are you looking at? What do you want? Strap me up, let them try, we'll see what happens, strap me up, won't let them—"

"Sir," said one of the police, holstering his baton and showing his empty hands, "I need you to calm down and look at me."

"Tarkinian scum!" Kormac picked up his chair and hurled it at the police officer, who stumbled back as it struck his upheld arms.

"Kormac, stop it!" Kaiya said, attention shifting between him and the Taskforce police.

The chair-struck officer continued to step forward. "Kormac, is it? I want you to look at me, Kormac. I want you to think about what you're seeing. You see my uniform?"

"You can't trick me," Kormac said, raising his fork. "I know how you work with all your lies and—"

"No one's lying," the officer said. "No one's trying to trick you. We just want to talk."

"I know what you're doing in Section C," Kormac said. "You're not taking me there! I won't be an experiment!"

The lead officer glanced at Kaiya. "Miss, I'm going to have to ask you to step away."

"No," she said. "I'm not going to let you hurt him."

"We have no intention of hurting him," the officer said. "Please step away."

Kaiya stood her ground, staring at the mild-faced Taskforce officer.

Then complied with the order.

"Kormac," the officer said, stepping forward again, "I need you to try really hard to focus on me, ok? Can you do that?"

The other two officers fanned out, blocking any potential path Kormac could take. As the lead officer neared the table, Kormac let out a roar and flipped it over, sending Kaiya's plate of *marashta* crashing to the floor along with the cutlery. The chill bottle and glasses smashed, shards flying.

The lead officer rummaged through his belt pack and pulled out a small square package, opening it to reveal some sort of medical patch. "I'm going to ask you one more time, Kormac. I want you to calm down and just look—"

Kormac charged forward with a scream and began stabbing with his fork. The lead officer parried the wild blows until his colleagues could rush forward and restrain him, a feat that took several attempts. As Kormac flailed around screaming and yelling that he had been betrayed, the lead officer stepped forward and thrust the medical patch onto his neck.

Within half a minute, Kormac fell silent and slumped to the floor, supported by the Taskforce police.

The restaurant was hushed, bar a few gentle sobs from the little girl with her family.

"What have you done to him?" Kaiya asked.

"Sedative," the lead officer said. "It'll wear off within a half hour."

Kaiya gazed down at Kormac's calm face. "He didn't mean it," she said. "I…"

The lead officer waited a few seconds, but Kaiya didn't know how to articulate her thoughts.

"I understand," the officer said. "It's not the first time we've had to deal with this." He bent down and placed his hands under Kormac's shoulders. "Let's get him outside."

The Taskforce police carried Kormac outside and deposited him against the wall.

"Does he have to… go somewhere, now?" Kaiya asked.

The lead officer shook his head. "There's nothing more we can do. He's staying with you?"

Kaiya nodded.

"Then all you can do is wait until he wakes up. After that… you'll have to figure it out."

The other officers glanced at each other. "I'm not comfortable with this," one of them said.

"Doesn't matter," the lead officer said. "Hospital doesn't want these ones. Besides, we follow the rules we're given. At least this one has some place to go back to."

Kaiya sat against the centuries-old stone wall and cradled Kormac's head.

"I…" she began, unable to look up at the officers. "Thank you."

The lead officer paused a few moments. "You be careful,

now," he said, then walked away, leaving Kaiya to guard Kormac's vulnerable body.

As the minutes passed, she returned time after time to the memory of a stun baton returning to its holster.

Kaiya stared up at the ceiling, a reflected ocean of dulled urban lights muted through her window's filtration layer. Kormac twisted in his sleep beside her, and every time she began to drift into semi-consciousness there would come the inevitable jolt, and panic would grip her for a few seconds until she came to and realised that no... no one else had come into her room.

What happened now? Kormac's despair had been written all over his face as they returned home. Nothing cheered him. The anticipation of a nice meal had been replaced with the reality of fast food, but he had barely touched his.

Even upon reaching bed, he didn't want to touch her, and simply lay soundlessly, not a single word spoken since waking from the sedative. She had tried half-heartedly to arouse him, but in the end she, too, was grateful not to face another night of shamed failure.

Perhaps in the morning...

No. She couldn't think like that anymore. Things were always going to be better tomorrow, but they just weren't. She'd never felt so disconnected from Kormac. All those dreams of returning to a peaceful existence seemed ridiculous to her, now, and something new had been stirring inside her since Joseph made his threat to uncover anything she didn't tell him.

This journey to Akheron would be more than just Joseph's police business.

In her fantasies, she inflicted pain...

Kormac gasped beside her, short and sharp. She watched his fingers quiver and his face attempt to contort itself, numb as it was from sleeping. His lips looked as though they were trying to form words. His face changed into a mask of pain, and the murmuring became muted whimpers. He had moved and made sound ever since he fell asleep, but now Kaiya became more concerned as she watched him draw himself into some ragged semblance of the foetal position.

Kormac had never been an unsound sleeper.

The memory of their former nights together crackled through her mind like lightning, pushing aside those silly night-time fears she had only just succumbed to minutes ago, reinvigorating the tender, troubled bond between them.

Kaiya rolled onto her side to parallel Kormac's body, reaching out to touch him. She stopped at the last moment and rested her hand on the bed, unsure if she should wake him. His body trembled, almost imperceptible, and his whimpering disappeared after a few minutes. Whatever thoughts floated through his mind had passed, and Kaiya felt a great responsibility towards him. She raised her hand again and placed it on his shoulder, light at first, a cat dipping its paw in water. She pulled it back as Kormac twitched, then tried again. The second touch didn't register, and she let the weight of her hand descend in full upon his shoulder.

Kormac seemed to relax, and she allowed herself to feel the gentle power that came from the knowledge that she had provided him with a relief no one else could. She smiled and moved closer to him. As she wrapped her arm around his body and positioned herself behind him, Kormac jerked awake with a frightened shout. The force of his movement shocked Kaiya, who withdrew, watching as he stared about in frantic panic, mouth open in almost voiceless scream. After the initial shout, all Kormac could achieve was a high-pitched whine. He stared at her, and in those few moments, she wondered if he could even see her. The panic of his waking began to recede, and he returned to his foetal half-ball, tighter now that he had woken, with the side of his face buried in the pillow.

She couldn't see his face, but she could recognise the gentle movement of silent, hidden crying.

Kaiya watched him for a minute before calling his name in a voice so mild it almost disappeared. He didn't answer. She called again and received the same lack of response, then touched his shoulder. She took his continued stillness as an indication of assent, and moved in once more, this time successful in her desire to hold him.

Kormac buried his face further into the pillow.

Kaiya could feel the detail of his breathing against her body, a progression of ragged unevenness. She spoke his name once more, which seemed only to increase his grief. Her voice had broken his wall of silence, and now the tears flew freer, accompanied by semi-choked lamentation. Kaiya could do nothing but lay there pressed against him, wondering what he had dreamed.

She stayed there for a few minutes until the heat between them became uncomfortable, then kicked the sheets off their legs and rolled onto her back. The air had grown thick with warmth and grief. She turned the windows to semi-night and listened as a faint trickle of distant chatter and roadworks drifted through on a cooling zephyr. Metallic chimes tinkled. Kaiya remained on her back, staring at the ceiling, and reached across to caress Kormac's hair with her fingertips.

He made no immediate response.

In time, he grew silent, and sounds of the outside world overtook her bedroom. A patrol passed below, questioning a man on the street. They pressed for several minutes, attempting to discern his motivation, then arrested him, dissatisfied with his answers. She listened to the man complain, and was grateful when his and the patrol's voices disappeared.

Time began to fall in and out of focus, and she closed her eyes. The breeze must have been all she needed. She glanced at

Kormac, wondering if perhaps he'd fallen back to sleep, and withdrew her hand. She rubbed her fingers together idly, dissipating the light sheen of oil they had gathered.

"I saw your father," Kormac whispered.

At first she didn't register the revelation. "In your dream?"

"No," he said.

The word hung between them, unfurling in her head as a dual seed of hope and trepidation. A large part of her wanted to forget he had said it, and even became angry that whatever illusions she had created might be shattered, whether the outcome were positive or negative. Before Kormac's arrival, she had known the best possible outcome was simply returning.

But that was before. Now she understood that returning was just the beginning.

"When?" she asked, glancing at Kormac from the corner of her eye. He remained on his side, turned away from her, the scars on his back almost glowing in the dull light.

"A few months after I arrived. He was on a truck, passing through our section. I didn't know if he was coming, or going, or staying, but as soon as I saw him I thought of you and..." he paused for a moment. The way he spoke told her that he had been over this story in his head many times before, stripping away its emotional content until only facts remained. "I tried to find him again, but I couldn't. I was surprised, actually. After, what – four and a half years? – he was still alive. I'm sorry, I didn't mean it to sound so blunt. I meant it as a compliment. He was a very tough man, your father."

Kaiya couldn't help but focus on the 'was' in Kormac's sentence and felt a few tears beginning to form. She took a breath and forced herself to stop. "So you only saw him once."

"No. I saw him again. I just couldn't find him the first time I looked. It was all luck. Maybe two months after, I was transferred to a different section, and there he was – the section leader. He noticed me, but he didn't know who I was. I wasn't even sure it was him. I tried to remember the holos you had, but it was difficult. He sat next to me at dinner one evening. Completely random. The Tarkinians are very strict – ordered. If I spoke to a section leader without being asked, I would be... Anyway, he sat next to me, and I had to look around, see if any guards were watching, and I just took a chance. I asked him if he was Harold. Had he been the Police Commissioner in Leth.

"I think it surprised him. He didn't do anything odd – he didn't even look at me – but something changed in his face. You have to understand, there weren't many people from Leth in my camp, or even the other border towns in Nymosen. Very few people spoke Nymian. They were all from Ropruss and the smaller states. Hundreds of thousands of them. It would have been surprising enough for him to meet someone who spoke Nymian, let alone someone who recognised him from Leth. Eventually he looked at me and said yes.

"I told him my name, said that I knew you. Then he wanted to know everything. He tried very hard to make himself appear as though we were having a normal conversation, but he completely ignored his food. I was worried we would attract attention. He asked me how long I had been there in the camp, then he asked about you. And your mother. I said that you were fine when I had last seen you, and that you missed him. He cried."

Kormac fell silent, leaving Kaiya to fight back her own trickle of tears. Her father had long ago become an idea more than anything. To know that Kormac had spoken to him, that he still thought of her, that he had still lived and could possibly still be alive – it all brought him back, as though he could once more be in the hallway, her still a child, opening her door ever so slightly to check that she was sleeping.

"He was so happy. I don't know if that's the right word, but I can't think of any other way to describe it. I couldn't tell him your mother had been taken. So I lied. I told him you were both here. I didn't even know if you were still alright. I can't tell you how afraid I was, Kaiya. I thought about you every day."

Kormac rolled onto his back and placed his hand on Kaiya's thigh. She took it in her own and clasped tight, as if the force of the gesture could stem the mixture of relieved happiness and grief. "I thought about you too," she said, and knew in that moment that she and Kormac had been separated to a degree far greater than she had hoped.

"Tell me more," she said. "Tell me what happened, please. I have to know."

Kormac stroked her wrist with his thumb. "There isn't much more to say. There were rumours that the Tarkinians were beginning to lose. They lifted our production quotas, but your father was never cruel like some of the others. A few weeks later I started the work day and he wasn't there anymore. I don't know where he went, or what happened. I... heard some people say he had been taken to... to Ledophas, but I don't believe that..."

Kaiya found no comfort in his tone of voice. He seemed reluctant. She wished she hadn't asked.

She had already lost one person tonight. She didn't want to know she'd lost another.

"Do you still love me?" Kormac whispered.

He stared at her with piercing, clear eyes, and Kaiya began to weep as she realised that they had come to the end she had struggled so hard to prevent.

"I do," she said, and didn't know if anything could be more true. Already memories and unfulfilled dreams floated through her mind, images of their happiness both real and imagined.

"Tell me I'm still the same," she said. "Please."

Kormac's lips quivered, his eyes shifting between her own as he traced a finger down her cheek. "But you're not," he said, "and I'm not."

Kaiya couldn't discern what hurt more – his rejection of her fantasy, or the fact that she knew he spoke truth. Three years of waiting had brought them to this moment, and now the dreams of a lifetime shared began to unravel fully, exposing a gaping hole filled with nightmares and questions she couldn't bear to confront.

What now? And with whom?

She had buried so many secrets over time, secrets she had told herself Kormac one day would know, secrets of a fleeting tenderness, or the transitory sensation of burning affection, but time and circumstance had betrayed them both, and now there was no one left to listen. In the morning, her home would be empty, and all those buried secrets would decay with time, disintegrating to ashes that would scatter across a lavender field of broken dreams.

And when Kaiya woke to the gentle sun, face tickled by a cooling breeze, she knew at once she was alone.

15

JOSEPH GAZED AT HER IN THE SILENCE. "SO HE LEFT."

"Yeah."

Kaiya sat across from the Chief Inspector, staring at the holos on his desk.

"How do you feel about that?"

She sighed. "I don't want to think about it." She no longer had the energy to delve within herself and confront what was there. All she wanted was to float away into some state of endless dreaming, disconnected from all the cares and concerns of humankind.

"I understand," Joseph said.

Kaiya closed her eyes in weariness and realised that she believed him.

"Did you bring your phone?" he asked.

"I still can't use it."

"Not here, no, but you'll have service again as we approach Akheron," Joseph said. "Non-Occupied areas managed to repair transmission nodes after the Network virus. We still have another week or so before we get any service here."

"I don't even know if I have the right address," Kaiya said.

"I checked it against our records from six years ago," Joseph said, "and it was accurate then. Your uncle has been living in the same place for thirty years – I doubt he's decided to move in the past six."

"He might not want to see me."

"Then again, he might," Joseph said. "Worry about that when it happens, ok?"

Kaiya nodded.

She watched the Chief Inspector, trying to piece together what kind of man he was behind the disparate parts of himself he had shown since they first met. He seemed contradictory, capable both of calm restraint and violence, of patience and of agitation, but then... so had Kormac, and Tilda, and Amelia, and Benjamin, and if she thought back, so had her parents.

So which part was the real Joseph?

"That's your wife, isn't it?" Kaiya asked, pointing to one of the holos. "What does she do?"

Joseph smiled softly at the holo. "Why do you ask?"

Kaiya shrugged. "Just... making conversation."

The Chief Inspector studied her. "She's a teacher," he said, "at SouthEast Public. Grade five."

"Does she like it?"

"She does."

"I don't mean to pry," Kaiya said.

"That's exactly what you mean," Joseph said, "but that doesn't make it wrong. Curiosity is good. It means you care."

"I don't know about that," she said.

The holo toddler boy gazed up at Joseph.

"Why are you taking me to Akheron?" Kaiya asked. "It's not to assist you in finding Bennett. You don't need me for that. And there's no way you'd want to bother keeping an eye on me while you do whatever it is you do, so if you want me to trust you, then tell me why you're really taking me."

Joseph considered her. "There is no single reason I am taking you, Kaiya. As your mentor under the restorative provisions set down in your sentence, I have a wide capacity to provide experiences and create contexts that I feel will be of benefit to you and, ultimately, the community. If it will make you feel better to know the multiple reasons I have made this choice, then I have no reason not to oblige. I want you to see your uncle Kytos. I want you to attend some of the hearings at the court of priority. I want you to be present when I make the arrest on Bennett. And I had wanted you to take someone with whom you could make a few positive memories in the capital. Is that a detailed enough answer for you? Do you... approve?"

"I don't really have a say in it," Kaiya said.

"No, you don't," Joseph said. "But you can still decide to approve or not."

Kaiya frowned. There was some kind of understanding just outside of her grasp. She could sense it.

"The only flaw in my plan," Joseph continued, "is that now you don't have Kormac. What about that other friend of yours, the girl... Tilda?"

Kaiya shook her head, offering no explanation. The Chief Inspector wouldn't understand.

"Do you have... *any* friends?" he asked.

She shot him a warning glance. She didn't need silly questions about irrelevant people.

"Why would you take me when you arrest Bennett?" she asked. "I still don't understand why you want to involve me. It's not... normal."

"There is something unique about the relationship between you and Bennett," Joseph said. "I didn't notice it until I reviewed the recording of your conversation with him in the concealed prison. He responds to you in a different way than anyone else we've had speak to him."

"So you're using me like... bait," Kaiya said.

"Is that a problem?"

Kaiya considered the statement. "No. I guess not. What am I supposed to do, though?"

"I don't know yet," Joseph said. "Leave that to the day. I'll figure something out."

Kaiya fidgeted in her chair, looking away from Joseph.

"Bennett said something when I talked to him," she said. "He said you... had an idea what happened to my father."

"Yes, he did say that," Joseph said. "But Bennett says a lot of things, and—"

"Don't lie to me," Kaiya said. "I hate Bennett, but I know he's not a liar. You had something to do with my father. You know where he is, don't you? That's why Benjamin put you with me. I know what Benjamin's like. He never tells you what he's thinking. He's manipulative."

"That's a pejorative way of putting it," Joseph said, "but you are correct in your analysis of Benjamin's character. And you are astute to recognise that there is a reason Benjamin placed me with you. What you are lacking, though, is the accuracy of that reason. I will not be providing that reason today."

Kaiya's stomach twisted at the dawning realisation Joseph really *did* have something to do with her father. She chided herself for having let Bennett go on with his silly notions of poetry when she should have pushed the truth out of him.

"I need to know," she said. "Please, I don't care what it is, I just need to know. I need—"

"Kaiya," Joseph warned. "I will not be changing my mind. There will be an opportunity for you to know the extent of my involvement with your father, but that opportunity is not today. If the next few days are going to work, I need you to place your trust in me. Not because I have shared information with you, but because I have not. That is the nature of trust."

"But I don't—" Kaiya said automatically. "You're..."

She didn't know what to say, and frowned.

"I'm what?" Joseph asked. "A collaborator? A traitor? A liar? Or are you tired of those labels?"

Kaiya remained silent, churning over the question.

"As much as you want me to tell you about your father," he said, "the person who needs to know something, in our situation, is me. I take it you've thought about what I said two days ago?"

A flurry of heat prickled across Kaiya's skin, descending into her stomach and crawling all the way up to her throat, where it threatened to choke her, demanding to escape from the inevitable disclosure she had realised must be made. She lost focus momentarily as she squirmed in her seat.

"Yes," she said.

Joseph was studying her again, his eyes irrepressible augers.

Kaiya sighed, just to let out the pent-up energy of anxiety. Already she could feel the shame. Joseph would look at her differently after this. If he even believed her in the first place.

"I was raped," she said at last.

The words hung in the air with no reaction. Joseph continued to stare at her. Her heart continued to thump against its prison. The world continued just as it had before. And in her mind, the event became a fact. A detached image in a sea of other moments of her life.

She sounded pathetic.

"It was a soldier," she added.

As if that made it any better.

Joseph nodded gently. "I'm sorry," he said.

Kaiya shrugged over-casually. "Not your fault."

"But deep down you blame us, don't you?" Joseph said. "If we had all stayed loyal, all fought back, then maybe we would have kept the Tarkinians out. There would never have been one there to do that."

Kaiya's eyes shot back to Joseph. Of course – she should have realised he would misunderstand.

"It wasn't a Tarkinian," she said. "He was Nymian."

"Sorry?" Joseph said.

"A Nymian," she repeated.

"No, I heard you..." he said. "That changes things."

"How?"

"Where was he from?" Joseph asked. "Do you know any details about him?"

Kaiya hesitated and told Joseph the soldier's name. "He was... from Akheron."

Joseph sat back in his chair and went quiet.

"That's why I stopped hosting," Kaiya added. "I never told Amelia."

"Why not?" Joseph asked. "You don't think she might have been able to help?"

"I don't know," she said, folding her arms. Sure, he made it sound so easy now...

"Doesn't matter," Joseph said. "Can't be changed."

He kept watching her. Thinking. Probably realising how much of a mistake he'd made by taking her on as mentor. How much time he'd already wasted with her.

"I have a question," he said, "that you don't have to answer. This Masuma girl, in the hospital. Is there something... extra that you feel you share with her. Something... beyond what you've already told me?"

Kaiya watched officers walking along the corridor outside, and gave a murmur of assent.

"And you..." Joseph began, raising his eyebrows. Kaiya murmured assent once more, and Joseph nodded. How Masuma would live with the reality of her situation, Kaiya didn't know. Even a year later, the realisation of what had existed inside herself made her feel dirty.

Corrupted.

Joseph would never understand.

"I sound like an idiot," Kaiya said.

"Why?"

"Because it's so... meaningless, isn't it? So what? Big deal, who cares, happens all the time."

"Are you trying to convince me of that, or convince yourself?" Joseph asked. "Cause the first one won't happen, and the second is a long way from happening."

Kaiya ventured her eyes to Joseph's placid face. "I just... I'm so... angry."

"I know," Joseph said. "I can tell."

"But *still*," Kaiya said. "All the time. And I can't stop... thinking about it. And then all these people, and they just don't care about anything. And... I want them to pay! I want them to suffer! They're the ones that let all this happen. They didn't fight back, and... and they should have... and I should have fought back, but I didn't. I didn't know how to, I was so... numb, and... I just let it happen, and everyone let everything happen, and you people all sitting here in your headquarters, like... I don't know what like! And those women! You know Tilda was one of them? And she *knew!* She was the only one I told, and she was fucking some Tarkinian the whole time. And all those people giving information, cowards, and then you tell me we shouldn't punish them? I hate them all! I want them to die! And you know where it starts? *Bennett!* Fucking *Bennett!* I want to hurt him. I want to... cut him, make him bleed... no, I don't know, it's not him. It's... '*him,*' too. It's always '*him.*' It's always been him. It's like he's laughing at me, like he knows he'll always have that part of me now. I want to... stab him in the throat, I want to tear his heart out, I want to watch him die. I want to feel his blood and knife his eyes. I want him to know I beat him! That's what I want. Nothing can be good again until he knows that *I* won – not him!"

Kaiya gasped, keeping her face tight to hold in the chaotic swell of emotions demanding voice. Thin, wet tracks glistened down her cheek. So *weak!* So *useless!*

"I wish I was like Amelia," she said, voice cracking. "I wish I could say things like she says them. I wish I had her words. I wish that people would listen to me and... love me like they loved her. But I just... I ruin everything. Because that's what I am. Like a disease."

Kaiya leaned forward, head in hands, and wept. Everything swam in her vision, a flood of things she'd never thought she would say. Joseph's office felt stifling, yet her chest was lighter than she could remember in a long time.

For the next several minutes Joseph stayed silent.

"Kaiya," he said at last.

She didn't respond straight away, but wiped her eyes and sat back up in her chair. The tiny scars on her face made her tears travel in odd directions.

"You're allowed to feel this way," Joseph said.

"I know that," Kaiya said, too quickly. "I don't need your permission."

"No, you don't," Joseph said, "but you have it anyway."

"Please don't pretend to care," Kaiya said. "I hate it when people lie. You have my *permission* to think I'm overreacting."

"Would it matter if I thought that?" Joseph asked. "Would that change how it feels to you?"

Kaiya frowned. "So you're saying that's what you think."

"You're being difficult," Joseph said.

She let out a snort of wet laughter. "I know."

Joseph grinned, and she began to compose herself.

"I'm not sure where to start with all those... thoughts," Joseph said, "but I'm glad you told me. You are much clearer, now. How do you feel?"

"I don't know," Kaiya said. "Tired."

"It takes a lot to hide all that from yourself," Joseph said. "You seem more surprised than I am."

"Maybe..."

"I don't have the power to... fix all the things you mentioned," Joseph said, "but there's one thing I might be able to do. What do you mean when you say you need to 'beat' him?"

Kaiya stumbled as she began to respond, trying to articulate for the first time thoughts that had rambled through her head for so long. "You can't just... what if someone came and robbed you? Took a bunch of stuff, or... something that meant a lot to you."

"Then I wouldn't have possession of those items anymore," Joseph said.

"Exactly," Kaiya said, and frowned to herself.

"You see the problem with the analogy?" Joseph asked.

She tried to pull her thoughts together into a coherent response. Now she was going to look like even more of a fool!

"You're trying to say he stole something from you," Joseph said, "but the problem with theft is that the material wrong is ongoing. In your scenario, I am separated from my possessions in that moment and in all the moments thereafter. But in your case, the event has happened. If you want to make the analogy work, you need to tell me what it is he has taken that you don't have anymore."

"But it's not about the physical," Kaiya said. "It's... other stuff. It's... dignity."

"So he possesses something of yours that is immaterial," Joseph said. "Something... intangible. Spiritual, even."

"Yes."

Joseph considered the ceiling for a short while. "But *how* does he possess it? The thief that steals from me – he can physically hold those items. But how can your attacker have possession of your dignity? Is dignity something you're born with and... you can lose it, or have it taken? Can you become a person without this intangible 'stuff' inside you?"

"I guess so," Kaiya said.

"Tell me what that means to you," Joseph said. "Dignity."

Kaiya fidgeted. Why did they have to go through all of this? What was he so curious about?

"You don't understand what it's like," Kaiya said. "It was so… humiliating. Like I was just… a thing. Like I was worthless."

"So dignity is your sense of self-worth," Joseph said. "Your inherent value as a human being?"

"Ok," she said. "If that's how you want to put it."

"Would you say that everyone has some kind of… inherent value?" Joseph said. "Does Kormac still have inherent value, even though the Tarkinians had him for three years? What about your little friend, Masuma?"

Kaiya made to speak, but held back. She needed to give this answer more thought.

"Let's take Masuma," Joseph continued. "Surely you look at her and see something of value, don't you? You don't just see a… shell, for want of a better word. Or is that the reason you spend time with her, because it makes you feel better that you're not as 'broken' as her?"

"That's not fair," Kaiya said.

"I'm not trying to be fair," Joseph said. "I'm trying to get to the bottom of what you think. We both know what happened to Masuma and how long it happened for. If you had your dignity stolen, and now you don't have it anymore, then what does that say about Masuma? She has even less value than you?"

"Of course not," Kaiya said, trying to grasp some stray thought that would bring together her argument. "Of course she has dignity, because… well, I guess cause I see her as having it. Dignity only matters if other people think you have it as well."

"I don't agree at all," Joseph said. "If it only matters what other people think, then you're saying that people aren't born with dignity. You're saying dignity is conditional."

"Maybe it is," Kaiya said.

"Then how does one attain dignity?" Joseph asked. "You'd have to have dignity in the first place for someone to steal it, which means you'd have to get it from somewhere, which means you'd be able to get some more, wouldn't it? Then it would be just like if someone stole my chair, and I went to buy a new one."

Kaiya frowned. "You can't just... buy dignity."

"No, I agree," Joseph said. "I much prefer the idea that we have dignity regardless of what anyone else does. Born with it. Can't take it. Can't steal it. Can't give it away. It can be disrespected, or you can disrespect it yourself, but it's not going anywhere. So maybe it's not a case of someone stealing your dignity. Maybe... you have no respect for it anymore."

"You're saying it's my fault?"

"Hang on," Joseph said, "I never said anything was your *fault*. Take a step back. I'm telling you that just because he did something bad to you, it doesn't mean your value is diminished. He disrespected your dignity, but he didn't steal it. And now I'm saying that every day you think that you don't have it anymore, you're the one disrespecting yourself. You're basing your entire sense of self on him and his actions."

Kaiya searched for something she could say in response. He had to be wrong. Why couldn't he just accept what she said and leave it at that? She hated having to explain herself.

"But even if you're right," she said, "it still hurts."

"Yes," Joseph said. "Yes, it does. And I don't want to take away from that, believe me. But my job isn't to help you feel more hurt."

"You're denying how I feel," Kaiya said. "You said it's ok for me to feel this way, and now you're saying I'm wrong for it."

"I'm not denying you anything," Joseph said. "I am challenging you to see beyond the confines you've created for yourself. You're allowed to feel any way you like, but why are we here in the first place?"

She waited for the Chief Inspector to go on, but realised he expected her to answer.

"It's not fair," she said.

"Why are we here in the first place?" Joseph repeated.

Kaiya sighed in frustration and held back for several seconds before finally responding. "Because I hurt someone."

"That's right," Joseph said. "Because you hurt someone. And the only reason you did that is because you didn't feel your life was worth anything. So as much as it's ok to feel the way you feel, the things you do because of that have consequences for people other than just you."

"But you're still saying—"

"Whatever you *think* I'm saying," Joseph said, "it's not what I'm really saying. The important thing is this, Kaiya – there is nothing about you that is any worse because of what he did."

"It doesn't feel that way."

"No, it doesn't," Joseph said, "but you've been thinking like this for a long time. You were born into thinking like this. It's all around you. The idea that you only have worth in relation to other people. But it's not true."

Kaiya studied the Chief Inspector's face, tracing the emerging lines and smattering of grey hair. "How did you get so wise?" she asked. "What happened to give you so many... opinions?"

Joseph laughed and adjusted himself in his chair. "Just life," he said. "Benjamin. My capstone mentor Alison Meer. If I say anything that is worthwhile, it's because they taught me."

"Always Benjamin," Kaiya said. "I don't remember him ever being interested in these sorts of thing. I just remember him being... weird."

"You can hardly expect the man to reveal the truth of himself to a child or a teenager," Joseph said. "You were too young to appreciate him. But your parents obviously did."

Kaiya smiled softly. "You know, mum said that he'd be the Commissioner one day. It was just in passing, and I laughed. But she was serious, and I didn't know why. I still don't, to be honest."

Joseph nodded. "Well, the force is still standing, and I can tell you that means a lot, right now. Every day feels like this building might explode. That everything might disintegrate... but I know exactly what you're doing – you're taking us off track."

He grinned at her and she couldn't help but snicker.

"I didn't think that..." she began. "I was afraid of today. Of what you'd say."

"Understandably so," Joseph said. "I'm not going to pretend that anyone else here would have reacted in the same way. The vast majority would have agreed with your analogy – end of story. But that goes back centuries. Thousands of years, even. It takes time for new mindsets to filter through society, especially into organisations like this one. It's never the people affected that change the minds of people in authority. Authority only ever listens to other authority. So the only way you can change those minds is to reach them from a place of authority."

"Then how did you come to change your mind, if you're part of that group?"

Joseph grinned. "I guess you could say I'm a bit... anti-establishment."

"But why?" Kaiya asked. "Why would you join the police if you didn't really approve of them?"

"I did, when I joined," Joseph said, "but you're taking us off track again."

Kaiya didn't pursue the matter, but couldn't help feeling that Joseph was hiding something.

"I want to see if there's another way we can look at what happened to you," he said. "You said it was like stealing, but what if I said that it's like being beaten up? Do you think it would have been different if he'd done that, instead?"

Kaiya stared back to the holos on Joseph's desk and tried to imagine the difference. "Yes. It would have been different."

"Why?"

"Because when you beat someone up, you hurt their body," Kaiya said. "But when... when someone rapes you they're... well they're not *taking* anything, I guess, but they're hurting the other parts of you. Your mind."

"Psychic harm," Joseph offered. "But rape can hurt you physically, can't it?"

"I guess it can."

"I've had cases like that," Joseph said. "And are you saying that there is no psychic harm done to someone who is beaten up? That their injuries are solely physical?"

Kaiya heard the desperate screams of a teenage girl in a night-darkened vestibule, and began to see where the Chief Inspector was leading.

"Well... I'm not saying there's none," she said, "but I still think it's different."

"How, though?" Joseph asked. "A perpetrator disrespects the victim's dignity in both cases. They both use their bodies as weapons, albeit different parts. They both can cause physical harm. They both can cause psychic harm. And both are events that occur at a specific moment in time and then are over, unlike your example of theft. Injuries can take time to heal, of course, but there is no question that they injuries *will* heal. In most cases, at least."

"But it's not like someone punched me in the face," Kaiya said. "Anyone can get punched in the face. This is specific. It's not just... an assault. It's an attack on who I am. *Because* of who I am."

"A woman?"

"Exactly," Kaiya said.

"So it's different because you're targeted for your identity," Joseph said. "Somewhat like Tilda was targeted for sleeping with a Tarkinian, or how certain people were targeted for giving the Tarkinians information. Collaborators, correct?"

"But people reacted to them doing something. I just had to exist."

"Yes," Joseph admitted. "That is a fair point. But couldn't we still say that every victim of assault is targeted for a specific reason?" Joseph continued. "Even if it is merely identity. What if you assaulted a Tarkinian for merely being a Tarkinian?"

"But it's not the same," Kaiya said. "It's not just who the person is, it's using who that person is against them."

"That I won't disagree with," Joseph said. "You're certainly right there. But is that all you are? A piece of anatomy? Is that how I'm supposed to see you – how you see yourself?"

"I'm still right, though," Kaiya said. "Even if it's not all of who I am, it's still a part of who I am. An important part."

"Only if we see our sexuality as sacred," Joseph said.

"But it *is* sacred," Kaiya said. "It's not the same as any other part of ourselves. You can't say your hand or your hair or your ear has the same value. It doesn't."

"And that's where the discussion ends," Joseph said. "Now we're in the domain of very personal judgments. I couldn't possibly tell you what is and is not sacred about your or anyone else's body. What if you were an artist? Then maybe you'd think your hands are the most important part of you. Or if your whole life revolved around some intellectual pursuit. Then maybe you'd value your mind more. The only thing I would suggest... is to think about this: do you see that part of yourself as sacred because you decided it is, or because you allowed someone or something else to decide it?"

Kaiya sat quietly for a short time as she gave the question serious consideration. There was a wider point Joseph was getting at, she could tell that much. Maybe it would become clear to her with time.

"I thought you had the answer," Kaiya said. "I thought you'd try to convince me I'm wrong, again."

Joseph laughed. "It's not about being wrong. This isn't a

lecture with definitive answers. Thinking you have the answers gets you into trouble. Think of this as... an invitation, instead. That you're allowed to see yourself and your life differently to how you might have before."

Kaiya nodded and looked over to the holo of Joseph's wife. What kind of conversations did they have at the dinner table? In bed? What kind of stuff did they argue about? After everything she and Joseph had discussed, she still knew almost nothing about him, yet her soul lay bare to his influence and gaze.

"So what now?" Kaiya asked.

The Chief Inspector gave a thoughtful sigh. "Do you still feel the need to 'beat' him?"

Kaiya licked her lips and stared at the table, conscious of the potential disappointment Joseph might express at her answer. "Yes."

"I'm not going to let you... do what you like to him, as you so eloquently described earlier," Joseph said drily, "but I think we can manage one more item on our agenda. If that's something you want."

He gazed at her with keen intensity, and slowly the whole world began to brighten. "Of course I want it," she said. She shouldn't have had to even say it. A new desire filled her, one she hadn't thought she'd ever experience: an eagerness to see the capital.

"I have only one condition," Joseph said. "Find someone to take Kormac's seat."

Kaiya already knew who to invite.

She was finally ready to face Akheron.

16

KAIYA STOOD BACKPACKED AT THE TRAIN STATION, A SMALL travelling bag by her feet. *Allied Atlantica* soldiers milled about, sometimes chatting in clumps, other times by themselves with heads buried in a tablet, all of them obviously on leave. They would pass by and greet her politely from time to time, and she would return the gesture. The soldiers made up the bulk of those waiting, but she could see pockets of Nymians here and there, most of them in business attire, and only a few families. The train would be far from full.

She checked her phone, useless for so long. Still useless. She dreaded the moment that reception returned and she would have to call her uncle. He might not even still be alive. The thought both terrified and relieved. If Kytos *were* dead, at least she wouldn't have to see him, but then... accommodation in Akheron was expensive.

She wasn't sure which would be worse.

"Where is he?" Joseph asked as he approached.

"Over there," Kaiya said.

Jonathan chatted with his countrymen.

Joseph looked at him and gave an approving nod. "Good selection. Your children will be magnificent."

Kaiya gave him a withering look. "Seriously? You're not going to turn comedian on me, are you?"

"Who said I was making a joke?" he said with a grin.

Kaiya rolled her eyes.

The hazard bells began to ring, and station wardens patrolled the platform making sure everyone was well clear of the opening hatch. The centre of the platform began to disappear, sliding off into either side, and the sound of charging magnets whirred over the station. Inch by inch the train levitated into position, each pod lifted individually before snapping together with its neighbours and stabilising.

Kaiya picked up her travelling bag and watched as soldiers and civilians readied themselves to board. Here and there a few people embraced loved ones, farewelling them to whatever business they had in Akheron or the smaller towns between.

Jonathan returned, duffel bag hanging over his shoulder.

"You must be Jonathan," Joseph said with an extended hand, and they made their introductions.

"Thanks for inviting me," Jonathan said. "I was lucky to get the leave. The Captain likes me, though, so that helps."

He glanced across at Kaiya, eyes sparkling in the midday sun.

She gave him a polite smile, then looked away. Hopefully this wouldn't turn out to be a terrible decision.

"You two are in carriage thirty-six," Joseph said, proffering his identity card. Kaiya took out her own and swiped it against Joseph's to complete the document transfer.

"You're not with us?" she said.

Joseph shook his head. "When I bought the tickets... well, the circumstances were different. Besides, I don't need to monitor your every move. You'd be stupid to try running away."

Jonathan didn't seem to notice the subtle hint that he wasn't originally intended to come, but his eyes flicked over at the mention of running away.

Kaiya forced a laugh and glared at Joseph. "Funny."

His response was amusement. "I'll see you in Akheron," he said, and gave Jonathan a casual salute. The Atlantican took it more seriously than Joseph must have intended it, and Kaiya smiled at the soldier's naïvete.

"Wait," she called to Joseph, "what if—"

"I'm sure you'll survive!" he called back.

The platform was emptying, and Kaiya scanned the detachable pods for number thirty-six. She and Jonathan stepped inside the four-person pod and sat on opposite sides. Visible through the crack separating platform and tracks, the magnets whirred beneath, fascinating her. That was the kind of thing she could see herself working on. None of those horrific energy conductors. A magnet had no biology – much better.

Preceded by warning beeps, the pod carriage doors began to close, softening the whir of the magnets until they were a barely-recognisable hum. Kaiya could only hear them because she listened, but soon enough her brain would make the sound a mere aspect of the background, and it would disappear.

"How long is the journey?" Jonathan asked.

"Can't be more than an hour straight through," Kaiya said. "But we have middle stops, so probably twice as long. Don't get to maximum speed, with stops."

The Atlantican nodded. How stupid of her – of course he knew how a train worked.

"What are the stops?" he asked.

Kaiya searched the map in her mind. "I think this is doing three, but I can only remember Flegeth. That's right in the middle. The other two are on either side, but..."

"Geography not your strong suit?" Jonathan said.

"Never saw the point in it," Kaiya said. "I'd be happy just staying where I am. Always have been."

"Yes, I seem to recall you saying you hated Akheron," Jonathan said. "And now you're coming to Headquarters and ordering me to go there with you."

"I didn't order you," Kaiya said.

"Suggested, then."

Kaiya grinned. "Strongly suggested."

Jonathan's face cracked open in cheer. "I'd hate to see your 'suggestions' unheeded."

She raised her eyebrows with a murmur. It was a good thing he hadn't.

"How's... Kormac, isn't it?" Jonathan asked. "Is he feeling better?"

Kaiya couldn't tell if the question was one of genuine interest, or a careful fishing line.

"He's doing better," she said, gazing out of the window. Where was he, right at that moment? Where would he sleep tonight? Would he come back while she was in Akheron? Would he have anywhere to go, anyone to see? Was he supposed to go back to the hospital for more of the supplements... had he even taken the supplements with him? Why hadn't she thought to check?

Not that they did anything.

Jonathan was watching her. "So why the trip to Akheron?"

"I have to," Kaiya said, but the answer didn't seem to satisfy Jonathan. "I'm going to see my uncle... and Joseph wants me to go watch the trials."

"You seem close with the Chief Inspector," Jonathan said.

"I barely know him," Kaiya sniggered.

And yet here she was. In truth, she had a deep sense that she could trust Joseph. Where that came from, she couldn't tell, but there was no denying its presence. He knew things – things that she knew he wasn't telling her – and yet... she understood that whatever reasons he had were good.

"And your uncle?" Jonathan asked. "What's he like?"

The pod descended a little as the train began to move.

"I barely know him, either," Kaiya said. "I haven't seen him since I was... six? That's three quarters of my life ago."

"Why so long?" Jonathan asked.

"I don't know, to be honest," Kaiya said. "I think something happened between him and mum, but I don't know. I never thought to ask... although I don't think mum would have told me."

"Why not?"

Kaiya shrugged. "Just not that kind of person? She's... not the kind that dwells on stuff like that. Always goes on about looking on the bright side, positive attitude, crap like that."

Just like Tilda...

No, she had to stop thinking about her.

"Good luck with that," Jonathan said.

Kaiya smiled and stared down at the wall-bounded portion of the river.

"So why Akheron?" she asked. "Of all the places you could see, why there?"

"Because it's beautiful," Jonathan said. His voice revealed the wonder of what he saw in his mind. "I've seen the holos of it. Magnificent. We have nothing like it in Atlantica."

"You have much bigger cities than here," Kaiya said.

"Of course we do. Much bigger. But nothing as unique as Akheron. All that glass, the hanging gardens. So much history."

"You don't think Leth is beautiful? Has history?" Kaiya asked.

"I do," Jonathan said. "But why does that mean I shouldn't visit Akheron, too? I'd hate to come all the way out to Nymosen and not see as much as I can. That's why I grabbed the opportunity. You never know if another one will come."

Kaiya grinned, though she couldn't let go of the feeling that his admiration for Akheron came at the expense of his admiration for Leth. People only had so much admiration to give.

"It was a long shot when I came to invite you," she said. "I didn't think you'd actually be able to."

"All luck," he said. "And being liked. If people like you, you can get away with all sorts of things. Besides, we're not a combat unit, so it's much easier to get the leave."

"You mean you never fight?" Kaiya asked.

"No, we fight," he said. "Just not right now. Some of the other guys were disappointed we wouldn't actually be in the war, but I don't mind it. I like reconstruction. It feels useful."

"So is fighting."

"Sometimes," Jonathan said. "I wouldn't have joined the army if I thought otherwise. But wars always end, don't they? You can't be fighting all the time."

Kaiya considered the statement. "I guess..."

She would have to give that greater thought.

Jonathan grinned. "It does make a difference when the locals let you help them, though."

Kaiya understood his remark and smirked. The train continued to creep forward, approaching the western wall.

"You know, I've never been on a train before," Kaiya said.

"Really? You prefer to drive?"

"I never got the chance to do much of that," she said acerbically. "I've just never been far enough to need one. I'm sure you've noticed Leth is rather small."

"It's... quaint," Jonathan said.

"Not like West Atlantica, I'm sure."

Jonathan laughed. "Not at all."

"Oh, look," Kaiya said.

The train passed over the western limits of Leth, leaving behind the ancient wall that stood guard and had been repaired for centuries on end. A great expanse of verdant valley stretched on either side, straddled by mountains to the north and south. The uncorrupted river wound its way from the north, disappearing from view into the distant mountain crevices and unaware of the role it would soon play in electricity production.

The image of her and Tilda's little stick boats floated through her mind, and she pushed it away with an angry sadness.

"Is it actually called the River of Sticks?" Jonathan asked. "I thought it was just a nickname when I first heard it, but everyone calls it that."

"No, that's its proper name," Kaiya said. "There's a forest in the mountains, it literally drops heaps of sticks and branches and leaves into the water. You can see them from here."

Jonathan chuckled. "Yes, I'm quite aware I can see them from here. I'm looking at them right now."

Kaiya looked at him archly.

"You don't really think very hard when it comes to naming things in this country, do you?" Jonathan said. "You could have called it anything, and you called it the River of Sticks."

"That's what it is, though," Kaiya said. "Why not just name it that way?"

Jonathan grunted. "If you say so. We would have named it after a president or a general. Someone important."

"Leth is older than presidents and generals," Kaiya said. "It's always been the River of Sticks, and it always will be."

"Until the forest dies," Jonathan said.

"That's centuries... thousands of years away," Kaiya said.

"But it's not infinite. So it won't always be the River of Sticks."

"Yeah, whatever," Kaiya said. "You know what I mean."

Jonathan smirked.

The Levway connected to Leth at the southwest corner and broke into tributaries leading to other border towns. Kaiya looked down at the almost empty road passing underneath, one lone car hovering along to the north. Few people had any desire to leave Leth, it seemed.

She glanced towards the southern mountains. Somewhere within them lay a field of lavender, a secret spot she had discovered weeks before the Tarkinians came, enclosed by protective peaks, innocent to the vicissitudes of human existence. She had only been there once, alone, but something tugged at the back of the memory, as if buried.

The image of Kormac returned to her, along with a flood of nostalgia for a love within the lavender that had never occurred. She hadn't known him, then, but... no, she couldn't quite put her finger on the feeling.

"You're very lucky to have all this green," Jonathan said. "We have a river, too, but it's dull. I'm surprised you stay in Leth so much. I'd always be outdoors if I lived here."

Kaiya kept her gaze on the mountains. She didn't appreciate being told how to live her life. "Where do you come from?"

"Astino," Jonathan said. "It's very large. Nice in its own way, but so much younger than Nymosen. It's too modern... and we don't have anything like this scenery nearby. I think... if I wasn't a soldier, I'd like to be a painter. I can see myself down there, painting the scenery. That's what I'd like to paint. Sceneries."

"A painter?" Kaiya asked. "Like in the museum? I didn't know people did that anymore. Except for houses and stuff."

"They don't," Jonathan said. "Not really. It's pretty useless, and not many people care. I'd never make money, but I think I'd like it. I'd have to come to Nymosen. Or anywhere but Astino, at least."

He smiled, but it seemed to Kaiya the gesture hid a great deal.

"I thought you said Astino is nice as well," she said.

"In its own way," Jonathan corrected, but he offered no further explanations.

Kaiya tried to imagine him as a painter, though she couldn't remember ever having seen one before. Perhaps he would dress like a holographer?

"How long have you been in the army?" she asked.

"Eight years serving," he said, "since my eighteenth birthday. Three years training before that."

"Long time," Kaiya said. "Why'd you join so young?"

"Because I could?" he said, shrugging, and then gave the question some more thought. "It got me out of Astino, I guess, for some of the year. I didn't have to spend holidays with my family."

"Oh," Kaiya said. "I see."

"Yes," he said, grinning. "My mother was a complete nutcase. Still is."

Kaiya laughed at Jonathan's joyousness as he spoke. "I'm sorry. I didn't mean to laugh."

"That's about all you can really do," he said. "I understand her better now that I'm older, but when I was a teenager... I just wanted to be anywhere but there. The army came around doing its recruiting, and I thought... why not? I'm guaranteed independence sooner than anything else I could have done. They paid me to train, and I got to walk straight out of high school into service."

"Do you still visit your family?"

"Of course," Jonathan said. "Just not as much as mum would like. It hasn't... clicked for her, yet. I'm not sure it ever will. She still can't understand why we all moved out as soon as we could. I have three brothers."

Kaiya watched his eyes, weighing up whether or not it would be appropriate to probe further.

"What exactly is wrong with her?"

Jonathan didn't respond straight away, and she cursed herself for overstepping the invisible boundary.

"She has the biggest mood swings," Jonathan said. "And she's completely delusional. She'll start talking about something that happened, except that it never happened. She had a complete meltdown when I was seventeen because I wanted to drive to a friend's house. She was crying, throwing things, yelling... going on and on about me having another car crash."

"But you can't crash a car," Kaiya said.

"I know, right? She was convinced I had the year before. I thought maybe it had happened to her or someone else when she was younger – before the anti-collision AI – but I couldn't find anything about it. She's never had one, dad's never had one, none of her friends have had one. She just... made it up out of thin air."

Kaiya murmured her amazement at the story.

"Has she tried to... get help?" she asked.

Jonathan shook his head. "She refuses. Says there's nothing wrong with her. Blames everyone else – *anyone* else – for whatever's going on. We don't even bother bringing it up nowadays. She'll never accept responsibility for herself."

"I wonder how it started," Kaiya mused.

"I don't really care, to be honest. I was over it a long time ago. Now I understand why dad does so much work outside of Astino."

The bitterness in Jonathan's voice was easy to detect.

Kaiya tried to imagine being in the situation Jonathan described, but something inside her resisted, a deep sense of incapability, or perhaps fear. But of what? Surely she could manage a brief period outside of her own existence.

"So how are the road tiles?" Jonathan asked.

"Fine without me," Kaiya said. "I kind of... stopped going."

"You mean you quit?"

"No," Kaiya said. "I just haven't gone back. Haven't spoken to anyone about it, either. I don't think they really care."

"I'm sure someone has noticed," Jonathan said. "What about the money?"

"Don't remind me," Kaiya said. "I've got a little bit saved up. But I'll be fine. I'll start working again when I get back from

Akheron. And my mum and dad will be back any day. Everything will be fine."

Jonathan didn't say anything, but nodded slowly as he watched her.

It unsettled Kaiya, and she gazed back out the window, wondering again what Kormac was doing at that moment.

"How long are you in Leth?" she asked.

Anything to take her mind off him.

Jonathan shrugged. "Could be a month. Could be six months. I've no idea."

"Do you have... someone to go back to?" Kaiya asked. "Or something? What will you do?"

"No one special, no," Jonathan said. "I guess I'll go back to Astino, visit my family. It's been a while, even before I came here. Then try to get deployment somewhere else. Maybe I'll give it all up and be a painter."

They grinned at each other, and Jonathan's eyes sparkled again as the train rounded a bend and the sun shone through the window.

"I think that'd be nice," Kaiya whispered. "Give it all up and be a painter..."

Somewhere beyond those mountains in the distance...

In a secret field of lavender.

———

Kaiya stood on a small side street, examining the old, cracked surface, relic of a time long before her existence. She knelt down and played with the loose, dark stones, pulling out bedraggled weeds here and there. It looked as though the street had travelled quite some distance behind her once upon a time. Now, the landscape had changed, a newer road cutting straight through the old and leaving a jagged mess where they would have intersected. The old street went nowhere, and served only as a makeshift bus stop bearing a faded sign from three years prior informing residents of an upcoming urban renewal project.

By the looks of things, the project had never happened.

Kytos still hadn't answered his phone. The bus journey from the train station had taken over an hour, and block by block Akheron's shining city centre, overwhelmed by glass, had been replaced by concrete brutalism. Kaiya stared around at the poorly-maintained towers and wondered if the entirety of Leth could fit into this single suburb.

A few people waited at the bus stop, staring blankly into the distance, and a few faces here and there made no effort to hide their interest in her arrival. Every window of a nearby ground floor had been smashed, a tattered curtain hanging limp amongst the stillness. The whole layout of the block seemed to stop any sort of breeze from entering, and the only tree in sight looked like it had been dead for years.

Kaiya walked towards one of the buildings, checked it was the correct number, and ascended the broken steps. The front door stood open, careless and defeated. Beside its frame an old, brown device had been attached, sporting oversized buttons with what looked to be long-faded names. She took out her phone, wondering if there was some localweb to which she could connect, but none existed. Even the Network signal was weak. Whatever the brown device was, it had no use to her.

She entered, cautious and quiet, and perused the lobby. The stench of staleness assaulted her. There really was no lobby – just a corridor. Doors to units stood closed, five on each side, with a stairwell visible at the end of the corridor. She approached it and began to climb the plain, aged concrete, lit by ancient-looking industrial lamps, some of them flickering or long dead.

Her scuffing footsteps echoed.

The entry to every floor looked the same, as did each corridor, except for variations in carpet condition and style. Each corridor contained a great, arched window where the first floor's door had been, all of them in various states of disrepair and grime. As she passed the seventh floor she noticed an old woman on a rocking chair, gazing out of the broken window. The woman looked back at her, still rocking, and gave a toothless, wild smile, followed by a cackle of maniacal exuberance.

Kaiya continued upstairs, a little quicker than before.

With fifty-three stories, why didn't the building have a lift? Kaiya didn't think she'd ever worked her legs so hard, and she only needed to go half way up. She wiped her face with the sleeves of her shirt, wanting to throttle whoever had designed the building. Though they were probably long dead. Kytos lived at the end of the corridor, if her details were correct and he was still alive. Upon reaching his floor, she walked to the end of the corridor and leaned against the window frame to catch her breath. Beyond it the Levway, in all its twenty lanes of glory, shone in mid-air, jammed with traffic, a giant holoboard floating on its side. A woman stared back at her from the holoboard, smiling, and Kaiya stepped back from the window in shock.

She was looking at herself.

RAPTURE
free yourself

She turned away from the vision, heart racing, and took off her backpack. She wiped her face with her sleeves again. Perhaps it was just the heat. She glanced back, and stared straight into her own eyes once more.

Kaiya picked up her backpack and stepped towards the door marked with a number nine, fleeing her own unwavering gaze, and knocked. She stayed close to the doorframe, hugging the corner of the corridor that remained outside of the holoboard's view. She waited, and began to realise that she couldn't hear anything from inside any of the apartments. Everyone was silent, it seemed. No conversations, no Vision Casters, no cooking – nothing.

Except for the distant shuffling of steps on the concrete stairs, coming inexorably closer to her level.

Had they been there before?

She knocked on the door again, cursing herself for ever going there. The footsteps on the stairs remained consistent in their approach, sounding faraway and just around the corner all at the same time. She wanted to call Kytos's name, but worried it might alert the stranger to her presence.

If he didn't already know…

Yes. Someone was coming for her.

She knew it.

Something moved inside the unit, grabbing her attention.

"Hang on," came a man's annoyed voice.

The stairwell footsteps gained pace.

Kaiya waited, playing with her thumbs, keeping her eyes on the entrance to the corridor and imagining the moment a face would appear. A series of metallic clinks came through the door beside her until it opened slightly, a metal chain hanging between it and the doorframe.

"Hello?" a man said. "Who are you?"

Kaiya looked through the crack at Uncle Kytos. He hadn't shaved for a fortnight or so and had dark shadows under his eyes, which stared somewhere over her shoulder.

"It's Kaiya," she said.

He made no reaction, at first.

"Your niece," she explained.

Kytos frowned. "How do I know that? I haven't seen her in years."

"I have a holo," she said, pulling out the holodisc Chief Benjamin had given her. She turned it on and showed Kytos the holo of him and her mother. He stared at it without expression, then turned his eyes to Kaiya's face, without reaching her eyes. He closed the door halfway to unlatch the metal chain, and stood back as he opened it. She picked up her bags, conscious of the still-approaching footsteps, and entered.

Before anything else, she noticed the darkness. Kytos had closed the faded, musty curtains of his window, for which Kaiya felt relieved. She walked in slowly, Kytos shutting the door behind her, and looked around at the odd mishmash of anti-quated, run-down furniture, a dining table taking the central position.

"Thanks," she said, as Kytos replaced the chain and locked the door in several ways.

"What are you doing in Akheron?" he said.

"Oh, I... just visiting," she said. "Nothing serious."

"I see."

He walked into a little corridor attached to the living room and hung up the keys.

"I tried to call you," Kaiya said, "but I'm not sure if I have the right number."

"So that was you," Kytos said. "Sorry. I don't answer calls from numbers I don't know. Where are your parents?"

"Tarkinia."

The words fell like boulders in the ocean.

Kytos stared at the wall. "I'm sorry to hear that."

"They'll be home soon," Kaiya said.

"Of course... of course. *Allied Atlantica*," he said dismissively.

Kytos walked over to the dining table and grabbed the ladder back of a chair. "Tarkinians," he snarled.

Kaiya murmured her agreement.

"So you want to stay?" Kytos said. His voice changed suddenly, becoming bright.

"Only if it's no trouble."

"I have a spare bedroom," he said.

Kaiya followed him down the corridor. A small window at its

end gave a view towards the city centre. Kytos opened a nearby door and indicated inside.

"Thanks," Kaiya said as she entered.

No one had been in the room for years, she was certain of it. She put her bags down on the small bed and stepped across to the window, opening its dusty curtains and allowing some light to penetrate the stuffy space. She stared towards Akheron's shining city centre, mostly blocked by the nearby monstrosities of architecture, but at least clear of any face-thieving holoboards. Distant towers nearly all of glass shot into the sky, piercing the heavens, drapes of greenery tumbling off their sides and waving in the air from home gardens pocketed throughout the buildings.

"It's very different to Leth," she said, and looked towards the door.

Kytos stood at the corridor window, gazing out.

He didn't respond at first, and Kaiya turned her attention back to the view, wondering if he were ignoring the question or had just not heard.

"It's a long time since I've been there," he said at last.

"To Leth?"

Kytos gave a long sigh. "Not since I last saw you."

"It probably hasn't changed much," Kaiya said. "Same as it's been for centuries."

"Oh?" Kytos said, his face piquing at the observation. "Even with the Occupation?"

Kaiya thought about the gutted houses and wrecked boulevard. "Well, there's damage, I guess. But it's not like it can't be rebuilt."

"Ah," Kytos said. "I didn't mean the infrastructure."

He looked worried as he stared out the window, but Kaiya couldn't tell if that was simply a result of the deep furrows that lined his face, or a genuine concern for something or other.

"Have you eaten?" he asked, looking over to her.

"No, I'm fine."

"Don't be ridiculous," he said, disappearing down the corridor and calling behind him. "It's a special occasion. We'll order."

Kaiya smiled to herself as she walked over to the doorframe and leaned against it. She had been wary, even after her admission, that her presence might be an unwanted burden, but there was something in Kytos's voice, despite his demeanour, that suggested an inkling of delight. Or perhaps it was all in her imagination, a projection of what she wished to see.

"What do you feel like?" he called.

"I don't mind," she said. A great deal of her was happy just to have been accepted. "Really. Whatever you want."

"Pick a number from one to nine," Kytos said.

"Why?"

"Humour me!"

Kaiya hesitated. "Five."

Kytos walked into the corridor from the kitchen, holding a worn-out tablet that looked as though it didn't even support holographics.

"Good choice," he said.

"What is it?"

"You'll see."

Kaiya was struck by the inflection in his voice. Exactly like her mother's. She followed him into the living room, where he sat in an old, squishy armchair that had seen better days, and looked at her, still avoiding her eyes.

"You look more like your father than your mother," he said.

She sat at the table and smirked. "Are you saying I look like a man?"

Kytos stared at her. "No?"

"I know," she said quickly. "Sorry. Joke."

"Oh, I see. Yes, very funny," he said without laughter.

The stale air suffocated with awkwardness.

"I don't think I look like either of my parents," she said.

Kytos shook his head. "Rubbish. You should look closer at that holo you showed me."

Kaiya filed away the suggestion, but couldn't help a small smile at the positive comparison. "I will."

They fell silent again and Kytos stared away at the wall.

"I can't believe you're here," he whispered.

For some reason Kaiya felt a trickle of responsibility for the length of time that had passed since their last meeting. She knew it had nothing to do with her but, then again, she hadn't been a child the entire time. She could have come at any point, had she really wanted to.

"Neither can I," she said.

"What would your mother think?" he mused.

What did that mean? She wished she had asked. She added it to the list of things she would find out as soon as her mother returned. In truth, his existence had barely ever registered in her mind, but now that they were together she found herself wondering even more why he had never returned to Leth. The only touch of memory she possessed from all those years ago had at least been positive enough for her to not outright dismiss the idea of going there in the first place.

"You could ask her?" she offered semi-humorously. "When she gets back."

Kytos glanced at her as if digging for some buried thought. "Maybe. It *would* be nice to see Leth again, even just to visit the mountains."

"Oh, I love the mountains," Kaiya gushed, latching on to some small aspect of commonality between them.

She felt immediately embarrassed at the revelation.

"Do you go often?" Kytos asked, his eyes betraying genuine interest.

"No," she said. In fact, it occurred to her just how rarely she ever went, despite her profession of love. "It was hard to leave

Leth during the Occupation," she explained, but whether for his or her benefit...

"Well, now you'll be able to go again," Kytos said.

"Yeah," she said, conscious of the excuses her mind was already making to avoid going to all that effort.

She stared away at her memory of the lavender field. Did anyone else know it was there? Surely there were others... but she liked the idea that her eyes had been the only human ones to gaze upon that sheet of waving purple.

There was something about that image that tugged in the back of her mind... something about her and Kormac buried beneath a sheet of unbreakable... no, it was connected to something else. A beach? She and Kormac on a beach, but also in the whispering lavender, though—

A sharp blade of pain sliced through her brain and she grabbed her head with a howl of agony.

"What is it?" Kytos asked.

Her vision swam as the pain dulled to a blunt throbbing. A table came into view beneath her – since when had she been at a table? She could have sworn she was somewhere else... but no, that wasn't right.

"I don't know," she said. The room returned to normal ever so slowly, and Kaiya felt as though something were slipping away – something tiny, something that had been important, once, but she couldn't figure out what it was.

He stared at her, frowning. "Do you need something?"

Kaiya thought about the question as she rubbed her forehead. "No, I don't think so."

She traced the conversation with Kytos in her head, wondering if the thought of Leth had somehow been responsible, but the idea seemed ludicrous. She wondered when she might go to the mountains again – she liked them, after all – but pushed aside the intrusion, marvelling at her mind's ability to present irrelevancies at such times, and after years of paying no heed to the object of the thought.

Later, she reflected on her experience as she lay in bed, and decided it had been nothing more than a chance moment. She smiled as she drifted to sleep.

She would be ready for another basic treatment by the time she returned home.

17

Kaiya woke, beams of glittering light piercing the stained window of her temporary bedroom. It felt stuffy. She stretched out, kicking one leg over the sheets, and stared at the window, wishing she could control it from the bed, which had been remarkably comfortable, given the general state of shabbiness in which Kytos kept his apartment. She hadn't expected him to possess anything of great comfort or quality.

The light sparkled against the wall, an odd spectacle. She stared at it, wondering what could give it such a quality, until she remembered the position Kytos's apartment held in relation to the sun and central Akheron. She sighed as she edged herself out of the bed, regretful of her decision to leave it, and walked over to the window.

At first glance, Akheron seemed ablaze with golden fire, too strong to look at for any length more than a few seconds. Kaiya averted her eyes, the image imprinted within them, and went about seeing if she could open the window. It had a metal fastening on the bottom, which she stared at for a few moments before twisting it about until the two components unlatched from each other. She struggled to pull the window up. It must have been years since anyone had opened it. A blast of breeze entered the room, giving her a shock that led to laughter. She had never felt anything like it! Perhaps her experience was affected by the height of the building, or the fact that the air was unfiltered by the kind of windows she had grown up with. Probably both.

She glanced towards the city again, allowing her eyes sufficient time to adjust before she placed them in the direction of the glass towers. She understood, now, why people called Akheron the City of Light. Everything shone, even the nearby concrete, it seemed. She gazed up into the cloudless sky towards the tops of Akheron's mighty skyscrapers, though they didn't scrape the sky so much as obliterate the concept of it. She poked her head out of the window and looked down, clutching onto the walls beside her as she realised just how far a drop of twenty-six storeys appeared. She pulled her head back inside and began to laugh again, half to dispel the fright of such height.

The breeze cooled the bedroom, sucking out years of stale air. In the glittering reflections of Akheron, the bedroom no longer seemed decrepit and unloved, but glowed with mystery and stories Kaiya knew nothing about. She sat back down on the bed, drinking in the transformation, and thought about what the day to come would offer. Joseph expected her at the police headquarters within the next few hours.

After a few minutes of consideration, she stood and opened the door to discover Kytos sitting just outside, staring out the window towards the city centre. The light illuminated the entire corridor, and crept into every crevice of his face, highlighting the lines of closed-off worry and splotches of silver against his receding hairline. He looked up at her, pensive, and lifted the edges of his clenched mouth into the lightest of smiles. "Morning," he mumbled, returning his gaze to the view outside.

"Morning," Kaiya said, and joined him in staring out the window. Even the years absent of cleaning made no difference to the power of the light, which streamed in and filled every place of darkness it could find.

"It won't last long, the light" Kytos said. "It's never quite so nice as it is right now."

"It's beautiful," Kaiya said.

"If only those bloody buildings didn't get in the way."

She hadn't noticed until Kytos mentioned them.

"At least you get some of it," she said.

They remained there for a few minutes, silent, until Kytos stood up, turned his back on the window, and carried his chair back to the dining table. Kaiya stayed, conscious of his variable mood. Perhaps she had become a burden already...

"Would you like some breakfast?" Kytos called. "I don't really have anything. Cereal – that's about it. I would have gone shopping if I'd known you were coming."

"That's fine," she said, pushing aside the fear that there had been a barb beneath his final remark. She walked into the kitchen and watched as Kytos pulled out the bowls and a cereal box. "Oh, I like that one."

"You do?" He finished pouring and looked up at her. "It's terrible for you, you know that, right?"

"Yeah, I know." She smiled. "Tastes good, though."

Kytos grinned. "I think I'm addicted. I've been eating it for decades. Sometimes I won't eat anything else for days."

"I know what you mean. I don't think I've gone that far, though."

"You shouldn't," Kytos said. "It's very hard to go back to eating normal food after this stuff." He picked up a chill bottle and poured some milk into each bowl. "You're still young. Get off it while you still can." He handed her a bowl.

"Thanks," she said, and moved into the dining room, where the reflections from Akheron's towers brought out the hidden gloss of Kytos's dark table. She grabbed a spoon from the holder and began to eat. The sweetness hit her like an explosion of joy, and she finished the bowl with little delicacy, Kytos a mirror.

"Do you want some more?" he said once their spoons hit the empty bowls.

"Only if you are."

"Of course I am."

Kaiya smiled, buoyed by the rush of sugar, and Kytos went to the kitchen. He returned soon after, and she saw that the second bowl had been filled higher than the first.

They ate in silence as Kytos perused his tablet. "Apparently there's a protest today."

"Oh? What about?"

"The trials, of course. Deportations. *Allied Atlantica* not doing enough."

Kaiya frowned. "I didn't think people in Akheron cared."

Kytos raised his eyebrows. "Really? We have more people missing here than the whole population of Leth."

She kept her spoon in the bowl and chewed on the remaining cereal in her mouth. "But the Tarkinians never got this far."

"Only because we surrendered," Kytos said. "We let them carve the country up. Surrendered! I fought, you know, in the last war. We *never* surrendered."

"You were a soldier?" she asked, filing away the new information into her meagre collection.

"A long time ago," Kytos said. "Joined as soon as I was old enough to start the training, even if I couldn't be deployed until I was older." He clenched his jaw and stared away at some distant memory. "I wanted your mother to join, but she was too focused on getting a scholarship for Nym State. We had our separate ways out, I guess."

She waited for some explanation, then realised none would be forthcoming. "What do you mean out?"

"Oh," he said, and glanced at her briefly for a few moments

while he considered his words. "Maybe another time. I shouldn't have assumed you knew."

"Mum never went to Nym State," she said.

"No, she went to Leth instead. Anyway, that's something you should ask her about."

"Kind of hard."

He sighed and shook his head. "I know."

Her mother had never said anything about Nym State. Now that she thought about it, her mother had never said much about Akheron at all. She wasn't sure her mother had told her anything, nor had she ever thought to ask. Another trickle of guilt gnawed away at her insides, and she cast her mind towards anything that would help to ignore it.

"I'm going to see the trials, today," she said.

Kytos scoffed. "Why bother? You'll never see the real collaborators in there, the ones who let the Tarkinians take over. It's a farce."

She felt an immediate connection with him, though she did think back to what Joseph had said, wondering which of them to believe. Joseph had said nothing for her to believe that he would lie, but Kytos's reaction tapped into something deep inside her.

"I guess we had to surrender, though, didn't we?" she said. "The Network and all..."

"What about it?" Kytos said, becoming angry. "They should never have been able to touch it! The Network should never have been so unprotected. We were asking for it!" He shook his head, eyes filled with frustration, and banged the table with his hand. "We should have known. The Tarkinians have always been the same. You *cannot* give them a chance – they'll just come back and destroy you again and again and again. We should have *learnt* that, as a country, but we haven't! And we should have kept fighting. I don't care if we all died, we should have kept fighting, rather than this... shame. That's what we have to live with, now. Shame. I am ashamed to be Nymian."

He left the table with a scowl, leaving Kaiya with silence and the fading of the glittery morning light.

Kytos was right.

Nothing she nor anyone else had done during the Occupation meant a thing. In truth, she and a collaborator held no difference. Nymosen's eventual victory held no value. They had all lost the moment they surrendered to the Tarkinians, and become nothing but symbols of shame for a man whose city had never even come under attack.

Kaiya glared at the table, unsettled by this line of thinking.

They should have known...

The Akheron Police Headquarters gleamed in mid-morning sun, a modest tower by the standards of the capital. The vast majority of glass had been made opaque, but a few panels here and there afforded uninterrupted views of those officers working inside. A man in uniform sat at a table against his window a few storeys above ground level, gazing dreamily into the distance. Kaiya watched him for a few minutes as she sat on one of the benches outside, waiting to see if he moved.

"You're on time," came Joseph's voice. He sounded almost surprised, striding up the wide parade in front of Headquarters.

"Actually, I'm early," Kaiya said. "If I were on time I'd be arriving... right about now."

Joseph gave a short laugh and indicated for her to rise. They walked up the middle of the symmetrical parade, benches placed equidistantly on its borders and creating a barrier – psychological more than physical – between the minor pedestrian traffic and two identical, mirror image gardens.

Kaiya looked back up at the dreaming officer before she lost sight of him. He still hadn't moved.

"So what are we doing?" Kaiya asked.

They stepped forward into the palatial reception.

"We are meeting Chief Inspector Alison Meer," Joseph said. "She's... well, you'll see."

They made their way through a security scan and Joseph occasionally greeted someone he knew. "I did my training here," he explained. "The woman we're meeting – Alison – was my interrogation instructor and my capstone mentor. Let's just say I didn't underestimate her after our first session. She could have been an Assistant Commissioner by now, if she'd played the politics."

"What, like Bennett?" Kaiya said.

"I have to say, I've never thought about it like that before," Joseph said. "But not quite what I mean. Bennett's a snake, Alison's more... an elephant. You always see her coming. She has no hesitation telling her colleagues off for minor infractions. She speaks directly to the media with no authorisation about internal affairs and corruption investigations. She made a speech when she hadn't even been an Inspector for a year, dressing down the Commissioner at the time for what she called his poor performance on female promotion. That didn't make her particularly popular. I think she's enjoyed the outsider status ever since."

Joseph led her up a corridor lined with the faces of previous Commissioners. They all looked stern. Men with solid statures and stately sensibilities.

"So why are we seeing her," Kaiya asked. "If no one likes her?"

"I didn't say no one likes her," Joseph said. "And even those who don't, respect her. We're seeing her for you. I'm the one looking for Bennett, and I'm not handing the investigation over to anyone, so all I need is someone with access to his file and enough authority to send a few resources my way. It's still a Leth investigation. But you? There's no one better than Alison Meer.

She takes a... special interest in these cases. Almost exclusive interest, as she's gained seniority."

The corridor seemed lighter, all of a sudden, though every step forward brought a greater sense of foreboding. So Joseph's friend was the best... that was validation enough. But she'd be expected to go through the details, there was no doubt about that. The new Chief Inspector would have seen heaps of women like her. What made her case so special?

They reached a waiting area on the western side of the building. Still relatively low, the surrounding towers of glass blocked most of Kaiya's view, but she could catch glimpses of the shimmering ocean and the expansive harbour area. Boats of all type dotted the water, distant specks. What would it be like to walk the deck of one of those? To feel the rocking of waves... at least, that's how she'd read them described. But what did it *really* feel like? She found it difficult to imagine the concept.

Beneath her a never-ending supply of cars hovered along the glossy black streets, the pavement on either side sparkling in a way that it didn't in Leth. Trees sprang up from the most random spots, and took pride of place in the centre of roundabouts, and everywhere Kaiya looked green drapery hung over glass. The building directly across from her had a garden at the same level she stood, a fascinating mixture of office space and encircling greenery.

Even here, on a relatively low floor, she was higher than the tallest building in Leth.

"Joseph," came a commanding female voice.

Kaiya turned around and watched the Chief Inspector greet a diminutive woman in uniform. Kaiya stared for a few moments, trying to figure out if she was a dwarf or simply very short. Joseph towered over her, yet still managed to look deferential.

"Top marks for punctuality," Alison Meer said. "I'm marking

you down for presentation. You need new clothes. Look, you have a stain. Not good enough, Balfour."

Joseph grinned but ignored the comments, instead indicating towards Kaiya.

"So you're the girl," Alison said before Joseph could speak. "Don't just stand there. I'm not coming to you."

Kaiya walked over to the Chief Inspectors, heart racing. She was already being told off!

"What's your name?" Alison asked.

"Kaiya."

Alison nodded curtly. "I like it. Follow me."

She turned and marched off to her office, short legs pumping fast. Joseph followed immediately, leaving Kaiya momentarily stunned. When she caught up, she gave a surreptitious glance at his shirt, trying to find this stain that Alison could see, but she couldn't find it.

Alison's office overlooked a wide boulevard leading all the way down to the harbour some distance away. Even her father's office – no, Benjamin's office – was smaller. And where Joseph's cubicle was void of almost anything, Alison's was cluttered with all sorts of knick-knacks and mementos. Her desk had been jammed into a corner and rendered unusable by an uncountable array of holodiscs, all active, and shelves lined the walls, all of them filled with holodiscs and minor pieces of art and craft, mostly handmade and of poor quality.

Kaiya stared at a child's simple painting in the centre of the wall, framed beautifully. It was supposed to be a sunflower, she thought, standing up from a blob of green and smiling proudly against a stark blue sky.

One by one in alternating randomness the holodiscs changed their displays.

"Take a seat," Alison said, pointing casually to a clump of rolling chairs on one side of the room. She took her own rolling chair and stared at them as she waited.

Kaiya sat, still taking in the contents of the room. However this Chief Inspector operated, it was nothing like what she was used to. Her father had always taught her to create boundaries. Separations. Symbols of status and power that would remind those present who is in control.

"So you're looking for Bennett," Alison said. "Open your localweb and we'll go through the data. You should have had it ready before you came in. That's wasted time. Slack, Balfour."

Joseph smirked as he placed his tablet on his lap and began typing on the light-projected keyboard. "Yes, Chief Inspector."

Kaiya averted her eyes as Alison stared, looking for something to break the discomfort.

"Did your daughter draw that?" she asked, nodding towards the sunflower.

"My daughter?" Alison said, looking back at the artwork. "No, I don't have children. One of my cases from years ago. Everything in this office is a case memory. I have no time for irrelevancies in my life. The force is a lifestyle, not a job. I try to drill that into everyone I train, but some people are just too stubborn to give themselves up for a greater cause."

She glanced at Joseph playfully, yet with a glint of seriousness.

"Yes, Chief Inspector," he said again.

"You see what I have to put up with?" Alison said. "He doesn't have the balls to argue his side. Just rolls over and takes it like a little bitch."

Kaiya's mouth dropped in shocked amusement.

Joseph laughed.

"Don't look so surprised," Alison said. "You think I got where I am playing nice with the big boys, girl? I don't have time for that crap. You want something, you take it, got it?"

Her eyes bore into Kaiya's.

"I said, got it?"

"Yes," Kaiya said, voice catching. "Got it."

"About time. You're not too quick on the uptake, are you?"

Alison gave her a once-over and turned her attention back to Joseph. Something about the statement sounded familiar. Who was it that had told her to take what she wanted?

"You ready yet, Balfour? I don't have all day."

"I'm connected," Joseph said. "I can see the data coming through."

"We think he's trying to smuggle himself out," Alison said. "We have keyword intercepts on all communication ever since the war started – no, don't start, I don't want to hear it, Balfour. I don't give a shit about 'privacy,' you're wasting my time. We have him pinned in three major locations, but it's sketchy, and the keyword trail goes dead two days ago."

"He'll have created codewords with whoever's helping him," Joseph said.

"Do I look like an idiot, Balfour?" Alison said. "Don't speak unless you have something useful to say."

"Yes, Chief Inspector."

Kaiya glanced between the pair, and Alison shook her head curtly. Disapprovingly.

"You know much about this *Rapture* thing, Balfour?" Alison asked.

Kaiya's ears pricked up.

"Somewhat, Chief Inspector," Joseph said.

"Good boy. Short and sweet. It's like a plague. They reckon it'll be the new insanity defence. That's bullshit! I'm not having a bar of it. Bring up the keyword location map."

Joseph did so, and the tablet projected a three-dimensional map of Akheron into the air, along with pulsing lights of varied brilliance. Three lights stood out in particular.

"Harbour, residential area, industrial area," Alison said. "What do you think that means? I want to know if you're any sharper than when you left here. It's not like you could have gotten worse."

Joseph smiled as he examined the map. "The harbour and residential area are easy. First is for the escape, second for the protection. Industrial area, though... anything special about that district?"

"You don't listen!" Alison said. "Think about *everything* I say, not just the question I ask."

Joseph frowned at the map. "Oh... *Rapture*. There's a *Rapture* clinic there."

"Exactly," Alison said. "Except?"

"Except there's no *Rapture* clinic there," Joseph said. He looked up at Alison with surprise. "You mean there's a black market already?"

"Everything's a black market until we say it's not," Alison said dismissively. "The question is: what's Bennett's involvement? Is he a patient? Does he run it? Know someone who runs it? Why is it a focal point of activity?"

"Why haven't you raided it?" Joseph asked.

"Because we're rounding up all these other damned collaborators, aren't we?" Alison said. "I told you not to ask stupid questions. Now I want to know: what's your plan?"

Joseph perused the map while he considered the question. "I want a shock team. Tomorrow. We shut down the clinic, extract information. I don't care about prosecuting them, we just need to know about Bennett."

Alison nodded curtly.

"Assuming he's not there, it's a matter of what new knowledge the raid gives," Joseph said. "His end game is obvious, but going to the harbour without knowing anything more than the fact he'll be there some day is failure waiting to happen. I don't need anyone else for the residential."

"You sure?" Alison interrupted.

"I'll take her," Joseph said with a grin.

Alison gave Kaiya a pointed look. "I hope you know what you're doing, Joseph. Can you defend yourself, girl?"

"Oh, I've seen what she can do," Joseph said. "She's more than capable. She's Harold's—

"I know who she is," Alison said. "You don't need to tell me twice. So that's your plan? You need anything else?"

"No," Joseph said.

"Good."

Alison stood up and walked over to the window.

"Thank you," Joseph said, dismissing the holomap.

"Your turn, girl," Alison said as she tapped on the window, turning it opaque and bringing up a green Network layer.

Kaiya hesitated. What was she supposed to say?

"I don't have all day," Alison said. "Give me a name!"

Joseph gave a brief, encouraging nod, and Kaiya gave over the soldier's first name. "That's all I know. Sorry."

"For what?" Alison said, typing on a projected keyboard. "Don't give me this 'sorry' bullshit. I'll decide what's enough and what's not enough to go on."

Kaiya remained silent as Alison flicked through Network layers, fingers rushing along. She grunted as she went, cursing the Network layer and beginning to ramble with great colour on what she thought of various people she had met from the defence forces in her lifetime.

Joseph began to laugh.

Alison gave him a pointed look.

"You might not think it's so funny when *you're* the one who has to deal with officer obfuscation," Alison said.

"Luckily for me I chose the backwaters, didn't I?" Joseph said drily.

Alison scoffed as she returned to flicking through files on the Network layer. "Waste of a life, if you ask me."

"Thankfully no one *did* ask you," Joseph said with a smile.

But the words were edged with steel.

Kaiya watched Alison process the admonition.

"Quite right," was all she said. "Well done, Balfour."

"It's like I'm twelve years old again," Joseph said with another laugh.

"Harden up," Alison said. "The real twelve year olds don't need your moaning. They need results."

"I know that, Chief Inspector."

"Damn straight," she said. "I'll give you a good whack around the ears if you ever forget. I don't want you going soft under that Benjamin fellow."

"We've spoken about this before," Joseph said. "You don't want to waste time, do you?"

Alison chuckled. "I hope he took my advice."

"Alison, if I do or say something because you taught me, Benjamin does it because it is natural to him."

Alison grunted and considered Joseph's statement. "I'll believe that when I see it. I think I'm due for a visit your way. To the backwaters."

They grinned at each other, and Kaiya went back to surveying the holos and childish artworks filling the Chief Inspector's office. No one was paying any attention to her anyway...

"Don't go vague on me, girl," Alison said.

"Sor—" Kaiya began, then stumbled at a stern glance from Alison.

"Good girl," she said. "This is going to take a day or two. We don't have immediate access to the military database, so you'll have to sit tight. I'll call Joseph when I have the information. I imagine you want to do this with him?"

"Uh... yes," Kaiya said. She guessed that was true?

"Then we're all done here," Alison said. "You both have fun with the collabo-scum."

Kaiya smirked. She'd have to remember that word.

"Call me tonight," Joseph said as he stood. "We'll finalise the shock team."

Alison dismissed the Network layer and tapped her windows

back to clear. "I'll call you when I'm ready to call you, Balfour. No sooner or later."

"Yes, Chief Inspector."

"Thank you for seeing me," Kaiya said.

Alison peered at her. "For what – doing my job? You think you're special or something?"

"Uh... no?" Kaiya ventured.

"What do you mean, 'no?'" Alison said. "The answer's 'yes.' It's a trick question, girl. The answer is always 'yes.'"

Kaiya gave up on trying to understand Chief Inspector Alison Meer. "Thank you?" she ventured once more.

"You're welcome," Alison said. "And Joseph..."

He stopped near the door.

"I'm sorry."

Joseph took a breath and nodded. "I know."

Kaiya watched them. Alison's demeanour had softened, albeit still hard.

"Life's not fair, is it?" she said. "But you always knew that."

"Only because you taught me."

The older Chief Inspector shook her head. "Give yourself some credit, Balfour. I just opened your eyes. You did the rest."

"There's plenty more still to do."

Alison smiled and indicated the breadth of her exquisite view. "There are victories along the way."

"I know that," Joseph said, "but they feel... outweighed, sometimes."

Kaiya waited for Alison's rebuke, but none came. Instead, the Chief Inspector gave him a sympathetic smile. What on earth were they talking about?

"You need faith," she said. "In yourself. In your capacity to influence the people around you. Don't ever let me hear you with this defeatist bullshit. You need to find a new purpose, Joseph, you can't... sit around wishing you'd made a different choice."

"It's not that—"

"Shut up and listen to me, boy," Alison said, eyes piercing. She stepped forward and lowered her voice. "You were just like the rest of the recruits, when you started. Blinkered. Brainwashed. Without really knowing it or understanding how. But you *listened*. You asked questions. I can count on one hand the men who've done that properly in the past thirty years of my teaching. But you know what I've noticed? They're becoming more frequent. Soon it'll be two hands. Then four. And one day, we won't even think it's something worth counting. The change is happening, if you take a step back."

"I don't doubt it," Joseph said.

Alison stared hard into his eyes. "We need you. I need you. The force is a lifestyle, Joseph. If you want to change something, make it your life. It's been nearly six years – time to start moving on. You could do magnificent things if you set your mind to it. I wish you'd start writing again."

"I have nothing to say."

"Bullshit. I still give your essay about the objectives of punishment to every recruit who studies under me. No one's ever written anything like it. I was so excited. I thought you were going to be the one that shakes up the establishment."

"That was sixteen years ago," he said.

"And haven't I been trying to push you in that direction ever since?" Alison asked. "Shit happens, Joseph."

"Alison—"

"Don't Alison me, Balfour," she said. "It's ok to grieve, but there's a point you need to let go and start searching for the silver lining. You *have* the silver lining. You've always had it. Go out and start exercising that brain of yours. Make things happen. Change things. Write stuff that challenges people. Undermine the system. Go back to being that person who refused to accept the way things were. Give people something to strive for."

"That's your job," he said.

Alison laughed. "I'll be dead within fifteen years, Balfour. Maybe senile before then. If you don't do it, who else will it be?"

Joseph fell silent and Kaiya wondered whether she should be listening, but Alison shot her a smile. "Get your phone out, girl. You should read what he was writing when he was younger than you."

"This is ridiculous," Joseph said, but Kaiya took out her phone and opened her localweb for short range transmissions. In a choice between defying Joseph and defying Alison... well, there was no choice. Alison called up a Network layer and ordered a file transfer to Kaiya's phone.

"You see all these holos, Balfour?" Alison said, pointing around the room. "All of these are people I helped because I had the balls to stand up to those in authority. When you go back to Leth, you start doing what you should have done at the beginning. And if you let me down this time, I swear I'll come to that backwater of yours and spank you."

"Yes, Chief Inspector," Joseph said, and they shared a brief, history-filled smile.

"Now go away," Alison said. "I'm busy!" and she corralled them outside, shutting her door.

Kaiya walked silently with Joseph through the corridors, glancing at the faces of important men in the history of Akheron's police force.

"So that was my teacher," Joseph said casually. "What did you think?"

Where did she begin with that?

"I can't tell if I like her or hate her," she said.

"I'm still figuring that out for myself," Joseph joked, "but in truth, I never really liked her until I'd finished my training and realised that I saw things differently to how the other new officers saw things. That's when I understood the value of Alison Meer."

"She's not very... friendly," Kaiya said. "I'd be terrified if I had to tell her my story."

"That's just because she knows me," Joseph said. "She's better with victims... somewhat. But imagine if you were the suspect or the advocate? I saw a senator piss himself in front of her."

"A senator?"

"She's incorruptible," Joseph said. "I think she *enjoys* taking on people like that."

They continued on in silence as Kaiya thought back to the painting of the sunflower. "She... had a lot of children in her holos."

Joseph merely murmured agreement.

They walked outside onto the parade, and Kaiya stopped halfway to the street to look up. The officer who had been staring dreamily out of his window was still there, now sleeping. She tittered, wondering if he ever got any work done.

"What's so funny?" Joseph asked.

She smiled back at the Chief Inspector. "I was just thinking... you got taken to school."

Joseph laughed and drew Kaiya in for a brief hug.

She offered no resistance.

"The important question," Joseph asked, "is did you go there with me?"

Kaiya wondered what the Chief Inspector meant as he took out his phone to order a taxi. With his attention elsewhere, she glanced down at her own phone and opened the document Alison Meer had sent her, reading the title page of Joseph's essay:

And the Righteous Shall Punish?

———

A ragtag few dozen stood in the park, calling for an overthrow of the government. Kaiya watched them, sitting against one of the great pillars dominating the steps of the Courts. They had erected tents and signs, and a scrawny, dreadlocked man with colourful clothes roamed around encouraging passersby to join them in occupying the city centre until, through their collective power and positive energy, they forced the government to resign. The passersby largely ignored him, though Kaiya found it entertaining to watch the occasional stream of abuse from the well-dressed, or the sycophantic nodding of someone who didn't look like they had any idea of what was being said.

A bus passed, an advertisement for *Rapture* glowing on its side. Kaiya looked away, thankful she'd seen no more holoboards like the one overlooking the Levway. She stood up, satisfied with her brief break from the endless legal shenanigans she had been witnessing in one of the smaller courtrooms, and cast another glance at the gathering in the park before turning around and walking back into the Courts. The high-ceilinged marble, filled with intricate carvings, glowed with some imbued substance similar to the glowstone in Leth's footpaths. Perhaps they were the same, and only the material on which it was applied made the difference.

The grandiose foyer sang with quietude, and Kaiya submitted herself to another security scan. The guard nodded at her to proceed, and she advanced towards the gigantic, polished oak doors of the main courtroom. Joseph had advised her not to watch those proceedings, but given he was tied up discussing the details of Bennett's case with some advocates...

Another guard stood by the doors and glanced at her. She thanked him as he opened one of the doors, and squeezed into the courtroom, the noise of an animated crowd overwhelming her.

A judge sat fully-gowned at the bench, sporting a black stole and banging a gavel repeatedly. "This court will come to order," he intoned with little effect. He maintained an expression of neutral disinterest, and Kaiya stared at him as she tried to make space for herself amongst the standing crowd.

An advocate in full court attire stood within the bar, staring at the ceiling with an expression of obvious frustration. "Your Honour, this is only a hearing. It is absolutely unheard of! I put to you, again, that we should move these proceedings in camera."

"I have heard your arguments, and I say to you – again – that I will not be party to the concealment of justice." The crowd applauded, and Kaiya wished she had some idea who could receive so much attention before a proper trial had even begun. "This court will come to order. I will not have proceedings delayed by public sentiment. If you wish to voice your concerns, I invite you to join the group across the road, who will be more than happy to have you, I'm sure." Slowly the noise subsided, though Kaiya didn't think anyone else had picked up on the acerbic humour in the judge's voice. Perhaps she was simply not yet invested enough for such inflections to pass beneath her notice. The focus of the courtroom remained firmly on whomever it was she could not see. "The accused will take the stand."

The judge's admonition of the crowd failed to quell them when the object of their loathing stood. All around her fists punctured the air and shouts of murderous retribution echoed against the walls. A woman stood crying nearby, clutching a holodisc from which the image of a well-dressed man protruded. The detainee beyond the bar held a curious expression as he approached the stand, calm and at ease in the torrent of abuse. The judge made a few gestures around the room and banged his gavel ineffectively. Kaiya couldn't even hear it, now.

Someone shoved her aside from behind. A guard. He cleared a path through the crowd until he reached a particularly vociferous man with a face full of hot temper and grabbed his arm with gloved hands. The man swung around in surprise and unloaded a stream of curses in the guard's face. The guard responded by activating shock pads on his gloves and forcing the man into submission. A few onlookers yelled their own abuse at the guard, who held up his hand near their faces, daring them to continue. None did. The man on the ground groaned as the guard dragged him out to the double doors, through which a steady stream of people had already slipped away.

The departure of onlookers gave her more space, and she travelled closer to the bar, as did the woman clutching the holodisc. Kaiya looked around, watching guards remove other troublesome spectators through doors she hadn't noticed before. The crowd settled, though she heard more than a few whispers accusing the judges and guards of being collaborators. The accused sat in the dock, looking somewhat oblivious to the events surrounding him or his centrality to them, his face a vacant pool of unawareness.

"Any further outbursts, and there will be no lenience," the judge said, only the slightest hint of annoyance emanating from his voice. "You may begin your questioning."

The advocate sitting nearest to her stood for the first time since her arrival. "Thank you, Your Honour." He glanced at the audience and waved his hand in a slight show of recognition. A smattering of light applause went around, the judge's warning no doubt fresh in everyone's minds. The advocate turned and faced the accused. "Please state your name for the record."

"My name is Peter Latain," he said in a pleasant voice, and was met with murmurs of disgust from the crowd.

"And please state your most recent occupation for the record."

"I held the title of Ambassador to the Occupied Territories."

Again the crowd made their feelings known, and the woman clutching the holodisc recommenced her sobbing.

"Will you tell the court the key responsibilities you held in your role as Ambassador?"

"To advocate for human rights protection in the Occupied Territories."

"Would you describe your performance of the role as successful?"

"Yes, I believe I played a strong and beneficial part in the protection of Nymians."

"Is it not true, however, that you cannot remember the majority of your time served as Ambassador?"

The former Ambassador cocked his head and smiled, adjusting his position in his seat. "That is an accurate statement, yes."

"So with what authority can you answer questions relating to your time as the Ambassador if you cannot remember vast sections of that period?"

"I assure you I will answer to the best of my ability."

He widened his genuine-looking smile.

The advocate for the prosecution glanced over at his colleague and raised his eyebrows. Kaiya thought the crowd might burst again at any moment, though the ever-present guards kept all in check. "In your recollection," the advocate said, "have you ever associated in any way with a Tarkinian?"

Peter Latain shifted in his seat again. "No, I have not."

A groan went around the room. A man nearby called him a liar under his breath, but from what Kaiya could see of the detainee's face, not a trace of dishonesty marred it.

"You were the Ambassador to the Occupied Territories, and you cannot remember ever meeting a Tarkinian in your life." The advocate turned and ambled towards the crowd, a sardonic expression over his face. "Truly a powerful operation you've had. It is quite evident that your memory has been altered irreparably. That I do not doubt. You are aware of the severity of the charges brought against you, correct?"

"I am, yes."

"And in light of the fact that you cannot remember much of the last six years, would it be safe to assume you *might* possess the capability to have carried out those crimes?"

"I don't think it is within my capability or character to commit the kinds of atrocities you are speaking of."

"You don't think," the advocate for the prosecution sniggered. "But how do you know? Can you, in fact, provide any reliable testimony regarding your own character if you cannot remember your own actions?"

"Objection, Your Honour," came the defence advocate's voice. "Two questions."

"Sustained. Restrict yourself, please."

"Apologies, Your Honour," the prosecution advocate said. "I repeat, can you provide reliable testimony regarding your own character if you cannot remember your own actions?"

"I believe I can," Latain said. "Yes, of course."

"I see. So in your mind the treatment named *Rapture*, while removing unwanted memories, allows a patient to retain the central elements of their character?"

"Objection, Your Honour," the defence advocate said. "Prejudicial."

The judge breathed out slowly and considered the former Ambassador. "Sustained, owing only to my knowledge of your prior submitted reasoning," he said, nodding at the advocate for the prosecution.

The advocate smirked at his defence counterpart and returned to his desk. "I have no more questions at this time, Your Honour."

"Very well. The accused is yours."

"Thank you, Your Honour," said the advocate for the defence, standing to a smattering of jeers. He ignored the crowd and walked over to the stand. "Peter, I understand this must be a traumatic time for you and your family, so I will attempt to keep this as brief and respectful as I can. Can you recall the reason you elected to undergo the *Rapture* treatment?"

"No, I cannot."

"That is a function of the treatment, correct?"

"Yes, that is correct."

"Now, forgive me for bringing up events that may cause pain," the advocate began, raising his voice further above the crowd, "but your daughter was a victim of the Tarkinians, was she not?"

Peter shifted in his chair again. "I'm not sure what you're talking about."

"You had a daughter, did you not?"

"No, I don't believe I've ever had any children."

"I see," the advocate said. He returned to his desk and turned on a holodisc, which he picked up and carried over to the stand, making sure the crowd could see it clearly. "Peter, do you recognise this woman?"

The former Ambassador stared at the holo. "No."

The advocate changed the holo to one containing the same woman, this time standing with the former Ambassador. "Do you recognise this man?"

"Of course. That is me."

"And you would agree that the woman you are standing with is the same woman as in the previous holo?"

"Yes."

"But you do not remember her?"

"No, I do not," he said, smiling.

The advocate nodded and turned off the holodisc, returning to his seat. "No further questions, Your Honour."

The judge glanced over at the advocate for the prosecution. "No new lines?"

"No, Your Honour."

"The accused may return to his seat," the judge said.

The former Ambassador smiled and thanked the judge

before returning to his seat next to the defence advocate. The woman clutching the holodisc trembled and was supported by a younger woman. The commotion in the crowd built again until a man lunged forward towards the bar, screaming "murderer!" at the former Ambassador. A guard rushed forward and neutralised the spectator before dragging him out of the court-room. Kaiya looked over at the former Ambassador and wondered if he really had done anything wrong.

"Prosecution, you may commence," the judge said.

The advocate for the prosecution stood, remaining behind his bench. "Your Honour, I would like to draw your attention to the stated objective of the *Rapture* treatment, namely the erasure and replacement of unwanted and or painful memories. Peter Latain was, by all accounts, a shrewd and calculating man in his career up to and including his role as the Ambassador to the Occupied Territories. I would ask Your Honour to consider why such a man, so successful in his professional life – and let us not forget, he is known to have been very close to Ministers of the previous government and some of our most celebrated enter-tainers – would throw away his memories if not for the fact that he was attempting to erase a guilty conscience. This is a calcu-lated move from an adept political tactician, and we must not allow ourselves to be hoodwinked by it."

The advocate for the defence stood in response. "Your Honour, I have shown clearly in the documents tendered previ-ously the crimes which befell the family of Peter Latain, particu-larly his daughter."

"A daughter over which he had no custody!" the prosecution said.

"Nevertheless," the defence continued, "I do not believe my colleague's denouncement of my client is appropriate or fair, given the concrete evidence of pain and suffering available to us. Is that not a primary motivator for undergoing this *Rapture* treatment?"

"Your Honour, my colleague likes to pretend that we have no evidence of our own. May I remind him, and the court, that we have documents signed by the accused in his capacity as Ambassador to the Occupied Territories. In fact, we have far more evidence that points to the commission of these crimes by the accused than my colleague has that he even retained a relationship with his daughter."

"This is absurd, Your Honour," the defence said. "To think that my colleague – or any of us, for that matter – have the capacity to comprehend the personal relationships of my client borders on the insulting."

"If I may return to my central argument, Your Honour, there is a clear statement of guilt in the very act of submitting one's self to this *Rapture* treatment. I say again, only one with a conscience of guilt will submit themselves to such a treatment."

"This is pure speculation!" the defence said.

"Unfortunately, Your Honour, the accused is unable to answer questions relating to his state of mind at the time of the alleged commission of these crimes, so we are all of us reduced to speculating on the reasons for his decision. But we reason based on the evidence in front of us. The defence's claim is no less speculative than mine and, if I may say so, Your Honour, based on less evidence."

"If we suppose, Your Honour, that my colleague is correct – which, I hasten to add, I highly doubt – then I fail to see the public interest in bringing such a case to trial."

"The public interest? Your Honour, I invite my colleague to look around this very room! The public interest in seeing collaborators of the highest rank committed to trial is very high."

"To what effect?" the defence said. "What could be achieved in trying a man with no memory? What form of rehabilitation could possibly occur?"

"I don't think that, given the severity of these crimes, the perpetrator holds any right to any form of consideration, particularly rehabilitation," the prosecution said drily.

"And of what use would it be, Your Honour, to commit a man to death who is not anymore the same man who commissioned the crime?"

"We cannot know that, Your Honour," the prosecution said. "Neither I nor my colleague can say with any accuracy that we know the effects of *Rapture* on any other aspect of one's life besides memory. Your Honour could subpoena the researchers involved, but I have my doubts they would shed any more light on the situation."

"Your Honour, my colleague is only attempting to do away with procedures that have served Nymosen well for over a thousand years."

"Your Honour, this is no ordinary criminal matter!" the prosecution said. "We are talking about the deportation of four hundred thousand Nymians, many of whom, we now know, have been butchered for organs and... bizarre experiments."

The crowd began to lose its composure, wailing and shouts echoing from the courtroom's high stone ceilings.

"We are talking about treason of the highest degree," the prosecution continued, "and day by day we learn more about the atrocities that have been committed *with the assistance of the accused*. Ledophas! A name that will haunt this continent for decades to come. Your Honour is aware of it, I assume? The people have heard its name whispered, but do they know the true extent? Do they know about the two and a half million bodies – so far! – from all across this continent? Slaughtered! Who knows how many Nymians among them? Who knows how many Nymians *deported by this man?*"

The prosecution advocate pointed at Peter Latain as the crowd erupted in fury.

The woman with the holodisc gasped as the atmosphere swelled.

"The public has a right to see this taken to trial," the advocate continued. "And to hell with *Rapture!*"

Ledophas.

Rumours, Kormac had said, that was all...

The room felt feverish, the crowd a sea of oppressive swaying and braying.

Kaiya glanced backwards, her heart beginning to race, and tried to edge her way through the inward-pressing bodies.

The woman with the holodisc screamed, a sound so piercing it forced Kaiya to turn and watch, along with a sizeable portion of the public gallery.

"Where is my husband?" the woman howled. "What have you done to him, you monster?"

She fell to the floor, weeping, and clutched the holodisc that showed her smiling husband.

Kaiya looked through the sea of heads to the former Ambassador. He sat, straight-backed and still, staring forward at the judge's bench, unflinching and oblivious. As Kaiya struggled to make her way to the doors of the court, the word Ledophas pulsed through her brain, reminding her again and again how little she knew, and how foolish she was to hope for her parents' return.

18

AKHERON GLOWED AT NIGHT, A CACOPHONY OF COLOURS THAT seemed to Kaiya an egregious assault on the public mood, if the feelings expressed in the courtroom that day could be considered the public mood. She wiped her face with the towel again and, after throwing it onto her bed, opened the bedroom window a little. There was only a slight breeze, but at least the previously trapped air that had been stirred into heat by the setting sun would have a chance to escape. She walked out into the dining room, where Kytos had separated into plates the *marashta* she had brought home.

She sat opposite Kytos and grabbed a fork. "You like *marashta*, right?"

"Mm, yes, I do," he said. "I haven't had it in a long time."

She savoured the exquisite flavours, pleased with her choice of establishment, and glanced now and then at Kytos, wondering what kind of thoughts ran through his head. Ledophas and everything else she had heard earlier still whirled in her own, but she had shoved it aside into a little corner of her mind, reserving a portion of her concentration on making sure it didn't leak back into the front of her consciousness. It remained there, however, ever present.

"Kytos, is there any particular reason you never open that curtain?" she asked, nodding towards the living room window.

Kytos looked at her and finished his mouthful. "You've not seen the sign?"

"Ah. I thought so." She poked the *marashta* with her fork. "So when you look at it, you see you?"

"Yes," he said. "I don't know how they do it, and I don't like it. It shouldn't be allowed. It's not right."

"How long has it been there?"

"Nearly a year. That's when Life Plus began treating people." Kytos shook his head and frowned. "And just look at them all. All these cowards, weak people, rushing out to get *Rapture*. What nonsense. It shouldn't be allowed, any of it. Country of cowards, we are."

He shoved a forkful of *marashta* into his mouth.

Kaiya stared down at her plate, chewing quietly. He was right, of course. People like her were cowards.

She finished her mouthful.

"It's good," she said.

Kytos made no indication that he had heard her remark. They ate in silence, he staring at his plate, and she at the motley collection of old furniture in the room. The fact of Kytos's absence in her life had unveiled itself of mystery, and stood in stark nakedness before her. Just to be around him felt awkward, try as she may to prod a happy thought from the prematurely aged man. Still, she had seen some glimmer of humour untouched by acid that morning, despite the rapidity of its disappearance, like a dinghy floating amongst torrid waves, failing to succumb to the ocean but invisible for some time after each attack.

She glanced at him again. It could still be possible, perhaps, to catch sight of the dinghy and hail it ever so slightly nearer to the shore. "Did you know," she said, "that the Tarkinians have a different type of *marashta*?"

At first she thought Kytos, who had just begun chewing on another forkful of his meal, would ignore her again. He glanced up and shook his head lightly, frowning, and finished the mouthful. "That's not right," he said. "It *came* from Tarkinia. Ages ago, hundreds of years."

She smiled, then realised he wasn't joking. "Are you being serious?"

"Of course I am. Why wouldn't I be?"

"Oh, I just... I didn't know."

"Now you do," he said. "It's fine. Most people don't."

He continued eating, leaving her to sit and ponder the revelation.

"But they're completely different dishes," she said.

"They are, but they came from the same one. The Tarkinian one."

Kaiya placed her fork down and stared at the *marashta*, unsure if she should eat any more, then looked over to Kytos's near-empty plate. "You hate Tarkinia, though."

"It's a horrible place," he said. "Horrible people. That's why I love *marashta*. It's a reminder of how much better we are."

He ate another mouthful and wiped his lips with a napkin, leaning back in his chair. "Let me explain. *Marashta* is a dessert in Tarkinia. Very sweet. It's disgusting, and incredibly unhealthy. You think our cereal this morning is bad? That's nothing in comparison. The *marashta* threads there are some kind of sugar compound. Then they have various sauces and toppings, like our *marashta*, but they're just all types of sweets. It's junk food. So someone, I don't know who, a long time ago, decided to make a healthier version of *marashta*, something you could eat as a proper meal, like we are now. And that's how we have two types of *marashta*."

"But we only have one here," Kaiya said. "I'd never even heard of the Tarkinian one."

"It was banned by the government for nearly fifty years," Kytos said. "About two hundred years ago, when the Tarkinians started getting aggressive again. I don't know how it worked. You can't have police in everyone's kitchens, but by the time some later government lifted the ban, no one wanted to eat it anymore. A lot of people probably didn't even know it existed, I'd say. So that's why you've only ever seen this one. The good one."

"I still don't see why you love it."

"Because we won," he said, looking up at her with a very serious expression. "Conquest isn't always done with military, you know. The Tarkinians gave us the unhealthiest food ever invented, and we changed it. To this. *We* made it better. Nymosen. Food is culture. It's conquest. Changing *marashta* was like winning a war. Eating it is like reminding them they lost."

Kaiya picked up her fork again and played with the *marashta* threads. How did Kytos know something like that? What else did he know about history? Or everything, for that matter? She recommenced eating, trying to feel as though doing so was a victory against the Tarkinians, but the thought brought about no change in feeling.

Kytos finished well before her and took his plate into the kitchen. When he returned he sat, as he always seemed to do, in the squishy armchair, though this time he didn't begin reading his tablet but began to tap its edges thoughtfully.

"Why exactly are you here?" he asked.

The question frightened her, and she stared away towards the window at corridor's end. After the history he had just told her, she almost felt a responsibility to tell the truth, though she didn't like the idea.

"There were some people in Leth," she said. "Soldiers.

They... hurt some people. I need to try to find them. You know...
for justice."

Kytos nodded and looked at her. "Important work, then.
These... other people must trust you very much."

She avoided his unsettling gaze. "They do," she said, and
played with her food a little longer. "I'm not sure I trust myself,
though, or the courts."

"They can be difficult, yes. And advocates are never the most
helpful people. But as for trusting yourself, well... whoever this
is all for, and why, I think you're doing the right thing. Justice is
always important. Some people need to be punished."

"Yes," she said, feeling suddenly closer to him. He understood, unlike everyone else. She continued eating the *marashta*,
feeling at once comfortable and still uneasy in his presence.

"Soldiers can be funny creatures, sometimes," he mused.

"What do you mean?"

"Not humorous, just strange. Odd. Don't get me wrong, I was
a soldier, and most of us were just normal people. But sometimes there are ones that shouldn't be there."

He scowled at nothing in particular and shifted his position.
"When I was in the war I had this superior, a lieutenant. He
was... not a good person."

Kytos fell silent and Kaiya waited, hoping he wouldn't
continue whatever story he had in mind. She was in no position
to feign sympathy for anyone, let alone a man she barely knew,
whatever his blood relationship may have been.

"He had always been a bit of a joker," Kytos said, "but he was
mean. You could laugh along, and it was probably better that
you did, because if you didn't, you might be the next one he
made a joke out of. I tried not to associate with him any more
than I had to, but he liked a crowd, so it was difficult to escape.

"I made a complaint to the major, but he didn't seem to think
it warranted an investigation. Told me it was just part of life – I
just had to deal with it. Nothing was quite the same after that.

The major told him. Now it wasn't just the lieutenant with his... comments, it was everyone, even the ones I was friends with. I asked for a transfer, but by then it was too late. We got deployed a few days later.

"We were somewhere on the western front. Each night the lieutenant would tell jokes, say that I was a coward and I would run away as soon as the fighting started, that I was a traitor, because I had gone to the major. I don't know who I hated more, him or the Tarkinians."

Kytos paused, his face a mask of memories.

"We were in a forest, one day. Got into a firefight, this was before sonic weaponry. We didn't have time to put on our vantum suits. The lieutenant didn't order a retreat until three of us had died, but all I could think about was what he had said the other night, that I would run away. I argued with him, and the Tarkinians shot me in the back. The lieutenant looked at me and said he couldn't take me, I was too much of a burden, that it was my fault anyway.

"I couldn't move my legs. When the Tarkinians came, I thought they would kill me, but they didn't. They took me to some prisoner of war camp instead. Gave me a wheelchair," he sniggered in disgust. "They gave me the same quota every day as everyone else, and if I didn't meet it, I would be punished. So I was punished a lot. I thought about killing myself, but I knew that eventually the war would be over. Wars always end, you know, and another one always comes. That lieutenant was all that kept me going. Knowing that one day I would get my revenge.

"I was right. Eventually the war ended, and I was brought back to Akheron. My spine was so badly damaged the surgery had to be done in stages over eight months. They gave me a medical discharge, the army. I think they got sick of me making complaints about the lieutenant, but I had to. They wouldn't do anything about him. Said that's the way things were, or didn't believe me, or said they'd look into it, but I'd never hear from them. When they gave me the discharge they said I should go and see a psychologist. They wanted me to see a psychologist," he sneered. "People just don't get it. I wasn't the problem."

Kaiya didn't know what to say, and probed the remaining *marashta* with her fork, unsure of whether it would be rude to continue eating. A storm cloud had descended on Kytos's face. He didn't look as though he were really present, but reliving once more his own injustices, still vivid after so many years. Kaiya chose at last to continue eating, hoping that the flavours would wash away the sharp bitterness soaking the room.

"I found him, eventually," Kytos said. "The lieutenant. Greeted me like an old friend! Didn't even think he'd done anything wrong. I went to punch him, but he stopped me. Didn't even hit me back, just told me to leave and never speak to him again. I never did, but I've kept tabs. He died two years ago. Bastard. I just wish I could've killed him myself. I despised him – I still do. I hope his children die, and their children, if he has any. But I got the last laugh in the end, though, didn't I – I'm still alive."

From what she saw on his face, Kaiya believed him. Kytos would no doubt have slaughtered the lieutenant were he there in the room. He might have been able to do it with his eyes. The intensity of his gaze and demeanour frightened her. The light that flooded in from the corridor window reached her at the table and danced about ever so gently, unable to penetrate the shadowed corner Kytos had created when he had chosen to place his chair there however many years ago.

She finished her *marashta*, eating as quietly as she could, and glanced back to Kytos. He now reclined in the armchair, his eyes closed and brow furrowed, resting his forehead on extended fingers. "I'm sorry," she said, hesitating. What could she say that would make any difference to him now?

"No, I am. I should have visited more." The dramatic change

in his mood surprised her. The eyes of fiery vengeance had softened to smoking ashes of regret. "I didn't even recognise you. I don't think I've seen you since you were six."

"Well, of course you wouldn't recognise me, then," she said, smiling a little so that the living room might begin to expel the shadow that had descended.

The slight attempt at humour seemed lost on Kytos, who kept his gaze fixed on the floor. The nature of her parents' relationship with him had always intrigued her, but she had assumed, for as long as she could remember, that Kytos would never again be part of their lives. Curiosity welled inside her, but she couldn't probe him on what she imagined was a sensitive issue – not after that display of decades-old emotion.

She stared at her plate. Would it be rude to leave the room? Kytos looked lost in his own world, and the truth was... he repulsed her. He was like a black hole of prickled anguish, radiating lamentation into the enforced darkness of his home.

Perhaps it was better that he hadn't been a part of her life.

She remained awake for many hours that night, unable to push aside the anxiety of ignorance. Every hour was an hour closer to Alison Meer's phone call. An hour closer to finding *him*. But what would happen? What would she do? Would she extract the kind of justice Kytos had failed to receive? Joseph's presence gave her some comfort, but... he was still only new in her life.

Kaiya reached over to grab the holodisc she had been using sporadically since going to bed. She turned it back on and lay on her side, arm under the pillow. Tilda stared back at her, face contorted in laughter and wearing a tiara that read *21*.

Had she been with the Tarkinian even then?

Kaiya flicked through the holos, searching for some sign... anything that would indicate when she had lost Tilda. But nothing could be found. She returned to the holo of the twenty-first birthday and stared at it until her eyes began to droop.

When Kaiya woke, the holodisc remained active, and Tilda sparkled in the glittering reflections of Akheron's morning.

Kaiya ascended the stairs of a modern residential tower in the southwestern suburbs of Akheron, distracted by the magnificent ocean view. Joseph took the steps two at a time, leaving her behind when she stopped paying attention, his earlier fury replaced with eagerness after he had finally found some useful information at the *Rapture* clinic.

Or warehouse, more accurately.

"This floor," he said, leaning against the railing and breathing hard.

In the distance, an ocean liner departed from the harbour. What if Bennett were on it? What if they were too late?

"What if no one's home?" she asked.

"Then we call Alison and get her to put an immediate arrest warrant out for everyone who lives here," Joseph said. "Anyone who's *visited* here in the last week. We scan every part of the Network we can and we find them, and we go to them, and we do whatever we have to."

The Chief Inspector sounded livid. Her father had always advocated distance between officer and case, but Joseph sounded like he was doing the exact opposite.

"Come on," he said, and they walked up an elegant corridor. "You're not to speak. I just want you to watch. Listen. Try to remember as much as you can. Stay near the door – that way you can stop anyone who tries to leave, or you can get out if things don't go down well. And yes, you have my permission to punch them in the face if they try the first one."

Kaiya tittered, then realised he was being serious.

Joseph banged on the door, and they waited.

An older woman opened it, silver-haired and wrinkled but spritely. Still relatively fit. "May I help you?" she asked.

"You are Felicity Danard, correct?"

"Yes?" she said.

"I am Chief Inspector Joseph Balfour of the Leth Police Force. I... worked with your son until recently."

The woman's face darkened. "I know you," she said. "You're one of those collaborators. My son told me all about you, don't think you can fool me. Get out of here, or I'll call the real police!"

Felicity Danard made to slam the door, but in a burst of temper Joseph kicked it back wide open, advancing into the frilly, primitively-decorated living room.

"What are you doing?" came a man's voice. He appeared from an adjoining room, at least forty years old, and picked up a poor quality stun baton, the kind that amateur arms companies sold to the general population.

"Don't even try it," Joseph warned, slipping on a pair of gloves and activating shock pads.

The man hesitated. He'd be the worse off in any competition between a stun baton and shock pads, and Joseph didn't look as though he would be holding back.

"Who are you?" Joseph demanded.

The man stood still, stun baton still primed, as Bennett's mother fell deeper into the living room, looking frightened next to the couch.

"Who are you?" Joseph repeated.

"Michael," the man said. "Michael Danard."

"What's your relationship to Bennett?"

"Don't answer him," Felicity said. "He's the one who's been trying to set him up."

Michael's eyes flicked over to Kaiya.

"I'm not afraid of death, you scum," Felicity said. "You should be ashamed of yourself."

"Sit down, you old bag," Joseph said, stepping towards her.

Michael advanced by obvious instinct, and stopped when Joseph's gaze returned to him.

"What's your relationship to Bennett?" Joseph asked again. "Close the door, Kaiya."

She did as he asked and stood guard in front of it.

"We're cousins," Michael said, placing his amateur stun baton down on a sideboard. His face indicated that he had accepted the position he was in, but Bennett's mother snarled at Joseph and snatched the stun baton for herself.

"Lis!" Michael said.

"You think you can barge in here and get away with it?" she said to Joseph. "What's your problem? What did my son ever do to you? He's a war hero, not some pig for hunting!"

Joseph glared at the woman, then turned his attention to Michael. "You want her to get hurt?"

"You scum," Felicity spat.

Kaiya watched Michael weigh up the situation. "Lis, be quiet."

"Disgusting traitor," Felicity continued.

"She sits down and shuts up or I make her," Joseph said to Michael.

Bennett's cousin licked his lips and moved to comfort his aunt.

"You traitor!" she said, backing away from Michael. "He told us this would happen. Don't you see? He told us they would come after him so he can't tell the truth about what happened in Leth."

"Maybe he doesn't know," Michael said, nodding to Joseph.

"He's one of the architects!" Felicity said. "I remember his name. He's the one that murdered the old Commissioner, Harold."

Kaiya froze.

Somebody was sucking all the oxygen out of the room.

Her vision danced as pinpricks of liquid hot nausea rained over her skin.

What had she just said?

"That's not true," came Joseph's voice, distant, as if floating through syrup.

No, no, no. She had to concentrate. Process what was happening.

"Kaiya," came Joseph's voice, and she managed to focus her eyes again to stare at the Chief Inspector. His head was turned towards her, oblivious to Felicity and Michael. "It's not true," he repeated.

"I..."

She wanted to say that she knew, but... what if he had? What if... no, why would Benjamin set her up like that? But Kormac had said... though Bennett had said something in the cells... he'd as good as *told* her Joseph had been involved with her father.

Joseph hadn't hidden it.

"Kaiya, look at me," Joseph said.

His command broke her back out of her reverie, and she watched as Felicity screamed, lifting the stun baton over her head.

Joseph glanced back in time to notice the attack and stumbled backwards, crashing into a coffee table. Felicity almost overbalanced, but regained her bearings and prepared another swing.

As the stun baton neared Joseph's face, he reached out and grabbed it with one of the shock pads. Sparks flew from the contact, and the stun baton began to overload, spitting energy. Joseph grabbed the baton with his other hand as well, tightening his grip, and the sparks leapt, threatening their faces.

Both Joseph and Felicity averted their gazes, closing their eyes against the electricity, until Joseph's shock pads managed to disable the cheap stun baton. Having sucked a large amount of the energy into his shock pads, he pushed the deactivated stun baton into Felicity's body.

Energy flowed from his shock pads into the baton, and arced into Felicity.

The old woman gasped as she was thrown backwards by the force, collapsing onto the floor.

Kaiya continued to stare at the scene, still trying to recall precisely what Bennett had said to her in the concealed prison about Joseph.

Felicity lay motionless on the floor.

Michael knelt down beside her and checked her pulse, glancing up at Joseph with fear.

"She'll be awake in a few minutes," Joseph said, and turned back around. "Kaiya, sit down."

She stared at Felicity's body.

"Kaiya, please," Joseph said. "Think this through. Has anything else this woman said been accurate? Does what Bennett's told her gel with your own experience?"

She frowned and followed Joseph's advice, sorting through the disparate threads of her confusion.

He was right.

At least... she had no better options right at this moment. But she would store that tidbit of information in the back of her mind.

She sat on one of the age-sunken couches, and Joseph shot her a strained smile.

"Thank you," he said.

"I don't want any more trouble," Michael said, and Joseph indicated to the couches. Bennett's cousin nodded and sat opposite Kaiya, unable to hide his curiosity.

She averted her gaze, but paid careful attention to Joseph, who circled the couch and looked out towards the ocean.

"I went to south-west four today," Joseph said. "Do you know why I would want to go there, Michael?"

Bennett's cousin made no immediate response.

"I should let you know," Joseph continued, "that I went there with a shock team. Disabled the entire operation."

Joseph turned his back to the wall-to-wall window and stared hard at Michael.

"I didn't come here with the intention of arresting a medical pirate," Joseph said, "but I'm a very flexible person. I'm quite content to... alter my schedule, if I don't get what I need."

Michael swallowed, eyes still flicking back to Kaiya.

"I told him I'd help him if he helped me," Michael said. "He just turned up here, I swear. Maybe four days ago."

"Help him with what?" Joseph asked.

"To get away from you," Michael said. "He told me what you did."

"And what's that?"

Michael swallowed. "That you killed the Commissioner, Harold. That you were working with the Tarkinians the whole time – that you still are. That you wanted to kill him."

Joseph considered the older, frightened man, and Kaiya waited for some shred of information that would still her heart.

"One of those is true," Joseph said, "and the other ones are lies. Or half-truths, at best."

He glanced across at her and gave an encouraging nod.

"Look, I don't care," Michael said. "I'm not stupid. I know how life works. All this bullshit about law and order, you don't believe in it either."

"Don't tell me what I—"

"What's your connection here?" Michael asked. "I've dealt with plenty of cops before. You go on about justice when it's someone else, but as soon as you're the one affected you're like everyone else. You just have better resources. You've already got me in a bind – you've won. You could at least not treat me like an idiot."

Joseph clenched his jaw and glanced over at Felicity.

Kaiya considered Michael's statement and realised he was right. Joseph *was* just like everyone else, and his reasons for hunting Bennett were more than he or Benjamin had let on.

"Did you believe him?" Joseph asked. "Bennett."

Michael shrugged. "I told you, I don't really care. It's got nothing to do with me. I'm a businessman."

"You're a medical pirate."

"Call it what you want," Michael said. "I'm not the one hurting people."

"How do you know that?" Joseph asked. "When I got to your warehouse, your surgeon was in the middle of an operation. I had to let him finish it, apparently, or the patient would die. Doesn't seem like your business venture is that free from harm, does it? I saw some of the people who were operated on yesterday. Like zombies."

"You don't know what you're talking about," Michael said. "The treatment takes a few days to take proper effect. And even if it were dangerous, what's it to you? Why's it your business what people do with their own lives?"

"It's not," Joseph said, "though it is my business when people set up warehouses offering cutting edge brain surgery with no regulatory oversight. Where you want me to go with that information is up to you, Danard."

Bennett's cousin considered his options, and Kaiya began to see hints of Alison Meer in Joseph's demeanour. Had they always been there, unnoticed? Was it only now that she had met Joseph's teacher that she saw the same specks of callous, brute force in his behaviour? The first time she had met him, he had told her he didn't mind stooping to her level. He had kicked her!

Just like any of Bennett's followers would have done...

"No prosecution?" Michael asked Joseph.

"Not even a file."

"I knew that bastard would get me in trouble," Michael said. "Selfish prick."

"Where is he?" Joseph demanded.

"He left this morning," Michael said with a smirk. "He'll be gone, by now."

Joseph glared. "You'd better hope he's not," he said, and glanced over towards Felicity, who staggered to her feet.

"Looks like Satan's mother pulled through," Joseph said darkly, and turned his attention back to Michael. "Tell me the ship. Tell me the dock."

"Don't you dare," Felicity said. "I will disown you so fast, you—"

"Shut up, you witch," Joseph said. "I can see where your son gets it, now. The arrogance. The disdain for anyone else's existence. I don't know what planet you live on, but let's get something straight: your son is a liar and a murderer. Whatever duty you had as a parent, you failed in it."

Felicity began to chuckle as she glared at him.

"Funny," she said. "He said something very similar about you."

Once again, Kaiya realised she had no idea what anyone was talking about, but she could tell straight away the effect Felicity's words had on Joseph. Dark fury descended across his face, and he became a magnet of tense trepidation.

The room roiled with storm cloud energy.

Then Joseph struck.

He strode towards Felicity, his gloved hand curling around the old woman's throat, and pushed her to her knees. She gurgled as her eyes turned to shock.

"What are you doing?" Michael yelled, rising.

"I've had enough of your family, Danard," Joseph said. "I'd sleep better at night knowing no one with your name existed anymore, but I'm a... forgiving man. So you tell me right now: what ship, and what dock?"

His hand tightened on Felicity's throat.

And Michael said nothing.

"I let the energy out of this shock pad," Joseph warned, "and I can't guarantee what will happen."

The shock of Joseph's actions subsided in Kaiya's brain, and she stood abruptly. "Stop it!" she told the Chief Inspector, but he stayed where he was, eyes fixed on Michael. "This... isn't right."

Joseph ignored her.

"I don't know the name of the ship," Michael said. "But it's dock thirteen. It was supposed to leave ten minutes ago."

Joseph held Felicity for a few more seconds as he stared at Michael, then shoved her to the floor. He took out his phone and commanded a call to Alison Meer, while Michael went to his aunt's side.

Felicity smacked his hands away and struggled to her feet, cursing her nephew.

She tried to reach Joseph again, but Michael pulled her back.

"Alison, I need a lockdown right now," Joseph said. "Dock thirteen. I don't have time for questions."

"I will hunt you," Felicity spat. "You touch my family, I promise I'll make you suffer."

Joseph raised a disdainful brow at the old woman, who was still restrained by Michael.

"Let's go," the Chief Inspector said to Kaiya.

She gazed at him, his body haloed by the peaceful ocean, and realised she didn't feel so safe anymore. But why? There was no way Joseph would hurt her, not like he had hurt Felicity, but... something had changed.

She was... afraid of him?

No.

She was disappointed.

Seagulls squawked, fighting over the remnants of hot potato

chips. Kaiya watched as the most dominant in the group spread its wings menacingly, beak stuck open as it defended... whatever it was that it was defending. The other seagulls scavenged nearby, only a few of them bothering to pay attention to the antics of the dominant, who didn't even have a chip to call its own. Kaiya could have understood the dominant's behaviour if it had stolen a bag of chips and didn't want to compete with the other birds, but all she could determine from its behaviour was that, truly, seagulls had small brains.

Nor did they care about the grand affairs of humanity.

"Don't make yourselves obvious," Joseph said to no one visible, his voice picked up by the tiny receiver module attached to his ear. "He'll already be on edge, so we don't want to spook him. Just pay attention. Make sure he doesn't sneak off."

Kaiya stared at the *Spirit of Liberty*, its departure delayed. How they were going to find Bennett on a ship that size was beyond her, especially when Joseph wanted no one else but them on it.

"He's going to know what's happening as soon as he sees me," she said to Joseph.

"Exactly," he said. "That's why I need you to make yourself as visible as possible. Once he sees you, he'll begin to calculate. He's risk-averse. There'll be too many variables he doesn't know. He'll assume the worst, and try to get off the ship."

"How can you know that, though?" she asked.

"I've spent a lot of time thinking and watching," Joseph said. "You get the measure of a man after all that time."

She studied him from the corner of her eyes. He had returned to his usual cool demeanour, but it was laced with edginess. A crisp preparedness for action.

"Don't let him know you've seen him," Joseph said. "You *must* let him find you."

"And when he does?" she asked.

"We'll be there," Joseph said. "Whatever you do, don't let

him surprise you. Keep your field of vision as wide as possible, put your back to the wall as much as possible. Crowds are your friend."

"Unless he has injectables," she said.

Joseph hesitated. "If something goes wrong, take out the contacts. As soon as the feed is disrupted, we'll know to come."

"And if I'm dead by then?"

"You won't be," Joseph said, pressing the point home with his eyes. "This is why you're here, Kaiya. Bennett can't resist you. You're like a magnet, for him."

"Why?"

"Because he needs to feel as though someone cares about the things he's done," Joseph said. "The more direct the relationship, the better."

"But—"

"We don't have time for this," Joseph said. "You'll get your answers when the time is right. I promise."

Kaiya frowned. Joseph's recent behaviour had removed some of the sheen of his persona, but she had no reason to disbelieve him. She sat on an iron-and-wood bench by the harbour railing and opened one of the contact packages.

The minuscule circuits providing a visual feed grew larger in Kaiya's vision as her finger approached. She pressed the silicone cup into her eye and waited for it to settle, the circuits having disappeared from her vision. She repeated the process on her other eye.

"Have you got that?" Joseph said to his receiver module.

He smiled at what must have been a humorous response.

"You're not going to give me a weapon?" Kaiya suggested.

"Nice try," Joseph said with a grin. "But in all seriousness, he'd turn that against you within the first six seconds. He didn't get to his position by luck."

She met the Chief Inspector's eyes, looking down at her with a hint of anxiety. Was the anxiety for her safety, or for the capture of Bennett? She had no way of knowing how deeply Joseph's own hatred of Bennett went.

"I'll be in your ear the whole time," Joseph said. "Just be casual. Try the public areas first. Good luck."

Kaiya nodded and turned to face the ship.

She glanced around as she walked down the pier, wondering which of the casually-dressed citizens were really police, and where those in uniform were hiding. A man in formal welcome attire nodded as she ascended the gangplank. Did he know what was going on? Did he even work on the ship, or was he a plant?

The main deck glistened in the sunlight, even brighter as a result of reflections from the copious glass used in constructing the ship.

No one else stood there.

Kaiya glanced at the empty helipad at the front of the ship, then made her way towards the enormous double doors nearby, entering a luxuriously-decorated entrance hall with... yes, that was definitely the softest carpet she'd ever felt. Why any ship needed—

No, she had to concentrate.

She walked through the entrance hall, attempting to look as though she belonged, but she could see the surreptitious glances of the receptionists. Did they know what was happening? She gave them a smile as she passed, and their lips turned up tightly in response.

Kaiya walked into another room with a bar, elegantly-furnished and only filled to about a tenth of its capacity. Slow, light-hearted music emanated from no place in particular. A giant mural on one of the walls gave the layout of the ship, and she studied it for several minutes. Parks, casinos, a theatre, a chapel, gymnasiums and swimming pools, souvenir shops, endless restaurants, an artificial beach... how was she supposed to find Bennett in all of that?

Perhaps he had the right idea... making a new identity and

coming to a place like this. Followed by a brand new life in Atlantica.

What could stand in her way? Besides the fake identity, of course.

"Stay on that map," Joseph's voice said in her ear.

She adjusted the receiver module, turning down the Chief Inspector's voice, and kept her gaze firmly on the mural. If the Akheron police already had access to every visual feed in the ship, surely it would have been simpler for them to pick up Bennett's position and extract him.

But no. Too dangerous, Joseph had said. Who knew what Bennett would do to defend himself?

And yet Joseph was fine with letting her walk around by herself.

Was this supposed to be a punishment?

All she saw was opportunity.

"Third level bar," Joseph said. "*The Laughing Dragon*. Go there."

Kaiya found the bar on the mural and left the one she was in, stepping into a marble-staired atrium with sparkling glass railings. She scanned the face of every passenger she saw – all of them smiling – but tried her best to avoid their eyes.

Her back was exposed. Joseph's words had made her paranoid.

"Wait there," Joseph said as she approached the polished doors of *The Laughing Dragon*. She leaned against the wall and tried to look casual. She wished she could speak to Joseph, but he hadn't given her that capability.

"Go inside," Joseph said. "Empty table right side, under window. Before lattice."

Kaiya followed his orders, walking into the sumptuous darkness of a polished, dark timber she didn't know the name of. The bar arced around to her left, and she made a beeline towards the table Joseph had mentioned, glancing at a wavy dividing lattice filled with traditional tribal masks. She sat with her back to the wall and waited, scanning the room.

"Bennett approaching," Joseph said, and Kaiya's muscles contracted.

Approaching where? What did that mean?

She didn't have to wait long for an answer to the question. The disgraced Commissioner appeared on the other side of the room and sat at the bar, unconcerned with his surroundings. Kaiya looked away by instinct, then tried to watch him from the corner of her eyes as the bartender placed a shot glass in front of him.

"Keep eyes directly on," Joseph said. "Scanning for weapons."

Trickles of anxiety dripped into Kaiya's chest as she did what Joseph told her to do. If Bennett turned his attention towards her, there would be no chance of hiding her gaze.

"Best guess shock pads," Joseph said. "Left pocket, half size. Possible injector pen shirt pocket. No sign of sonic weaponry. Too much distance to analyse for explosives."

There wasn't a great deal of comfort in those words.

"You can take eyes off, now," Joseph said, "unless you like the look of him."

If she could have slapped him, she would have. She could hear someone laughing in the background!

"We're sending two in," he continued. "Can't act 'til space clear. Hold tight 'til he moves."

Kaiya did as he said.

Every minute seemed like eternity as she waited for Bennett to turn his head in her direction, but not once did he do so. When he finally left, her shoulders lifted free of the weights that had constricted her. She breathed easier.

"Stay there for now," Joseph said.

Now that Bennett was gone, her mind began reconstructing the scenario of his existence there, playing scenes of her tackling him to the floor, smashing some glass and shoving it into his neck. Watching him struggle underneath her victorious weight.

If only she had been so confident when he was there.

"He's moving to deck level," Joseph said. "Exit starboard, take middle atrium down to deck. Plainclothes are onboard."

Kaiya followed the Chief Inspector's directions, gazing out over the ocean as she did so.

The middle atrium was structured similarly to the first, but was significantly larger. A fountain took pride of place in the centre, water streaming down from every floor in dazzling patterns, creating a mist that cooled Kaiya's face as she walked down the stairs.

Children laughed below, splashing in the basin.

Their parents scolded them.

When she reached the basin, she gazed at her reflection in the water and waited for further instructions.

None came.

Kaiya looked around. On one side of the fountain was a park full of children, on the other a busy cafe. Passengers moved freely throughout, bustling and noisy.

A blur of faces.

"Get back onto second level," Joseph said. "Now."

The urgency of Joseph's voice caught Kaiya around the throat, and she froze momentarily before setting her gaze back on one side of the curving staircase.

"He's slipped out of vision," Joseph said. "Nothing to worry about. He'll come back in. But get to some space until then."

Great. He couldn't make up his mind. One minute it was crowds are friends, the next it was find space.

A laughing girl about seven years old ran into her leg, and stumbled back in shock. Kaiya gave her a reassuring smile, and the girl's shy face brightened. She ran off, chasing her friends.

Kaiya watched as the girl disappeared into the park area.

And gasped as a hand grabbed her own wrist.

"I don't want to kill you," Bennett said, squeezing tight, "so the first thing you're going to do is take that receiver module out of your ear."

Kaiya stood still, racing mind trapped in thick honey.

"Come on, Brown, work with me here. Don't be like your father."

The temerity of his words reactivated her brain, and she reached up to take out the receiver module.

"Plainclothes are in the—" Joseph said, cutting out as she deactivated the tiny device.

"Good. Now give it to me," Bennett said.

She followed his order, closing her eyes in some vain attempt to feel his presence more clearly.

"Do you know what I have in my hand?" he asked.

Kaiya swallowed, beads of sweat forming on her face. No one around her seemed to have noticed that the man behind her meant harm. "Atropine," she guessed. "That's how you killed the woman in the town square. I was there. I saw what happened to her. I knew what you'd done as soon as I saw the symptoms."

"It's a pity your father had to die," Bennett said. "I hate wasting resources, and he was excellent at his job."

"Is that why you hated him so much?"

"That's cute," Bennett said. "Trying to take control. Shift the power dynamics. Not going to work on me... *Kaiya*."

His breath whispered against her ear, sending a chill down her neck.

He was toying with her.

"I knew what was happening when I saw you in that bar," Bennett said. "I'd already suspected something was up when our departure was delayed. The question I have... is why did they send *you*?"

"Because I'm irresistible," Kaiya said.

She didn't even understand what Joseph had meant by that,

but Bennett laughed. "I'm not interested in you like that," he said.

Whatever Joseph *had* meant, she knew it wasn't that. Had he set her up for this exact encounter?

"Who put you up to this?" Bennett asked. "It couldn't be Benjamin. He'd never risk you. Not his style."

Kaiya's mind raced, trying to determine if holding onto the information gave her any leverage. Bennett was clever, but a braggart. Maybe there was some tidbit of information she could glean from him.

"It was Joseph," she said.

Bennett grunted. "Makes sense. His reasons are personal, after all. But it still doesn't explain *you*."

She wished Bennett would explain *Joseph*.

"How much do you think the Chief Inspector cares about you, Kaiya Brown?" Bennett said. "What would he do if he knew I had you like this? If he knew I could kill you?"

All around them the passengers continued talking and laughing and walking, oblivious to the crime that was occurring right in front of them.

"Why would he care about me?" Kaiya said.

"I'd like to know that, myself," Bennett said. "Now, as much as I love talking to you, Brown, your puppeteers must be wondering why you've been in the same position so long. Or were you hoping I wouldn't consider the fact you're wearing contacts?"

Kaiya closed her eyes. If she could just take one out...

"Move," Bennett said, prodding towards the bow of the ship. "You run, you die."

He let go of her wrist slowly, and Kaiya walked forward, conscious of Bennett's presence. The collabo-scum Commissioner was quick on his feet. Strong reflexes. She didn't want to risk him thinking she was trying to escape.

How far a drop was it to the ocean?

"I've always found the best way to resolve a situation is to bring it to a head," Bennett said. "That way, every side knows what's at stake. Then they can negotiate accordingly. Did your father teach you that?"

Kaiya kept moving forward, searching for the cameras that would give Joseph a clear shot of the situation, but a ship like this wouldn't have its cameras visible. She could only hope. Bennett was trying to goad her, just like he had in the concealed prison. Why not play along?

"Whatever lessons my father gave me," she said, "they weren't the same ones your mother Felicity gave you."

She regretted the words as soon as they left her mouth, and braced herself for some kind of reaction.

None came.

Instead, Bennett chuckled. "The trick to getting on someone's nerves," he said, "is you have to poke the ones they care about. But your father was never the best interrogator, so I can't blame you for failing."

Kaiya clenched her jaw. Had Bennett always been like this?

They neared the helipad at the front of the ship.

"Stop," Bennett said.

Kaiya gazed forward towards the peaceful-looking harbourside, the sound of gentle waves lapping against the side of the ship.

Not a cloud in the sky.

Not a Joseph or a uniform in sight.

"And now we wait for them to come to me," Bennett whispered in her ear.

How long would that take?

"They won't," she said, but who knew what they would do, in truth?

Bennett stayed silent, and they waited.

The sun prickled Kaiya's skin.

The proximity of Bennett's body, the pressure of his menacing presence, made her sweat.

Salt touched her lips.

And they continued to wait.

Maybe this had been the point all along? Maybe this entire series of events with Joseph had been a charade, his way of scheming to bring his own special, personal vengeance on the former Commissioner. She should have known she was being played.

And to think Masuma would never know what happened...

The thought of the girl sharpened Kaiya's thoughts. She didn't have to accept this.

She *knew* Bennett. She *knew* what he was like. She had to find the right topic to keep him talking...

"Why does Joseph hate you?" she asked. "If you're going to kill me, I want to know what for."

Bennett tittered and pressed the side of the injectable against her body. Kaiya stiffened, understanding his reassertion of power.

"Joseph blames me for things I didn't do," Bennett said.

"Like what?"

"Does it matter?" Bennett said. "If you die, you won't care, and if you don't... then I'd rather know that he has to choose to relive it once more, or risk losing your faith in him. In either case, I win, don't I?"

"My father was right to never promote you," she said.

"Now that... would be a fascinating thought experiment, wouldn't it, Brown? Would I have done what I've done had I been given what I deserved to begin with. Who can tell?"

He lingered on every word, drawing them out poetically with great inflection.

It was all a game, to him.

"And here he comes," Bennett said.

Joseph walked down the pier towards the ship.

Kaiya began to panic as her opportunity to extract some kind of information from Bennett disappeared step by Joseph step.

"What did Joseph do to my father?" she demanded, twisting her head so she could just see the edge of Bennett's face. "Tell me."

"You should learn to let things go," Bennett said. "Whoever came up with the idea that we need to know every truth was a fool."

"Why can you never answer me?" Kaiya asked.

"I don't owe you any answers."

Kaiya gasped as Bennett grabbed her wrist again.

Joseph approached the gangplank, handgun raised. "Let her go, Bennett. Aren't you tired of this by now?"

"Bit dangerous from that distance, don't you think?" Bennett said. "Wouldn't want to hit her by... mistake, would you?"

"I have impeccable accuracy."

Bennett's laugh boomed in Kaiya's ear. "At short range," he said. "In fact, I'd say you have a talent for point-blank, wouldn't you?"

"Not nearly as well-developed as you give me credit for," Joseph said, stepping onto the gangplank.

"Uh-uh-uh," Bennett warned, and Kaiya felt the injectable pressing against her side.

Joseph stopped.

"Good boy. *Inspector.*"

Seagulls squawked...

The sun beat down...

Beads of liquid salt ran down Kaiya's lips...

"So what do you think your chances are?" Bennett called to Joseph. "And what about you, Kaiya Brown? Are you going to trust the man that killed your father? The man who executed him?"

"Don't listen to him, Kaiya," Joseph said.

"She's going to find out eventually, Balfour!" Bennett

laughed. "Stop lying to the poor girl. Tell her how you put that gun to his head and blew his brains out all over the southern pass."

Kaiya squeezed her eyes shut, trying to block out the stinging sweat.

"How do you imagine this is going to play out?" Joseph called. "Some kind of swap? You give me Kaiya and you get your freedom?"

"Don't be stupid," Bennett said. "I know I won't be going anywhere. I just wanted you here to watch the Brown girl die."

Kaiya breathed in sharply. Now she understood.

She couldn't wait any longer.

Her body exploded with adrenaline.

Her skin prickled with energy as she picked up on Bennett's tiniest movements.

His hand appeared on the edge of her vision, holding the pen-like syringe. Kaiya saw the opportunity burst into her consciousness, instinct kicking in, and she drove her elbow up into Bennett's shoulder, sending her weight backwards into him.

They fell together onto the deck, and Kaiya scrambled to untangle herself from the former Commissioner. He wrapped a leg around both of hers, squeezing them, and stabbed downwards with the syringe.

She grabbed at his arm instinctively, pushing against his superior strength. He grunted and brought his other hand around to her neck, pressing down until she spluttered, gasping for air that would not come.

The injectable lingered in her blurry sight as she rolled back and forth as best she could, pinned within Bennett's death role embrace.

People were moving in the distance...

Kaiya gurgled.

Masuma looked up at her...

The injectable pressed down inexorably.

The scars on Kormac's back…

Shadows.

Blue sky fading.

"You can't beat me, Kaiya," someone whispered, distant… breath tickling her ear… "I'm a better poet than you'll ever be."

Pinpricks of light burst in her vision.

Tilda laughing…

Spattered blood on stalks of lavender…

19

SOFT GOLD SHIMMERED IN THE AIR, TINGED WITH DEEP CRIMSON. Kaiya watched the glass-towered reflections of dawn dance into her bedroom and stretched out on the bed, head still heavy. Her throat ached, and she pressed the skin gently, wincing as she relished the pain.

The memory of coming to this moment was hazy, but she could pick out points of reference, bright stars in the darkness after Bennett. She remembered Joseph's face, but where that had been, she couldn't tell. She remembered the floating sensation of travelling up the stairs of Kytos's building on a lev-powered stretcher. Kytos watching her in the midnight darkness...

She draped her legs out of the bed and waited for the room to stop spinning. When the world had righted itself, she went to the unlatched window and stuck her hands out into the as yet unheated open air.

Akheron glowed.

She edged her head out of the window and gazed towards the east, squinting at the rising sun.

Her door opened.

"I thought I heard you," Kytos said. "It's early."

Kaiya pulled her head back in and smiled.

"It's nice," she said.

"How are you feeling?"

Kaiya searched her body to figure out how to answer that question. She didn't really know.

"Tired?" she said.

"You should get some more sleep," Kytos suggested.

"No, not like that," Kaiya said. "I think I just... want to sit for a while."

Kytos nodded and stood silent for a few moments before leaving the room awkwardly and closing the door behind him. Kaiya found his demeanour amusing, as well as the assumption that she wanted to be alone, and instead followed him out through the corridor and into the living room. He looked up with glum surprise as she entered.

"I'd rather be out here, if that's ok with you?" Kaiya said.

"Oh... yes. Of course."

She sat on a lounge chair that captured some of the dawn reflections, glancing occasionally at Kytos in his dark corner. His tablet illuminated his face and the light-sucking wall behind him. If only they could have opened the curtain in the living room, but who wanted to look at a holoboard of themselves staring back at them?

Like a beckoning, judgmental mirror.

"What are you reading?" Kaiya asked.

Kytos glanced up at her and back at the tablet. Was he finishing a paragraph?

"There's a columnist in the Akheron Herald that I like," he said. "A historian. Writes extended essays about the historical basis of contemporary events. I've read all his books. He's just written a piece criticising Nymosen's public health response to the prisoners from Tarkinia. Your hometown gets a special mention."

Kytos shook his head disapprovingly.

"But will anyone listen?" he said. "No. Of course not. People never learn. The future can be sitting right there in front of them, and they'll still think they're the first ones who've ever walked that path."

Kaiya watched him frown at the tablet and continue reading, his body engulfed by the chair that had so long ago sunk under the years of his daily weight.

He looked like her mother had when the Tarkinians first came – creased by constant concern.

"So what are they doing wrong?" Kaiya asked.

"Everything," Kytos said. "Not enough funding, not enough doctors, not enough psychological assessment, not enough time under supervision, releasing patients too quickly... but you know what'll happen? There'll be a review in twenty years. People will look around and see the consequences of pushing people through the system, and they'll say 'we' didn't do enough! There'll be apologies. There'll be campaigns for recognition. People will tell stories. And then everyone will forget. And the next time it happens? We'll do the same thing we did this time. And the last time. And the time before that. People never learn."

The doctor who had treated Kormac came into Kaiya's mind. She had been blinded, then, she saw that now. But with the clarity of hindsight, she realised he had known something. He had been so adamant about the supplements and... bitter, now she thought about it.

What had that Taskforce officer said about the hospital not wanting Kormac...

"I don't think people *never* learn," Kaiya said.

Kytos shook his head. "I should have been clearer. People – individuals – they can learn. But people as a group? There's nothing more stupid or more dangerous than that."

Kaiya leaned back in her chair and gazed out into the distant, brightening dawn. If the past two days had taught her anything, it was that Kytos had a more active intellectual life than she ever would have given him credit for. He would have fit in well around the dining table at home, but... obviously there were things she didn't know.

She couldn't remember what she had seen, as consciousness faded in Bennett's grasp, but the imprint of her mind's desperate grasping stood firm. Regrets and realisations had pushed to the front as she watched the needle approaching, as the blackness came. As Bennett's grip weakened and the shouts of Joseph and others whispered in her mind while lucidity faded away.

So many things she hadn't yet done. Words she wished she'd said. Things she wished she'd known.

"What happened?" Kaiya asked, eyes resting hesitantly on Kytos. "Between you and mum."

Kytos stared at the tablet, eyes unmoving, and shrugged. "We never saw eye to eye on certain things."

Kaiya waited for more information, but he offered none.

"What kind of things?" she pressed.

Kytos shifted in his seat, obviously uncomfortable at her questioning. But she wasn't going to let the information go, anymore. She wanted to know.

"I didn't like that she married your father, to be honest. He was one of those... anti-war protestors. Refused to serve, while I was out there defending his right to be morally superior. We hated each other, in the beginning. I would call him a traitor, he would call me a baby killer. It's just the language we used back then. Your mother and I stopped talking for a while, and the next thing I know, your father's joined the police."

Kytos lifted his hands dismissively.

"He apologised, in the end, your father. I ended up liking him – at least, when I knew him – but I don't think I ever told him that."

Kaiya waited, eager for more information. "Is that all? What happened after that?"

"It's not about what happened after that," Kytos said. "It's about before, as well. It's about the way your mother is. The way she's always been. I don't blame her for not staying in Akheron, even though she worked so hard to get into Nym State. But I thought... I thought she would at least take me. She left me on my own, with him. And after she left, he was even worse."

The dark look on Kytos's face warned Kaiya against asking for further details, but she could already make more sense of why there had never been any holos of her maternal grandfather, even if she didn't have all the pieces of that puzzle.

"It's funny, you know," Kytos said. "After all this time, I understand why he was so angry. He fought the Tarkinians in the northern province changeovers. He was at the massacre of Sandaweir. But understanding something when you're older doesn't make it any better when you're younger. It doesn't change what happened. After I was old enough to move to the barracks, I'd go to see your mother from time to time, but it was like she'd completely forgotten about our entire lives up until that point. Everything was good times and sunshine, like that could make the past disappear. I wanted to talk, but she didn't. She never has.

"The only thing she *did* want to talk about was the future. She'd always be telling me I needed a plan. Something to 'strive' for, but why should I ignore the past? That's what she wanted me to do. Act as though it never happened. Then the war came. Another one. I've told you about that already."

Kaiya nodded softly to indicate that she remembered.

"I blamed her for a long time," Kytos said, "for not understanding. But it wasn't really her fault. People never understand. She tried to be supportive at the beginning, I think, but I didn't want to hear about the things she was talking about. It was the same as always – talking about the future, about moving on. But not once did she acknowledge what had happened. Not once did she say that I had been wronged. She never wanted to hear about the past. Only the future. She thought this was 'encouraging.'

"But I did what she wanted, for a while. I saw the people. I took the medications. It's all bullshit, though. That's the truth she didn't want to see – that there's no cure. You either get justice or you don't. There's no in between."

Kytos stared at the closed curtains hiding the outside world, the lines of his face etched deep with memory.

"The last time I was in Leth," he said, "we had a fight, your mother and me. She told me I was a bad influence. That she didn't want me around you. I haven't spoken to her since then."

He rested his forehead on the tips of his fingers and began to cry.

"I wish I could see her again."

Kaiya turned her head away, hiding the leak of her own memories.

Any day now, she would return.

Everything would be fine.

Kaiya lay on the grass of Akheron's central park, gazing up at the tower-pierced expanse of blue. The grass prickled her skin, both that which was exposed and that which was covered. She scratched herself idly, touching her tender throat from time to time and enjoying the occasional salt-tinged gust of air that dampened the effect of constant sunshine.

Here, in the centre of the capital, birdsong conquered the incessant chatter of speech, the constant hum of traffic, the screeching of magnetic pads in need of repair. She had debated whether or not to tell Joseph her plan for the day, but decided the Chief Inspector didn't deserve that knowledge. He hadn't stayed. He hadn't come back to visit her. She had fulfilled her role, a pawn in his greater plan to exact his own revenge on Bennett. What had happened to Bennett?

She would have to face Joseph eventually...

"I've been wanting to come here," Jonathan said, sitting beside her.

"Why haven't you?" Kaiya asked.

She turned her face towards Jonathan, who frowned.

"What happened to—"

"It's fine," Kaiya said.

"Shouldn't you be in hospital?"

Kaiya shrugged. "You'd think so. But apparently my uncle's place is just as good."

"If I'd known you were injured I wouldn't have come," Jonathan said.

"You think that would have made me stay inside?" Kaiya asked. "I don't want to talk about this. I'm sick of... morbid stuff. What have you been doing?"

Jonathan considered her and took a long, relaxed sigh. "Going to museums. Visiting galleries. Learning about architecture."

"All stuff I'd expect to hear from a soldier," Kaiya said.

He grinned.

"I enjoyed myself," he said. "I like seeing how differently you portray events that I read about in school. You have a very... revisionist streak, in this country."

"And you don't?"

"That's a fair point," Jonathan conceded, "but we're not in Atlantica. This is your country."

"I don't know about that," Kaiya said. "Leth used to be independent."

Jonathan gave her a disbelieving look. "You're not still going on about that, are you?"

"What do you mean, still?"

"You told me how you felt the day I... met your friend, Tilda," Jonathan said.

Kaiya cast her mind back, but all that came was Kormac smashing a chair against the wall.

"You told me I wouldn't understand," Jonathan said, "then tried to say Leth had never had anything to do with Tarkinia."

"But we haven't!" she said.

"Where exactly did you learn that?" he asked.

"What do you mean where did I learn it? Everyone knows that."

"So the Nymians decided just to waltz in one day and take over?" Jonathan said. "Don't be naïve. Leth was always under the protection of Tarkinia. The Tarkinians let you have your 'independence' and you gave them access to mineral deposits in the mountains. Sure, the duke surrendered to Nymosen, but the Nymians weren't just coming along saying they wanted to take over little towns."

Kaiya stared at the points of dazzling light coming from the towers.

"Besides," Jonathan continued, "that was eight hundred years ago. Don't you think it's time to let it go? Just accept you're a Nymian and be done with it."

Kaiya didn't have the heart to argue the point any further. She supposed he was right. It didn't really matter. None of those things mattered anymore, in truth. Alison Meer would put everything right again. Maybe she'd even called Joseph already.

Surely Joseph wouldn't have gone to all that trouble with his own teacher if he didn't mean to go through with it...

"My uncle told me something about *marashta* the other day," Kaiya said, and passed on her newfound information.

"I didn't know that at all," Jonathan said.

"I thought you'd find it interesting."

The accuracy of that thought pleased her.

"Don't you wish you had one book," Jonathan said, "and that

book told you everything about the history of a place, or a person, or a thing? Every detail, all completely objective. No distortions or lies or... bending the truth."

"I guess," Kaiya said. "Do you think it's possible? Would you write it if you had the chance?"

Jonathan chuckled and lay down on the grass beside her. "I don't think it is possible. You'd have to be able to live the life of everyone who's ever existed. But it's a nice idea. Some kind of story that isn't affected by what the reader thinks or feels."

"Then I could prove I'm right," Kaiya said.

She grinned across at Jonathan, tracing the glint of sunlight in his hair, and realised she was glad for his presence.

"And what if it proved you wrong?" he said.

"Then we'd know the book's not accurate."

They laughed together, and Kaiya warmed through some combination of the sun, the prickling grass, and the knowledge – foreign as it felt – that she was safe, here, with Jonathan.

"I think you've thoroughly demonstrated why the book could never work," he said.

She continued to memorise the visible side of his face, all the while hiding the fact she was doing so. With Kormac and Tilda gone, she was either child to Joseph or adult to Masuma, and in truth she felt like neither. Rather, she was lost in some middle ground, stuck in a prolonged moment of time between the two stages.

With Kormac there had been expectation; with Tilda, judgment. And with Jonathan there was simply grass, and sky, and breeze, and sun. She knew he had deeper thoughts and intentions than her, but she could ignore that for the moment and enjoy the presence of someone who she could sense was struggling with the same inability to move beyond the middle ground.

A bird glided across her vision.

"Have you changed your mind about Akheron?" Jonathan asked.

Kaiya let the question linger for a long time, mulling over all she'd seen there so far, from Kytos's decrepit concrete suburb, to the beauty of a city centre reclaimed for nature. "It has some nice bits," she said.

She could see Jonathan's face crack open in a grin, and couldn't help mimicking his response.

"That's a big improvement," he said.

"I'm trying to be more... open-minded," she conceded. "I still love Leth more than anything, but... it doesn't feel the same anymore. It feels empty."

Jonathan looked across at her. "That's not Leth, Kaiya. That's you. Towns don't feel like anything. You make it feel like something."

She somewhat grasped his meaning, and stopped herself from automatically looking for a rebuttal to what he'd said.

"Do you really think so?" she asked, more mildly. "Why do you like visiting different places, then?"

He considered the question. "I know what you're trying to say. But even when I go somewhere new, it's not the place itself that affects me, it's what I bring to it. It's the state of mind I'm in at the time, it's the things I choose to see there, it's the people I meet. So when I think of Leth, it's... charming. I'll probably always think it one of the most beautiful places I've been."

Kaiya allowed the subtle compliment to float without any immediate response. She would have to address the diversion of interest between them rather than just ignore it and simply hope that her rejection would not drive yet another person away from her. Though did she really deserve anyone's interest to begin with?

"I don't want to lead you on," she said.

"If I took your behaviour so far as you trying to lead me on," Jonathan said, "I'd be a masochist of a man."

She laughed, harder than the joke warranted, expelling the tension of not having known how he would respond to her boundary-setting.

"I'm well aware how you feel about soldiers," Jonathan said.

"It's not about that," Kaiya said. "If it were, there wouldn't be an issue – you're an exception. I'm just not up to anything. With anyone. I'm too tired."

"And there's Kormac," Jonathan offered, more a hesitant probe than a statement.

Kaiya closed her eyes and sighed. "Not really. Not anymore. But even that... it's too confusing to think about. Can't we talk about something else? Tell me about painting or Atlantican food or how you think road tiles should be healed."

"Is that really what you want to talk about?" Jonathan asked. "I assumed there'd be something else on your mind, otherwise you wouldn't have called me."

"Maybe I want to talk about both," Kaiya said. "The nothing stuff *and* the important stuff."

"So which is the nothing stuff?" Jonathan asked.

Kaiya smiled at the subversion of her dichotomy. She would have to ponder whether the subversion had merit but, until then, she might as well bring up the one thing she had thought to ask.

"I went to the courts the other day," she said, "and I heard someone talking about Ledophas."

She glanced across to see if he gave any reaction, but his face remained still.

"I thought that maybe you'd know something," she said. "Anything, even. Maybe not even about there specifically. Just about the people who haven't come back yet."

Jonathan shook his head. "I don't know, Kaiya. I'm sorry. I have no authority. I just do my job and don't get in anyone's way. These are the kind of things you need higher clearance for. I don't even try to find out. Don't you think some things are better just to not know?"

"*Some* things, sure," she said. "But not other things. You found out about the first convoy, didn't you? So obviously you're able to find stuff out when you want to."

"Not whenever I want," he said. "That was luck more than anything. The fact that the first convoy was so close is really the only reason I got the information. Everyone was going to know the next day, and I knew what to ask for. But this? This isn't the kind of thing I know how to ask for."

They stayed silent for a short while, and Kaiya listened to a distant group of passing school children chattering away about imaginary creatures.

"I wish I could be more helpful," Jonathan said.

Kaiya pushed aside the disappointment at his lack of knowledge – she was too tired to care – and smiled across at the Atlantican. "You can't even fix a road tile right."

Jonathan chuckled. "Funny what you remember and what you don't."

"You would tell me, wouldn't you?" Kaiya asked. "If you heard something..."

"Of course I would," he said. "But I don't hear much. And what I do hear is nearly all official. Standard diplomatic news. Prisoner swaps, visas for foreign partners, that kind of thing."

"They're doing that now?"

Jonathan nodded. "Nymosen finally agreed to release its prisoners. Tarkinia's created a special visa category for their soldiers to bring over Nymian partners and—"

"Hold on," Kaiya said. "What prisoners?"

Jonathan peered at her. "From the camps in central Nymosen," he said. "Where do you think you put Tarkinian prisoners for the past six years?"

"I didn't know we had any," Kaiya said.

Jonathan shook his head. "You're strange. I figured everyone knew about that. They're nowhere near as big as the Tarkinian camps, but that's this time. It used to be the other way around, two wars ago. Honestly, I'm surprised you and Tarkinia don't just agree to leave each other alone. Neither of you are ever going to win."

"If they stopped attacking us—"

"Go read a book!" Jonathan said. "You're as bad as each other."

"I don't care," Kaiya said. "I don't want to be in either country."

"But you are in one," Jonathan said. "That's reality."

He looked at her and she sighed.

"I'm sick of talking about Tarkinia," she said.

"Then tell me what you want to talk about," Jonathan said. "I'm all ears."

Kaiya took a deep breath and focused on the tiny prickles of grass in her back. "You still haven't told me about the paintings or Atlantican food," she said.

Jonathan grinned and began to regale her with stories and facts. Kaiya listened, allowing time to flow across the stillness of her body, and her mind to float away into the endless, shining blue. Jonathan's words were meaningless, but the fact of him speaking brought her comfort as the constant concern of the day pressed harder and harder against her consciousness.

Every minute ticking by was one closer to Joseph's testimony – testimony that he had failed to mention he was giving – and, as far as he knew, she would be in bed under Kytos's care. Joseph knew things. Things he wouldn't tell her.

And some things *were* better to know.

Kaiya sat near the rear of the courtroom, a smaller one than that which had displayed the former Ambassador to the Occupied Territories. Most of the room was filled with onlookers, but not so many that every seat was taken as people squeezed together trying to catch a glimpse of a common enemy. She had examined the interactive list of hearings for each courtroom before entering, and while the main courtroom contained the combative cases, this one told stories from those who had been affected in this way or that.

There were no sides, only a public examination.

The mood of the room was sombre.

"Doctor Samuel Taylor, we thank you for agreeing to provide this testimony today," the advocate said.

The doctor sat in the witness box and nodded gravely.

"For the purposes of these proceedings' records, can I confirm that you are the chief cardiologist of the Nymosen Defence Force medical division and a senior research fellow at Nymosen State University?"

"That is correct."

Kaiya leaned back on her bench, heart eased only slightly by the knowledge that she was early. She had worried about missing Joseph's testimony, but he came after the doctor.

Though the anticipation still niggled. She wanted it to come and not to at the same time.

"Thank you," the advocate said. "I would like, with Your Honour's permission, to give warning to those in the gallery regarding the contents of this witness's testimony."

The judge nodded, and the advocate turned to face the crowd.

"Doctor Taylor will be providing a type of testimony today that this court has not yet heard. I warn that this testimony will be explicit in the nature of its description of Tarkinian torture tools and methods. I would invite those of you who feel they may prefer to remain ignorant of these details to return for future witnesses."

A low murmur washed through the courtroom, and several spectators stood to leave.

The advocate nodded to himself when the doors closed once more.

"Doctor Taylor, I want to first ask with what reliability you are able to give your evidence today? Can you describe to us how it is you have come to acquire the knowledge you will be sharing?"

"We were first made aware that the Tarkinians were using multiple electro-based torture methods about one year into the war," the doctor said. "When the province of Vyalet was reclaimed, we liberated several hundred prisoners of war and subjected them to rigorous interviewing. Through this process we learnt to some degree the type of things the Tarkinians were doing, but... those were early applications of emerging technology. Our work has been largely theoretical, using the testimony of escaped and liberated prisoners, until last week, when we were finally able to deconstruct and analyse one of the Tarkinian tools."

"The name of this tool, for the record?"

"We cannot determine if the Tarkinians called the tool something specific, but colloquially it is known as 'the boards.'"

Kaiya sat straighter on her bench, skin prickling as though she were still laying on the grass.

"This is not the only discovery our team has made," the doctor continued, "but it is the key finding for which I am capable of discussing today, given my area of expertise."

"And your area of expertise as a research fellow is the use of electricity on biological organisms?"

"That is correct," the doctor said. "My colleagues will be giving evidence tomorrow on other Tarkinian techniques. Janet Fyfe is a leading biochemist and brain physiologist, and Julian Quay an expert on organ engineering and remodelling."

The advocate cleared his throat and glanced at the gallery.

"You mentioned that the first batch of prisoners you interviewed five years ago were exposed to an early application of these 'boards.' I understand you haven't yet described what this machine does, but can you speculate at all why its function changed over the years? Was it ineffective in its earlier incarnation?"

The doctor shook his head. "Not at all. From all reports, the boards were highly effective in their early incarnation, but improvements were made, as far as we can tell, to maximise pain while minimising the chance of permanent cardiac arrest or the subject slipping into unconsciousness. It seems the function of the boards was punishment. Other tools had uses to the Tarkinians in their various... research programs, but the boards were purely for punishment. And entertainment, according to some reports."

"So the Tarkinians were applying this tool to prisoners as a kind of sport?" the advocate asked.

"You could put it that way, yes. My understanding is that while there were regular public applications of boarding for misdemeanours, there were also private sessions in which officers or visiting delegates could... be in control of the machine, somewhat. Give them a firsthand experience of being in charge of its effects. We have stories, too, of the boards being popular in certain... how shall I put this... 'group activities' with primarily female prisoners."

The advocate cleared his throat again.

Kaiya clenched the muscles in her legs.

Pressed her interlocked fingers tightly together.

"Thank you for enlightening us," the advocate said. "Can you describe to us this process of 'boarding?'"

"To understand the process, you need to understand the construction," the doctor said. "The boards are quite literally based around a single, upright-standing plank of wood. There are other constructions based on more flexible materials for some of the private uses I mentioned earlier, but the simple construction is the most common. The subject is placed against the plank, facing it, and his head is secured by a conductive helmet attached to this plank. This stops the head from drooping. The second support comes in the form of a mechanism that protrudes from the plank and covers the subject's chest. In this way, the subject may be lowered towards the ground along with the board, which has the capacity to angle further than the subject, whose feet will also have been secured. This ability to place the subject at an angle, and at varying distances from the board, seems to have been important for regulating the subject's experience of pain by adjusting natural blood flow and promoting a certain feeling of imbalance."

Murmurs of revulsion trickled through the gallery, and Kaiya forced herself to stay present. She couldn't let the image of Kormac enter her head.

"The plank is fixed with a number of extendable, electricity-conducting components," the doctor continued. "The most obvious is a series of very fine wires that are wrapped around the back of the subject and placed into latches on the other side of the board. This creates, as far as we can tell, a near-perfect series of lines on the subject's back, which assists in magnifying minute control of the subject's experience of the electricity that will later be flowing into their body. As the subject is held at his or her angle by the helmet and chest support, the board can be lowered further, tautening the wires around the subject's back. This intensifies the pain experience for the subject, and can lead to permanent scarring, something which has been quite common in those returned prisoners we have seen so far."

"How serious is this scarring?" the advocate asked.

"It ranges from mild discolouration to major hypertrophy," the doctor said. "Those who were subjected to minor punishment seem to recover well, as the wires make no permanent mark on the skin and simply deliver the electricity. Those subjected to more extreme punishment, however, often experience not only the electricity of each wire, but the wire cutting into their skin as the board pulls away and pressure increases. Combined with the near non-existence of adequate medical care at these facilities, hypertrophic scarring is relatively common in those who have been subject to this process. The majority of this scarring is discrete, meaning we can see each scar and the line it appeared from, but there are some cases where the subject's back is entirely covered in scar tissue."

Kaiya forced herself to stay seated as the doctor spoke. Nearby, a handful more spectators shuffled out of the courtroom.

"I take it," the advocate said, "that this is the core method of inflicting punishment with the boards?"

The doctor licked his lips as he thought about the question. "It would be fair to say that all subjects to boarding go through this process, so in that sense it forms a core aspect of the experience, but I would reject the notion that the electrified wires are the worst aspect of this punishment."

Another trickle of the gallery left, and the advocate cleared his throat again.

"I would class the wires as part of the exterior experience," the doctor said, "and minor punishments may use merely this exterior experience, but many subjects of boarding also go through what I will call an internal experience. You must understand that the current applied through the wires attached to the subject's back is very low, and the size of the wires aids in the localisation of the pain experience. The Tarkinians perfected minute electrical control with the boards, and were able to increase or decrease at tiny increments depending on the subject's height and weight, and whether or not water was being applied – this is a technique that can be used to create a more general feeling of the shock. No new technology needed, merely someone with water and a rag to drip the water onto the subject's back. But the real... genius, I hate to say... of the boards is how well the Tarkinians have perfected control over the heart's electrical system.

"Even small amounts of current placed through the body can result in ventricular fibrillation, which is why the current from the wires is so delicately controlled. The Tarkinians found a way to balance the maximum amount of pain possible with their desire to maintain regular internal electrical functioning. They developed a specific method of altering that internal electrical functioning. You will recall the support mechanism on which the subject's chest is placed?"

"Yes," the advocate said.

"While the wires provide tiny currents in a specific location, the chest mechanism provide a more generalised burst of electricity. It is somewhat flexible, and is placed in such a way as to cover the majority of the lungs, and pass next to each side of the heart. In this way, the Tarkinians can control function and dysfunction of the entire cardio-pulmonary system."

"They stopped the subject's heart?" the advocate asked.

"It's not that simple," the doctor said. "The Tarkinians didn't stop and start organs, though it may be simpler to think of it that way. Most defibrillation or cardio-pulmonary resuscitation occurs while the heart is electrically-impaired as opposed to not working at all. What the Tarkinians achieved was control over putting a subject into cardiac arrest and then pulling them out of that arrest. They would then repeat the process multiple times, though it wasn't perfect. The Tarkinians managed a degree of control we've never seen before, but reports suggest that deaths still occurred during the act of boarding."

"Is this the primary cause of death?"

"Actually, no. We have done a very preliminary analysis of some victims, and found a range of causes that relate to longer-term damage not only to the cardio-pulmonary system, but other organs as well. The level of stress this procedure places on the heart is extraordinary, so we're not surprised that the leading cause of subsequent death is *future* cardiac arrest. Occasionally the Tarkinians could not control current application completely, which has led to damage of the nervous system in some subjects. The vast majority of these subjects have died either through extermination, having become useless to the Tarkinians, or from related organ failure. There are also cases of infection in those subjects that were injured by the wires. We have no evidence that any medical care was provided in these cases. I also want to add, for the record, that there are obvious effects on subjects that are not directly related to the physical aspect of boarding—"

"You mean psychological effects?"

"Yes, with boarding a highly contributing factor in these effects. I am concerned that the political and medical response to these effects have been inadequate."

Kaiya shut her eyes, wiping away the few tears she wouldn't allow to fall. If she could simply open a portal and step through to Kormac. Touch him. Hold him. Never let him out of her sight again.

The courtroom air suffocated.

"Doctor Taylor," the advocate said after a significant pause, "exactly how painful is this procedure?"

The doctor hesitated before answering.

"I will answer your question," he said, "but I want to preface by saying that straight pain is the wrong way in which to think about boarding or measure its impact. A subject who goes through the core aspect of boarding, the wires, will begin by experiencing an... itch, across their back. That itch will progress to a generalised feeling of heat, and finally to a searing sensation located specifically on the points the wire touches. The next step is the application of pressure as the board lowers faster than the subject. As the wires cut into the skin, the pain becomes more generalised again, and the subject experiences muscle spasms and the sensation that they are burning. In many cases, this is precisely what is happening to them. Given the practice of holding subjects at an angle, occasionally the body will spasm suddenly enough that the spine will break, though this seems to have been uncommon, as the Tarkinians minimised internal electrical interference when using this technique.

"We have yet to hear, however, a single subject of boarding complain that these external processes are worse than the internal. The effect of what I am going to call cardio-pulmonary 'pulsing' – the act of stopping and starting the system, for ease of expression – is profoundly psychological. The specific physical experiences are different across subjects, but common ones include a generalised feeling of tightness in the chest. When the heart is returned to its normal functioning, the subject experiences a flooding sensation of fatigue, but these are merely side-effects of the procedure. The true aim is to make the subject believe they are about to die.

"The Tarkinians achieve this in two ways. By creating electrical dysfunction in the heart, blood flow is compromised and the subject experiences a... spreading numbness in his or her extremities, which is compounded by the fact they have been placed on an angle. Blood flow is enough to maintain vital organs, meaning that the subject cannot pass out, and is forced to continue experiencing the procedure. In a typical case of cardiac arrest, oxygen is not delivered correctly to the body, but the Tarkinians were able to 'pulse' in such a manner as to maintain enough oxygen in the brain to counteract this phenomenon. Maintaining subject consciousness while this occurred was of supreme importance to those carrying out the procedure. The subject's brain realises that bodily function is irregular, but is powerless to either fix the situation or to place the subject into an unconscious state. A subject effectively chokes as he attempts to breathe. These pulmonary pulses typically last one to two minutes."

"And how long does the entire procedure last?" the advocate asked.

"Typically five to seven minutes," the doctor said, "but I have heard of cases lasting thirty to forty. The Tarkinians would simply alternate between the various components of the board to ensure the subject remained conscious and alive the entire time."

Kaiya sat motionless.

And all through her mind ran the image of Kormac's bound and twitching body.

The drowning gasp for hollow air.

The guilt of experiential comparison.

What had she ever been thinking?

20

An elderly woman smiled at her as they waited to return to the courtroom after a short recess. Kaiya returned the gesture and studied the woman's aged face, tracing cheerful lines and silver hair. Why was the woman there? What had she thought of the doctor's testimony? Was any of this even new to her?

The questions were mere moments of fleeting curiosity, but left Kaiya with a profound sense that, in truth, she knew nothing of anything.

She lingered until the majority of the gallery had entered, then stepped through the doors and positioned herself as far away and as hidden from the witness box as she could manage. She picked a tall man to sit behind, making sure that she could peek around him to watch Joseph when she wanted to.

The bailiff announced the judge's entry and Kaiya performed the ritual standing and sitting, trying to see where Joseph was at that moment.

"We invite to the stand Chief Inspector Joseph Balfour of the Leth Police Force to provide testimony for the public record," the advocate announced.

Blood pumped in Kaiya's ears. The reality of the situation

was beginning to dawn on her. Six years of questions and mystery, of a thousand imagined scenarios.

Joseph appeared through a door to a back room and sat in the witness box.

"The court thanks you, Chief Inspector, for agreeing to provide your testimony in a public forum," the advocate said. "I also hear congratulations are in order for yesterday's recapture of Bennett Danard, who will be a primary focus of your testimony today. I have no doubt it will be of great use to the court in its deliberations on the fate of Mr. Danard."

"Thank you," Joseph said.

"Can you describe for us, Chief Inspector, the overall culture of the Leth Police Force under the leadership of Bennett Danard?"

Joseph took a moment to compose his thoughts.

"Bennett Danard was never so much concerned with his role as Commissioner as he was with the titles the Tarkinians gave him," he said. "I had little to do with him before he took on the role of Commissioner. I hadn't been an Inspector very long when the Tarkinians came, but I did have a strong relationship with both the former Commissioner, Edward Brown, and the current Commissioner, Benjamin Laveau."

"Why was that?" the advocate asked. "You would have been quite young to have developed relationships with both men."

"Leth is small," Joseph said, "and to be friends with one was to be friends with the other, though I wouldn't characterise my relationship with either of them as friendship. More... well-acquainted colleagues who shared broadly similar attitudes and ideas. Commissioner Brown recruited me into the Leth force directly after I finished my training in Akheron. My understanding is that he had been swayed towards a view that the force required cultural change, and began to read some of the work by Alison Meer. He was heavily influenced by Benjamin Laveau, in that regard."

"You completed capstone training under Alison Meer, did you not?"

"Yes," Joseph said.

The advocate smirked. "I applaud you for surviving," he said, receiving a few titters from the gallery for his effort.

Joseph gave a polite smile.

"You became an Inspector four years after joining the Leth Police Force," the advocate said. "At what point did you begin your professional relationship with Bennett Danard?"

"I knew about him fairly soon after I joined the force," Joseph said. "He was legendary to a certain group of officers, and there's no question that he deserved that reputation. He's the kind of person who 'got things done,' and if certain rules needed to be bent to do that, so be it. Commissioner Brown didn't like him at all, and the feeling was mutual. Edward was trying to create a much less hierarchical environment within the force, as well as cultivate an idea that we were members *of* the community as opposed to members *from* the community. There was a lot of pushback within the force, and Bennett was held up by many as a model for effective policing. I never personally met him until a year after I became an Inspector, when I worked under him on a murder case."

"But he was the head of the narcotics division, wasn't he?"

"Yes," Joseph said, "but you're forgetting how small Leth is. Our divisions are more fluid. They denote tendencies towards particular types of investigations, more than anything. Bennett has an academic background in chemistry, so he took the lead on anything related to that. In this particular case, the murder was done by injectable."

"What was that experience like under him?" the advocate asked.

Joseph searched the ceiling as though the answer were hidden somewhere inside.

"Eye-opening," he said. "Bennett was... magnetic. He was

charming. He could coax information out of anyone, and if he couldn't do it through more manipulative means, he would resort to straight out force. Threats of police action, physical intimidation. I saw him take a razor to one of the perpetrator's friends, hold him down and make a small cut on his arm, then apply some sort of liquid to the wound. He had the location of the perpetrator within two minutes."

"Did you report this?"

"No," Joseph said. "I was afraid of the repercussions, either directly from Bennett or from other officers who supported him. Word travels quickly in Leth. Bennett caught the murderer, there was a conviction, and a lot of people questioned why Edward was trying to move the force away from a 'results' focus to a more 'process' focus. Then when he passed on Bennett for one of the Assistant Commissioner roles, the Headquarters really split. There were officers who refused to work together."

"Do you think this dynamic played a role in Bennett coming to power?"

"No, I don't," Joseph said. "I think it played a role in what happened *after* he got his position, but there was never any question that Edward's time as Commissioner had ended, when the Tarkinians came. Edward really believed in what he was doing, but Bennett was something else. Even in the murder case, I got no sense that Bennett cared about *why* he was pursuing the murderer. There was no sense that he was doing this for any particular person or principle. He made a comment to me one day, just off the cuff, that the only thing that mattered was winning."

"Winning what?" the advocate asked.

Joseph shrugged. "Everything, I suppose. Everything to Bennett was competition. Complete victory. Complete conquest. If he rose, it must have been at the expense of someone else. If someone else was given a promotion, then it was a direct attack on him. So I think... I speculate... that he came into the position of Commissioner with a sense that he had 'beaten' Edward."

"And after he got that position, how did the dynamic you mentioned earlier play into it?"

"There was complete control from day one," Joseph said. "Bennett gave every officer an ultimatum: they were to return to their positions and comply with the force's new policies and direction, or they would be exterminated. That's the exact word he used: exterminated. Nearly everyone returned, but there were some who held out. Anyone who had participated in the defence of Leth was put under supervision from an officer who had supported Bennett."

"I assume you were a member of the group that followed Commissioner Brown's call to fight the Tarkinians?"

"I was," Joseph said, "but it was clear that we had lost. I was afraid, to be honest, of not going back. I had a wife and a young child at that stage, but Benjamin Laveau encouraged me to return to the force with him. That it was ok to do that. That dying was pointless."

"What about Commissioner Brown?"

"He couldn't return," Joseph said. "We knew that he would be killed. There was no question about that. He simply told us to keep up as much morale as we could amongst those who didn't support Bennett, and try to minimise the harm we caused while Bennett was in that position."

"What happened to Commissioner Brown?" the advocate asked. "There is no mention of him in any documentation, official or otherwise. It's like he disappears from existence."

Apprehension pulsed through Kaiya's body, rising to her throat.

Making her eyes flood with weary imbalance.

Joseph took a long breath.

"I was ordered to execute Commissioner Brown," he said.

Kaiya closed her eyes, apprehension turning to the heat of churning sickness.

Bennett laughing.

Joseph's gun.

Blood on the lavender stalks.

"I'm sorry?" the advocate said.

Joseph frowned, taking an excruciating few seconds deciding what next to say.

"Bennett chose me," he said. "I didn't know what had happened to Edward. No one ever said anything about him, but Benjamin figured that they hadn't caught him yet, given that the Brown house was still being watched twenty-four seven. Nine weeks after Bennett had signed the agreement with the Tarkinians, no one was watching the house anymore. Benjamin confronted Bennett, demanding to know what they had done with Edward. He was disciplined, and I made the mistake of questioning that disciplinary action. I believe that's the only reason I came back to Bennett's attention.

"A week after that I was working late. Very late. Bennett came to my office and told me I was to accompany some Tarkinian soldiers on an exercise. I didn't question the order, but Bennett grabbed me as I left and told me to think carefully about how I wanted my career to go. To decide how much my life meant to me, and that the Tarkinians would never be as forgiving as he would. I knew something was up – I could feel it – and the Tarkinians took me to an encampment south of Leth. They had prisoners there. Not many, and I'm not sure why, but that seemed to be what the camp was for. The Tarkinians took me to a secluded spot and brought a man out. I couldn't see him at first, but then I realised it was Commissioner Brown."

"Did he appear to be in good health?" the advocate asked.

"As well as could be expected," Joseph said. "He didn't look as though he had been tortured, if that's what you're getting at. The Tarkinians said they had treated this as a domestic matter and given jurisdiction to Bennett. Bennett's response was to give me the 'opportunity' to rectify my stance against him by executing Commissioner Brown, and the Tarkinians complied, as Bennett had been given some authority as a Tarkinian officer."

"I don't understand something," the advocate said. "Why did Bennett Danard not do this himself? The conflict between him and Commissioner Brown was quite personal, was it not?"

"I've thought about that for a long time," Joseph said, "and there's only one answer that's ever made sense to me: Bennett wanted to show that Edward was meaningless to him. He wanted to show *Edward* that. Bennett was always playing these games with the officers. Creating uncertainty."

"Would that not indicate that Commissioner Brown was in fact quite meaningful to Bennett Danard?" the advocate asked.

Joseph smiled softly. "That tends to be my thinking, yes. In any case, I did not comply with Bennett's order."

The silent mortars of war in Kaiya's mind halted, leaving behind a hollow ringing of terror. She had barely begun to process the idea that both Joseph and Kormac had lied, and now fire seared her synapses, locking her body tightly to the bench as she merely existed in broken thought, waiting for a new indication of what she should believe.

"The Tarkinians handed me a gun, and I said no," Joseph said. "They laughed, and they insisted, and I said no again. They got impatient. Roughed me up a bit, but nothing serious. Then they told me to shoot him, again. And I said no. I was sure they would kill me. I kept trying to think what Benjamin would do. Was it worth it to die there when they were probably just going to kill him anyway? I thought about my family, but I just couldn't do it. Edward looked at me, and I looked at him, and... I don't know how to describe it, but I knew that he was grateful. I don't think that he was afraid of dying. Not that. He was grateful that I was choosing to not be the one who killed him. And then... it was over. The Tarkinians dragged him off back to the encampment, and took me back to Headquarters. I never found out what happened to him, but I keep my eye on the convoy reports. I always wonder if I'll see his name."

Kaiya forced stillness on her face as her mouth began to quiver.

"So there is a possibility that Commissioner Brown is still alive, you think?" the advocate asked.

"My Tarkinian is not strong," Joseph said, "but from the little I gathered as I left, they didn't seem to think much of what Bennett had asked me to do. I don't think they comprehended Edward's significance, and treated him like any other prisoner. The reality is that the chances of Edward still being alive are minimal. But I like to think it from time to time."

The advocate gave an understanding grunt. "Now I have some indication, thanks to the brief you provided before today's evidence, of the rest of this story," he said. "Are you comfortable to continue sharing in this public forum?"

Joseph hesitated.

"Yes," he said, not entirely convincingly.

The advocate nodded. "What happened after you returned to Headquarters that night?"

"Nothing," Joseph said. "Nothing happened that night. And nothing happened the next day. Or the day after that. Nothing happened for eight days, and I thought that was the end of it. But it wasn't. They came while we were eating dinner. Bennett and three Tarkinian soldiers. I knew I should have gone. I should have taken us all and found a way out of Leth, somehow. Even gone to a friend's house to hide. But I didn't."

Joseph cleared his throat, composing his face.

"I told my wife to take Samuel away, but Bennett ordered the soldiers to keep us there. He was nearly two, Samuel. I knew Bennett was there to kill me. I should have known he would come, it was just the way he works. He lets things go cold, then strikes when you think he's forgotten. He took his gun out and pressed it to my forehead. Told me I should have listened to him. Then he said he wouldn't kill me. That he wasn't that forgiving. One of the soldiers took... one of the soldiers took Samuel from my wife. They were both crying. The soldier told Samuel to stand against the wall. Bennett walked over to my son and put the gun against his head. He smiled at me, and pulled the trigger."

Having restrained himself throughout his explanation, Joseph began to cry, filling the courtroom with gasps of desolation. Kaiya watched, too filled with conflicting emotion to react in any way but simply soak up Joseph's agony.

"My wife screamed like hell was being pulled through her body," Joseph said. "Then Bennett turned to me and said... 'you see? It's not that hard,' and he left. My wife couldn't move. She just sat against the wall screaming. I had to pick up my son and wrap him in a sheet just to feel like I was doing something useful. There's still a stain on my wall."

Kaiya glanced around the gallery at glistening faces and locked her eyes on the elderly woman who had smiled at her before they walked in. She clutched an old, physical photograph, eyes closed as if in meditation, wrinkled skin wet with her own memory.

Her own stories that Kaiya would never know.

"My wife blamed me," Joseph continued, "once the initial shock had passed, after a few days, when we were able to function again. She said it was my fault. And I believed her. I could have made a different choice. I could have simply done what Bennett ordered me to do, and none of this would have ever happened. I thought like that for years, until I realised... Bennett could have made a different choice as well. I didn't kill my son. Bennett did. In any case, I didn't know how to respond to my wife's blame, because deep down I knew she was right. Even today part of me still thinks she was right. She changed after that. She had always been... cheerful. Interested in everything. She would read all the time, but then she stopped. She didn't want to do anything, or go anywhere. She never talked, except to tell me how much she hated me. I thought it would pass. But it didn't."

The advocate paced in front of the bench, allowing Joseph to regain some small measure of composure.

"How long after your son's death did your wife commit suicide, Chief Inspector?"

"Nine weeks," Joseph said. "I found her hanging in Samuel's bedroom. She left a note, very short. She wanted me to know that I had killed her. That was her way of punishing me."

Kaiya made no attempt to hide herself as Joseph surveyed the room for the first time, locking his gaze in her direction.

———

They ambled amongst the gravestones and variegated shrubbery, breeze tickling Kaiya's ears. Small birds chattered in weeping branches of green, flitting about merrily and giving only cursory attention to the complex lives of those below.

Kaiya had sat outside the courtroom, waiting, and stood humbled in Joseph's presence when he finally emerged. What could she possibly say, she had thought, but the Chief Inspector's only allusion to what had just passed was a warning that it was not the time nor the place to discuss such matters.

She deferred to his judgment, relieved that she would not be required to offer any comfort she didn't know how to give.

"There is a section devoted to military personnel," Joseph said as they entered that portion of the graveyard.

Kaiya read the gravestones as she passed them. The vast majority listed men younger than her. There had been a time when she wondered if death would be superior to the steady trudging of life, but what would those who lay in the ground have given to stand where she was now?

The thought forced her to stop.

She stared at a brand new, gloss-black monumental grave adorned with fresh flowers. The gravestone bore the face of a uniformed man of nineteen, cheeks high with mirth as he smiled. Joseph waited silently nearby, and Kaiya felt no pressure to continue on their journey to the place she feared he was taking her.

Who had placed the flowers there, where this man could never know they had been given? Who visited this memory to a fact that no longer existed, and wished there was something they could give to crack the glossy stone and resurrect he who lay within?

If she had escaped the trudging, would anyone still alive have stood to wish the same for her?

Kaiya continued, taking note of the faces on each gravestone, reading the too-close years of birth and death. She played through the past few years in her mind, wondering what facts would have changed were her existence to have ended at any particular point. Perhaps there would have been one less guerrilla attack on the Tarkinians, but then... Amelia could always have found a replacement. Perhaps Kormac would not have suffered her incapability of caring for...

Kaiya stopped again, stunned. How long had she hidden that realisation from herself?

A new and powerful guilt swept through her body, and she sifted through memory after memory of the short time she had spent with Kormac since his return, drenching herself with stinging regret. When she returned to Leth, she would make that right. Whatever they were, she and Kormac, she would make right all her previous failures. Give him all that he had required and she had ignored.

And Tilda...

No, that was too much to face. Not when the suspicion of Joseph's reason for taking her there continued to grow.

She contented herself with taking another face from her mind, one that always swam just below the surface, emerging constantly to remind her of its existence.

Masuma.

She no longer cared why the girl had imprinted herself so strongly on her, nor whether it was right or wrong, good or bad. It simply was, and more than any regret, the child shone brightly in her mind. A beacon that made the trudging worthwhile.

A fact that would have changed had existence ended.

A fact she could still have the power to change.

Kaiya smiled shyly at Joseph, who returned the gesture, and they walked on in silence until her eyes fell on the first female soldier she had seen thus far. She had died at the same age Kaiya was now. Kaiya wondered what had been the final thing those eyes had seen. When her holo was taken, had she thought it might grace a block of veined and glossy white?

A message of how deeply loved she was by those who remained was followed by a quote Kaiya immediately recognised:

> though I'm not strong, nor wise,
> and not always am I smart,
> but what I have is loyalty,
> and kindness for your heart

She smiled at the reference, and wondered if that had been a childhood favourite. She, herself, had not read it for years until she passed the story on to Masuma, and after so long that reading had raised questions in her mind about whether or not she had ever truly understood the story.

She would need to read it again, when she returned to Leth.

"Do you know why we are here?" Joseph asked her softly as they resumed their slow journey through the field of those fallen.

Kaiya didn't respond straight away, trying to push aside her apprehension with thoughts of Masuma and all the pretty flowers smiling in the sun.

A little bird landed on a gravestone and cocked its head at her, beginning to tweet.

"I'm afraid to answer that," Kaiya said.

Joseph glanced at her, and she turned her head away.

"Alison Meer called me this morning," he said.

Kaiya's lips trembled as she did her best to restrain the grief that pounded against the thin doorway between heart and eyes. She kept walking as the world began to blur, one step after another, and finally stopped, defeated by the confirmation of her fear.

Fragments of a woman.

Joseph murmured her name, and she shrugged off his hesitant hand, an unwanted mark of supposed comfort.

For unmeasured minutes she stood and cried, the anguish of an unmet need escaping her mouth to mix with the birds and breeze. She clenched her fists and wailed, driving her nails into her skin, relishing the points of pain that forced her to remember that she still walked on this broken, malevolent earth, that she would remain unfulfilled, that all the foolish hopes she had held to were gone, buried underneath a moment of final, unchangeable destruction.

That the Occupation had never ended, and never would.

Joseph murmured her name once more, but she kicked the ground and howled in fury. She wanted nothing more to do with him, or any other person, or life, or existence, unless she were undoing it. Unmaking herself. Unmaking all that ever had been and ever could be.

But in the end, what was she? Victory didn't belong to her or people like her. All of her life was another's to be conquered. That's all it had ever been.

She had never been anything.

Always nothing.

Meaningless.

The same, repeated thoughts whirled in Kaiya's mind as she withdrew into the darkness of her own blindness, until Joseph once more spoke her name, and she allowed herself to let in a tiny spark of his care. The Kaiya within her mind struggled to see the spark, but slowly it grew brighter, and Kaiya dared to open her eyes, wiping away the film of grief that blocked out normal perception.

A flock of birds ascended from the distant, weeping branches, squawking joyously as the sun glistened on their feathers.

"Why did you bring me here?" Kaiya breathed.

"So you'd know I was telling the truth," Joseph said, and Kaiya looked up at his honest face. "Come with me."

She accepted his offer and followed him through some more of the gravestones, wiping away the final traces of her tears. They hadn't disappeared, she could tell that much, but they were held back for the moment by a grudging acceptance that she had to complete this ritual of knowing.

Joseph led her to the grave, and Kaiya stared.

The holo of *him* had been taken before he had ever entered her life. He stared so proudly at the world, so full of radiant joy, and all Kaiya could feel was rising nausea at this monument to a fake memory. This was not the truth of him!

She studied the engraving of his name on the headstone as Joseph walked away and left her alone. She studied his name and the names of those who had been in his life. What had they done to allow him to become who he had been? What did they know about who he really was?

He had died six months ago. The knowledge only brought

more questions to her mind, and she wondered how he had died. Where had he died... who had been the one to kill him... would anything have changed had she known? Would she be any different, or have felt differently about the knowledge had she acquired it then as opposed to now?

That knowledge was beginning to filter through her body, and though the same despair and fury remained, it was now joined by an insatiable curiosity over the circumstances of his departure from this world.

She hoped he had suffered.

A woman approached bearing a wreath, one of the few other people Kaiya could see. She ignored the woman at first and returned to punishing herself with recollections and questions she would never be able to answer, but soon realised the woman was coming closer not just to the area she inhabited, but to *her*.

Kaiya glanced back at Joseph as horror sank through her body, trying to glean some kind of indication that this had been planned.

But Joseph's face betrayed concern.

The woman came closer to Kaiya and stopped nearby, glancing down at the monument. The lines of her drawn face fell downwards in regret, and she gave Kaiya a strained, cautious smile.

"Hello," she murmured.

Kaiya greeted the woman likewise, stunned, and watched as she placed the wreath on the memorial. They stayed silent for a long stretch of time as the woman gazed down, and Kaiya managed to find her bearings, taking a long breath to calm herself.

"This is your son?" she ventured.

The woman nodded shyly.

Kaiya could almost have laughed, though it would have been the bitterest sound she could imagine. Of all that could have occurred, life had given her this.

And yet... as soon as the thought shot through her mind, so did Joseph's story. The doctor's evidence and Kormac's unspoken pain. Masuma's incapability of connecting the enormity of her own horror to an emotional response Kaiya would have thought more appropriate.

Part of her reeled with shame, and another part resisted, insisting on the right to revel in her own bitterness, unrelated from anyone else's existence.

"You knew him?" the woman said softly.

Kaiya hesitated, and shook her head. "He stayed at my house in Leth. That's all."

The mother accepted her answer and they returned to silence.

Sun glistened on the memorial stone.

Another flock of birds descended on the weeping branches.

The wreathed flowers lay in ignorance of their eventual withering.

"You must be proud of him," Kaiya said.

"My pride's not much use to either of us now, is it?" the mother said, wiping away a tear. "It won't bring him back."

Kaiya watched her, studying the shadows beneath her eyes, the few strands of grey hair. How much did she really know about her son? What fantasy did she live when she thought of him?

"Tell me about him," Kaiya said.

"He was my son," the woman said. "There's nothing more to say than that."

Kaiya could tell the woman wanted to be left alone, but she waited a little longer, wondering what had existed between these two people who were strangers to her in almost every way. She was an intruder, here, on something that didn't belong to her, but then... had he not also been an intruder?

Why should she be protected from knowing the truth of her son?

Kaiya readied herself to tell the woman, a large part of her relishing the pain that she would be able to inflict in doing so, and looked down at the wreath of flowers.

The woman bent down and rearranged them, making sure they were positioned perfectly on the monument. Making sure they gave as much beauty as they could.

Kaiya's breath caught in her throat, and she realised...

"I'm sorry for your loss," she said to the woman, who thanked her and gave a courteous nod.

Joseph stood not so far away, and Kaiya strode across to him, arms folded as she tried to contain the crumbling, temporary walls within her. He grew hazy in her vision and she stepped forward into his arms, allowing herself at last to be broken within his presence, to reject the part of her that demanded a fortitude of iron.

"I couldn't tell her," she cried. "It would have been like... killing him all over again, but he *still* wouldn't be the one that suffers."

"It's over now," he comforted.

"But it's not," she said. "He's dead. It can't ever be over."

Joseph remained quiet, and Kaiya shifted her head against his chest so she could see the sunshine with a single clouded eye.

"I'm proud of you," he said, but whatever his intention had been in saying that, she only cried harder, accepting ever so slowly that she would never receive the satisfaction that she deserved.

21

KYTOS LOOKED UNCOMFORTABLE IN THE CAVERNOUS TRAIN station. Neither of them had said a word throughout the entire journey by bus from his squalid circumstances. He hadn't even told her he would be coming, but Kaiya was grateful to some extent. His company was welcome, especially given the fact he had not forced her into any sort of inane conversation, or probed for information.

They reached the ticket gate and Kaiya hesitated. She never again wished to see Akheron, and who knew if Kytos would ever leave it. The realisation they might not see each other even once more affected her in some minute way. She still couldn't tell what was what inside of herself, as if everything had fused into one ball of uncertainty. Or perhaps it was something else. She couldn't tell.

She turned and faced Kytos, avoiding his eyes. "Thanks for letting me stay."

"It's no problem," he said.

She flicked her eyes towards his face. He was looking out at some point behind her. They stood silent for a few moments as people passed them, and the soft ding of ticket gates reading identity cards floated through the early morning air. Rainbows of refracted light danced off the sides of the buildings, unnoticed by those arriving early to work and too busy to consider them. Kaiya tried to ignore the dazzling arrays, but they assaulted her eyes wherever she looked. Even the ground, coated in some mixture of concrete and glass, offered no relief from the relentless light, sparkling wherever a shadow had not blocked the sun.

"What will you do when you get home?" he asked.

Kaiya shrugged. "I don't know," she said, but already the nervousness came upon her as she thought of Tilda and what she would say to her. If there *were* anything she could say to her that would make up for what she had done. And how would she find Kormac?

Perhaps new convoys had returned. There was a chance her father was still alive, Joseph had said in his evidence, and there was even more that her mother would be. There was always that to look forward to, but at the same time... Kormac had not worked out the way she had thought it would. How could she be sure of this?

But there was Masuma. At least one thing she hadn't ruined.

"You can call me if you need anything," Kytos said.

"Likewise."

But she doubted they ever would.

Kytos swallowed. "I..." he began, then gazed around for a few moments at the scenery, as if nothing more than a casual exploration of the atmosphere. "I liked having you here."

She didn't know what to say to that, though she suspected Kytos was just saying it to cheer her up. "Thanks," she murmured, deciding that was better than nothing. They lingered longer, and Kaiya wondered exactly what they were doing, though something inside her resisted the idea of leaving just yet. "It was good to see you," she added.

Kytos grinned half-heartedly. "I'm old and boring, Kaiya. You don't have to make me feel better."

"I meant it," she said.

Kytos licked his lips and gazed up at the sky. "As I said, I liked having you here."

"You could come to Leth some time," she said.

He seemed to consider the proposal, a delicate smile on his face. "Maybe. We'll see what happens. Akheron's not as bad as you think it is, and I like being here."

"I know." They waited a little longer until she glanced at her phone and saw the time. "I should go."

"Yes." Kytos stepped forward, hesitant, and they hugged each other awkwardly. When they finished, Kaiya nodded to herself and picked up her travel bag, walking a few steps towards the ticket gates.

She turned around and glanced at Kytos, who stared at her, face shadowed, half-silhouetted in Akheron's morning blaze of colour. "Bye," she called.

Kytos smiled and raised his hand in farewell.

Kaiya turned and went through the ticket gates, descending the grand steps onto the platform below. Joseph and Jonathan waited by the train, watching her as she approached. She greeted them both, noting the unhidden attraction in Jonathan's eyes, and the aloofness in Joseph's demeanour.

"We're all going to travel together, today," Joseph said, and Kaiya took out her phone to accept the ticket.

Kaiya was grateful that no one wanted to speak much, and flicked through her phone, looking for Joseph's essay that Alison Meer had given her. Perhaps that would take her mind off things during the journey.

"I spoke to Headquarters at Leth," Joseph said, holding up his own phone.

"The Network is back up?" Kaiya asked.

Joseph shook his head. "Just some of the more important places. Like the hospital."

He gave her a significant look, and Kaiya's mood began to shift.

"How long do we have 'til we leave?" she asked, and for the first time she could remember the extended wait pleased her.

She walked to a private section of the platform and called the hospital, speaking to multiple receptionists before finally reaching the person she desired.

"Hello?" came Masuma's timid voice.

"Hi," Kaiya said, face breaking open with warmth she hoped the girl could sense. "It's Kaiya."

"I know," Masuma said, a little less hesitant. "I can tell."

Kaiya laughed, mostly from an awkward sense that she was somehow special. "I'm coming home," she said.

There was a small pause on the other end of the line, then Masuma's voice returned. "Really?" she said, already more lively. "When?"

"Right now," Kaiya said with a laugh, and Masuma giggled in response.

She had no idea what was so funny, but for some reason... they simply continued, laughing and giggling for no apparent reason.

"I'm bored," Masuma said, and Kaiya grinned at the empty space around her before giving Masuma the offer she knew the girl was waiting for.

With a promise that she would visit her that day, Kaiya talked with Masuma until the train arrived, listening to the girl's complaints about nurses and the other children around her, confidence increasing bit by bit until Kaiya could barely say a word herself.

The journey home remained silent, but Kaiya watched the scenery outside and smiled.

Kaiya stepped out of Joseph's car and onto the footpath of a side street connected to southern boulevard. By the look of the road tiles, the boulevard would be able to reopen within perhaps the next week, if it were given priority. As far as she had learnt on her journey home, the presence of the Taskforce police had quelled the majority of public sentiment.

Though she didn't really care to know, anymore.

She grabbed her bag from the back seat and paused for a moment to stare at a child's mobile still laying idle. It had taken her aback the first time she saw it, and even now, even with the knowledge that those limply-hanging, fluffy animals were there waiting to be held, she still froze. She tried to imagine the face of the child who had played with the mobile, the face she had seen herself in Joseph's office.

A face that explod—

"That everything?" Joseph asked.

Kaiya closed the door and tried to pretend she hadn't been mesmerised by the mobile.

"Yeah," she said, and waited for some kind of direction or dismissal from the Chief Inspector.

"What will you do now?" he asked.

Kaiya sighed. "I don't know. I haven't even thought about it."

"I suggest you do."

"Is that what you mean," Kaiya asked, "or are you saying it's a requirement that I think about it?"

Joseph grinned. "They're not mutually exclusive. I suggest you think about it precisely because it is a requirement."

Kaiya tittered and avoided the Chief Inspector's gaze.

"What do you expect from me?" she asked.

Joseph took a few moments in consideration. "I expect you to see Benjamin as soon as possible."

"Benjamin?" she said. "Why?"

"He will be interested to hear about your experience in

Akheron," Joseph said. "In your own words, not the ones I give him."

"But when do I have to see you?" Kaiya asked. "What other 'requirements' do I have for this... program?"

"I'll have a think about that," Joseph said, "but that will depend on what happens with Benjamin."

Kaiya raised a brow at the Chief Inspector's reticence. "If you say so."

"I do," Joseph said, and they stood silently together on the footpath, the sound of playing children echoing from the boulevard.

Kaiya sensed there was nothing more to say, but it felt strange to leave the Chief Inspector, despite their time in Akheron being only a few days, and much of it apart. She wished she had the right words to ease whatever hidden pains he still possessed after Bennett's atrocity, but everything that came to mind seemed a shadow in comparison to what she desired it to be.

He had said outside the courtroom that it wasn't the right place or time, but hadn't said a word about his testimony since. Perhaps he had meant it would never be the right place or time?

She grimaced at her failure to put the odd feeling inside her into words, and instead stepped forward to hug the Chief Inspector. He returned the gesture.

"Thank you," Kaiya whispered, though she wasn't quite sure for what. It seemed like the right thing to say, though, and surprisingly it filled the gap of words she had been trying to find.

They farewelled each other and Kaiya waited to watch Joseph depart, waving as he disappeared around the corner.

The sound of children became clearer as she went in the opposite direction to the Chief Inspector. Kaiya took a moment to survey the boulevard she had lived on for most of her life. She couldn't remember ever having done so, before, simply standing and drinking in the shape of the buildings, the different tinges to each one, the sometimes-bold, sometimes-elegant decorations that adorned windows and doors. The detail of statuettes on stone railings of stairs.

Already the units occupied by colla— no, the units that had been gutted by protestors — were mostly boarded neatly up. Someone had painted huge flowers on the timber, and Kaiya smiled at the thought of Jonathan standing there with a paint-brush and a crowd of bemused onlookers.

Perhaps she would visit him soon.

Despite the shattered windows here and there, the gaping maws of blackened terrace houses, the boulevard looked cheerful, ringing with the voices of the red and blue-ribboned boys playing soccer. Kaiya walked towards her building, watching them kick the ball through makeshift hat and bag goalposts. The smallest boy took possession of the ball and weaved his way through the opposition while his captain ran alongside calling for the pass. But there seemed no reason to do so – the small boy had everything under control.

The captain tripped the small boy over, stealing the ball and thumping it through the opposition goalpost bags. He cheered along with his teammates, ignoring the small boy who limped off to the edge of the terrace blocks and began to cry.

Kaiya stopped on the concrete steps of her building and sat, pretending to ignore the boys' game.

One of the small boy's teammates approached him and spoke, but the small boy snapped back, holding his knees against his chest, and the teammate returned to the game with a backward glance.

The captain pranced about as if he owned the world, and Kaiya glared. Part of her wanted to march right over there and give the boy a good whack, though another thought of the comfort she could give to the injured one. She couldn't do both at the same time, so which would be first? Or rather... which would be first had she the courage to stand up and do anything in the first place?

The conflict had nothing to do with her.

In the distance, a pair of maintenance workers appeared and began to work on a portion of the boulevard.

The game ended soon after, and the victorious captain relished the adulation of his teammates. They continued to ignore the small boy, except for the one who had tried to speak with him. He stayed behind, holding the ball, and approached the injured boy once more and sat beside him.

Soon they laughed together, and kicked the ball between themselves. Each kick became progressively harder, until the ball came flying across towards Kaiya, who stood up and stopped it with her foot. The boys lifted their hands, and Kaiya shot them a brief smile, returning their ball with just the right amount of force to elicit two shouts of gratitude.

Now that she was standing, it seemed silly to sit back down, and she picked up her bags to walk inside. The friendly boy asked the small one how his leg was doing. Apparently it still hurt.

But he seemed much better now.

Kaiya dropped her bags as she closed the front door behind her, and stood to take in the silent assault of emptiness. She had become accustomed, even after such a short time, to the gentle Levway hum near Kytos's apartment. Here in the 'backwaters,' as Alison Meer thought of Leth, there was no such barrage of civilisation.

She went to the window and tapped it open for both light and air, and the chatter of the two boys lifted up to her ears, fading as they walked away towards the river. The maintenance workers shared jokes, their laughs boisterous, but they were too far away for Kaiya to hear the content.

A pair of Taskforce police ambled up the boulevard, but from all she had seen since her return, the uprising was over.

Kaiya took her bags to her bedroom and threw them on the bed, sighing at the prospect of having to unpack. She procrastinated for a while, placing a stack of unworn clothes on her pillows and studying the patterns on the quilt with great interest, then resigned herself to the fact she would probably live out of the backpack for a week before dealing with it properly.

So Joseph wanted her to speak with Benjamin. She had a growing suspicion that this would not be the only conversation required of her. She could barely remember what Stephen looked like – he'd been nothing but shadows when they met – and whenever his face came into her mind, it was the face of her father, perhaps younger and not so friendly, but still her father.

She did her best not to think about Stephen.

But there could be no doubting there would be an expectation she would face him. She had realised it on the journey home. Until that humiliation came, she would do her best to avert her mind, to focus on the things she needed to do. To find Tilda and Kormac. To speak with Masuma.

Anything to prolong the space between now and feigning apology to that collab—

Kaiya kicked her bed in frustration and went to the bathroom to wash her face.

Tiny scars stared back at her.

She touched the one on her lip and wondered how the doctors had been unable to heal it. *Old* people had scars, from well before wounds were simple to heal, not people her age.

Well... no, that wasn't so true anymore...

Kaiya stepped back from the mirror, still examining her face, and watched as the scars became nothing but small parts of the whole.

Tilda's house stood broken. The flame-gutted shell of her childhood overlooked the street like an altar to some god of destruction, wooden teeth blackened and piercing the sky. Kaiya stared at the ruins, picturing everything she had seen over so many years of being inside those walls. Childhood games of stuck in the mud on the small patch of now-dead lawn. Parties with a handful of friends and cheap decorations. The cake always simple, like everything else they had owned. Practical, never beautiful.

Except for the piano in the front sunroom, which now leaned on two semi-intact legs. Ruined, but recognisable for what it had once been. The one great material possession protected and loved by Tilda's parents, as destroyed as they likely were.

Kaiya closed her eyes.

No. There was still a chance. Everything would be fine.

A woman walked along the footpath, minding her own business.

"Excuse me," Kaiya said, waiting for the woman to recognise she was being addressed, "there was a girl who lived here. Tilda. Do you know where she is?"

The woman stopped and looked suspicious. "What's that got to do with you?" she said. "You a whore as well?"

"What?" Kaiya said as a flood of automatic nausea went through her body. Not Tilda, surely...

"You should pick better friends," the woman sneered. "That girl was a collaborator through and through."

Kaiya stood frozen as the woman continued on her way, but thawed as she realised what kind of whore she had meant. The idea of Tilda—

She didn't want to think about that.

Kaiya loitered for a while longer, probing for information from anyone who passed. People either knew nothing or gave the same suspicious look, but finally a group of children stopped and gave their full attention, deliberating with each other as to what they knew and did not know.

"I saw her the other day," one of the boys said, "over by the river on west side."

"She's *always* on west side, you idiot," a girl said, "that's where they *all* are. Don't you know *anything*?"

The boy rolled his eyes, but was clearly embarrassed. He blushed as the other kids laughed at him. Kaiya probed the children some more, and they gave frank answers as to the whereabouts of the community that allegedly existed on the western side of Leth where the river flowed between the wall.

By the time the children left, the first helpful boy was glancing at the girl who had insulted him. Kaiya laughed to herself as the girl responded in kind, but only when the boy turned his head.

Kaiya gave the street one last appraisal, noting the spot where she had succumbed to the stun batons, and began her trek to the riverside. The streets were badly damaged where the fighting had taken place – not that long ago, now that she thought of it, even though it felt like weeks or months – and the rubble from the building hit by the Obsidian Tank had been mostly shoved back into a pile. The few workers she saw on the roads didn't seem to be doing much work. Mainly they just chatted while they fiddled with the road tiles, one of them watching the inactivity with great attention. Supervising, as they liked to call it.

The streets were much better as she approached the riverside. Well enough for cars to use them. A plaza appeared on the other side of the street she walked on, full of people and life and colourful market stalls. The 'back to nature' section of Leth, she thought with a grin. Most of the nearby terrace houses sported strange ornaments that hung from olden-style windows like the ones in Kytos's house. A man sat behind one with a guitar, singing along with two women from separate houses who both poked their heads out of their windows to make music over the space below.

Here and there within the plaza, Kaiya could see women either with decorative headscarves or simply showing their shaved heads, and no one seemed to care. She crossed the road that separated riverside and terrace houses. A few people sat eating on the tree-shaded benches and tables, but Kaiya's attention was caught by a section of broken balustrade surrounded by police barriers. On closer inspection, it wasn't just the balustrade, but a chunk of the riverside construction itself, and water lapped in through the breach.

Kaiya gazed down at the ravenous energy conductors.

They returned her attention, mocking and arrogant.

To fall into their tendrils was said to be painless, but how anyone could choose to feed themselves to such evil contraptions was beyond her. Any death but that one, surely.

She stepped away from the balustrade and continued along the riverside towards the western wall, glancing occasionally down at the water. Watching the conductors watch her.

Laneways on the other side of the road disappeared into shadowy bivouacs. Somewhere inside that hidden warren, there would be answers. Kaiya walked nearly to the wall and then began retracing her steps, trying to figure out which was the right one.

She made a random decision and crossed the road, scanning her surroundings as she entered the narrow darkness between two buildings.

The sound of her footsteps echoed, but she didn't have to walk long before the laneway became a small square with other laneways leading from it. She looked down each one, but there was nothing particularly distinctive about any of them, so she continued deeper into the maze, dodging mossy puddles as she did so. She came to a circle, this time, with even more possible exits, and frowned.

There had to be some sort of pattern she didn't know.

Anyone could be hiding in there...

She made another random selection, beginning to walk faster, and came to yet another circle, though this one at least gave her some bearings. The riverside was visible far in the distance through one of the laneways, an unbroken line. She was somewhere further east of where she had entered.

Who on earth had designed the area in such a way as to allow this rabbit warren to begin with?

Footsteps echoed from one of the nearby laneways, and Kaiya became alert. So that was one advantage of the laneways. Advance notice.

She gazed down a few of them until she saw a long-haired man approaching.

"Hello," he said, and Kaiya glanced around as her neck prickled with distrust.

Making ready to run.

"Are you lost?" the man asked, stopping within the laneway.

Kaiya checked the other laneways, wondering if anyone else was hiding there ready to ambush, but no... they were alone, which wasn't that great a comfort.

"No," she said.

The man cocked his head, long hair swaying as he did so. "Are you looking for someone in particular?"

Kaiya furrowed her brow. "Did you know I was here?" she asked.

"We have security measures, yes," came the answer.

Kaiya hesitated. The man didn't look so threatening now that she'd had a few moments to analyse his movements. He had stopped in the laneway. He didn't *seem* to pose any immediate threat...

"Do you know someone called Tilda?" she asked. "Matilda, maybe?"

"It's hard to say," the man said, "we have people coming and going all the time. Does she know you're looking for her?"

"No," Kaiya said. "I'm not even sure she'll want to see me."

The man considered her. "Follow me," he said. "I'll take you inside. You can stay back a little if you like."

His readiness to accommodate eased her apprehension, and she did just that, following the man from a safe distance behind. He led her through the maze of laneways, and signs of life began to emerge – a bit of rubbish here, discarded cloth there.

Slowly the sound of voices came to her ears.

"Sally-Anne knows everyone," the man said, pointing to a woman with a bright floral headscarf. "Talk to her and she'll point you in the right direction."

Kaiya walked forward into a clearing in what must have been the middle of the rabbit warren block. Awnings stretched out from poles of all different sizes, some attached to hooks built into the building walls, making a mishmash of faded colour and shade. Beds, couches, cabinets, crockery, and back-packs littered the ground underneath, and a crowd of mostly women chattered amongst themselves, read tablets, played games.

Existing in a pocket of acceptance.

Kaiya approached Sally-Anne, who stood behind a battered old credenza that had lost half its drawers. She was using it as a workstation, evidently, and looked up at Kaiya as she came closer.

"I remember you," Sally-Anne said. "I have a knack for faces."

"Oh?"

"In the hospital last week. You were speaking to a doctor. He got angry at you."

Kaiya thought back to her encounter with the doctor, and realised she was speaking to the coll— to the woman who had so brazenly flaunted her status as an escort or lover to the

Tarkinians. She felt immediately guilty, but then... that was silly. The woman couldn't have read her mind.

"I was angry with him, too," Kaiya said.

"Why's that?"

Kaiya tried to answer, but she didn't know what to say anymore. In fact, she could feel her face tinging red as she thought back on the event.

"Nothing important," was all she said.

Sally-Anne gave a knowing expression. "You must be looking for someone. There aren't many of your kind who'd come in here by themselves."

"My kind?" Kaiya asked. "Do people even know this place exists?"

"Of course they do," Sally-Anne said. "The western maze is old as Leth itself. There's always some group hiding here. Some group the rest of the town doesn't like. This time it's our turn. So who do you want?"

"Tilda."

Sally-Anne flicked through her tablet and frowned.

"Matilda Morant," Kaiya said, and waited as Sally-Anne continued to search.

"Here she is. Let me just pull up..."

Sally-Anne went quiet as she read something on the tablet. Her eyes flicked over to Kaiya, betraying a sense of deep judgment. "You really want to see her?"

"Yes," Kaiya said, doing her best to hide her apprehension.

Sally-Anne considered her for a few more seconds. "I hope I don't regret this. I hope you don't either. I'll show you where she stays, but I'll be watching you. If there's any trouble, you'll be out of here quicksmart. Understood?"

"Yes."

If she could just read whatever it was that Sally-Anne had read...

"This way," Sally-Anne said as she stood.

Kaiya followed through the clearing and another laneway, much shorter than the others. Here and there coll— the women glanced at her with suspicion or outright loathing. Did all of them know who she was? No, that was absurd. She tried to tell herself she was just imagining it, but she couldn't have been dreaming the faces on some of them.

"Hair-heads aren't welcome here," Sally-Anne explained.

"Not the most original insult," Kaiya said drily. "They don't even know me."

Sally-Anne shrugged. "There's a lot of anger. It's not really anything to do with you, but it's common behaviour, attributing blame to groups. A lot of the women here find a deeper sense of community when they're able to point to one type of person, like people with hair, and say that they're the reason everything's bad. People think lumping people together into 'them' is just about those other people, but it's not. It's just as much to do with the 'us' group being able to identify with each other and form tighter social connections. It's all about identity."

"I think I get what you mean," Kaiya said. The explanation seemed strangely familiar. "Where'd you hear all that?"

"I taught at the university," she said. "Sociology, but half my published material is in social psychology journals."

"There's a difference?" Kaiya said.

Sally-Anne gave a short laugh. "Big enough that someone like me can laugh, small enough someone like you can ask."

Kaiya flushed. Now she looked stupid. "Yeah, well I never got the chance to learn, did I?"

"Would you have taken the chance if you had it?"

"I was planning to go," Kaiya said, "then... I don't know. I kept saying I'd still go, once the Tarkinians had gone."

"And now they've gone," Sally-Anne said. "So maybe you should think about it again."

Kaiya was already plucking out reasons not to, but recognised she was doing just that and forced herself to stop. "Would you be teaching me?"

Sally-Anne laughed. "No, not any time soon. I was at the top of my game when the Tarkinians came. I didn't care at all about those kinds of things, who was in charge, just as long as I could get my work done. But they started stacking the university, and I realised the only way I could keep my job is if I pretended to be in love with one of them. It wasn't so bad, to be honest, and I got a lot of useful material. I'm going to do a series of articles on the relationship between institutional structures and group behaviour when all this has eased up."

She indicated to the messy lifestyle around them.

"I made so many notes during the Occupation. Really, I think it will make me a leader in the field, if I can ever get a post again. The academics who didn't play ball, the ones who lost their jobs – even some of the ones that didn't – they don't want me back. They say it's because I'm a collaborator, but that's not it. They're envious that I was able to keep publishing, keep researching. I'm not sure why that should be held against me. I simply did what was necessary to do my job. They weren't prepared to do that."

Kaiya did her best not to frown. The woman had no shame at all!

It must have been nice to have so much confidence in one's choices.

"Do you think it was worth it?" Kaiya asked.

"I don't think it's a relevant question," Sally-Anne said. "You're asking me to compare against a hypothetical past, and hypotheticals are meaningless to me. I did what I did, and that's that."

"But now you don't have a job. Everyone who sees you knows what you did."

"Do I look like I care? People who see me *think* they know what I did. They *imagine* they know what I did. People never stop to think that maybe other people don't see the world exactly the same as they do. We always have trouble believing that it's possible for someone else to value things differently than us. So when they see me, they don't see how I might weigh options differently than them. They apply their own personal moralities to my choices, and they imagine that the disgust they would feel must also be felt by me. Or that if I don't feel that disgust, then I must be a fundamentally bad person. But they still know nothing about me. That entire thought process is about themselves."

Kaiya mulled over both the content of Sally-Anne's statement, and the fact that the woman seemed wholly detached as she delivered it, as though she didn't truly connect her own experience to what she was describing.

"I'm going to be fine," Sally-Anne continued. "The people who don't like me will forget why. They'll find other things to complain about. A year or two from now, everyone will move on with their lives. Maybe some of them will get *Rapture*."

"You think people forget that easily?"

"When the reason they hated what they hated is taken away, yes. The Tarkinians are gone, and once these trials are over, and the prisoners are back, then people will go back to hating what's immediate."

"Unless some of the prisoners don't come back," Kaiya said.

"That's always a possibility," the older woman said. "But not having someone around anymore isn't quite the same as being constantly aware of someone's presence. Or the presence of an idea. You'll see, once this is all over. I think it's already started, and it's nothing to do with *Rapture*."

Kaiya thought there was truth in Sally-Anne's words. She had noticed the difference in atmosphere after only a few days away in Akheron. A sense of calm had descended on the town. A sense that there was something to look forward to, that a balance had shifted and people were beginning to see with new eyes. But then, was it really the town? Or was she just once more convincing herself that something inside her was something outside?

Sally-Anne stopped and turned to Kaiya. "I meant it when I said I'll be watching you. These people have been through enough, they don't need anyone causing trouble."

Kaiya resented the notion that she was the one who would cause trouble.

Sally-Anne nodded towards a plain, haggard tarpaulin hung limp over a section of laneway. Beneath it was a makeshift bed of thick blanket, and a few bits of familiar clothing hanging from a flimsy, single-poled rack.

Tilda stared, fists clenched at her side, and stayed silent as Kaiya approached. Her body language confirmed what Kaiya had feared, that there would be more than a little resistance to this attempt at rapprochement.

There didn't seem to be any point in the niceties of greeting.

"I don't want to see you," Tilda said.

Kaiya froze. Where did she possibly go from there?

"I just want to talk," she said.

"But *I* don't want to talk to *you*," Tilda said. She looked away, as if she couldn't handle Kaiya's presence, but turned around just as quick, face painted with bitterness. "It's just like you, isn't it? Coming here, telling me you want to talk, like it doesn't even matter that I don't want to."

"I know you're upset," Kaiya said, conscious of judgment from those around her who may hear the exchange. "That's why I came. Because I—"

"I told you," Tilda said. "I don't want to see you."

And yet she didn't look away. Whatever hurt lay behind Tilda's eyes, she was still looking at her. That had to mean something.

"Just give me five minutes," Kaiya said. "Please, Tilda."

But Tilda's face darkened even further.

"My name's Matilda," she said. "Use it."

Kaiya understood, then, that Tilda's feelings were deeper than she had imagined.

"Ok," she said. "Matilda. I'll call you Matilda. Anything you want. Please just listen to me. I need you to listen to me."

Even as she said the words, a trickle of bitterness crept inside at the humiliation of having to plead. It wasn't like Tilda was totally innocent. If she hadn't—

"Then talk," Tilda said as she folded her arms. "You want to say something, say it. Just... get it over with." She stood there all closed off, a shining beacon of restrained and trembling fury, and yet... again, she hadn't followed through with her initial statement. Despite her protestations, some part of her must have wanted to talk.

"I was wrong," Kaiya said. Three simple words of abasement that bore down on her with unexplainable weight. Three words of weakness. "I shouldn't have let them take you. I should have stopped them. I was just so angry and—"

"There we go," Tilda said. "Already trying to justify yourself. You always do this. You twist everything around and make it about you, about what you're feeling and what you want. You can never just say that you were wrong."

"I— ok, fine, you're right," she said instead, biting back the desire to defend herself from the untrue accusation. Why couldn't Tilda understand how difficult it was to do something like this? She didn't have to make it worse.

"Was that it?" Tilda said. "You wanted to come and tell me how it's my fault you did what you did?"

"It's not your fault. Please, Ti— Matilda. I didn't mean to make it about me. Believe me."

"Why should I?" Tilda said. "Why should I have any faith in you at all? You go on about other people being traitors, but you've got no loyalty yourself. You betrayed me."

"I... was wrong," she repeated.

"You can't even admit it!" Tilda said. "You're too much of a coward to say it. You know what I just realised? That's what I want. I want you to *say* it. That you betrayed me. You're a traitor."

Tilda's eyes blazed out of a face that still showed bruises, then she smirked.

"You can't even do that, can you?" she said. "You know why? Cause you don't think you were wrong. You still think I'm the one who—"

"Ok!" Kaiya said. "I betrayed you. I let you down. I... I'm a traitor. And I *was* wrong. I know that I— I don't know what to say, Tilda! I'm doing my best. Just tell me what I need to do, what I need to say. Tell me how to convince you that I mean what I'm saying. I was wrong."

The accidental slip over her name didn't seem to have drawn any ire from Tilda. Kaiya was grateful for that. She didn't really even know what she was saying anymore. There was a note of panic in her voice. None of this was happening how she had imagined it would, but then... when did it ever?

What if Tilda was right?

"I don't believe you," she said.

Kaiya nodded in the too-quiet laneway, conscious of judging eyes and holding back a rising sense of failure and despair. "I guess that's a fair punishment," she said. "I don't deserve your belief."

Her voice cracked as she tried to look at Tilda, but shame weighed her eyes down to the level of the grimy laneway, and she realised that she had just spoken the truth.

She was unworthy.

Tilda made no comment for a short time. Could she sense the honesty in her words?

"At least you can see it," Tilda said. Her softer tone – if still laced with acid – gave Kaiya some measure of hope that there was a way to win Tilda back.

"I just wanted you to know," Kaiya said. "So you don't think that I'm the same person I was when they... when I hurt you."

Kaiya stood still, neck prickling with anticipation and the eyeballs of those who pretended not to look, watching as Tilda considered her words.

"Is that all?" Tilda asked blankly.

Kaiya did her best to keep her face straight, but a stray tear still escaped. "Please, Ti— Matilda. I mean it. Please believe—"

"It's nothing to do with that," Tilda said. "What else do you want to say?"

Kaiya hesitated. "I don't understand."

"You can't think of anything else you might want to say?" Tilda pressed. "Nothing at all that you think you might *need* to say? Something you don't *want* to say?"

Kaiya understood, then, what she had done wrong, and the floor of her stomach disappeared in a sea of boiling trepidation that bubbled up through her veins. She had made a fatal error.

And yet she still struggled to say what she knew Tilda wanted to hear.

"I'm sorry," she managed at last, but Tilda just shook her head.

"I don't think you even know what that means," Tilda said. "That's the problem, Kaiya. It didn't even cross your mind. You don't care about anyone else."

"I do," she said. "I do, I really do. Why do you think I'm here? Because I care about you. Because I want to make things better. I... did the wrong thing, I know, but—"

"Do you really think it's just about that?" Tilda said. "You still don't get it. You always think it's about these big events, as if one event means everything, but it's not about the big things. It wasn't that you betrayed me once. It's about all the other times you didn't listen, the times you made me afraid, made me feel unwanted, all the times you could have come and spent time with me because *I* was upset and you didn't, because you were always so absorbed in what's happening in your own life that you just never bothered to think about what was happening to everyone else around you."

Tilda had begun, at last, to cry.

"You still don't understand," Tilda said. "Do you know what *I* lost? I know everything about what you've been through, but how much do you know about how I feel? You don't even know the name of the man I fell in love with. And I don't care if you don't like the Tarkinians! You were supposed to be my best friend. I should have been able to *trust* you, but I never could. There were so many clues, Kaiya. So many opportunities for you to find out, but you never paid attention to anyone but yourself. So don't come here thinking that it's about one time that you made a mistake. That's just the topping on the *marashta*. It's about who you are. You're a bad person, Kaiya."

Kaiya closed her eyes and allowed herself a few moments of quiet grief, still doing her best not to show how affected she was by Tilda's words. What could she say to deny this charge? Tilda was right.

"And it's not just me," Tilda continued. "After all that time, after everything you said about Kormac. All that waiting and telling me how much better things would be once he returned. After all of that, he comes back, and you just... discard him."

"I didn't discard him!"

"No, that's exactly what you did, Kaiya. You went out picking fights and getting put in hospital while he's sitting there at home wondering what the hell he's supposed to do with his life now. Wondering if you actually care that he's there. You barely ever remembered his medication. You actually tried to convince him to get *Rapture*? I almost couldn't believe it when he told me that. But you know what? I can, now. Cause I can believe anything of you, except the things you want me to believe. He's better off without you in his life."

"You saw Kormac?"

"Don't even think about it, Kaiya! If there's one thing I can do, it's keep you away from him."

"That's not your choice to make," Kaiya said.

"He's not capable of making a choice, Kaiya. Don't you see that? He *needed* you, and you failed him."

"Fine! Ok! Ok..."

Kaiya covered her face in surrender. She couldn't bear the slicing truth of Tilda's tongue any longer. All of those fanciful ideas she had imagined on the train were crashing down around her in a smoking heap of consequence and reality.

"Are you done?" Tilda said.

Another lashing of venom.

Kaiya wiped her face and caught her breath. "I want you to tell me his name," she said. "I care, I really do. I want to make up for everything. Please let me."

Tilda studied her, wiping away her own stream of pent-up anger and regret.

"Rainer," she said at last.

Kaiya couldn't help but smile gently at the tiny offering Tilda had given her. Just the shadow of an indication that not all was lost.

"It's a good name," she said. "You think I would have liked him?"

"Only if you didn't try to kill him first."

Kaiya almost chuckled, but wasn't sure if that was an appropriate response, or if Tilda were even making a joke. She seemed to have calmed, but the laneway was still covered with eggshells.

"You must miss him," Kaiya said.

Tilda's face scrunched up in ugly grief once more. "Took you long enough to figure that out."

"Do you still want to be with him? The Tarkinians are giving people visas, if they were with a soldier. Jonathan told me."

"I'm surprised you haven't driven him away yet," Tilda said.

"So am I."

And for the first time, the crack of a smile broke Tilda's face. "I heard something about that. It's real?"

"Yes!" Kaiya said, and dared to take a step closer. "It's real, they're doing it right now. You could... go to Tarkinia. If that's what you wanted."

"What, you can't bear the idea of me being near you?"

Kaiya didn't respond. There was no real malice behind the words. They felt more like a flailing attempt to hold onto a feeling that was fading away to irrelevance.

"I don't want you to leave," Kaiya said. "But I want you to be happy. I know I don't deserve you, Tilda. I just want to make things better."

Tilda looked at her for the first time without a sense of loathing.

"Thank you," she said.

They stayed silent for some time afterwards as Kaiya wondered if there were anything she could say that would strengthen the fragile thread she had salvaged between them.

"You know you can come back any time," she offered. "I promise it will be different."

But Tilda shook her head. "I need time. It's too much right now."

"I understand," Kaiya said, though she wasn't sure if that were the truth, looking around at the faded concrete and patches of moss. "Any time. I promise."

Tilda gave a short nod, and Kaiya understood that it was time for her to leave. The other collab— women sleeping near Tilda made concerted efforts not to watch. Even Sally-Anne pretended she hadn't been paying close attention to the exchange.

"Feel better?" she said as Kaiya walked away.

"I do, actually. Almost... lighter."

Sally-Anne grinned.

"Kaiya," came Tilda's voice from behind.

She turned to face her, hopeful for a quick change of heart. Already imagining her apartment lit up with company returned.

"I saw him yesterday," Tilda said. "Not far from here. I don't know where he's sleeping, but I've asked around. He seems to stay near south wall, on the opposite side of the river. If you asked... I'm sure someone would help you."

It took Kaiya a few moment to process the gift that Tilda had given her, and she wished she could find better words for her gratitude. "Thank you," she said, already relishing in the glow of a new hope, and they each gave each other half a smile.

22

KAIYA STARED UP AT THE HOLOBOARD AS THE *RAPTURE* advertisement melted away. People bustled around her on the side street, intent on whatever chores they had to do, ignoring one another yet somehow avoiding collision. Kaiya's stillness provided obstacle to several people who must have assumed she would move as they approached and were stunned when they had to stop and pay attention to precisely what was happening around them.

Every one of them cursed her for getting in their way.

She ignored the comments, though, and watched through a window the man behind the counter of a convenience store. Something about his behaviour was odd, and though she wanted nothing more than to find Kormac, the curiosity was too great to resist, and she walked inside, trying to catch his eye.

"Welcome to my emporium of delights," he boomed.

Kaiya grinned at him and indicated that she would look around. An older woman glanced across at her and smirked as she nodded towards the man behind the counter.

"I think he's lost it at last," she said. "Two days now he's been like this. Can you believe it?"

"I've never been here before," Kaiya said.

"Oh, I'm sorry." The woman laughed. "I just assume everyone here's a local. I didn't think I'd seen you before, but you never can tell."

The woman laughed again, and Kaiya categorised her as one of those people she avoided, or smiled at for extended periods of time if she were unlucky enough to catch their attention.

"Welcome to my emporium of delights," the man's voice came again.

The customer who had just walked in walked straight back out.

"It's funny, you know," the woman said, "we always used to like coming here because Victor was so taciturn. He'd say the strangest things. He was always complaining about something. Didn't trust anyone. Now he's scaring people away cause he's too happy. It doesn't make sense."

Kaiya nodded and studied the shelves, slowly extricating herself from the woman without appearing so rude as to simply turn her back. She walked up to the counter, picked up a chocolate bar, and placed it on the counter.

"What a beautiful day," Victor said.

Kaiya gazed out of the grimy windows. Half of the day's light dissipated on entry.

"Yes. Beautiful."

She studied the man with the smile plastered across his face as he completed the transaction. He stared at her every spare moment, but Kaiya had the strangest feeling he was completely blind.

"Is everything ok?" she asked.

"All things are perfect," he said. "What a beautiful day!"

Kaiya put back her identity card and frowned.

"Thanks," she said, unwrapping the chocolate bar as she left the convenience store.

Victor continued beaming at nothing.

There was something familiar about that expression. She'd seen it somewhere before.

She wandered the streets for well over an hour, looking through shop windows, peeking down alleyways and trying to find anyone who looked as though they weren't sleeping in a proper bed. Someone was bound to know something. She asked here and there, but half didn't know anything, and the other half were downright rude.

A woman pointed her in the direction of a shelter further within the southwest quadrant. Kaiya went there, rehearsing the things she wanted to say, and dismissing the apprehension that Kormac would not want to listen by placing him firm within an image of a full and lively home. He would come back, and Tilda would change her mind, and even Masuma had begun to intrude on the image, and everyone would laugh and eat and forget that anything else had ever existed.

The walls of the surrounding buildings glowed in warm sun, and Kaiya's footsteps sprung with anticipation.

She found the shelter surrounded by those who looked like its clientele, and became conscious of anyone who even glanced in her direction. Men sat outside against the wall or on the curb, chatting softly in small groups, while one man laughed raucously by himself. The topic of his conversation changed as Kaiya approached the front door, and he gave her a wide grin when she came nearby. His teeth looked perfectly healthy, and his hair was relatively neat. Not quite what she would have expected from one with such behaviour. She did her best to ignore him as she entered the shelter, but glanced down as she did so, taking in the man's shoeless feet.

Thick scars stood tall on the back of his ankles.

Kaiya averted her gaze.

"Can I help you?" a man said from behind a desk. Kaiya told him who she was looking for and gave a description. The man checked his documentation and frowned.

"You say you're a friend of his?" he said.

"I... yes. A friend. I heard he'd come back. I've been trying to find him."

The man studied her briefly. "As far as I'm aware, he's due at the *Rapture* clinic in a couple of hours."

"What?" Kaiya said. "That can't be right. Are you sure?"

"That's what I have here," he said. "Apparently he has elected to undergo the procedure under the returnee program."

All that glowing warmth turned to spreading nausea.

"Do you know where he is now?" she said. "Right now. I have to see him. It's important."

The man looked disbelieving, but gave a tired shrug, as if he couldn't be bothered dealing with this kind of nonsense anymore. "Clinic would be your best bet, wouldn't it? Otherwise, he tends to loiter around the park two blocks that way."

Kaiya thanked the man and strode off in the direction he had pointed.

The dishevelled stranger with bare, scarred feet sang from his position by the wall.

> *Will you pick the lavender,*
> *the young and blooming lavender,*
> *will you pick the lavender,*
> *before its time has come?*

Kaiya remembered the lullaby from her own childhood...

> *Will you pick the lavender,*
> *the purple, lilting lavender,*
> *will you pick the lavender,*
> *and give it for my love?*

Her mother's voice... and now the stranger's voice fading behind her...

Will you pick the lavender,
the dry and dying lavender,
will you pick the lavender,
to tear it all apart?

The words became indistinct as Kaiya rounded a corner, and she tried to put the song out of her mind. It made her nostalgic in a sad, hope-sucking way. How sweet it would have been to return to knowing nothing more than pretty pictures in the mind, having songs sung to her in bed as she travelled the meadows and flowers and soared far above the rooftops of Leth hunting dragons and trading jokes with bumblebees.

But all things came to dust, in the end. Every flower died.

Kaiya stopped beside the park and gazed around for some sign of Kormac. Children swung, laughing as parents pushed them. Young mothers chattered as baby eyes swallowed the endlessness of a new world. An old couple helped each other walk the faded paths, steadying one another step after shared step.

A holoboard beamed down over the street.

RAPTURE
free yourself

The thought of Kormac forgetting her made her sick. She circumnavigated the park, studying the face of every man she saw, but never his. Each one was a moment of dashed hope, and she returned to her original vantage point, watching the children swing.

The only thing she could do was wait at the clinic.

She strode down the footpaths, glancing at the faces of those she passed, those on the other side of the street. She came to the opposite corner of Victor's convenience store and stopped to stare inside. Victor beamed as a customer walked out without having purchased anything.

Kormac.

Her heart skipped a beat as she watched him glance suspiciously at those around him and cross the street. He was going towards the river. Kaiya wanted to rush over there and surprise him from behind, and imagined how pleased he would be to see her again, but... perhaps that wasn't the way it would go.

Would he be angry with her?

She decided to follow at a distance.

From time to time she bumped into other pedestrians, ignoring their verbal retribution as she kept her eyes firm on Kormac's back. He stopped at random intervals and muttered to himself, and kept looking up suddenly as he walked. There didn't seem to be any particular sounds that were catching his attention, but something was. Maybe she just couldn't hear it.

Kaiya went over the different things she could say to him depending on his reaction. Whatever happened, she simply had to stop him from having the *Rapture*. Maybe there would be time for that in the future, when she could maximise the chance that she would stay there afterwards, but that was then. She had to do just enough for him to come back to her.

She emerged onto the boulevard that divided riverside and the southern quadrants.

Kormac stopped on the other side, at the entrance of the western bridge, and turned around to face her.

"Why are you following me?" he called.

The realisation that he had known she was there stunned her momentarily. "I need to talk to you," she said at last. "Let's—"

"Don't come any closer," he warned as she stepped onto the boulevard.

Kaiya complied with his demand, and felt an immediate rush of disappointment. "Kormac, what's wrong?" she probed.

"Why are you following me?" he asked again.

"I just want to talk."

"You're lying," he said, pacing back and forth over a few metres of the opposite footpath. "You're lying, you're lying."

"I'm not lying, Kormac. I know I should have taken better care of you. Please just—"

"Don't come any closer!"

Kaiya stopped again, one step nearer to Kormac. Of all the reactions she had expected, this hadn't been one of them. They had hardly left on terms of hatred or anger. The realisation of their distance – perceived though it may have been – had been mutual, when he left. Perhaps he was bitter that she had refused to try harder. Perhaps if she could just prove—

"I knew they'd gotten to you," he said. "The night I got back, and you were there. I knew it. I should've trusted my instinct, but I didn't. I trusted you, like an idiot."

Kaiya gazed nonplussed. "What are you talking about?"

"Don't lie to me!" he said. "You can't trick me anymore. I know what you're doing, and I won't let you do it."

A few passersby had stopped to watch the commotion. In the distance, Kaiya could see approaching police.

"Kormac, can we please talk about this somewhere else? You're scaring people."

"You can't fool me. I know how you work. You're all in it together, aren't you? Every one of you! I should have known, I should have known. I should have trusted my instinct. I knew you were with them. I knew this was all a set up. Why are you doing this? Why can't you leave me alone?"

He began to cry, the sound of his heaving sobs flooding their surroundings.

Kaiya began to realise the truth of the matter.

"Kormac," she said very carefully, "look at me. You know who I am, don't you? It's Kaiya. You know I'd never hurt you, right? You know I'd..."

She wanted to say that she would never betray him, but she couldn't bring herself to lie after what Tilda had said to her. The claim that she would never hurt him had been hard enough to say. Her arsenal of truth seemed very limited, all of a sudden.

"I trusted you," he cried, "and you were with them the whole time."

"With who, Kormac?"

"The Tarkinians!" he shouted. "Don't pretend like I don't know. I know how you work. You've been trying to get me back this entire time. Trying to put me back in *there*. Don't you know what it's like, Kaiya? Do you have any idea what it feels like?"

The police were coming closer.

"Kormac, you have to trust me right now," she said. "I'm here to help you."

She began to cross the boulevard again, and Kormac cursed at the top his lungs, yelling for her to stop, that he would kill himself, that he would kill all of them. The police approached faster, now, but like hell she was going to give responsibility over Kormac to them. She ignored Kormac's yells and came ever closer to the bridge, pushing Kormac back into the middle.

Tears sprang to her eyes as he detailed the ways in which he would slaughter her.

Now Kormac stood in the middle of the bridge, stalking from side to side. Three police stood guard on the northern end, approaching slowly, as the police on the southern end did likewise.

"I told you, you bitch!" he said. "You treacherous bitch. Fucking whore bitch slut. Thought you could lie to me, thought you could fool me. I know you, I know what you're doing."

"Kormac, just stop. Look at me, please. Look at me."

He still paced furiously back and forth, but a little of the energy dissipated, and he at least glanced at her.

"Don't you remember how we used to talk about going up to that place I told you about in the mountains? Remember?

Before all of this happened, before I'd even met you. I went up and I found that field, and there was no one there. Just endless flowers. You remember I told you?"

He didn't say anything, just stared at her and behind her.

"We always talked about how I'd take you there. And we'd stay there. We'd completely run away and live our whole lives away from the war and all the things we were afraid of. And talking about it... it was like we were there. Do you remember?"

Kormac shook his head as if he refused to listen to any more. "It's all fake. You can't run away. It's always there. You can't escape it, you can't run away."

"Of course you can't," Kaiya said. "Not completely. But it wasn't about it being realistic. Don't you remember what it felt like? All those dreams about things we could never do. The stories we told each other about what life would be like once the Tarkinians were gone. The places we'd go and the things we'd do. It was like we weren't really alive, like we were waiting for the day we'd get a chance for life to really begin and we were just living in our imaginary little world. But it's not imaginary anymore. It's here. I didn't understand, Kormac, I didn't realise, and I'm so sorry. I was so caught up in these things that I thought mattered. I was so concerned that things weren't 'perfect.' I should have been there for you, I should have been more grateful that I had you back, but I wasn't. Because I didn't understand what was happening around me. I didn't understand what was happening *to* me. I didn't think about what you were thinking or feeling, only how it affected me. I never stopped to realise that all of those things we'd dreamed about... they were possible, now. They're still possible. And I want it, Kormac. I want to have the life we always dreamed about."

"No," Kormac said, still stalking the bridge. "No, I don't trust you. You're lying to me. I know you are. I know how you work, I know how you get in people's heads. It won't work with me! Get away from me!" he yelled at the police on either side of him. "You're not taking me back there!"

Kaiya turned to the police and begged them to stop. "I can help him," she said, "if he doesn't feel like you're about to attack him."

"Miss, we need to contain this situation," called one of the officers. "Please allow us to do our jobs."

Kaiya turned back to Kormac. "I'm going to come closer," she said. "You understand, Kormac? I'm going to come closer. I want you to see that I'm not lying to you. I want to prove—"

Kormac gave a furious shout and backed away towards the balustrades.

Kaiya stopped, realising that perhaps the police were right. Kormac didn't want to listen to her. What had she done that made him believe she would ever be allied with the Tarkinians? Surely there was *something* she could find in her behaviour, but no matter how much she tried, she couldn't locate anything that remotely resembled anything that would have given rise to Kormac's paranoia.

He gazed around by the balustrade, and Kaiya grieved how like a frightened boy he looked.

"Miss, please step away," one of the officers said, but how could she? How could she stand there and tell him how much she wanted to prove that she would be there for him and then turn around and leave him to them? All she wanted to do was care for him. Take him back home and build a world together piece by challenging piece, until he could look at her and know that whatever happened, she would always be there for him.

That she'd never hurt or betray him again.

"Kormac," she said, stepping forward in placation, "think about everything we wanted. We can still have it."

He glanced down at the river and began to cry. "You're not taking me back there. You will *never* put me in that thing again."

"No one's taking—"

"Get away from me!"

He lunged towards Kaiya, and punched her hard in the face.

She collapsed against the balustrade, dizzy with both physical and psychological shock. The world blurred around her as men shouted from all different directions. Kormac replicated himself in her vision, tied inextricably with multiple versions of the balustrade, shifting in and out of her comprehension.

She tasted blood.

"Fall back," came an unfamiliar voice as Kaiya's eyes returned to normal.

She pushed herself up to her feet, leaning against the balustrade, and looked up at Kormac.

He stared down at the arcing, hesitant police, head flicking fervently between them.

On top of the balustrade.

"Get away from me!" he said. "I'm not going back!"

Kaiya wiped her face and stared down at a torrent of rich blood smudging her hand.

"Kormac…" she whispered. "Please."

He fixed his panicked eyes on her own. She wished she could see behind them, to understand what it was he saw as he stood there halfway between the solidity of stone and the ravenous energy conductors. If she could only know what she had done to arouse his suspicion, she could help him. She could bring him back to reality.

Kormac's lips trembled as his voice cracked wetly. "I won't let you take me…"

She smiled up at him, feeling blood ooze down her lips.

"I love you," she said, moving forward and reaching for his hand.

But whoever it was that looked back at her didn't see what she had hoped he would see.

Kormac stepped backward, and tumbled off the balustrade.

23

KAIYA SAT ACROSS FROM BENJAMIN IN THE LOUNGE THAT HAD SEEN three Commissioners in the past six years. She took a deep breath as she wiped away the remnants of her grief, feeling the rawness of her staring eyes. On the street below, people marched to another day of work, the morning sun casting long shadows.

The cenotaph in the middle of the grassy commons loomed, and Amelia came laughing into her head.

"Do you feel ready to talk, now?" Benjamin asked.

Kaiya watched an advertisement for *Rapture* play on a distant holoboard, then turned her attention back to Benjamin with a final, ragged breath. "I guess so?"

He regarded her with that thoughtful inscrutability she both hated and admired.

"Have you ever played *Choice* before?" he asked.

"Played what?"

"It's a card game." Benjamin grabbed a deck from a drawer in one of the cabinets, and pulled his couch closer to Kaiya's, shifting the coffee table between them. He shuffled the cards and divided them into two decks. "It's very simple. We each have a deck, but the cards are hidden to us. I will go first. I place a card on the table, then you place a card." They did so. "Your king beats my five. So now you take my five and place it at the bottom of your deck. But I take your king and place it at the bottom of mine."

"Why?"

"It's just the way to game works. Those are the rules."

"But how do you win?" Kaiya asked. "What's the point of it?"

"That will become clear in time."

Kaiya gave him a sceptical glance but accepted the odd rules, and they played a few more silent turns. He would explain some trick later in the game. She just had to be patient.

"I take it you didn't sleep much?" Benjamin asked.

She shook her head. "I couldn't stop thinking about it. Over and over and over. I kept wondering if I'd said the wrong thing, if there was something else I could have done. It was like he couldn't even hear what I was saying."

"I know," Benjamin said. "I spoke to one of the officers who was there. He said you were... less than cooperative, afterwards."

"If they hadn't been there..."

"Do you really think it was their fault?"

"Oh, I don't know," Kaiya said as she rubbed her forehead. She had been drained of any emotional connection to the experience. Everything was just exhaustion, now.

"How's your nose?" Benjamin asked.

"Fine. Not that I had much say in it, did I?"

"Do you believe the officer who incapacitated you was wrong to do so?"

Kaiya shrugged. "I would have gone to the hospital eventually. Maybe he... hurried me along."

She could only manage a weak smile, but Benjamin appreciated the joke.

"You saw the girl?" he said.

Kaiya played another card. "Joseph told you about her?"

"Joseph tells me many things. But I want to know about the girl. How is she?"

Kaiya stayed silent, conscious of the heavy resistance she felt at giving Benjamin any details regarding Masuma. She probed that feeling, trying to discern precisely what it was that she was trying to preserve. Some sense of... authority? Ownership?

No, that wasn't it. Not completely.

"She's much better physically," Kaiya said, "and she talks more often, now."

"What does she talk about?"

"She likes to make up stories," Kaiya said, "and she tells me what happens in the hospital. Things she sees other people doing. Things she hears."

"She never talks about the past few years?"

"No."

"What about the future?"

"No."

Benjamin nodded as he played a card.

"She's spoken about how things were when she was little," Kaiya said, "but just in passing."

"How does she feel about the child?"

"I... haven't asked her. I don't know how."

"You want to pretend it doesn't exist."

Kaiya hesitated. "I always imagine her without it."

The confession embarrassed her somewhat, as though it cast doubt on the way she related to Masuma. Or was she simply over-conscious of Benjamin's judgment?

"Do you ever think about your own?" he said.

Kaiya stalled as she went to take a card from her deck, recovering from the momentary rush of blood upon realisation that Benjamin, this man she had known since she was small, knew about that aspect of her life. Her feelings must have shown on her face.

"Joseph reports to me, Kaiya. I am the one who decided to put him with you. Don't forget that."

She couldn't help but feel a sense that Joseph had betrayed her, though she had always known that anything she said to him would be repeated to Benjamin. The fact that Benjamin knew, though, these things that she had never told him, made it clear in her mind how naked she was before him.

"Of course I think about it," she said at last. "Not as much anymore, but... it's there in the back of my mind."

"Have you considered the notion that you refuse to acknowledge Masuma's child because it reminds you of your own?"

Kaiya stared at the cards.

"Oh," she said.

"Which leads me to wonder if you regret that decision."

"Of course not," she said straight away. "Although... I wonder what it would have been like, sometimes. If it would have made a difference, either good or bad. But I think I made the right choice. What do you think?"

"You want me to validate your choice?" he said. "Reassure you?"

"I don't need reassurance," she said. "I just want..."

She avoided Benjamin's gaze as she took his winning card and placed it under her deck.

"Something for you to consider," he said, "as you think about how to raise this issue with Masuma."

"I'm not sure I want to."

"Do you think that's more for your benefit or for hers?"

Kaiya hated the fact that she deserved to feel the guilt Benjamin's insight gave. She needed him on side if she was ever going to float the idea she could be a more permanent fixture in the girl's life. Slips like these only put her further from that ideal.

"I don't know what I'm supposed to say to her," she said. "I'm afraid of making her upset. What if she doesn't want to talk about it?"

"Then you don't talk about it," Benjamin said. "But at least she knows that she *can* talk about it."

"Well of course she can talk about it."

"But you haven't made that explicit, have you?" he said, playing another card. "Would you have known, at that age, in those circumstances? Put yourself in her shoes. Maybe she's just as afraid of saying the wrong thing as you are. Afraid of making *you* upset, somehow. She's not your friend, Kaiya. She's a child. You have to give her the permission to talk to you."

Had she done *anything* right in her interactions with Masuma?

"You're afraid she'll stop needing you," Benjamin said with a sigh of consideration. "You have developed quite a deep attachment in a short time, yes?"

"We have," she said, uncertain if it were acceptable to say so. "I don't know why, but she trusts me, and... I think about her a lot."

"Why do you think she has this effect on you?"

Kaiya thought about the question as they continued to swap cards.

"You already have the answer, don't you," she said.

Benjamin chuckled. "You're not getting out of it that easily."

"Fine," she groaned. "I don't know. I guess I... like the fact that she *wants* to be around me. I like the fact that she doesn't know everything about me, all the things I've done."

"She sees you how you wish to be seen?"

"Something like that."

Benjamin considered her. "Admired, like Amelia was. You like the fact that she looks up to you. Do you think that's it, or something more? Do you like to think that she *needs* you, Kaiya?"

She refused to answer the question straight away, playing

her next card. Benjamin didn't budge, however, and sat waiting for her response.

"I do," she grudgingly whispered.

Benjamin played his next card, and they swapped. "Thank you. I'm glad you can admit that. The thing is, she may have attached herself to you like a magnet, but you've done the same thing in return. Wouldn't it be fair to say that you feel you need her?"

"I do," she said. Was this an acknowledgment that they should share a more intertwined future?

"And so you both receive the same thing – the sense that you are special. And both of you are afraid of the same thing – that you'll stop being special. Given the circumstances, I see no oddity in the fact that you would latch on to each other in such a manner. Consider what she represents to you – the opportunity to recreate your sense of identity and importance. What do you think you mean to her?"

She had never thought to wonder, but she saw an opportunity to place another seed of her thinking in Benjamin's head.

"Her parents had the *Rapture*, so maybe I'm like a replacement?"

"That's a fair thought," Benjamin said, "but I think it's more fundamental than that. In fact, I would contend that your position is not quite the same. In a child's mind, a parent bears natural responsibility. There is a set of expectations that goes along with that. You, however, have no such natural responsibility, and yet there you are. Maybe it was nothing more than pure chance that you met when you did, but you made a choice when you sought her out. You went to her, and you gave her something very special – time."

"She spends more time with the nurses and other patients," Kaiya said.

"But that time doesn't belong solely to her. The nurses, the children, they interact because they have to. You interact with her because you *want* to, and that makes a world of difference, don't you think?"

"I guess so," she said, slipping Benjamin's card of lower value under her deck. Of course, he was completely correct. Everything he said was a revelation. Admiration and annoyance, all at the same time; the story of her entire relationship with him.

"So we have established," he said as he played a card, "that it is natural for you both to feel the way you feel, and that you are going to address the matter of her feelings on the child she carries. The question is – what happens to her, and what happens to her child? She can't stay in a hospital forever."

He watched her with piercing intensity as she prepared to launch into an explanation of why she thought Masuma should stay with her, but something irked her about Benjamin's approach to the issue. He was always a step ahead, making sure she came to the conclusions that he had already come to. He was drawing her in to something, bringing her to a place where she would say something he already expected her to say...

"You already know what I want, don't you?" she said.

Benjamin smiled gently. "You've been trying to convince me of it this whole time. You made it clear what you wanted without ever having to say it. And the only reason you tried to ease me towards your way of thinking is that you already know what the answer is, don't you?"

Kaiya pushed down the abrupt sense of disappointment that swelled within her throat. "But you said we both needed each other."

"That's not quite what I said, actually. I said you both *feel* that you need each other, which presents a problem, notwithstanding the simple fact that you are in no position to care for someone in her state."

"I can, though. I know I can. I'll—"

"I have already decided this," Benjamin said. "You will not change my mind."

"Who said you get to choose, though?"

"You think I wouldn't have influence? No, I don't want to turn this into an argument. The decision is made, and you will accept it."

Kaiya sulked as Benjamin waited patiently opposite.

"I don't understand why it's a problem," she said. "Isn't that a good thing, for people to need each other? It's like... glue."

"Sometimes the glue can be too tight, Kaiya. It binds people too close together, so they're unable to be separate individuals. Everything that happens to one affects the other. If I allowed this to happen, you would create an entire world around sacrificing your own wellbeing for her. Not even *for* her but because you are running away from yourself. And Masuma? How would she know what you are? Are you a sister? A friend? Would she feel that you have authority, as she grows up? Who would be her point of reference for what it is to be a functioning, active member of society? Don't try to tell me you could fulfil that role. And then you add the child. You don't even know Masuma's feelings on the matter. You're afraid to ask the questions that she needs someone to ask. Do you know what options are available? Do you know where to find that information? Do you know how to guide her in that decision-making process? What will be the effect on her if she gives up the child? What if she wants to keep it? Who would be the primary caregiver? Would the child grow up thinking that Masuma is mummy, or you? But you haven't thought about these things. The fact of the matter is, Kaiya, that you're not putting her best interests first. You're only thinking of how you can make yourself feel better."

The criticism cut deep, and Kaiya couldn't help reflecting on what Tilda had said the day before. "You're saying I'm a bad person."

"Don't be dramatic," Benjamin said. "I never said anything of the sort. Your way of thinking is a completely normal reaction to your circumstances. But I would be failing in my duty both to you and to Masuma if I even countenanced the idea that this could work. You need to rebuild your own life, and she needs someone who already has theirs together."

Kaiya played a card as she searched for some rebuttal to Benjamin's litany of concerns, but she knew any such argument would be pointless. Besides, she had an uncomfortable sense that he could be right. Her mind was already readjusting to encompass the notion that she would return to an empty home, pressing tighter and tighter. A cavernous entrapment.

"How can you be so sure all of that would happen?" she asked.

"Rigorous study, and a great deal of introspection." He seemed to find his response quite amusing, and took Kaiya's winning card to place at the bottom of his deck. "You know, I was always a person who cared too much. At least, that's the way I like to put it. I would put a great deal of effort into my girlfriends when I was younger. I could never find someone who needed me as much as I needed them, and after a while I began to wonder, why did I feel this way? So I stopped, and I focused on my work, and I read a lot. I changed the pattern of my behaviour, and realised that it was easier for me to be alone than to face dissatisfaction every day. I became less anxious. I became more perceptive. I understood, in time, that my dissatisfaction came from me, not from them. The very thing I wanted to use to fix myself was the thing that harmed me. Now I know the context is very different, but the underlying tendency is the same. The trouble is, Kaiya, in your case it's not just you who is trying to fulfil yourself through another person. That other person will be doing the same through you. In the end, you'll destroy yourselves."

"So you don't want me to see her anymore."

"On the contrary," Benjamin said. "I agree that you can both be very good for each other and, whether or not you intended to, you've placed yourself in a position of responsibility in her life. I would be disappointed if you abandoned that responsibility. The question I ask is merely where the line is drawn on how much responsibility you take on."

"You're assuming that whoever takes guardianship of her will accept me as well."

"A Commissioner's recommendation is not one to be lightly dismissed," Benjamin said, "and I can think of someone very specific who could provide what Masuma needs. Someone who has spent enough time preparing himself to take on such a role once more. You would agree with me, I hope?"

Kaiya reflected on Benjamin's choice.

"I do," she said.

"Then it is settled."

"Has Joseph even said anything about it?" she asked.

"I have raised the issue in passing. If you were to... give him a promise of your support, I think that would ease some of his apprehensions."

Kaiya played another card as she thought over the way their conversation had progressed. She could see Benjamin's breadcrumbs stark in front of her, yet felt no sense of manipulation. He had taken her on the journey she needed, and she glanced at the Commissioner, this man she had known since childhood, and wondered if she had been wrong to doubt his capacity.

"Ok," she said, "but I want one thing. I want to be the one to introduce him to her."

Benjamin laughed. "You get that from your father. He always pushed hard, even when he was in a corner. You can be the one to introduce them, Kaiya, that's fine."

She grinned to herself as they continued the card game in silence. In time, Kaiya realised that the order of the cards being played seemed very familiar. "Aren't we back to the beginning? These are exactly the same cards in reverse."

"Very astute," Benjamin said, "but the game continues."

He would give an explanation at some point, surely. She

just had to wait. Besides, the game was relaxing. She didn't have to think much while she played it, and could begin to reimagine her life in the near future. She fixed the image of Masuma with Joseph in her mind, and found that she had begun to picture the girl as she really was, not how she should have been.

Yes, she needed to address the reality of her situation.

"I met Alison Meer," she said, glancing up to see Benjamin's grin in response. "She gave me an essay Joseph wrote."

"I remember that," Benjamin said. "One of the reasons I poached him to Leth. Did you want to share your thoughts?"

Kaiya steeled herself with a breath. "I think I know what I have to do. You've been leading me to this point the entire time, haven't you? Putting me with Joseph. Making me go to Akheron. You want me to speak to Stephen."

Benjamin leaned back in his couch. "I do. That is the end point of this process for you, as an offender – to confront the person you have wronged. Do you feel you are ready for that?"

"I don't know," she said. "I'm... afraid."

"Why?"

Kaiya stared down at the cards as she tried to make her admission sound as casual as possible. "Because I'm ashamed."

"Good," Benjamin said. "That means you are ready. The only problem is that Stephen does not wish to see you."

"Why?"

"Because he believes that you are irrelevant to him."

She frowned at Benjamin.

"What does that even mean?"

Benjamin placed a card under his deck and reclined. "I have spoken to Stephen at length on some... esoteric matters. This case was only a small element of that discussion, but I will convey his feelings regarding it. You say you feel ashamed now, but in the days after you assaulted him, did you feel any shame then?"

"Well... no. Because I thought he deserved it. To be honest I... still feel like he did, somehow."

"That is simply your mind attempting to justify the behaviour you now feel ashamed of," Benjamin said. "We never like to identify ourselves as being a person of lowered character. It damages self-perception. But it's fair to say that you weren't really aware of Stephen at all, or how he felt about you, after that night?"

"Of course I thought about it," she said. "You made me go to court!"

"Your actions placed you in court," Benjamin corrected, "but that is not the point. Stephen was merely a fact of your case, but my question was whether or not you were aware of his feelings regarding you."

"I guess not."

"So how he felt had no impact on you, correct?"

Kaiya followed the breadcrumbs in her mind. "That's correct."

"Then that's established. Now, he couldn't hurt you back, could he? He had no power to make you suffer. And if that was the case, thinking about you would be a waste of his time, would it not?"

"But how can I know that?" Kaiya said. "I'm not him."

"Exactly. You're not him. So why should he think about you at all? What would it change?"

Kaiya scrunched her face in frustrated concentration. "I don't understand. What does he want from me?"

"You're not listening to me, Kaiya. He doesn't want anything from you. He doesn't want anything to do with you. He doesn't even want to acknowledge your existence."

"But *why*?" she said. "It makes no sense."

"Bear with me," Benjamin said. "What you did caused Stephen a great deal of harm, correct?"

"Yes."

"Now... I have seen him, and he looks very well, but there is still some damage inside. The doctors, however, have said he will be fine. So he will return to normal, with time. Are you a doctor?"

"What? No..."

"So you have nothing to offer him as he recovers, correct? You can't heal him, can you?"

"No."

"Are you still hurting him?"

"What do you mean?" Kaiya said. "Obviously I am. You said he isn't fully recovered yet."

"He isn't. But that night has passed, hasn't it? In this moment, you are not in his home beating him in front of his daughter, are you?"

Kaiya glared briefly at Benjamin. "No."

"Exactly. So you're no longer hurting him, correct?"

"But you said he's not better yet!"

"Are you stopping him from getting better?"

"How would I know that?"

"You would know because you would be stopping him. Physically. Literally."

Kaiya scowled. "But what about what he thinks?"

"Can you force him to think about anything in particular?"

"I guess not?"

"So why should he think about you?" Benjamin said. "We've established you can't help him. And we've established you're no longer harming him. What use do you have in his life?"

"He's the same as everyone else, though. You can't move on without justice."

"Who are you to decide that?" Benjamin said. "What if justice is irrelevant. Does Stephen's body know whether or not you have paid for your crime?"

"His head does, though."

"Then you're saying his satisfaction should be based on something he has no control over."

Kaiya let the statement sink in. She had never thought about it like that.

"You have to understand, Kaiya, that it's not about you. None of it is about you."

"This is what I don't understand," she said. "If you think I did something wrong, and then I'm not punished for it, wouldn't you think I should be?"

"In what capacity are you asking that, though?" Benjamin said. "This is key in Stephen's argument. That question is relevant only to the state and its legal system."

"But it's not! What courts and other people do has an effect on you."

"Only if one allows them to. They cannot make Stephen better. They cannot take back what you did. They could distract him, if he were given to thinking in such a manner, but he's not. You are not within his direct control, Kaiya, therefore you must become irrelevant."

She gave a deep and weary sigh. After everything she had experienced over the past day, she simply didn't have the energy to spend on understanding this pointless perspective.

"So you agree with him?" she said.

"I wouldn't go that far. I think that he truly believes what he says, but unless he is a machine, I struggle to see how he could never, at any point, at any time, feel anger or loss or the desire for revenge, just like you or I would. I grant that his view is intellectually sound, and I admire that, and I wish it were simple to just 'believe,' as he purports to, but I question whether flesh and blood can truly achieve it. Perhaps it's a little too... logical."

"Then why did you bother telling me?"

"Because even if perfection cannot be achieved, there is merit in striving for it. I found his clarity refreshing. He has a calm mind."

"But I don't want to be a machine," Kaiya said.

"You don't have to be. You simply take aspects of Stephen's thinking and apply them how you wish."

"Why should I, though? What if I don't want to be calm? What if I want that... intensity? All he's trying to do is convince himself that he's not affected, but he still is. He *has* to be. He's only lying to himself."

"And you're always honest?"

Kaiya glanced down at her constantly-replenishing deck of cards, mulling over Benjamin's appreciation of Stephen's logic. "So where does that leave me?"

"That depends," Benjamin said. "What do you want from your life?"

"I don't want to talk about that. I want you to tell me what happens now that Stephen won't talk to me. You and Joseph must have some plan."

"The two subjects are inextricably linked, Kaiya. I need an answer."

"I don't know!" she said. "How am I supposed to know? Kormac's gone. Tilda's going to Tarkinia. I still dream about... *him*. And now I keep wondering about Ledophas, and the boards, and... all the things I still don't know, that I'm afraid I'll never know."

"Why not have the *Rapture*?"

"Because I'm tired of running away. It doesn't matter how far I go, there's always something new. Everything I'm running from is just as fast, like a shadow. I used to think maybe I could get rid of the shadow, but... I don't want it to win. I have to win."

Benjamin considered her as they played a few more cards. "What does winning look like, to you?"

"I can't win," she said. "Winning looks like something I can't have."

"Then you have to change what winning means."

"You make it sound so simple."

"It's simpler than attaining something you can't have, though, don't you think? So make a decision. What do you want from your life?"

"Benjamin, please. Just give me some time to figure it out."

They played a few more cards, and Kaiya allowed her mind to watch Kormac disintegrating as he touched the water.

Again.

And again.

"Bennett will be executed on Thursday," Benjamin said, "if that makes you feel any better."

"That was quick."

"He pleaded guilty. To everything. Things I didn't even know about, although I wonder if perhaps he was lying about some of those charges."

"To make himself look more important," Kaiya said.

Benjamin grinned. "Precisely. I'm sure he loves the idea of being immortalised. It doesn't matter what for."

Kaiya looked around at the space that had belonged to Bennett for three years. Apart from the furniture, it was almost bare, devoid of the holos and framed certificates and ornaments that had littered the place when her father was Commissioner. Benjamin hadn't yet made the space his own. How much longer would he be there?

"Do you think that if Joseph could go back in time, he would make a different choice?" Kaiya asked.

"You're asking me because you don't believe he'd give you an honest answer," Benjamin said, "but you know I can't give you an answer either. What would having an answer to that question mean to you? Who knows what Joseph would do if he could turn back time? You could waste your entire life speculating over those kind of questions."

"I just wondered if maybe he looks around and questions if it was really worth it," she said. "If dad never comes back, then... it was all for nothing, wasn't it? Everything that Joseph went through."

"I am certain that Joseph would beg to differ."

Benjamin's voice maintained its usual calmness, but Kaiya sensed conviction behind the statement.

"I don't hate Bennett as much anymore," she said. "I mean that... I don't feel it as strongly anymore, since I heard Joseph's story. Like I'm not justified in feeling that strongly in comparison to him."

"What does a comparison have to do with anything?" Benjamin asked.

"Bennett hurt him worse than me. He has a right to hate Bennett more than I do."

"The recognition of another's suffering doesn't require you to minimise your own. I am pleased that you have gained some insight into the people around you, Kaiya, but don't do it at the expense of looking inwards. Then you will simply have swapped one extreme for the other."

There was something comforting about Benjamin's words. Validating.

"But perhaps you are finding," Benjamin continued, "that Bennett is less relevant to you."

"I wish I'd been strong enough to kill him myself," she said.

Benjamin placed Kaiya's card of higher value beneath his own deck. "If you'd been able to do that, he would have died the winner. The last thing he would have known is that he was powerful enough to make you want to kill him."

"I would have beaten him, though. He'd know I won."

"But would you have? Truly? Or would you merely have been playing by the rules he created? If you win a game, but the entire game is set up for the amusement of the other player, then can your victory ever mean anything other than victory for that other player? You fell into Bennett's trap, Kaiya. You allowed yourself to play a game that he created. His death would have been an acceptable part of that game, because it still existed within the boundaries of what he created."

Kaiya frowned as she took Benjamin's card and placed it under her own pile.

"Then how was I supposed to stop playing his game?"

"By refusing to give him what he wanted. When he was here, still, in the concealed prison, I kept him under such tight control for a reason. Yes, part of that reason was to track anyone who wanted to see him, but those people didn't feed Bennett quite the same as someone like you could. You were the only person since his capture to give him any sense that he still had power. He latched on like a starving child, and you fed him. He dangled information, you bit. He was taunting you and you reacted precisely how he wanted. For all of his chest-beating about being a poet, he still failed at that, in the end."

"I don't understand what that means."

"A poet creates from nothing," Benjamin said, "though even that is a contentious statement. But that is the nature of Bennett – as long as a statement works for him, he will use it, no matter its accuracy. To Bennett, his existence is virtue enough to create an entire rulebook of morality. He wanted you to own your desire to kill him, you remember? To Bennett, it is a greater blasphemy to be dishonest about achieving what you desire than it is to desire something the greater community would determine is immoral. The greater community, after all, is irrelevant to one's striving for self-creation. But consider this, Kaiya – if Bennett were truly a poet, then why did he feel so much need to have power over you? The answer, of course, is that he was never a poet. He existed in relation to the people he could make suffer. His sense of power stemmed not from himself, but from how others acted in response to his behaviour."

"Unlike Stephen," Kaiya said.

"Precisely. This is what Stephen understands, though the context is different. You do not defeat the enemy by giving them your attention – you defeat them by making them irrelevant to you."

"Someone hurting you isn't irrelevant, though. If you're in a cage and someone's beating you every day, you can tell yourself all you want that it doesn't matter, but it's still happening. You still feel it. All you're doing is lying to yourself."

"Would lying to yourself be the worst thing you could do?" Benjamin asked.

"Maybe it would be. Maybe it would make you less likely to find a way to escape."

"And if one could not escape?"

"You remember what they did to you while you were there, so you can give it back to them when you can. You can't give them what they deserve if what they did doesn't still burn inside you."

"Then your wellbeing is determined by how effectively you can exact revenge on the person who hurt you."

"It doesn't matter!" Kaiya said. "At least then I'm better because of something *real*, not because I convinced myself I'm better when in reality nothing changed and they were never punished."

"Then we're simply trading principles, are we not? Stephen's is the principle of psychological self-preservation, yours is the principle of truth."

"And you believe in Stephen's principle."

"I told you I wouldn't go that far," Benjamin said, "but I do believe it is an ideal we should strive for."

"Why, though? Why should we strive for that? Shouldn't we be striving to make people pay for what they've done?"

"That is a separate goal, Kaiya, one that I have in my mind in my role as Commissioner. As a human being, however, I have to decide if what a person has done to me is worthy of my time. I have to do my best to put aside the feelings that others' actions provoke and consider if I am allowing them to rule my life."

"But it's not natural," Kaiya said. "We're not machines, just like you said. Doesn't that mean that we should embrace all of those feelings that you want to put aside? Shouldn't we be proud of the fact that we can be angry and hurt, and keep pushing until we've made things right?"

"And if you are unable to make things right?" Benjamin said. "What will *you* do now, for instance?"

Kaiya shrugged with as much nonchalance as she could feign. A sliver of familiar anger slid back into her heart. "I don't want to believe that you're right."

"Nor should you," Benjamin said. "I don't believe either approach in its extreme is appropriate. Being a machine is no way to live, but neither should we be a grenade exploding at the slightest provocation. In truth, we are both at various times in our life. You saw how intensely Joseph still feels about Bennett, and Joseph is a calm man."

Kaiya slipped Benjamin's card under her own deck, appreciating the intellectual olive branch he proffered.

"Do you think the officers respect you?" she asked. "Are they still trying to kill you?"

Benjamin laughed. "Who is 'they,' exactly, Kaiya? As with all organisations, there are people who like me and people who dislike me, and each of those for their own particular reasons. If you are expressing further doubt in my capacity to lead, however, you should know that I will not be going anywhere."

Kaiya met his firm eyes for a moment, but had to look away, embarrassed by his understanding of how she had felt without ever having explicitly told him.

"Your father was more of a bulldozer," Benjamin said, "albeit one who was capable of holding the respect of most of those he ran over. I will never be that type of Commissioner, and you shouldn't judge me in the same way as him. Weakness in your eyes can be strength in another's, and that is if you even decide to use that framework. I hope you will understand my value in time."

She stayed silent, uncertain of her ability to say something appropriate.

"Now I have a great deal of work to do, Kaiya, so what can you tell me about this game that we are playing?"

Benjamin's statement focused her mind onto the cards. "We're back to the beginning again. Am I supposed to be seeing something? Cause I have no idea why we're playing this game."

"Why do you suppose it's called *Choice*?"

"I have no idea. You never actually make any choices. You just put a card down, then swap, over and over again."

"Except there is one choice staring you in the face," Benjamin said. "Why is it that you keep playing?"

"The game hasn't ended."

"But we've established it cannot end, haven't we? There are no tricks. We have been playing the game precisely as it is meant to be played. There is nothing more to it."

"So how are you supposed to win?"

"You can't."

"Then what's the point of playing it?"

"I like to think it's educative."

"But I haven't learnt anything!" Kaiya said.

"You're being stubborn. Why don't you just stop playing?"

"I don't want to lose."

"Of course," Benjamin said. "No one likes to lose. But what exactly are you losing if you stop playing? We could go on forever, you know..."

Kaiya stared at the cards and began to smile.

24

MASUMA TURNED ANOTHER PAGE IN HER BOOK, READING SLOWLY to Kaiya.

"Although most citizens of Leth were happy with their conditions, there was a growing group who believed that the border town should not be a part of Nymosen. Led by a young and out... outspoken woman, the Eman... Emank..."

"Emancipators," Kaiya said.

"...the Emancipators began a conflict that lasted eight years and saw a... acc-u-say... zay... accusations of treachery on both sides. The true story of the Emancipators, however, and their lasting influence, would not be revealed until more than sixty years after the execution of its leader."

The chapter ended, and Masuma turned the page, looking up hopefully at Kaiya.

"You know I can't," Kaiya said. "I have to be there to watch."

"Can I come?"

"Not to that. But you'll see me afterwards. You can get ready while I'm gone, how does that sound?"

Masuma looked back down at the chapter title, *Punishment and Purification*, disappointed.

"It'll be fun," Kaiya said.

"People will look at me."

"That's right," Kaiya said. "They'll look at you and wonder where you got such a pretty skirt. And they'll see your hair done up all nicely, and all the other girls will be jealous cause you're the birthday girl and they're not."

Masuma giggled shyly, touching the flared wool and felt skirt and matching blouse Kaiya had found deep within her wardrobe. Kaiya had barely worn the outfit before she grew out of it.

"What if he doesn't like me?" Masuma asked.

"Don't be silly, of course he'll like you."

Kaiya slotted the book back into the shelf, and realised her answer had failed to provide any comfort to the girl.

"Trust me," she said, and sat back beside her. Masuma huddled close, staring at the distant wall. "You saw him once, remember? He said hello to you. He is a very... kind man."

Masuma still looked a little doubtful. "Do I have to talk to him?"

"I think that would be a good idea, if you think you can. See how you feel at the time. But he won't be angry if you don't."

"Will I have to be alone with him?"

Kaiya shook her head. "It's a party, remember? There'll be lots of people. And dancing, and *food*, Masuma – so much food!"

Just the thought of it filled her with hungry anticipation, but Masuma's forced smile betrayed lingering unease.

"What's wrong?" Kaiya asked.

She watched Masuma play with the skirt, both of them silent.

"When my son is old enough," Masuma said at last, "I'm going to read him all the things you've read me."

Kaiya looked sadly at the girl, composing her response as gently as possible.

"Masuma, we've talked about this already," she said. "The scans say it's a girl."

"But maybe they're wrong."

She looked up at Kaiya, quiet desperation in her eyes.

"They're not wrong," Kaiya said.

She should have known that morning's ultrasound was still playing on the girl's mind. The overly-cheery doctor had been so rapt – not to mention relieved – that everything looked healthy and normal, though Masuma's demeanour signalled a conflicting mixture of feelings. As for the question of the child's sex, Kaiya doubted that Masuma had even given it much thought until the doctor asked if she wanted to know.

"I don't want a girl."

"But what do you mean?" Kaiya said. "What's so bad about having a girl?"

"No, I mean... I don't want her to be a girl."

Kaiya readied herself to launch into a defence of girls, but held back, reflecting on Masuma's statement. There really was nothing she could possibly say. Her mother would have known, if she were there...

Another two convoys, and still no mention...

"It'll be fine," she said, and drew the girl in for a hug. What else could she do? Maybe Masuma was right.

She gave her a kiss on the forehead and a promise to be straight back, then exited the children's ward, wondering whether it would be any use to – once more – harass the front desk staff for any details on new arrivals matching a description of her parents.

One look at the overcrowded waiting room convinced her otherwise.

Outside, Kaiya ambled towards the southeast CBD, where Bennett's execution would take place. Even as far back as the hospital, the Taskforce police were on edge. Kaiya ignored them as best she could, hands in pockets, and stared up at the sky. She paused from time to time to examine a window, or a colour of paint, or a bird, that took her fancy. The late afternoon clouds had begun to part, allowing sun to shine through for moments at a time before covering it back up again. Kaiya wondered which force of nature would be victorious. She had never been good at telling the weather.

"Kaiya," came a man's voice.

She looked across to a maintenance worker kneeling on the road. She'd forgotten his name, despite working with him several times.

"I was wondering if I'd see you again," he said. "Heard you quit."

"Not even that," she said as she approached. "Just got... caught up in other things."

The man nodded, pretending to understand. "You coming back?"

"I haven't decided. I'll think about it."

He grinned and proffered a road tile. "Here, let's see if you've still got the touch."

Kaiya accepted the challenge and took the man's electroscalpel, automatically beginning to take apart the repellent layer. She stopped herself and surveyed the circuitry layer at length. The damage was not too extensive. The biological component was most likely intact. She took the electroscalpel and prodded the layer in a few places, watching the electricity work its way through.

She smirked to herself and replaced the protective layer. No difference in overall time, indeed.

"You're quicker than the others I work with," the man said. "You should come back."

Kaiya shrugged. "We'll see. I feel like doing something different."

She bade her farewell to the maintenance worker and continued deeper into southeast quadrant. Joseph would likely be waiting, and no doubt there would be a significant crowd. She didn't need to worry about that, thanks to her position within the police cordon, but it was never pleasant having to push one's way through a crowd and hope they accepted the inconvenience.

But the size of that crowd she had not expected.

Kaiya slowed as she approached the southeast CBD. People were jammed together, spilling out onto the feeder road she was on. The roar of murmuring thousands echoed between buildings, heating the air with expectation.

Still stunned by the turnout, Kaiya crept through the crowd, apologising as best she could as she neared the space set aside for the police delegation.

"I was concerned you'd miss it," said Joseph as she approached.

"Never."

The air was clearer, here, and while a few people glared at the extra space afforded to the police delegation, most ignored them.

"Nothing like a bit of old-style vengeance, don't you think?" Joseph said.

Kaiya followed the direction of his glance, staring at the high gallows.

"What time is he due?" she asked.

"Any minute now. You missed the celebrations, though. Some enterprising individuals decided selling pies and hot dogs would create a more festive atmosphere."

"I *am* a bit hungry."

Joseph peered across at her. "Too late, unfortunately. I'm sure they're wishing they'd brought more, though, after how quick they sold out. Look at that – streamers."

Kaiya grinned at the Chief Inspector's sardonic demeanour. Coloured streamers arced through the air a short way away, followed by laughter.

"It's not the atmosphere I expected," Kaiya said.

"I always find it best to avoid expectations, when it comes to groups. They're as random as a coin toss."

Kaiya looked at the Chief Inspector, whose ironically cheery disposition betrayed a tense nervousness. She immediately thought better of asking if he knew anything about the convoys.

"How was your visit?" he asked, too casual.

"We're reading *A Very Brief History of Leth*."

"On her birthday? How exciting."

"She's enjoying it," she said defensively.

Joseph frowned. "She is? You think that... I should buy it? For her, I mean..."

Kaiya smiled at the Chief Inspector, both admiring and jealous.

"I guess it's not so much the book," she admitted. "More the fact that she's able to read most of it. I think she'll read anything right now."

Joseph accepted the answer, still looking nervous. Kaiya stared at him, noticing for the first time how well-dressed he was. Crisp shirt, polished boots, what looked like brand new jeans.

And he'd had a haircut.

"Something on your mind?" he said.

Kaiya looked away.

"Is Benjamin coming?" she asked.

"No, he's watching from up there."

Kaiya looked up towards the Commissioner's lounge. Benjamin stood behind the windows, arms clasped pensively behind his back.

From somewhere distant in the crowd, a chorus of hatred arose.

"So this cafe place," Joseph began. "It's just beyond the east gate intersection?"

Kaiya nodded. "I'll be there about six. After Tilda's convoy leaves."

The crowd parted on the opposite side of the gallows, two lines of police with activated energy shields providing a barrier between them and the corridor they were creating.

Escorted by fully-armoured Taskforce police, Bennett walked towards the gallows.

"And if she doesn't like me?"

It took a few seconds for Joseph's soft voice to impress itself upon Kaiya's mind. She looked across at the Chief Inspector, who stood tall and imposing, staring at the former Commissioner. She could have laughed at the irony, but restrained herself out of sympathetic admiration for the honest trepidation in Joseph's voice.

"Then I'll put you where Bennett's going," she said.

They smiled at each other, and Kaiya hoped the joke would break the awkwardness of the question. It didn't feel right, for some reason, for Joseph to express such uncertainty.

As Bennett mounted the gallows and an officer slipped the noose around his neck, force shielding flickered into existence. Whether more to keep Bennett in, or to keep the crowd out, Kaiya couldn't tell. A general hush fell, broken intermittently by angry yells, but even they dissipated, replaced by a heavy solemnity that Kaiya found more fitting for the occasion.

A lone bird flew overhead, calling to its flock far away.

Bennett gazed around at his audience, the shadow of a proud smirk glued onto his face. Kaiya stared at him, wondering if now, at the end of his life, he held any regret for the choices he had made. Surely there was some flicker of it behind that plastered-on expression. There had to be some recognition of who and what he was.

"Bennett Danard," came the voice of a fully-robed Justice, echoing throughout the southeast CBD, "you have been sentenced by the highest court in this land to pay penalty for your crimes: treason, murder, aiding the enemy, corruption, evading arrest, and crimes against humanity. You stand before those you have wronged. Under the law of this land, you may think on your crimes and plead for your life. Should the voice of the people be unanimous, it shall be spared."

"I didn't know that was possible," Kaiya said to Joseph. From the smattering of whispers all throughout the crowd, neither did many others.

"Formalities," Joseph said. "Witnesses very rarely forgive the criminal, and with a crowd this large…"

By what some were shouting, it would have been pointless for Bennett to ask.

Instead he laughed, a dry, unconvincing sound, thin when compared to the amplified voice of the Justice. "You're all hypocrites," Bennett shouted, and gazed at his audience.

Gazed right at Kaiya.

She expected to feel some kind of revulsion or hatred or anger, but… nothing much happened. The former Commissioner stared at her, and her at him, but all she could muster was a gentle appreciation that this event was happening. Truly, Bennett had barely been in her mind since she returned to Leth.

The clouds covered the sun, and Kaiya pulled herself inwards at the sudden coldness.

"Bennett Danard," the Justice intoned, "may you find peace in the grave."

The tension in the crowd was palpable as one of the Task-force officers approached the trapdoor mechanism. He looked up at Bennett, as Bennett looked to Kaiya, and Kaiya looked to Bennett, all in a sea of eyes that were hardened to the sight of death.

The officer opened the trapdoor, and Bennett fell. His neck snapped as the rope jerked upwards, and he began to sway gently. The rope turned him this way and that, so that the majority of the audience could see his still-open, life-drained eyes. As he steadied, he rotated back to his original position.

Kaiya gazed at the traitor, and the traitor gazed into her.

———

The last sunlight of the day cast Kaiya's shadow across Tilda's face. The clouds had relented at last, leaving late victory to the disappearing ball of fire. Already the footlights had begun to glow, sensing that their duty would soon be required.

"And you're... completely certain you don't want to stay?" Kaiya asked.

"Would you be happy to have him here?" Tilda challenged.

Kaiya hesitated.

"We could never make a life in Leth," Tilda said. "I have to go, and to be honest..."

Whatever it is that she wanted to say, she shook her head and decided against it. Kaiya had a fair idea that Tilda's remaining, barely-contained rage underpinned the sentiment, but she could at least pretend that they were old friends saying sweet goodbyes.

"Tarkinia's not a bad place," Tilda said. "And they're not bad people."

Kaiya tried to accept the honest belief in Tilda's words, and nodded. "Maybe I'll come and visit you one day."

The first breath of Tilda's laughter seemed sarcastically cruel, but by the end of her humour it had changed to something genuine. "If you were able to manage that, Kaiya, I'd forgive you for anything."

She slotted the information away, wondering if it were really true.

"I have something for you." Kaiya pulled out a holodisc and turned it on. She and Tilda stared out, all of nine years old and making faces. Kaiya flicked through holos of them both until she came to a section just of Tilda and her parents.

Tilda grabbed the holodisc and stared at the floating images.

"I thought we'd lost them all when the Network crashed."

"We had them on a backup drive," Kaiya said. "I... never even thought to look until today."

Tilda held the holodisc tight. "Thank you." Her words were restrained, but genuine.

Kaiya did her best to put away the wild imaginings of earlier, that Tilda would embrace her and tell her how much she appreciated the gift and how could she ever leave?

This journey would be good for Tilda. She just had to keep telling herself that.

"I hope everything... goes well," Tilda said, glancing briefly at Masuma, who stood nearby.

"I think it will. I think it's good for everyone."

"Good," Tilda said, and the two of them nodded in agreement. Kaiya wasn't quite sure what they were agreeing on, but it felt good to do it in unison.

Jonathan stepped forward from a conversation with his countrymen. "Forgive me, but it's time to go."

Tilda smiled and thanked him for bringing her to the bus that floated ready to leave. She took the first step and turned back to face Kaiya, struggling for what to say.

"I don't..." she began, and shook her head. "I'll keep in touch, ok?"

"I'd like that," Kaiya said, and with a final, brief smile Tilda found a seat on the bus full of women just like her.

Flanked by Jonathan and Masuma, Kaiya watched the bus depart through east gate, and disappear into the night towards Tarkinia.

She took a breath to dispel a rising sadness.

"Let's go have some fun, hey?"

Masuma smiled at the suggestion, face glowing, while Jonathan's reaction showed a greater cognisance of Kaiya's internal distractions. They ambled into the snaking side street she had stumbled upon the day of the first convoy arrivals, decorated now with festive lights and quaint, old-style gas heaters. They drew Masuma like a firefly, and she held her palms up near the flame. Kaiya didn't feel much in the mood, but followed suit. It had a curious quality, the flame, flickering between too warm and too distant, shifting in strength with the tiniest puff of wind, never stable like the everyday heating panels within windows. And yet it was so full of... life. A different kind of heat than she was used to.

She left Masuma by the gaslight, stepping back to Jonathan. His curiosity regarding Masuma had been evident since he arrived.

"I'll tell you another time," Kaiya said.

"Is that an invitation?"

She couldn't help but smile. "I ask too much of you."

"Or perhaps I give too much."

"More than I deserve. That much I know."

"Careful, now," Jonathan said. "You don't want to develop *too* much insight. It's unhealthy."

They continued down the alleyway, stopping as Masuma went to compare the different gaslights.

"She's stalling," Kaiya said. The realisation reminded her that, for all the cheerfulness the child displayed, she was still deeply afraid. Perhaps everyone was inclined to that, beneath the surface...

"This is the cafe?" Jonathan asked.

Cecilie's Coffeepot stood nearby, glimmering with fairy lights and packed with raucous customers. They spilled out into the alleyway, as did the customers of other shops, and occupied a collection of scattered and mismatched tables and chairs. A five-piece band with instruments Kaiya had never seen before was setting up on a small stage not too far away.

The air was warm with memory and affection.

"I wanted to ask you," Kaiya said, "before all of this. I was at the hospital earlier, when the convoy came, and... I just wanted to know if you know anything. If you know anything about any more, or when the next ones are coming, or... just anything."

Jonathan looked at her quite seriously. "I think it's best that you enjoy the evening," he said. "I wouldn't... I don't think there will be much more to look forward to. Not in this regard."

He looked quite uncomfortable as he said it.

"I see," Kaiya said.

But even so, there was a chance... perhaps she didn't fully understand him, or maybe his information was incomplete. There was still...

"Masuma," she called. She couldn't think about that, not tonight.

The girl came to her.

A few of the outside revellers stood to dance as the band began to play, and Kaiya glanced inside Cecilie's cafe, scanning the boisterous crowd. She found Joseph sitting by the wall, straight-backed and very aware of his surroundings. He held something in his lap.

Jonathan pointed down the alleyway. "How about I see you later? I'm going to speak to him."

Kaiya smiled her thanks and watched as Jonathan went to speak to a rather elderly man who stood behind a canvas. Already a small crowd surrounded him, watching the oddity with great interest.

"Let's go," she said to Masuma, who took her hand. They walked into *Cecilie's Coffeepot*, staying close together. The cafe was a melting pot of Nymian and Tarkinian and what sounded like dialects of each. Cecilie's voice rose above the crowd announcing that some food Kaiya had never heard of was ready, and the collective pitch of the room raised along with their inter-est. Kaiya led Masuma through the crowd, catching Joseph's eye as she approached.

He placed a package on his chair as he stood, and shared a greeting with Kaiya.

Masuma positioned herself half-hidden behind Kaiya's back, but Kaiya put her hand on Masuma's shoulders and turned to reveal the girl. "Masuma, this is Joseph."

She stood silent, staring at Joseph's chest.

"Hello again, Masuma," he said.

Kaiya waited a few seconds for Masuma to say something. "Joseph is a Chief Inspector, remember?"

"That's right. They even give me a badge to say so."

He took the badge out of his pocket and held it in front of Masuma.

She stared. "It's shiny," she said at last.

"Yes. It is," Joseph said. "Why don't you take it?"

Masuma glanced up at his face and reached out delicately for the badge. "It's heavy," she said as she studied it.

"Heavier than you thought it would be?" he asked.

Masuma nodded. "It must be uncomfortable."

"I used to think that," Joseph said, "until I realised that was the point."

Masuma handed the badge back, and gave Joseph a very brief smile.

"Kaiya tells me it's your birthday," Joseph said. "I... got you something, though I don't know if you'll like it." He picked up a small package wrapped perfectly in rainbow-striped paper and a golden bow.

Masuma didn't seem to know how to react. She stared at the package, then at Joseph, and thanked him in a very serious tone of voice before accepting it with great delicacy. She unwrapped the package carefully, ensuring that the bow was untied properly and almost no damage came to the paper, as if they themselves were great treasures.

Kaiya knew by instinct it was a book. A real, old-style paper one. When Masuma finally revealed the cover, she ran her fingers across the bright artwork, reading the title slowly.

"It's mine?" she said. "Like... properly mine?"

"Of course it is," Joseph said. "The wrapping paper, too."

Kaiya sensed the hint of amusement in Joseph's voice, but it was lost on Masuma, who held the book tight against her swollen body.

"Thank you," she said, still serious, then looked up at Kaiya. "Can we go outside? There's too many people."

"As long as I can eat something," Kaiya said, and the three of them walked outside. Already a good portion of the alleyway was taken up with some traditional dance, people watching and laughing as the women stepped off every so often to their next partner. Masuma stood by the nearest gaslight and watched the dancers, still clutching her book.

Flames danced in the silver-plated hairpiece Kaiya had given her earlier.

Bar the tattered rags she had returned to Leth in, Masuma either wore or held every item that truly belonged to her. A skirt, a blouse, a book, a silver-plated hairpiece, and a delicately-salvaged piece of wrapping paper and bow ribbon.

"Have you eaten?" Kaiya asked Joseph.

"Just some finger foods. As far as I can tell that's all anyone eats here. It must cost them a bit, the cafe owners."

"What do you mean?"

"They just give it away. The food comes, people eat, more comes, people eat that. All free. They do this every week, you said?"

"Apparently."

A colourfully-dressed woman, assisted by a boy of about ten, walked by with a serving platter. "Is like some?" she said in a thick Tarkinian accent. Kaiya had no idea what the little filo-crusted morsels were, but she and Joseph took some and dipped them in the gooey sauce.

Kaiya waited until Joseph had tasted one.

"They're good," he said, surprised, and Kaiya followed his lead. They really were.

"So where's your soldier boy?"

She rolled her eyes. "Over there. Watching some guy paint."

"Oh? I didn't know people did that anymore."

Kaiya watched Jonathan, studying his complete enrapture with the process unfolding before him. The whole activity seemed so pointless. Holographics gave a much more accurate rendition of scenery, so why bother with something so laborious that gave inferior results?

Oh well. Each to their own. At least he had found something of value from another evening with her.

The music from the band ended, and the dancers laughed breathlessly with each other. Still standing by the gaslight, Masuma stared at the dancers, who soon began a new pattern of steps.

Masuma continued to stare.

Kaiya finished her food and tapped Masuma on the shoulder. "Did you want to dance?"

The girl didn't respond straight away, but looked back over at the dancers. She shook her head. "It's ok."

"But do you *want* to dance?" Kaiya pressed. "That's what I asked."

"I can't."

"Don't be silly. Of course you can. Why don't you go dance?"

For all of her nervous prevarication, Masuma looked quite happy with the prospect. "Only if you do it with me."

"This should be good," Joseph said.

Kaiya kicked him lightly in the shin. "You deserved that."

They smiled at each other, and Kaiya resigned herself to Masuma's fancy.

"You can come, too, if you want," the girl said to Joseph, who glanced at Kaiya as he finished his food.

"I would be delighted to accompany you, mademoiselle," he said, "though perhaps I am best placed guarding your most recent acquisition."

Masuma looked to the dancers again, considering her position, and reluctantly handed over the book and packaging to Joseph.

They approached the rounded rectangle of dancers, and Kaiya paid careful attention to their movements. "It doesn't look too hard," she said, tapping her fingers along with the simple rhythm, *a-step, step, clap-clap-clap* repeatedly until the women twirled along and met their next partner.

Masuma mimicked them, twirling on her own and giggling when her skirt flew upwards. She brushed her hair from her eyes and looked around nervously, but only a few old ladies paid her any mind, each smiling encouragement. She looked back to Kaiya, and for the first time that evening, perhaps because of the light or the skirt or the hairpiece or maybe it was something else, Kaiya realised that Masuma was slowly becoming the age she had turned that day. Bit by cautious bit, her mind caught up to her body.

Two young men stood ready to join the dance, waiting for partners. Kaiya made eye contact, and nodded briefly to indicate she and Masuma would join them.

"You ready?" Kaiya said.

"Only if you are."

Kaiya led Masuma to the rectangle, hand pressed gently on her back, and the dancers parted almost unconsciously with their steps and twirls, admitting the new arrivals. The young men gave polite smiles to their unspoken-to acquaintances, the one partnered with Masuma showing great care. Kaiya looked back at Joseph, who apparently thought the spectacle rather amusing, and then suddenly she was stepping and clapping, laughing as she embarrassed herself in front of Masuma, who was picking the steps up far quicker.

Kaiya looked up at the twinkle of fairy lights, and twirled towards her next chance to do better.

ALEXANDER FORBES

To find out more about Alexander Forbes, join the monthly newsletter, and view his latest works, go to alexanderforbes.com.au.